Faith and Fiction

ROBERT DETWEILER is Director of the Graduate Institute of the Liberal Arts, at Emory University in Atlanta. He is the author of a highly regarded study of John Updike.

GLENN MEETER teaches English at Northern Illinois University, DeKalb. His stories have appeared in a wide variety of publications, including the *Atlantic* and *Redbook*.

Faith and Fiction

The Modern Short Story

edited by
ROBERT DETWEILER
and
GLENN MEETER

WILLIAM B. EERDMANS PUBLISHING COMPANY
GRAND RAPIDS, MICHIGAN

Copyright © 1979 by Wm. B. Eerdmans Publishing Co.
255 Jefferson Ave. S.E., Grand Rapids, Mich. 49503
All rights reserved
Printed in the United States of America

Library of Congress Cataloging in Publication Data

Main entry under title:

Faith and fiction.

    1.   Short stories. 2.   Religious fiction.
I.   Detweiler, Robert. II.   Meeter, Glenn.
PZ1.F1854 [PN6071.R4] 808.83'1 78-32082
ISBN 0-8028-1737-8

For Barbara, Nancy, Joel, Alison,
Bettina, and Dirk

Acknowledgments

"Gorilla, My Love," copyright © 1971 by Toni Cade Bambara. Reprinted from *Gorilla, My Love*, by Toni Cade Bambara, by permission of Random House, Inc.

"The Face of Evil," copyright 1954 by Frank O'Connor. Reprinted from *More Stories by Frank O'Connor*, by permission of Alfred A. Knopf, Inc. This story first appeared in *The New Yorker*.

"A Temple of the Holy Ghost," copyright, 1954, by Flannery O'Connor. Reprinted from her volume *A Good Man is Hard to Find and Other Stories* by permission of Harcourt Brace Jovanovich, Inc.

"A Young Man, Gleaming, White," from *The Third Bank of the River and Other Stories*, by Guimarães Rosa. Copyright © 1968 by Alfred A. Knopf, Inc. Reprinted by permission of the publisher.

"One Day After Saturday," from *No One Writes to the Colonel and Other Stories*, by Gabriel García Márquez, translated from the Spanish by J. S. Bernstein. Copyright © 1962 by Universidad Veracruzana, Vera Cruz, Mexico. Copyright © 1968 in the English translation by Harper & Row, Publishers, Inc. Reprinted by permission of the publisher.

"In the Blue Country," by Ralph Blum. Copyright © 1970 by Ralph Blum. Reprinted by permission of the author from the *New American Review*, 1970.

"The Kool-Aid Wino," excerpted from *Trout Fishing in America*, by Richard Brautigan. Copyright © 1967 by Richard Brautigan. Reprinted by permission of Delacorte Press/Seymour Lawrence.

"Don't You Remember Me?" by Glenn Meeter. This story originally appeared in *The South Dakota Review*, Spring 1968. Used by permission of the author.

"Oh Happy Eyes," a translation of "Ihr Glücklichen Augen," from *Simultan*, by Ingeborg Bachmann. Reprinted by permission of Joan Daves. Copyright © 1972 by R. Piper & Co. Verlag, München.

"Shōjū," by Nobuo Kojima, translated from Japanese by Elizabeth Baldwin. Copyright © 1952 by Nobuo Kojima. Reprinted by permission of Japan Uni Agency, Inc.

"The Deacon," copyright © 1970 by John Updike. Reprinted from *Museums and Women and Other Stories*, by John Updike, by permission of Alfred A. Knopf, Inc. Originally appeared in *The New Yorker*.

"A City of Churches," from *Sadness*, by Donald Barthelme. Copyright © 1972 by Donald Barthelme. This selection appeared originally in *The New Yorker*. Reprinted with the permission of Farrar, Straus & Giroux, Inc.

"Conversation with My Child on the Nazis' Deeds in the Jungle," a translation of "Gespräch mit meinem Kind über das Treiben der Nazis im Wald," from *Vom Fenster meines Hauses aus,* by Urs Widmer. Copyright © 1977 by Diogenes Verlag AG, Zürich.

"The Suitor," by Larry Woiwode. The story first appeared in *McCall's.* Reprinted by permission of Candida Donadio & Associates, Inc. Copyright © 1970 by L. Woiwode.

"Lazarus," by Lawrence Dorr. Copyright © 1973 by Wm. B. Eerdmans Publishing Co.

Story #6 from *Stories and Texts for Nothing,* by Samuel Beckett. Reprinted by permission of Grove Press, Inc. Copyright © 1967 by Samuel Beckett.

Contents

Preface

IN REGARD TO A COLLECTION which groups its stories under such headings as "Powers Governing the World," "The Moral Law," "Revelation," and "Community," a word of explanation may be in order.

Ordinarily one expects anthologies of short fiction to organize themselves according to either form or content. If according to form, one expects to see sections labelled, say, "The Tradition" or "The Older Masters," followed by others which concern Experiment or New Developments; or if the method is formal analysis rather than form-history, one expects to see sections on Characterization and Setting, followed by others on Symbol and Style, or to see Suspense, Scene, and Summary following Plot and Point-of-View. If, on the other hand, the organization is according to content—that is, according to what in the nonliterary world the stories are *about*—one will expect to see stories about The South followed by others about The West; or stories about Love and stories about Growing Old; or stories about Communism, Capitalism, Catholicism, Protestantism; and so on.

In this collection, however, we have tried instead to focus on what may be called, without too much presumption, we hope, the meaning of stories—a meaning that derives from both form and content. We have therefore grouped the stories in categories that are theological in origin—not primarily because so many of them are "about" religion as a subject (though a certain religiosity of subject matter is in fact characteristic of much contemporary fiction), but rather because we feel such terms are useful for discovering the meaning of any story regardless of content. The use of categories with a theological origin is meant, then, as an effort in intrinsic, not extrinsic, literary criticism. Our anthology is concerned not so much with religion and literature as with the religion *of* literature.

Thirty years ago Wellek and Warren, in their *Theory of Literature,* spoke of the absurdity of defining the meaning of literature merely in terms of ideology. Rather than comparing an author's creed with our own, they went on to say, "what we can legitimately compare is the total world of Dickens, Kafka, Balzac, or Tolstoy with our total experience, that is, our own thought and felt 'world.'" That kind of comparison surely is the aim of all interpretation of fiction. And we can best make such comparisons, we believe, in terms that are shared by both the created worlds of fictions and our own "real" worlds of thought and feeling.

Our four categories, then, originate in literary criticism as much as in theology. They belong to both because they are first of all categories of our human experience in building the cognitive and affective worlds of our own lives. Each category represents a question we habitually address to the "worlds" of our own lives and of fiction. The answers—at least as these involve fictional worlds—fall generally into two major kinds. One kind of answer is implied, in stories, by the formal mode of realism in presentation; a second kind of answer is implied by anti-realism in presentation. Thus the American story "Eve in Darkness" and the Russian story "Kabiasy" share, despite obvious differences in their content, some common attitudes toward life that we can intuit from the full and realistic texture of their presentation; on the other hand, "The Woman and the Mighty Bird," from Africa, and "A Young Man, Gleaming, White," from South America, have in common some attitudes that we can intuit from their similarly anti-realistic mode of presentation.

Mode of presentation is of course not the only fact of
form about a given story: the act of interpretation will always
be more complicated, more challenging, and more interesting and rewarding than the act of pigeon-holing. Our collection includes twenty-five stories by modern and contemporary writers of widely differing national background and
ideological persuasion. Each of them offers its own distinctive delights of form and of content. Taken together, they
offer an excellent opportunity for comparing fictional
"worlds" with each other and with our own: that is, an
opportunity for exercising our skills of interpretation.

Since we have wished to be generative and provocative
rather than prescriptive about the interpretation of the
stories, we are offering brief analyses of them in an afterword
rather than in an introduction. We mean "afterword" in a
double sense: after the words of the stories themselves and
after the reader's own interpretation. Our readings of the
tales are supplemental and might be used as extensions of
and contrasts to the reader's own; this is true as well for the
general introduction, which explains the anthology's con-
ceptual framework. In any case, whether the reader chooses
to read the stories before, after, or instead of our supplemen-
tary material, we believe that he or she will find the stories'
best rewards in seeking and discussing the meaning of the
worlds they create.

This preface would not be complete without an expression of gratitude to two of our co-workers: to Mr. Jon Pott, of
Wm. B. Eerdmans Publishing Company, for his steady en-
couragement and enthusiasm; and to Mrs. June Mann, of the
Graduate Institute of the Liberal Arts at Emory, for her
devoted and genial efforts in getting the book to press.

R. D.
G. M.

Introduction

I
The Religion of Literature

DURING THE MODERN PERIOD there has been general agreement that literature and religion are related—but little agreement as to what their relationship is.

Almost a hundred years ago Matthew Arnold observed that institutionalized religion was waning as a force in man's life; and he predicted that it would be in "poetry," in literature, that the soul of a religionless mankind would in the future find its best support. But T. S. Eliot, writing some thirty years into the twentieth century, observed to the contrary that modern literature had been corrupted by what he called "secularism"; that it preached a "gospel of this world, and of this world alone." Far from being a substitute for religion, modern literature, as Eliot saw it, needed itself to be "completed" by criticism from a "definite ethical and theological standpoint."

More recently another critic, Northrop Frye, has seen a third kind of relationship. All of modern literature, according to Frye, descends from the religious or "mythic" literature of the past—and all of it, even the most secular, bears traces of its origins. Furthermore, Frye speculates that the current literary period (which he calls the "ironic" phase of the literary cycle) is itself a preparation for a new phase of religious myth-making.

Literature in Frye's view, then, is neither a substitute for religion nor a renegade from it; instead it is both the descendant and the ancestor of religion, reminding us of the old even as it prepares a way for the new.

Meanwhile, modern literature after the Second World War has become more insistently religious, and more pluralistically and eclectically so, than ever. And although literary criticism has tried to match this religious insistence with a concern for religion of its own, its efforts have not always been successful. "The search for religious elements in literature," wrote R. W. B. Lewis in 1959, "has become a phenomenon that would have startled and bewildered Matthew Arnold, who did not have this sort of thing in mind at all."

But there is another approach to the problem which does not speak of religion *and* literature at all. Rather it speaks of the religion *of* literature.

"There are religions without a literature," Howard Mumford Jones writes in his *Belief and Disbelief in American Literature;* but, he goes on to say, "I cannot think of a literature without a religion, not even in Russia. . . ."

Every literature, then, and every work of literature, must embody something that may be called its religion. In this view religion and literature are seen not as consecutive or parallel but rather as *concentric* concepts. At the heart or center of every work of literature is something sacred— something that other critics might call the work's "vision" (like Murray Krieger) or its "intuition" (like Benedetto Croce), but that we like Howard Mumford Jones may call its religion. Even Eliot, after all, though he spoke of modern literature as being "secular," did think of secularism as one kind of "gospel." And he admits that "the author of a work of imagination is trying to affect us wholly, as human beings"—therefore, presumably, as religious beings too.

The idea that literature has its own kind of religion may be both liberating and foreboding to the reader. Once we recognize that the religion of literature may be quite separate from that of institutions—in the words of R. W. B. Lewis, that when a religious cause is put into the language of literature "something happens to the cause as well as to the language"—we are able to respond to works of many times and places much more openly than before. We may respond, however, with more perplexity as well. If literature has its own kind of religion, how are we as readers to think about, give a name to, the kind of religion which we find there?

II
Clues to the Religion of Literature

Author and Subject

Literary criticism has tried to answer this question in a number of ways. The most obvious approach to the religion of a work of literature is through the religion of the writer—assuming we know something about it. Milton scholars trying to express something of the religion of *Paradise Lost* refer to Milton's prose tract on Christian doctrine, *De Doctrina Christiana*. In the contemporary period, knowing that Philip Roth is Jewish (or, better still, knowing that he has read Martin Buber), we may seek in his work some aspect of Judaism or of Martin Buber's thought. Knowing that Flannery O'Connor was Catholic and had read Teilhard de Chardin, we seek in her work something of Catholicism or of the thought of Teilhard. Knowing that John Updike is Protestant and has read Karl Barth, we look in his work for aspects of Barth and of Protestantism.

The difficulties with this approach are also obvious. What if the writer has no clear religious affiliation or commitment—or if, as in the case of Norman Mailer, his "affiliations" are as extensive and as varied as the books themselves? What if the writer, like the early Solzhenitsyn, has chosen to keep his religious commitments hidden? Further, supposing we know something about the writer's extra-literary religion, where precisely should we seek for its reflection in the work itself? If in the characters, what do we make of the fact that the characters of the Catholic Flannery O'Connor are predominantly Protestant fundamentalists? Or that Roth sometimes writes about Protestants and Catholics, and Updike about Jews? If we seek for a reflection of the author's religion in the themes of his works—a likely place to look—we must face the fact that the theme or spirit of a writer's work often runs counter to that of his co-religionists. Many Protestants find Updike objectionable; some of the strongest objections to Roth's work have come from Jews; and at least one critic who knows Teilhard finds that the spirit of Flannery O'Connor's work is alien to his.

Reader

The presence of such writers, those whose orthodoxy is denied by the orthodox, has led some critics to describe the religion of literature by reference to their own, the critics', religion. Perhaps the best known of such essays is Lionel Trilling's "Wordsworth and the Rabbis." The strength of this approach is its honesty. Its difficulty is that such a personal vision of a writer's work is hard to communicate convincingly to others. Though you cannot very well quarrel with what a work happens to remind me of, you may very well wonder whether I am reading *from* or *into* the work. It is Christians, after all, who are most likely to see Christianity in Shakespeare; it is Marxists who are most likely to see Marxism. If I know your sect, Emerson said, I anticipate your argument.

The Spirit of the Age

Another way to deal with the religion of a work of literature is to define it by reference to the *Zeitgeist*, the Spirit of the Age. That spirit, of course, must always be accounted an influence on a literary work, and especially so in a period like the contemporary "post-Christian" one, in which there is no officially-authenticated spirit to oppose that of the age. No one can question the usefulness of terms like "Deism" and "Romanticism" in enabling us to understand something of the religion of Western literature in the eighteenth and nineteenth centuries.

A difficulty with this sort of term appears, however, when we reflect that a great writer may be said to form the spirit of an age as much as he is informed by it. To speak of the spirit of the *Lyrical Ballads* as "Romantic" may seem almost as circular an elucidation as to call that spirit "Wordsworthian." Another kind of difficulty is posed by those writers who seem immune to the spirit of their own age. Emily Dickinson, whose work was at first explained as a kind of throw-back to the work of Emerson and Blake, was later seen as a precursor of Imagism and Modernism. The work of Solzhenitsyn, another writer whose publication was delayed, is often called "nineteenth century" in spirit—even though one of his earliest critics, Georg Lukács, saw in him an "overture" to the literature of the future. One wonders whether these writers are really immune to the spirit of their age or only more deeply in tune with it than scholarship can recognize.

The Spirit of Place

The name of Solzhenitsyn suggests another way in which to define the religion of literature, and that is through reference to the spirit of place—or, better, a nation. It is this spirit to which R. W. B. Lewis refers when he speaks of the concept of "The American Adam" as a "native American mythology." That a mythology can be national in origin seems likely in the case of America—born as it was in opposition to or in isolation from many Old World mythologies—but other nations have developed their own mythologies as well. The spirit of Solzhenitsyn's work is sometimes defined by reference to the "myth of Holy Russia," a myth which animated the work of Tolstoy and Dostoevsky, among others, during the last century. National mythologies of course lie partly in the eye of the beholder. Lukács, a non-Russian Marxist, calls the spirit of Solzhenitsyn's work "socialist realism"; Alexander Schmemann, a Western critic, sees it as Christian; and the keepers of the official Soviet national mythology have denounced it as decadent and Western. Finally, a great writer will have as much to do with creating a national mythology as he does with creating the spirit of the age. As Solzhenitsyn himself has written, a country which has a great writer has a second government.

The Spirit of Form

The approaches mentioned so far are open to the objection that they avoid dealing with the work of literature itself, more specifically with the form of the work. For if literature has its own kind of religion, must it not reveal itself above all where literature is most distinctive, that is, in its form?

In the formalist approach the matter of Shakespeare's ideology, of his personal commitment, belief, or state of grace, and the matter of the spirit of his age or the mythology of his nation—all of these are less important for the spirit of a given work than the fact that that work happens to be, let us say, a tragedy. For tragedy has its own laws of form and thus its own spirit. As Keats put it, the poet is a "camelion." He has no "religion" beyond that demanded by the form of his work.

The formalist approach does force us to depend on the work and only on the work for our evidence. But if it is to be useful for the literature of our own period, when few generic labels are felt to be prescriptive, and when there is in fact a tradition of subverting such labels, the formal distinctions we make must be of a very broad sort.

One critic who has made such distinctions is Joseph Frank. In his essay "Spatial Form in Modern Literature," Frank suggests that there are only two basic forms of narrative literature; he calls these the *chronological* and the *spatial*, since the first follows the flow of time in the ordering of its materials, while the second attempts to stop or freeze the flow of time. He suggests further that each of the two basic narrative forms is associated with its own kind of "spiritual climate." The chronological or time-oriented form of narrative is associated with a spiritual climate of "confidence and intimacy with the universe." The other form of narrative is associated with a spiritual climate of "disharmony and disequilibrium" with the universe. It is no accident, says Frank, that in the modern period we have many more examples of "spatial" narrative than previously. The typically modern spiritual climate, that of disharmony and disequilibrium with the universe, demands expression in the form that orders its materials in patterns transcending the flux of time. "History," says Joyce in *Ulysses*, itself a novel of spatial form, "is a nightmare from which I am trying to awake."

III
The Two Religions of Literature

We are presented, then, with two basic literary religions (or "spiritual climates"), each associated with one of the two basic forms of narrative. The two basic forms have been much elaborated upon, and in dealing with them literary criticism has given us a number of pairs of opposed terms. Beginning in the eighteenth century we hear much of the "novel" and the "romance"; in the second half of the nineteenth century the terms become "realism" and "antirealism." Among contemporary writers, Philip Roth refers to novels of "society" and novels of the "self," while John Barth prefers to think of "technically conventional" and "technically up-to-date" novels.

But much less has been said to elaborate upon the religions or spiritual climates associated with these two forms. If we wish to elaborate on this side of the matter we must look beyond literary criticism to the fields of philosophy, psychology, theology, and anthropology.

We may choose, for example, to elaborate upon the two religions of literature by seeing them reflected in the philosophical terms "immanence" and "transcendence." Or, appealing to psychology, we may think of the two religions of literature as related to the religions of the "healthy-minded" and of the "sick soul," as these are described by William James in his *The Varieties of Religious Experience.* Or we may take our terms from Paul Tillich's discussion of the types of religious faith, and think of these two religions as representing the "moral" and "ontological" types of faith. Or, finally, taking our terms from Joseph Campbell's anthropological series called *The Masks of God,* we may relate the two literary religions to what Campbell calls "Occidental Mythology" and "Oriental Mythology."

In each case what we will have done is to set up for ourselves a framework for the discussion of the religion of an author or work, a framework which follows the boundaries set by form but cuts across the boundaries set by institution or creed. On the basis of their realism or anti-realism in form, for example, we can begin to make some comparison of the religions of such pairs of opposed writers as Solzhenitsyn and Nabokov, Eliot and Hardy, James and Hawthorne, Tolstoy and Dostoevsky. At the same time we can allow for each writer's personal allegiance to such diverse ideologies as Marxism, Humanism, Orthodoxy, and Transcendentalism.

IV
The Two Religions of Literature: "Canaan" and "Rome"

The framework for discussion put forward in this anthology is based on the book *Two Types of Faith,* by the Jewish philosopher Martin Buber. The two types of faith of which

Buber speaks are, first of all, *types* of faith—ideal and general rather than specific and actual. In fact they are related to the other pairs of opposed general concepts which have already been discussed: immanence/transcendence, moral/ontological, the healthy-minded/the sick soul, Occidental/Oriental.

Buber's two types of faith, however, are more fully worked out in concrete religious terms than are any of the others. They are related, for example, to the faiths of specific individuals in the history of faith: Buber calls them the faiths of Abraham and of Paul. They are related to specifically religious texts, Buber having developed them out of his study of the Old and New Testaments. They are related in fact to the origins of two religious traditions, Judaism and Christianity.

As a treatment of two living religions Buber's work has been criticized on the grounds that both Judaism and Christianity during their long histories have come to share many elements which Buber ascribes exclusively to one or the other. For the analysis of the religion of literature, however, both the clarity and the concreteness of Buber's definitions are useful. In this book the concept of the two types of faith is used to indicate differences that are always theoretically present, though in practice they may not be so.

In general outline, the two types of faith are as follows. The first kind of faith has its origin during the migration of groups of people into a land that has been promised to them. It is a migration which is experienced as being led by God for purposes which are ultimately divine. For those of this faith, God is associated with the community memory of this leading and its purposes. God reveals himself in the laws that govern everyday life within the community. He reveals himself within the everyday events of community life—especially events of historical significance regarding the community and its land. His purposes in guiding his people within their history have to do with establishing a nation which shall be holy, that is, established according to the rule of justice and righteousness. As for the individual, his faith is felt as a matter of trust in the guidance that has been given and in the ultimate fulfilling of the divine purpose. His will is bent toward persevering in that trust, that is, in "keeping" the faith.

One can see in this outline much of the religious experience of mankind and especially of Western man. Not only Abraham and Moses and David, but Russians, Englishmen, and Americans, among others, have experienced something of this kind of faith. Not only Hebrews but many peoples have experienced their land and its history as that of "Canaan." Not only Judaism but Christianity and Marxism, Humanism, Mohammedanism, and, in our day, Buddhism, have accommodated themselves to religious experiences such as these.

Further, one can see in Buber's outline of the faith of "Canaan" an elaboration of that religion of realism in literary form, that spiritual climate which has been described, though in overly simple terms, as "confidence and intimacy with the universe."

The second kind of faith has its origin during a time when individual nations and their sense of their own organic history have broken down. It originates during a time when men, losing sight of the divinely-ordained purposes of tribe or nation, recognize themselves to exist as part of a vast, impersonal, bureaucratically-controlled world-empire. The laws that govern one's daily life are felt to have been imposed from without, by powers and principalities which are remote from any divine purpose or indeed any intelligible purpose whatsoever. In the psychological realm as well, men feel that their lives are controlled by alien, demonic forces. The moral law is not a means of salvation but another aspect of bondage. In this situation God reveals himself in a special way as having purposes for individuals apart from the purposelessness of history. He reveals himself apart from the anarchic, contradictory "laws" of the world-empire. His purposes have to do with freeing individuals from the bondage of their psychological and social situation. For the redeemed or rescued individual, faith is felt as a matter of belief in the new revelation or insight by which he or she has been rescued. His will is bent not toward persevering in the "guidance" of the past, but rather toward the conversion of his soul from the old and now irrelevant loyalties toward the formation of a new self. His community is found in association with others who have accepted the new revelation, regardless of their past or their origin.

Again, one can see in the outline of this second kind of faith much of the religious experience of mankind, not only during the Roman Empire of the first and second centuries but in many nations and in many times. This is especially true when we recognize that the new revelation or insight may assume an immense variety of forms, from the most degrading superstitions and the most perverse cults of mystery to the highest forms of philosophy and mysticism. It may assume the forms of popular self-indulgence in astrology, drugs, sex, or various "Eastern" rituals, or the form of the lofty self-control of the Stoic or the ascetic. Men of many times and places have experienced their historical and psychological situation as that of "Rome," and the particular forms of the faith they have developed in response to that world-vision vary even more widely.

Further, one can see in the outline of the faith of "Rome" an elaboration of that religion of anti-realism in literary form, that spiritual climate which has been called a "feeling of disharmony and disequilibrium" between oneself and the universe, and the consequent search for joys and truths which are beyond those of earth, to be seized by the imagination or by special insight.

The fact that at any given moment we may experience our human situation as that of "Canaan" or of "Rome" allows us to see Buber's two types of faith as elaborations of the literary religions of realism and anti-realism. It allows us also to see them as elaborations of the two basic kinds of national mythology—and of the two basic kinds of time-spirit. In addition, we can see in them the two kinds of faith that have moved many individuals—authors, characters, and readers—of many religious or ideological traditions. They may serve, then, as a set of categories under which we may discuss the religion of many stories from many times and places.

V
Aspects of the Two Religions of Literature

The short stories in this book are arranged according to some of the general aspects of religion about which our two major types of literary religion may be said to differ. Put another way, each heading represents a question which we habitually address to the world of our own life as we experience it—and also to the created worlds of fiction as they are presented to us. They are questions about the powers in final control of the world's destiny; about the nature of the moral law; about how truths, especially truths of an ultimate nature, are revealed to us; and—a question which relates to all of the others—about the nature of human communities.

In the case of each of these questions, the answer which a given story implies can be intuited from its mode of presentation. In each case the literary world which is closest to the religious world of "Canaan" will tend to be represented to us in the mode of realism: in events which are probable, in characters who are "like ourselves" (that is, characters who have personality and free will), in a style which is neutral in serving as a window to the characters and events, and in a narration whose aim is to be "clear," that is, to lay bare or discover to us the meaning of the characters' lives. Likewise in the case of each question the literary world closest to the religious world of "Rome" will tend to be represented to us in the mode of anti-realism: in supernatural, improbable, dreamlike, or surrealistic events; in characters who seem conformed to some imposed pattern rather than growing organically outward; in a style that attracts attention to itself rather than "serving" character and event; and in a narration which is often puzzling or obfuscating, whose aim is to create meaning rather than to discover it—or perhaps to deny that meaning can be merely "discovered."

The four headings are as follows.

1. *The powers governing the world.* Stories whose world is that of "Canaan" imply that God (or Providence, or the equivalent—perhaps History or the Life-force) is in direct, intimate contact with the working out of events. Stories whose world is that of "Rome" imply that intermediate powers of some sort, perhaps demonic but certainly not divine or human, are in control.

Among war novels, for example, one thinks of *War and Peace*, in which the major action, the defeat of Napoleon's forces by Russia, is worked out by a beneficent force larger than that of any individual or even nation, as an example of the religion of "Canaan" in literature. One thinks of Thomas Pynchon's *Gravity's Rainbow*, on the other hand, in which the Second World War is "determined" by competing supra-human powers variously called Technology, Chance, Probability, and The Rocket, and by multi-national corporations under no perceptible human control (and generally referred to as "They" or "The Firm"), as an example of the literary religion of "Rome."

2. *Concepts of the moral law.* Stories implying the first kind of religion show the moral law as beneficent, as a means of salvation or grace. Stories written in the perspective of the second kind of religion see the moral law as problematic, as a burden or as bondage. Among contemporary novels, Malamud's *The Assistant* is an example of the first kind of story; in it, the hero's task is precisely to learn to follow the

moral law exemplified in the person of the storekeeper to whom he appears first as assailant and then as "assistant." Joseph Heller's *Catch-22* is an example of the second kind of story. Its very title has become a synonym for the law of bondage or absurdity; its hero's task is to escape from the realm of operation of this law.

Further, the style of *Catch-22*, in its obsessive and mechanical repetitions, and the book's narration, in its abrupt and confusing shifts out of chronological sequence, are themselves impositions of an external and inorganic sort, like the bureaucratic law; whereas the style of *The Assistant*, though it ranges from the comically ironic to the lyrical and poetic, always stays within the bounds of the language of men speaking to men—echoing the fact that the law to Frank, the title character, is represented not by a text (still less a hidden or mythical text like "Catch-22") but by its human embodiment in his employer, Morris Bober.

Of the stories in this collection three in particular form an interesting sequence in relation to their vision of the law. In "The Woman and the Mighty Bird" the bird, like the military law in Heller's book, is mysterious, powerful, other-than-human, inescapable. But, by way of contrast to "Catch-22," this law is within its own terms entirely just and predictable. And though the style in Jordan's telling of the tale is, like Heller's, patterned, its pattern is ritualistic and meaningful, the repetitions incremental, though indeed incrementally terrifying; those in *Catch-22* are unexpected and yet have an infuriating logic, the logic of a machine gone out of control.

The language in DeVries's "Every Leave That Falls" is the language of ordinary speech; but it becomes marked by something of the compulsive repetitiousness of *Catch-22* precisely where the human representative of the law—the narrator's father—assumes some of the inhumaneness of the bureaucratic law. And the style of "Gorilla, My Love," certainly an organic style which grows from the character, is

not so much the language of common human speech or even
of the narrator's community as it is simply her *own*—an echo
of the story's action, in which Hazel (the narrator's "real"
name) discovers painfully that her trust in the moral law and
her understanding of it may be *only* her own—not shared
by the wider community represented by the theatre owner
or even by the adults in her family.

   3. *Concepts of divine manifestation or revelation.* Stories
embodying the first kind of religion see the divine manifested
in daily, "mundane" events, particularly in human
relationships—as in most of the novels of George Eliot.
Stories embodying the second kind of religion see the divine
revealed in special or "supernatural" events—as in the fan-
tasies of C. S. Lewis or Tolkien, or, on a more realistic level,
in the malignant "coincidences" of Thomas Hardy.

   Short stories, concentrating as they do on revelatory
moments, moments that we have learned to call along with
James Joyce "epiphanies," perhaps illustrate this aspect of
the fictional world better than do novels. Certainly they
provide good examples of irony and complexity. Although
one may arrange stories in a sequence of revelation that
moves from supernatural to natural (as we have done here),
it is also true that among the most complex and interesting
stories are those which seemingly use a transcendent mes-
senger to send us (or the characters) back into the natural
world—and those which on the other hand seem to generate
a supernatural manifestation from the materials of the merely
natural life. Two of the most surrealistic of these stories, for
example, "The Woman and the Mighty Bird" and "Conversations with My Child on the Nazis' Deeds in the Jungle,"
lay thematic stress on the importance of the "merely human"
community; and a number of the realistic, fully-textured
stories, among them "Eve in Darkness" and "In the Blue
Country," are shot through with hints of transcendence.
Especially interesting in this regard is "The Seventh House,"
in which a patiently trusting kind of narrative style seems to

discover at last not a Providential design but rather one that has been engineered by Fate.

4. *Concepts of the community.* Stories written in the perspective of the first kind of religion see the separation of an individual from his organic community (that is, his family, village, nation) as tragic or pathetic—unless indeed his separation is that of a prophet who means to bring a message back to the community. Stories written in the perspective of the second kind of religion regard the separation of an individual from his organic community as necessary to his own redemption or rescue. In John Updike's *Rabbit, Run,* there is an almost perfect tension between the two opposed views of the community: Rabbit's parents, wife, and children appear to him alternately as God-given responsibilities and as the destroyers of his own soul.

Short stories more often than the novel take the family as the largest form of community they can deal with. In Woiwode's "The Suitor" the family as a community is seen as the center and the purpose of divine interest. In Brautigan's "The Kool-Aid Wino," though, the boy's family and its impoverished life represents that which he escapes from when he creates "his own" reality. (Or should one rather guess from the narrator's tone of quiet pathos that he is attempting somehow to hallow his family's existence rather than to escape it?)

Nevertheless, stories such as those by Barthelme, Bambara, Kojima, Kasakov, Mrozek, Updike, and Widmer, among others, show that the shorter fiction can deal as well with communities such as the town, the church, the nation, the West—and can see in them aspects of the communities of "Canaan" and of "Rome."

It will have been noticed by now that not all short stories share all aspects of either of the two religions. Though art must be more patterned than life, it must also be less patterned than any critical theory. One final illustration, this one from outside the stories collected here, may serve to show how the fictional world can be complicated by its author in order to counterpoint some of the possibilities of the two kinds of religions. Washington Irving's "Rip Van Winkle" brings its hero back into his community, and it presents its characters in full realistic detail as to their manner of speech, their personality, habits, dress, and so on. Both of these are characteristics of the literary religion of "Canaan." Yet the story also exposes Rip to a supernatural experience of sorts—his mountaintop visit to Henry Hudson's ghostly crew—and his twenty-year sleep does rescue him from the harsh work-ethic of his village, for he returns having reached that age when a man may be "idle with impunity." And when he observes that a new "King George," George Washington, has taken the place of the old, any easy confidence of the reader in the "progress" of American history is apt to be troubled. In short, the essential religion of the story can be gotten at only by a thoughtful comparison of all the elements—plot, theme, structure, texture, tone—of the whole story.

The editors hope that the stories in this book will prove equally complex and enjoyable, and equally fruitful in stimulating discussion, not only of the two general types of religion in literature but of all the intermediate colorings of human faith which the stories in their variousness reflect.

G. M.

I
POWERS GOVERNING
THE WORLD:
PROVIDENCE OR FATE?

Eve in Darkness

KAATJE HURLBUT

Kaatje Schuyler Hurlbut was born in Manhattan and studied at Columbia University and the College of William and Mary. Over the past two decades her short stories have appeared in a large number of literary journals, large-circulation magazines, and anthologies in the United States, England, the European continent, South Africa, and Australia. Mrs. Hurlbut, married and the mother of three children, lives in Albany, New York.

THAT LITTLE MARBLE NUDE was so lovely. She was the loveliest thing I had ever seen. In a corner of my grandmother's dim, austere living room she stood on a pedestal like a small, bright ghost.

I was about five when I used to stand and gaze up at her with admiration and delight. I thought that her toes and fingers were as beautiful as anything about her: they were long and narrow and expressive. She stood slightly bowed and the delicate slenderness of her emphasized the roundness of her little breasts, which were like the apple she held in her fingers.

I wonder now who she was. I think she may have been Aphrodite and the apple was the golden prize, "for the fairest"—the fateful judgment of Paris. But Victoria, my cousin, who was older than I, said that she was Eve. And I believed her.

We observed the quietness of that room, Eve and I, as though we were conspirators. I never talked to her or even whispered to her (as I did to the blackened bronze of Pallas Athene in the hall), but in the quietness I considered many things standing before her and she received my considerations with a faint, musing smile I found infinitely satisfying. Others came into the room and talked as though the quietness was nothing. Molly, the Irishwoman who cleaned, bustled about with a dustcloth, muttering and sighing. Victoria even shouted there. Only my grandmother did not shatter the quietness because she had the kind of voice that only brushed against it. Callers were the worst for, sitting with teacups and smelling of strange scents, they threatened never to leave but to sit forever and say in old continuous voices, "We really must go now" and "My dear, promise you will come soon" and "Where have I put my gloves?"

But leave they did. And after the teacups had been removed and the carpet sweeper run over the crumbs I would go back to the room alone and stand before Eve to consider, often as not, the reason for one of the callers wearing a velvet band around her wrinkled old throat. My cousin Victoria said that it was because her throat had been cut by a maniac and she wore the velvet band to hide the terrible scar. I suspected that this was not the truth. But it was interesting to consider. Eve smiled. It might have been true.

Eve smiled because of the things she knew. She knew that I had handled the snuffboxes I had been forbidden to touch: some of them were silver but some were enamel with radiant miniatures painted on the lids and when I looked closely at the faces the eyes gazed back at me, bold and bright. Eve knew that at four-thirty I went to the front window to stick out my tongue at the wolfish paper boy, to whom I had been told to be very kind because he was so much less fortunate than I. She knew that I was deathly afraid of the ragman, who drove over from the East Side now and then, bawling, "I cash old clothes." You couldn't really tell what he was saying but that was what he was supposed to be saying. Victoria told me that he took little girls when he could get them and smothered them under the mound of dirty rags and papers piled high on his rickety old cart. I laughed at Victoria and hoped she didn't know how afraid I was. But Eve knew. Sometimes I only considered Eve herself because of her loveliness. When the room was dim she gleamed in the shadowy corner; but when the sun came into the room in the morning she dazzled until she seemed to be made of light pressed into hardness. And the cleanness of her was cleaner than anything I could think of: cleaner than my grandmother's kid gloves; cleaner than witch hazel on a white handkerchief.

As I stood before Eve one afternoon Victoria came up behind me so silently I did not hear her.

"What are you doing?" she asked suddenly.

I jumped and turned to find her smiling a wide, fixed smile, with her eyes fully open and glassy.

"Nothing," I said, and an instinctive flash of guilt died away, for it was true: I was doing nothing. But she continued to stare at me and smile fixedly until I lowered my eyes and started to move away.

"Wait."

"What?"

"Do you know what that is?" she asked slyly and touched the apple Eve held in her fingers.

"An apple."

"No," she said, smiling more intensely. "That," she thrust her face close to mine and almost whispered, "that is the forbidden fruit." She enunciated each syllable slowly and somehow dreadfully.

"What kind of fruit?" I asked, backing away.

She stopped smiling and looked steadily at me, her eyes growing wider and wider. And then with a kind of hushed violence, as when she would tell me about the murders in the Rue Morgue and about an insane man who howled and swung a club in a nearby alley on moonless nights, she told me about the Garden of Eden; and about the tree and the serpent; and about the man, Adam, and the woman, Eve.

"And the forbidden fruit," she said at last in a harsh flat whisper, "is *sin!*"

"Sin." She whispered the word again and gazed balefully at the little marble statue of Eve. I followed her gaze with dread, knowing all at once that sin was not any kind of fruit but something else: something that filled me with alarm and grief because I loved Eve. And as I stared she only looked past me with her blind marble eyes and smiled.

I suppose it was the first time in my life that I experienced sorrow. For I remember the strangeness of what I felt: regret and helplessness and a deeper love.

"Sin."

My mind tried to embrace the word and find its meaning, for it belonged to Eve now. But I could not grasp it. So I said the word to myself and listened to it.

"Sin."

It was beautiful. It was a word like "rain" and "sleep": lovely but of sorrowful loveliness. "Sin": it was lovely and sorrowful and it belonged to Eve.

Victoria, who had been watching me, asked with a sudden, writhing delight: "Do you know what sin is?"

"No," I said, wishing fiercely that she would go away.

"And I won't tell you," she said slyly. "You're much too little to know."

For a time after that I was so preoccupied with the vague sorrow that surrounded Eve that I went to the room only out of a reluctant sense of duty. I felt that I might somehow console her. And there she would be, holding the apple in her delicate fingers, smiling. And I wondered how she could be smiling with sorrow all around her. I looked long at her, until her smile almost hypnotized me, and all at once it occurred to me that she did not know about Sin. Poor little Eve. She didn't even know that Sin was all around her, belonging to her. She was only white and beautiful and smiling.

But as Christmas drew near I went to her again as I had gone before: out of need. I went to consider the curious and wonderful things I had seen in the German toy store over on Amsterdam Avenue. There was the old German himself, fat and gentle and sad. My grandmother had told me people had stopped going to his store during the First World War because the Americans and the Germans were enemies. And I hoped earnestly that he did not think I was his enemy. Eve smiled. She knew that I wasn't. And she smiled about the bold colors of the toys trimmed in gold; and about the ugly laughing faces of the carved wooden dolls, too real for dolls' faces but more like the faces of dried shrunken little people, as Victoria said they were.

Someone who had made the grand tour had brought home, along with the laces and lava carvings and watercolor scenes of Cairo, an exquisitely small manger in which the Infant Christ lay wrapped in swaddling clothes. His arms were flung out bravely and his palms were open. He was always taken from the box at Christmastime and placed on a low table where I might play with him if I did not take him from the table. But he was so small and beautiful and brave-looking that I could not bring myself to play with him as I would a toy. Overcome with enchantment one afternoon, I took him up and carried him across the room to Eve. I held him up before her blind marble eyes and she smiled. It was a tremendous relief to have her smile at him.

I looked regretfully at the apple and turned away from her. I held the baby Christ close to my lips and whispered the lovely sorrowful word to him.

"Sin."

But little and brave as ever, with his arms flung out and his palms open, he seemed not to have heard me.

That night I wandered aimlessly down to the basement where the kitchen was and when I approached the kitchen door in the darkness of the hall I bumped into Victoria, who was standing at the closed door listening to the hum of voices that came from inside the kitchen.

She grabbed me and quickly clamped her hand over my mouth.

"Go," she whispered fiercely. "Go back."

But I was frightened and clung to her helplessly. Still holding her hand over my mouth, she led me back down the hall and up the dark stairs, stumbling, into the hall above. By that time I was crying and she tried to quiet me, still whispering fiercely.

"Listen," she hissed, "if you won't tell you saw me there I'll tell you something *horrible.*"

"I won't tell," I said into her palm. I hadn't thought of telling; I was too frightened.

"Do you know who that was in the kitchen? It was Molly."

Molly, I remembered, was to come that night: my grandmother had put crisp new bills in an envelope and had said Molly was coming for her Christmas present.

"Molly," said Victoria, "was crying. A horrible thing has happened. Her daughter—" she stared at me with wide frightening eyes that I wanted to turn from but couldn't, "—her daughter *sinned!*"

"What do you mean?" I asked in alarm, thinking of Eve. I was afraid I was going to cry again and I clenched my fists and doubled up my toes so that I wouldn't.

"She had a baby!" She looked hard at me, fierce and accusing. I backed away from her.

"You won't tell you saw me there?"

"How did she sin?" I asked, thinking of the brave baby and Eve gleaming in the dark corner smiling at him.

"She had a baby, I told you," she replied impatiently. And then, as she looked at me, an expression of evasive cunning crept into her eyes. "King David sinned also."

"King David in the Bible?" I asked.

"Yes. Now promise you won't tell you saw me."

"I promise," I said.

I tried to remember something about King David, but all I could think of was the beginning of a poem: "King David and King Solomon led merry, merry lives."

He sounded happy and grand like Old King Cole was-a-merry-old-soul. I tried to imagine how the sadness of Sin belonged to him: I wondered if he held an apple, like Eve; I didn't think he could have a baby, like Molly's daughter.

I thought about Sin when I lay in bed that night sniffing the lavender scent of the sheets. I whispered the word to myself, carefully separating it from other words and considering all that I knew about it: Eve held Sin in her slender fingers and looked past it with blind marble eyes. Molly's daughter sinned (I wondered if she was as beautiful as Eve); she sinned and had a baby: a little brave baby with his arms flung out and his palms open. Sin. Why, it was hardly sorrowful at all.

When my grandmother came in to say good night I sat up to kiss the fragrant velvet cheek and whispered privately: "What did King David do?"

"What did King David do? King David played his harp!" she answered gaily, and it sounded like the beginning of a song:

King David played his harp! He sinned and played his harp! Lovely, lovely Sin: he played his harp!

Slowly at first and then swiftly, the remains of the vague sorrow spiraled out of sight and rejoicing came up in its place.

Over and over I beheld them, bright in the darkness on a hidden merry-go-round, swinging past me, friendly and gay: King David holding aloft his harp; Molly's daughter's little baby with his arms flung out so bravely; and brightest of all came Eve with her apple, smiling and shining with Sin.

The Gospel According to Mark

JORGE LUIS BORGES

Jorge Luis Borges was born in Buenos Aires in 1899 and has achieved an international reputation for his poetry, essays, and short stories. His works include *Ficciones, Labyrinths, The Book of Imaginary Beings,* and *The Aleph and Other Stories 1933–1969.* "The Gospel According to Mark" is taken from his 1972 collection, translated by Norman Thomas di Giovanni, entitled *Doctor Brodie's Report.*

THESE EVENTS TOOK PLACE at La Colorada ranch, in the southern part of the township of Junín, during the last days of March, 1928. The protagonist was a medical student named Baltasar Espinosa. We may describe him, for now, as one of the common run of young men from Buenos Aires, with nothing more noteworthy about him than an almost unlimited kindness and a capacity for public speaking that had earned him several prizes at the English school in Ramos Mejía. He did not like arguing, and preferred having his listener rather than himself in the right. Although he was fascinated by the probabilities of chance in any game he played, he was a bad player because it gave him no pleasure to win. His wide intelligence was undirected; at the age of

10

thirty-three, he still lacked credit for graduation, by one course—the course to which he was most drawn. His father, who was a freethinker (like all the gentlemen of his day), had introduced him to the lessons of Herbert Spencer, but his mother, before leaving on a trip for Montevideo, once asked him to say the Lord's Prayer and make the sign of the cross every night. Through the years, he had never gone back on that promise.

Espinosa was not lacking in spirit; one day, with more indifference than anger, he had exchanged two or three punches with a group of fellow-students who were trying to force him to take part in a university demonstration. Owing to an acquiescent nature, he was full of opinions, or habits of mind, that were questionable: Argentina mattered less to him than a fear that in other parts of the world people might think of us as Indians; he worshiped France but despised the French; he thought little of Americans but approved the fact that there were tall buildings, like theirs, in Buenos Aires; he believed the gauchos of the plains to be better riders than those of hill or mountain country. When his cousin Daniel invited him to spend the summer months out at La Colorada, he said yes at once—not because he was really fond of the country, but more out of his natural complacency and also because it was easier to say yes than to dream up reasons for saying no.

The ranch's main house was big and slightly run-down; the quarters of the foreman, whose name was Gutre, were close by. The Gutres were three: the father, an unusually uncouth son, and a daughter of uncertain paternity. They were tall, strong, and bony, and had hair that was on the reddish side and faces that showed traces of Indian blood. They were barely articulate. The foreman's wife had died years before.

There in the country, Espinosa began learning things he never knew, or even suspected—for example, that you do

not gallop a horse when approaching settlements, and that
you never go out riding except for some special purpose. In
time, he was to come to tell the birds apart by their calls.

After a few days, Daniel had to leave for Buenos Aires to
close a deal on some cattle. At most, this bit of business
might take him a week. Espinosa, who was already somewhat
weary of hearing about his cousin's incessant luck with
women and his tireless interest in the minute details of men's
fashions, preferred staying on at the ranch with his
textbooks. But the heat was unbearable, and even the night
brought no relief. One morning at daybreak, thunder woke
him. Outside, the wind was rocking the Australian pines.
Listening to the first heavy drops of rain, Espinosa thanked
God. All at once, cold air rolled in. That afternoon, the
Salado overflowed its banks.

The next day, looking out over the flooded fields from
the gallery of the main house, Baltasar Espinosa thought that
the stock metaphor comparing the pampa to the sea was not
altogether false—at least, not that morning—though W. H.
Hudson had remarked that the sea seems wider because we
view it from a ship's deck and not from a horse or from eye
level.

The rain did not let up. The Gutres, helped or hindered
by Espinosa, the town dweller, rescued a good part of the
livestock, but many animals were drowned. There were four
roads leading to La Colorada; all of them were under water.
On the third day, when a leak threatened the foreman's
house, Espinosa gave the Gutres a room near the tool shed,
at the back of the main house. This drew them all closer;
they ate together in the big dining room. Conversation
turned out to be difficult. The Gutres, who knew so much
about country things, were hard put to it to explain them.
One night, Espinosa asked them if people still remembered
the Indian raids from back when the frontier command was
located there in Junín. They told him yes, but they would

have given the same answer to a question about the behead-
ing of Charles I. Espinosa recalled his father's saying that
almost every case of longevity that was cited in the country
was really a case of bad memory or of a dim notion of dates.
Gauchos are apt to be ignorant of the year of their birth or of
the name of the man who begot them.

In the whole house, there was apparently no other reading matter than a set of the *Farm Journal*, a handbook of
veterinary medicine, a deluxe edition of the Uruguayan epic
Tabaré, a *History of Shorthorn Cattle in Argentina*, a number
of erotic or detective stories, and a recent novel called *Don
Segundo Sombra*. Espinosa, trying in some way to bridge the
inevitable after-dinner gap, read a couple of chapters of this
novel to the Gutres, none of whom could read or write.
Unfortunately, the foreman had been a cattle drover, and
the doings of the hero, another cattle drover, failed to whet
his interest. He said that the work was light, that drovers
always traveled with a packhorse that carried everything they
needed, and that, had he not been a drover, he would never
have seen such far-flung places as the Laguna de Gómez, the
town of Bragado, and the spread of the Núñez family in
Chacabuco. There was a guitar in the kitchen; the ranch
hands, before the time of the events I am describing, used to
sit around in a circle. Someone would tune the instrument
without ever getting around to playing it. This was known as
a guitarfest.

Espinosa, who had grown a beard, began dallying in front
of the mirror to study his new face, and he smiled to think
how, back in Buenos Aires, he would bore his friends by
telling them the story of the Salado flood. Strangely enough,
he missed places he never frequented and never would: a
corner of Cabrera Street on which there was a mailbox; one
of the cement lions of a gateway on Jujuy Street, a few blocks
from the Plaza del Once; an old barroom with a tiled floor,
whose exact whereabouts he was unsure of. As for his

brothers and his father, they would already have learned
from Daniel that he was isolated—etymologically, the word
was perfect—by the floodwaters.

Exploring the house, still hemmed in by the watery
waste, Espinosa came across an English Bible. Among the
blank pages at the end, the Guthries—such was their original name—had left a handwritten record of their lineage.
They were natives of Inverness; had reached the New
World, no doubt as common laborers, in the early part of the
nineteenth century; and had intermarried with Indians. The
chronicle broke off sometime during the eighteen-seventies,
when they no longer knew how to write. After a few generations, they had forgotten English; their Spanish, at the time
Espinosa knew them, gave them trouble. They lacked any
religious faith, but there survived in their blood, like faint
tracks, the rigid fanaticism of the Calvinist and the superstitions of the pampa Indian. Espinosa later told them of his
find, but they barely took notice.

Leafing through the volume, his fingers opened it at the
beginning of the Gospel according to St. Mark. As an exercise in translation, and maybe to find out whether the Gutres
understood any of it, Espinosa decided to begin reading them
that text after their evening meal. It surprised him that they
listened attentively, absorbed. Maybe the gold letters on the
cover lent the book authority. It's still there in their blood,
Espinosa thought. It also occurred to him that the generations of men, throughout recorded time, have always told
and retold two stories—that of a lost ship which searches the
Mediterranean seas for a dearly loved island, and that of a
god who is crucified on Golgotha. Remembering his lessons
in elocution from his schooldays in Ramos Mejía, Espinosa
got to his feet when he came to the parables.

The Gutres took to bolting their barbecued meat and
their sardines so as not to delay the Gospel. A pet lamb that
the girl adorned with a small blue ribbon had injured itself on
a strand of barbed wire. To stop the bleeding, the three had

wanted to apply a cobweb to the wound, but Espinosa treated the animal with some pills. The gratitude that this treatment awakened in them took him aback. (Not trusting the Gutres at first, he'd hidden away in one of his books the two hundred and forty pesos he had brought with him.) Now, the owner of the place away, Espinosa took over and gave timid orders, which were immediately obeyed. The Gutres, as if lost without him, liked following him from room to room and along the gallery that ran around the house. While he read to them, he noticed that they were secretly stealing the crumbs he had dropped on the table. One evening, he caught them unawares, talking about him respectfully, in very few words.

Having finished the Gospel according to St. Mark, he wanted to read another of the three Gospels that remained, but the father asked him to repeat the one he had just read, so that they could understand it better. Espinosa felt that they were like children, to whom repetition is more pleasing than variations or novelty. That night—this is not to be wondered at—he dreamed of the Flood; the hammer blows of the building of the Ark woke him up, and he thought that perhaps they were thunder. In fact, the rain, which had let up, started again. The cold was bitter. The Gutres had told him that the storm had damaged the roof of the tool shed, and that they would show it to him when the beams were fixed. No longer a stranger now, he was treated by them with special attention, almost to the point of spoiling him. None of them liked coffee, but for him there was always a small cup into which they heaped sugar.

The new storm had broken out on a Tuesday. Thursday night, Espinosa was awakened by a soft knock at his door, which—just in case—he always kept locked. He got out of bed and opened it; there was the girl. In the dark he could hardly make her out, but by her footsteps he could tell she was barefoot, and moments later, in bed, that she must have come all the way from the other end of the house naked. She did not embrace him or speak a single word; she lay beside him, trembling. It was the first time she had known a man. When she left, she did not kiss him; Espinosa realized that he didn't even know her name. For some reason that he did not want to pry into, he made up his mind that upon returning to Buenos Aires he would tell no one about what had taken place.

The next day began like the previous ones, except that the father spoke to Espinosa and asked him if Christ had let Himself be killed so as to save all other men on earth. Espinosa, who was a freethinker but who felt committed to what he had read to the Gutres, answered, "Yes, to save everyone from Hell."

Gutre then asked, "What's Hell?"

"A place under the ground where souls burn and burn."

"And the Roman soldiers who hammered in the nails— were they saved, too?"

"Yes," said Espinosa, whose theology was rather dim.

All along, he was afraid that the foreman might ask him about what had gone on the night before with his daughter. After lunch, they asked him to read the last chapters over again.

Espinosa slept a long nap that afternoon. It was a light sleep, disturbed by persistent hammering and by vague premonitions. Toward evening, he got up and went out onto the gallery. He said, as if thinking aloud, "The waters have dropped. It won't be long now."

"It won't be long now," Gutre repeated, like an echo.

The three had been following him. Bowing their knees to the stone pavement, they asked his blessing. Then they mocked at him, spat on him, and shoved him toward the back part of the house. The girl wept. Espinosa understood what awaited him on the other side of the door. When they opened it, he saw a patch of sky. A bird sang out. A goldfinch, he thought. The shed was without a roof; they had pulled down the beams to make the cross.

Night-Sea Journey

JOHN BARTH

John Barth was born in 1930 in Cambridge, Maryland. He has taught at Pennsylvania State University, the State University of New York at Buffalo, and Johns Hopkins University. His novels include *Giles Goat-Boy* (1966); *The End of the Road, The Floating Opera,* and *The Sot-Weed Factor* (revised editions, 1967); and *Chimera,* for which he was named co-winner of the National Book Award for 1972. "Night-Sea Journey" is taken from his 1968 collection of short fiction *Lost in the Funhouse.*

"ONE WAY OR ANOTHER, no matter which theory of our journey is correct, it's myself I address; to whom I rehearse as to a stranger our history and condition, and will disclose my secret hope though I sink for it.

"Is the journey my invention? Do the night, the sea, exist at all, I ask myself, apart from my experience of them? Do I myself exist, or is this a dream? Sometimes I wonder. And if I am, who am I? The Heritage I supposedly transport? But how can I be both vessel and contents? Such are the questions that beset my intervals of rest.

"My trouble is, I lack conviction. Many accounts of our situation seem plausible to me—where and what we are, why we swim and whither. But implausible ones as well, perhaps especially those, I must admit as possibly correct. Even likely. If at times, in certain humors—stroking in unison,

17

say, with my neighbors and chanting with them 'Onward! Upward!'—I have supposed that we have after all a common Maker, Whose nature and motives we may not know, but Who engendered us in some mysterious wise and launched us forth toward some end known but to Him—if (for a moodslength only) I have been able to entertain such notions, very popular in certain quarters, it is because our night-sea journey partakes of their absurdity. One might even say: I can believe them *because* they are absurd.

"Has that been said before?

"Another paradox: it appears to be these recesses from swimming that sustain me in the swim. Two measures onward and upward, flailing with the rest, then I float exhausted and dispirited, brood upon the night, the sea, the journey, while the flood bears me a measure back and down: slow progress, but I live, I live, and make my way, aye, past many a drownèd comrade in the end, stronger, worthier than I, victims of their unremitting *joie de nager*. I have seen the best swimmers of my generation go under. Numberless the number of the dead! Thousands drown as I think this thought, millions as I rest before returning to the swim. And scores, hundreds of millions have expired since we surged forth, brave in our innocence, upon our dreadful way. 'Love! Love!' we sang then, a quarter-billion strong, and churned the warm sea white with joy of swimming! Now all are gone down—the buoyant, the sodden, leaders and followers, all gone under, while wretched I swim on. Yet these same reflective intervals that keep me afloat have led me into wonder, doubt, despair—strange emotions for a swimmer!—have led me, even, to suspect . . . that our night-sea journey is without meaning.

"Indeed, if I have yet to join the hosts of the suicides, it is because (fatigue apart) I find it no meaningfuller to drown myself than to go on swimming.

"I know that there are those who seem actually to enjoy the night-sea; who claim to love swimming for its own sake, or sincerely believe that 'reaching the Shore,' 'transmitting the Heritage' (*Whose* Heritage, I'd like to know? And to whom?) is worth the staggering cost. I do not. Swimming itself I find at best not actively unpleasant, more often tiresome, not infrequently a torment. Arguments from function and design don't impress me: granted that we can and do swim, that in a manner of speaking our long tails and streamlined heads are 'meant for' swimming; it by no means follows—for me, at least—that we *should* swim, or otherwise endeavor to 'fulfill our destiny.' Which is to say, Someone Else's destiny, since ours, so far as I can see, is merely to perish, one way or another, soon or late. The heartless zeal of our (departed) leaders, like the blind ambition and good cheer of my own youth, appalls me now; for the death of my comrades I am inconsolable. If the night-sea journey has justification, it is not for us swimmers ever to discover it.

"Oh, to be sure, 'Love!' one heard on every side: 'Love it is that drives and sustains us!' I translate: we don't know *what* drives and sustains us, only that we are most miserably driven and, imperfectly, sustained. *Love* is how we call our ignorance of what whips us. 'To reach the Shore,' then: but what if the Shore exists in the fancies of us swimmers merely, who dream it to account for the dreadful fact that we swim, have always and only swum, and continue swimming without respite (myself excepted) until we die? Supposing even that there *were* a Shore—that, as a cynical companion of mine once imagined, we rise from the drowned to discover all those vulgar superstitions and exalted metaphors to be literal truth: the giant Maker of us all, the Shore of Light beyond our night-sea journey?—whatever would a swimmer do there? The fact is, when we imagine the Shore, what comes to mind is just the opposite of our condition: no more night, no more sea, no more journeying. In short, the blissful estate of the drowned.

"'Ours not to stop and think; ours but to swim and sink. . . .' Because a moment's thought reveals the pointless-

ness of swimming. 'No matter,' I've heard some say, even as
they gulped their last: 'The night-sea journey may be absurd,
but here we swim, will-we nill-we, against the flood, onward
and upward, toward a Shore that may not exist and couldn't
be reached if it did.' The thoughtful swimmer's choices,
then, they say, are two: give over thrashing and go under for
good, or embrace the absurdity; affirm in and for itself the
night-sea journey; swim on with neither motive nor destination, for the sake of swimming, and compassionate moreover
with your fellow swimmer, we being all at sea and equally in
the dark. I find neither course acceptable. If not even the
hypothetical Shore can justify a sea-full of drownèd comrades, to speak of the swim-in-itself as somehow doing so
strikes me as obscene. I continue to swim—but only because
blind habit, blind instinct, blind fear of drowning are still
more strong than the horror of our journey. And if on occasion I have assisted a fellow-thrasher, joined in the cheers
and songs, even passed along to others strokes of genius from
the drownèd great, it's that I shrink by temperament from
making myself conspicuous. To paddle off in one's own direction, assert one's independent right-of-way, overrun one's
fellows without compunction, or dedicate oneself entirely to
pleasures and diversions without regard for conscience—I
can't finally condemn those who journey in this wise; in half
my moods I envy them and despise the weak vitality that
keeps me from following their example. But in reasonabler
moments I remind myself that it's their very freedom and
self-responsibility I reject, as more dramatically absurd, in
our senseless circumstances, than tailing along in conventional fashion. Suicides, rebels, affirmers of the paradox—
nay-sayers and yea-sayers alike to our fatal journey—I finally
shake my head at them. And splash sighing past their corpses,
one by one, as past a hundred sorts of others: friends, enemies,
brothers; fools, sages, brutes—and nobodies, million upon
million. I envy them all.

"A poor irony: that I, who find abhorrent and tautological the doctrine of survival of the fittest (*fitness* meaning, in my experience, nothing more than survival-ability, a talent whose only demonstration is the fact of survival, but whose chief ingredients seem to be strength, guile, callousness), may be the sole remaining swimmer! But the doctrine is false as well as repellent: Chance drowns the worthy with the unworthy, bears up the unfit with the fit by whatever definition, and makes the night-sea journey essentially *haphazard* as well as murderous and unjustified.

"'You only swim once.' Why bother, then?

"'Except ye drown, ye shall not reach the Shore of Light.' Poppycock.

"One of my late companions—that same cynic with the curious fancy, among the first to drown—entertained us with odd conjectures while we waited to begin our journey. A favorite theory of his was that the Father does exist, and did indeed make us and the sea we swim—but not a-purpose or even consciously; He made us, as it were, despite Himself, as we make waves with every tail-thrash, and may be unaware of our existence. Another was that He knows we're here but doesn't care what happens to us, inasmuch as He creates (voluntarily or not) other seas and swimmers at more or less regular intervals. In bitterer moments, such as just before he drowned, my friend even supposed that our Maker wished us unmade; there was indeed a Shore, he'd argue, which could save at least some of us from drowning and toward which it was our function to struggle—but for reasons unknowable to us He wanted desperately to prevent our reaching that happy place and fulfilling our destiny. Our 'Father,' in short, was our adversary and would-be killer! No less outrageous, and offensive to traditional opinion, were the fellow's speculations on the nature of our Maker: that He might well be no swimmer Himself at all, but some sort of monstrosity, perhaps even tailless; that He might be stupid, malicious, insensible, perverse, or asleep and dreaming; that the end for which He created and launched us forth, and which we flagellate ourselves to fathom, was perhaps immoral, even obscene. Et cetera, et cetera: there was no end to the chap's conjectures, or the impoliteness of his fancy; I have reason to suspect that his early demise, whether planned by 'our Maker' or not, was expedited by certain fellow-swimmers indignant at his blasphemies.

"In other moods, however (he was as given to moods as I), his theorizing would become half-serious, so it seemed to me, especially upon the subjects of Fate and Immortality, to which our youthful conversations often turned. Then his harangues, if no less fantastical, grew solemn and obscure, and if he was still baiting us, his passion undid the joke. His objection to popular opinions of the hereafter, he would declare, was their claim to general validity. Why need believers hold that *all* the drownèd rise to be judged at journey's end, and non-believers that drowning is final without exception? In *his* opinion (so he'd vow at least), nearly everyone's fate was permanent death; indeed he took a sour pleasure in supposing that every 'Maker' made thousands of separate seas in His creative lifetime, each populated like ours with millions of swimmers, and that in almost every instance both sea and swimmers were utterly annihilated, whether accidentally or by malevolent design. (Nothing if not pluralistical, he imagined there might be millions and billions of 'Fathers,' perhaps in some 'night-sea' of their own!) However—and here he turned infidels against him with the faithful—he professed to believe that in possibly a single night-sea per thousand, say, one of its quarter-billion swimmers (that is, one swimmer in two hundred fifty billion) achieved a qualified immortality. In some cases the rate might be slightly higher; in others it was vastly lower, for just as there are swimmers of every degree of proficiency, including some who drown before the journey starts, unable to swim at all, and others created drowned, as it were, so he imagined what can only be termed impotent Creators, Makers unable to Make, as well as uncommonly fertile ones and all grades between. And it pleased him to deny any necessary relation between a Maker's productivity and His other virtues—including, even, the quality of His creatures.

"I could go on (*he* surely did) with his elaboration of these mad notions—such as that swimmers in other night-seas needn't be of our kind; that Makers themselves might belong to different *species*, so to speak; that our particular Maker mightn't Himself be immortal, or that we might be not only His emissaries but His 'immortality,' continuing His life and our own, transmogrified, beyond our individual deaths. Even this modified immortality (meaningless to me) he conceived as relative and contingent, subject to accident or deliberate termination: his pet hypothesis was that Makers and swimmers *each generate the other*— against all odds, their number being so great—and that any given 'immortality-chain' could terminate after any number of cycles, so that what was 'immortal' (still speaking relatively) was only the cyclic process of incarnation, which itself might have a beginning and an end. Alternatively he liked to imagine cycles within cycles, either finite or infinite: for example, the 'night-sea,' as it were, in which Makers 'swam' and created night-seas and swimmers like ourselves, might be the creation of a larger Maker, Himself one of many, Who in turn et cetera. Time itself he regarded as relative to our experience, like magnitude: who knew but what, with each thrash of our tails, minuscule seas and swimmers, whole eternities, came to pass—as ours, perhaps, and our Maker's Maker's, was elapsing between the strokes of some supertail, in a slower order of time?

Naturally I hooted with the others at this nonsense. We were young then, and had only the dimmest notion of what lay ahead; in our ignorance we imagined night-sea journeying to be a positively heroic enterprise. Its meaning and value we never questioned; to be sure, some must go down by the way, a pity no doubt, but to win a race requires that others lose, and like all my fellows I took for granted that I would be the winner. We milled and swarmed, impatient to be off, never mind where or why, only to try our youth against the realities of night and sea; if we indulged the skeptic at all, it was as a droll, half-contemptible mascot. When he died in the initial slaughter, no one cared.

"And even now I don't subscribe to all his views—but I no longer scoff. The horror of our history has purged me of opinions, as of vanity, confidence, spirit, charity, hope, vitality, everything—except dull dread and a kind of melancholy, stunned persistence. What leads me to recall his fancies is my growing suspicion that I, of all swimmers, may be the sole survivor of this fell journey, tale-bearer of a generation. This suspicion, together with the recent sea-change, suggests to me now that nothing is impossible, not even my late companion's wildest visions, and brings me to a certain desperate resolve, the point of my chronicling.

"Very likely I have lost my senses. The carnage at our setting out; our decimation by whirlpool, poisoned cataract, sea-convulsion; the panic stampedes, mutinies, slaughters, mass suicides; the mounting evidence that none will survive the journey—add to these anguish and fatigue; it were a miracle if sanity stayed afloat. Thus I admit, with the other possibilities, that the present sweetening and calming of the sea, and what seems to be a kind of vasty presence, song, or summons from the near upstream, may be hallucinations of disordered sensibility. . . .

"Perhaps, even, I am drowned already. Surely I was never meant for the rough-and-tumble of the swim; not impossibly I perished at the outset and have only imaged the night-sea journey from some final deep. In any case, I'm no longer young, and it is we spent old swimmers, disabused of every illusion, who are most vulnerable to dreams.

"Sometimes I think I am my drowned friend.

"Out with it: I've begun to believe, not only that *She* exists, but that She lies not far ahead, and stills the sea, and draws me Herward! Aghast, I recollect his maddest notion:

that our destination (which existed, mind, in but one night-sea out of hundreds and thousands) was no Shore, as commonly conceived, but a mysterious being, indescribable except by paradox and vaguest figure: wholly different from us swimmers, yet our complement; the death of us, yet our salvation and resurrection; simultaneously our journey's end, mid-point, and commencement; not membered and thrashing like us, but a motionless or hugely gliding sphere of unimaginable dimension; self-contained, yet dependent absolutely, in some wise, upon the chance (always monstrously improbable) that one of us will survive the night-sea journey and reach . . . Her! *Her*, he called it, or *She*, which is to say, Other-than-a-he. I shake my head; the thing is too preposterous; it is myself I talk to, to keep my reason in this awful darkness. There is no She! There is no You! I rave to myself; it's Death alone that hears and summons. To the drowned, all seas are calm. . . .

"Listen: my friend maintained that in every order of creation there are two sorts of creators, contrary yet complementary, one of which gives rise to seas and swimmers, the other to the Night-which-contains-the-sea and to What-waits-at-the-journey's-end: the former, in short, to destiny, the latter to destination (and both profligately, involuntarily, perhaps indifferently or unwittingly). The 'purpose' of the night-sea journey—but not necessarily of the journeyer or of either Maker!—my friend could describe only in abstractions: *consummation, transfiguration, union of contraries, transcension of categories*. When we laughed, he would shrug and admit that he understood the business no better than we, and thought it ridiculous, dreary, possibly obscene. 'But one of you,' he'd add with his wry smile, 'may be the Hero destined to complete the night-sea journey and be one with Her. Chances are, of course, you won't make it.' He himself, he declared, was not even going to try; the whole idea repelled him; if we chose to dismiss it as an ugly fiction, so much the better for us; thrash, splash, and be merry, we were soon enough drowned. But there it was, he could not say how he knew or why he bothered to tell us, any more than he could say what would happen after She and Hero, Shore and Swimmer, 'merged identities' to become something both and neither. He quite agreed with me that if the issue of that magical union had no memory of the night-sea journey, for example, it enjoyed a poor sort of immortality; even poorer if, as he rather imagined, a swimmer-hero plus a She equaled or became merely another Maker of future night-seas and the rest, at such incredible expense of life. This being the case—he was persuaded it was—the merciful thing to do was refuse to participate; the genuine heroes, in his opinion, were the suicides, and the hero of heroes would be the swimmer who, in the very presence of the Other, refused Her proffered 'immortality' and thus put an end to at least one cycle of catastrophes.

"How we mocked him! Our moment came, we hurtled forth, pretending to glory in the adventure, thrashing, singing, cursing, strangling, rationalizing, rescuing, killing, inventing rules and stories and relationships, giving up, struggling on, but dying all, and still in darkness, until only a battered remnant was left to croak 'Onward, upward,' like a bitter echo. Then they too feel silent—victim, I can only presume, of the last frightful wave—and the moment came when I also, utterly desolate and spent, thrashed my last and gave myself over to the current, to sink or float as might be, but swim no more. Whereupon, marvelous to tell, in an instant the sea grew still! Then warmly, gently, the great tide turned, began to bear me, as it does now, onward and upward will-I nill-I, like a flood of joy—and I recalled with dismay my dead friend's teaching.

"I am not deceived. This new emotion is Her doing; the desire that possesses me is Her bewitchment. Lucidity passes from me; in a moment I'll cry 'Love!' bury myself in Her side, and be 'transfigured.' Which is to say, I die already; this fellow transported by passion is not I; *I am he who abjures and rejects the night-sea journey!* I. . . .

"I am all love. 'Come!' She whispers, and I have no will.

"You who I may be about to become, whatever You are: with the last twitch of my real self I beg You to listen. It is *not* love that sustains me! No; though Her magic makes me burn to sing the contrary, and though I drown even now for the blasphemy, I will say truth. What has fetched me across this dreadful sea is a single hope, gift of my poor dead comrade: that You may be stronger-willed than I, and that by sheer force of concentration I may transmit to You, along with Your official Heritage, a private legacy of awful recollection and negative resolve. Mad as it may be, my dream is that some unimaginable embodiment of myself (or myself plus Her if that's how it must be) will come to find itself expressing, in however garbled or radical a translation, some reflection of these reflections. If against all odds this comes to pass, may You to whom, through whom I speak, do what I cannot: terminate this aimless, brutal business! Stop Your hearing against Her song! Hate love!

"Still alive, afloat, afire. Farewell then my penultimate hope: that one may be sunk for direst blasphemy on the very shore of the Shore. Can it be (my old friend would smile) that only utterest nay-sayers survive the night? But even that were Sense, and there is no sense, only senseless love, senseless death. Whoever echoes these reflections: be more courageous than their author! An end to night-sea journeys! Make no more! And forswear me when I shall forswear myself, deny myself, plunge into Her who summons, singing . . .

" 'Love! Love! Love!' "

The Butterfly and the Traffic Light

CYNTHIA OZICK

Cynthia Ozick has been a teacher of literature and writing at Ohio State University, New York University, the Chautauqua Fiction Workshop, and Indiana University. Her fiction, poetry, essays, criticism, reviews, and translations have appeared in many periodicals, and her work is included in numerous anthologies, including *The Best American Short Stories* (ed. Martha Foley) for 1970 and 1972. She is the author of a novel, *Trust* (1966), and a volume of short stories, *The Pagan Rabbi and Other Stories*, in which "The Butterfly and the Traffic Light," originally published in *The Literary Review* (Autumn, 1961), appears.

> *. . . the moth for the star.*
> —Shelley

JERUSALEM, THAT PHOENIX CITY, is not known by its street-names. Neither is Baghdad, Copenhagen, Rio de Janeiro, Camelot, or Athens; nor Peking, Florence, Babylon, St. Petersburg. These fabled capitals rise up ready-spired, story-domed and filigreed; they come to us at the end of a plain, behind hill or cloud, walled and moated by myths and antique rumors. They are built of copper, silver, and gold; they

are founded on milkwhite stone; the bright thrones of ideal
kings jewel them. Balconies, parks, little gates, columns and
statuary, carriage-houses and stables, attics, kitchens, gables,
tiles, yards, rubied steeples, brilliant roofs, peacocks, lap-
dogs, grand ladies, beggars, towers, bowers, harbors, barbers,
wigs, judges, courts, and wines of all sorts fill them. Yet,
though we see the shimmer of the smallest pebble beneath
the humblest foot in all the great seats of legend, still not a
single street is celebrated. The thoroughfares of beautiful
cities are somehow obscure, unless, of course, we count Ven-
ice: but a canal is not really the same as a street. The ways,
avenues, plazas, and squares of old cities are lost to us, we do
not like to think of them, they move like wicked scratches
upon the smooth enamel of our golden towns; we have forgotten most of them. There is no beauty in cross-section—
we take our cities, like our wishes, whole.

It is different with places of small repute or where time
has not yet deigned to be an inhabitant. It is different especially in America. They tell us that Boston is our Jerusalem;
but, as anyone who has ever lived there knows, Boston owns
only half a history. Honor, pomp, hallowed scenes, proud
families, the Athenaeum and the Symphony are Boston's;
but Boston has no tragic tradition. Boston has never wept.
No Bostonian has ever sung, mourning for his city, "If I do
not remember thee, let my tongue cleave to the roof of my
mouth"—for, to manage his accent, the Bostonian's tongue
is already in that position. We hear of Beacon Hill and Back
Bay, of Faneuil market and State Street: it is all cross-
section, all map. And the State House with its gilt dome (it
counts for nothing that Paul Revere supplied the bottom-
most layer of gold leaf: he was businessman, not horseman,
then) throws back furious sunsets garishly, boastfully, as no
power-rich Carthage, for shame, would dare. There is no
fairy mist in Boston. True, its street-names are notable:
Boylston, Washington, Commonwealth, Marlborough, Tre-
mont, Beacon; and then the Squares, Kenmore, Copley,

Louisburg, and Scollay—evidence enough that the whole, unlike Jerusalem, has not transcended its material parts. Boston has a history of neighborhoods. Jerusalem has a history of histories. The other American towns are even less fortunate. It is not merely that they lack rudimentary legends, that their names are homely and unimaginative, half ending in -burg and half in -ville, or that nothing has ever happened in them. Unlike the ancient capitals, they are not infixed in our vision, we are not born knowing them, as though, in some earlier migration, we had been dwellers there: for no one is a stranger to Jerusalem. And unlike even Boston, most cities in America have no landmarks, no age-enshrined graveyards (although death is famous everywhere), no green park to show a massacre, poet's murder, or high marriage. The American town, alas, has no identity hinting at immortality; we recognize it only by its ubiquitous street-names: sometimes Main Street, sometimes High Street, and frequently Central Avenue. Grandeur shuns such streets. It is all ambition and aspiration there, and nothing to look back at. Cicero said that men who know nothing of what has gone before them are like children. But Main, High, and Central have no past; rather, their past is now. It is not the fault of the inhabitants that nothing has gone before them. Nor are they to be condemned if they make their spinal streets conspicuous, and confer egregious luster and false acclaim on Central, High, or Main, and erect minarets and marquees indeed as though their city were already in dream and fable. But it is where one street in particular is regarded as the central life, the high spot, the main drag, that we know the city to be a prenatal trace only. The kiln of history bakes out these prides and these divisions. When the streets have been forgotten a thousand years, the divine city is born.

In the farm-village where the brewer Buldenquist had chosen to establish his Mighty College, the primitive commercial artery was called, not surprisingly, "downtown," and then, more respectably, Main Street, and then, rather covetously looking to civic improvement, Buldenquist Road. But the Sacred Bull had dedicated himself to the foundation and perpetuation of scientific farming, and had a prejudice against putting money into pavements and other citifications. So the town fathers (for by that time the place *was* a town, swollen by the boarding houses and saloons frequented by crowds of young farm students)—the town fathers scratched their heads for historical allusions embedded in local folklore, but found nothing except two or three old family scandals, until one day a traveling salesman named Rogers sold the mayor an "archive"—a wrinkled, torn, doused, singed, and otherwise quite ancient-looking holographic volume purporting to hold the records and diaries of one Colonel Elihu Bigghe. This rather obscure officer had by gratifying coincidence passed through the neighborhood during the war with a force of two hundred, the document claimed, encountering a skirmish with the enemy on the very spot of the present firehouse—the "war" being, according to some, the Civil War, and in the positive authority of others, one of the lesser Indian Wars—in his private diary Bigghe was not, after all, expected to drop hints. At any rate, the skirmish was there in detail—one hundred or more of the enemy dead; not one of ours; ninety-seven of theirs wounded; our survivors all hale but three; the bravery of our side; the cowardice and brutality of the foe; and further pious and patriotic remarks on Country, Creator, and Christian Charity. A decade or so after this remarkable discovery the mayor heard of Rogers' arrest, somewhere in the East, for forgery, and in his secret heart began to wonder whether he might not have been taken in: but by then the Bigghe diaries were under glass in the antiseptic-smelling lobby of the town hall, school children were being herded regularly by their teachers to view it, boring Fourth of July speeches had been droned before the firehouse in annual commemoration, and most people had forgotten that Bigghe Road had ever been called after the grudging brewer. And who could blame the inhabitants if, after half a hundred years, they began to spell it Big Road? For by then the town had grown into a city, wide and clamorous.

For Fishbein it was an imitation of a city. He claimed (not altogether correctly) that he had seen all the capitals of Europe, and yet had never come upon anything to match Big Road in name or character. He liked to tell how the streets of Europe were "employed," as he put it: he would people them with beggars and derelicts—"they keep their cash and their beds in the streets"; and with crowds assembled for riot or amusement or politics—"in Moscow they filled, the revolutionaries I mean, three troikas with White Russians and shot them, the White Russians I mean, and let them run wild in the street, the horses I mean, to spill all the corpses" (but he had never been to Moscow); and with travelers determined on objective and destination—"they use the streets there to go from one place to another, the original design of streets, n'est-ce pas?" Fishbein considered that, while a city exists for its own sake, a street is utilitarian. The uses of Big Road, on the contrary, were plainly secondary. In Fishbein's view Big Road had come into being only that the city might have a conscious center—much as the nucleus of a cell demonstrates the cell's character and maintains its well-being ("although," Fishbein argued, "in the cell it is a moot question whether the nucleus exists for the sake of the cell or the cell for the sake of the nucleus: whereas it is clear that a formless city such as this requires a centrality from which to learn the idea of form"). But if the city were to have modeled itself after Big Road, it would have grown long, like a serpent, and unreliable in its sudden coilings. This had not happened. Big Road crept, toiled, and ran, but the city nibbled at this farmhouse and that, and spread and spread with no pattern other than exuberance and greed. And if

Fishbein had to go to biology or botany or history for his analogies, the city was proud that it had Big Road to stimulate such comparisons.

Big Road was different by day and by night, weekday and weekend. Daylight, sunlight, and even rainlight gave everything its shadow, winter and summer, so that every person and every object had its Doppelgänger, persistent and hopeless. There was a kind of doubleness that clung to the street, as though one remembered having seen this and this and this before. The stores, hung with signs, had it, the lazy-walking old women had it (all of them uniformly rouged in the geometric centers of their cheeks like victims of some senile fever already dangerously epidemic), the traffic lights suspended from their wires had it, the air dense with the local accent had it.

This insistent sense of recognition was the subject of one of Fishbein's favorite lectures to his walking companion. It's America repeating itself! Imitating its own worst habits! Haven't I seen the same thing everywhere? It's a simultaneous urbanization all over, you can almost hear the coxswain crow 'Now all together, boys!'—This lamppost, I saw it years ago in Birmingham, that same scalloped bowl teetering on a wrought-iron stick. At least in Europe the lampposts look different in each place, they have individual characters. And this traffic light! There's no cross-street there, so what do they want it for in such a desert? I'll tell you: they put it up to pretend they're a real city—to tease the transients who might be naïve enough to stop for it. And that click and buzz, that flash and blink, why do they all do that in just the same way? Repeat and repeat, nothing meaningful by itself. . . ."

"I don't mind them, they're like abstract statues," Isabel once replied to this. "As though we were strangers from another part of the world and thought them some kind of religious icon with a red and a green eye. The ones on poles especially."

He recognized his own fancifulness, coarsened, labored,

and made literal. He had taught her to think like this. But she had a distressing disinclination to shake off logic; she did not know how to ride her intuition.

"No, no," he objected, "then you don't know what an icon is! A traffic light could never be anything but a traffic light.—What kind of religion would it be which had only one version of its deity—a whole row of identical icons in every city?"

She considered rapidly. "An advanced religion. I mean a monotheistic one."

"And what makes you certain that monotheism is 'advanced'? On the contrary, little dear! It's as foolish to be fixed on one God as it is to be fixed on one idea, isn't that plain? The index of advancement is flexibility. Human temperaments are so variable, how could one God satisfy them all? The Greeks and Romans had a god for every personality the way the Church has a saint for every mood. Savages, Hindus, and Roman Catholics understand all that. It's only the Jews and their imitators who insist on a rigid unitarian God—I can't think of anything more unfortunate for history: it's the narrow way, like God imposing his will on Job. The disgrace of the fable is that Job didn't turn to another god, one more germane to his illusions. It's what any sensible man would have done. And then wouldn't the boils have gone away of their own accord?—the Bible states clearly that they were simply a psychogenic nervous disorder—isn't that what's meant by 'Satan'? There's no disaster that doesn't come of missing an imagination: I've told you that before, little dear. Now the Maccabean War for instance, for an altogether unintelligible occasion! All Antiochus the Fourth intended—he was Emperor of Syria at the time—was to set up a statue of Zeus on the altar of the Temple of Jerusalem, a harmless affair—who would be hurt by it? It wasn't that Antiochus cared anything for Zeus himself—he was nothing if not an agnostic: a philosopher, anyway—the whole movement was only to symbolize the Syrian hegemony. It wasn't worth a war to get rid of the

thing! A little breadth of vision, you see, a little imagination, a little *flexibility*, I mean—there ought to be room for
Zeus *and* God under one roof.... That's why traffic lights
won't do for icons! They haven't been conceived in a
pluralistic spirit, they're all exactly alike. Icons ought to
differ from one another, don't you see? An icon's only a
mask, that's the point, a representational mask which stands
for an idea."

"In that case," Isabel tried it, "if a traffic light were an
icon it would stand for two ideas, stop and go—"

"Stop and go, virtue and vice, logic and law!—Why are
you always on the verge of moralizing, little dear, when it's a
fever, not morals, that keeps the world spinning! Are masks
only for showing the truth? But no, they're for hiding,
they're for misleading, too.... It's a maxim, you see: one
mask reveals, another conceals."

"Which kind is better?"

"Whichever you happen to be wearing at the moment,"
he told her.

Often he spoke to her in this manner among night
crowds on Big Road. Sometimes, too argumentative to be
touched, she kept her hands in her pockets and, unexpectedly choosing a corner to turn, he would wind a rope of hair
around his finger and draw her leashed after him. She always
went easily; she scarcely needed to be led. Among all those
night walkers the two of them seemed obscure, dimmed-out,
and under a heat-screened autumn moon, one of those
shimmering country-moons indigenous to midwestern America, he came to a kind of truce with the street. It was
no reconcilement, nothing so friendly as that, not even a
cessation of warfare, only of present aggression. To come to
terms with Big Road would have been to come to terms with
America. And since this was impossible, he dallied instead
with masks and icons, and Isabel's long brown hair.

After twilight on the advent of the weekend the clutter of
banners, the parades, the caravans of curiously outfitted

convertibles vanished, and the students came out to roam. They sought each other with antics and capers, brilliantly tantalizing in the beginning darkness. Voices hung in the air, shot upward all along the street, and celebrated the Friday madness. It was a grand posture of relief: the stores already closed but the display-windows still lit, and the mannequins leaning forward from their glass cages with leers of painted horror and malignant eyeballs; and then the pirate movie letting out (this is 1949, my hearties), and the clusters of students flowing in gleaming rows, like pearls on a string, past posters raging with crimson seas and tall-masted ships and black-haired beauties shrieking, out of the scented palace into drugstores and ice cream parlors. Sweet, sweet, it was all sweet there before the shops and among the crawling automobiles and under the repetitious street lamps and below the singular moon. On the sidewalks the girls sprouted like tapestry blossoms, their heads rising from slender necks like woven petals swaying on the stems. They wore thin dresses, and short capelike coats over them; they wore no stockings, and their round bare legs moved boldly through an eddy of rainbow skirts; the swift white bone of ankle cut into the breath of the wind. A kind of greed drove Fishbein among them. "See that one," he would say, consumed with yearning, turning back in the wake of the young lasses to observe their gait, and how the filaments of their dresses seemed to float below their arms caught in a gesture, and how the dry sparks of their eyes flickered with the sheen of spiders.

And he would halt until Isabel too had looked. "Are you envious?" he asked, "because you are not one of them? Then console yourself." But he saw that she studied his greed and read his admiration. "Take comfort," he said again. "They are not free to become themselves. They are different from you." "Yes," Isabel answered, "they are prettier." "They will grow corrupt. Time will overwhelm them. They have only their one moment, like the butterflies." "Looking at butterflies gives pleasure." "Yes, it is a kind of joy, little dear, but full of poison. It belongs to the knowledge of rapid death. The butterfly lures us not only because he is beautiful, but because he is transitory. The caterpillar is uglier, but in him we can regard the better joy of becoming. The caterpillar's fate is bloom. The butterfly's is waste."

They stopped, and around them milled and murmured the girls in their wispy dresses and their little cut-off capes, and their yellow hair, whitish hair, tan hair, hair of brown-and-pink. The lithe, O the ladies young! It was all sweet there among the tousled bevies wormy with ribbon streamers and sashes, mock-tricked with make-believe gems, gems pinned over the breast, on the bar of a barrette, aflash even in the rims of their glasses. The alien gaiety took Fishbein in; he rocked in their strong sea-wave. From a record shop came a wild shiver of jazz, eyes unwound like coils of silk and groped for other eyes: the street churned with the laughter of girls. And Fishbein, arrested in the heart of the whirlpool, was all at once plunged again into war with the street and with America, where everything was illusion and all illusion led to disillusion. What use was it then for him to call O lyric ladies, what use to chant O languorous lovely November ladies, O lilting, lolling, lissome ladies—while corrosion sat waiting in their ears, he saw the maggots breeding in their dissolving jewels?

Meanwhile Isabel frowned with logic. "But it's only that the caterpillar's future is longer and his fate farther off. In the end he will die too." "Never, never, never," said Fishbein; "it is only the butterfly who dies, and then he has long since ceased to be a caterpillar. The caterpillar never dies.— Neither to die nor to be immortal, it is the enviable state, little dear, to live always at the point of beautiful change! That is what it means to be extraordinary—when did I tell you that?—" He bethought himself. "The first day, of course. It's always best to begin with the end—with the image of what is desired. If I had begun with the beginning I would have bored you, you would have gone away. . . . In my ideal kingdom, little dear, everyone, even the very old, will be passionately in the process of guessing at and preparing for his essential self. Boredom will be unnatural, like a curse, or unhealthy, like a plague. Everyone will be extraordinary."

"But if the whole population were extraordinary," Isabel objected, "then nobody would be extraordinary."

"Ssh, little dear, why must you insist on dialectics? Nothing true is ever found by that road. There are millions of caterpillars, and not one of them is intended to die, and they are all of them extraordinary. *Your* aim," he admonished, as they came into the darkened neighborhood beyond Big Road, "is to avoid growing into a butterfly. Come," he said, and took her hand, "let us live for that."

Kabiasy

YURI KAZAKOV

Yuri Kazakov was born in Moscow in 1927 and published his first book of short stories, *Teddy*, in 1957. English versions of his work include stories in *Going to Town and Other Stories* (1964), translated by Gabriella Azrael, and in *The New Writing in Russia* (1964), translated by T. P. Whitney, from which "Kabiasy" is taken.

THE CLUB MANAGER, Zhukov, overstayed his visit at the nearby collective farm. It was August. He had come during the day on business. He had gone all about and talked a lot—but it was an unsuccessful trip. Everyone was in a hurry because it was a busy season.

Quite a young chap, Zhukov had worked in the club hardly a year, and he understood his duties still rather vaguely. They had appointed him because he played well on the accordion and had taken an active part in each district sport competition. He still played on the soccer team for his native Zubatovo, though he now lived in Dubki in a little room in the club.

He should have gone home sooner when there was a car going to Dubki. He started to, but then he had changed his mind and paid a visit to a teacher who was an acquaintance. He wanted to talk about the volleyball team and in general about cultural activities. The teacher was out hunting. He

39

should have returned long before but was late for some reason, and Zhukov stayed waiting dolefully. He understood that it was silly and that he should have left.

He sat two hours in this way, smoking out the window and chatting uninterestedly with the mistress of the house. He had even dozed off a bit, but voices outside awakened him: they were driving the herd and the women were calling the cows.

Finally, there was no sense in waiting any longer and Zhukov, irritated at his failure, having gulped down for the road some sour kvas which put his teeth on edge, set out for his own collective farm. It was 12 kilometers away.

Zhukov ran into the night watchman, Matvei, on the bridge. Matvei was standing there in a raggedy winter cap and a well-worn sheepskin coat with his feet set wide apart, holding a gun over his elbow. The old man rolled himself a cigarette and looked up from beneath his brows at the passing Zhukov.

"Ah, Matvei!" Zhukov recognized him even though he had seen him only a couple of times. "Are you going hunting too?"

Matvei, without answering, walked along beside him slowly, squinting at his cigarette. He got out his matches and lit up, inhaled several times, and coughed. Then, scratching the flap of the sheepskin coat with his fingernails, he put away his matches and finally said:

"What hunting? I'm guarding the orchard at night. From my blind where I am hidden."

Zhukov still had a bad taste in his mouth from the kvas. He spit and then also lit a cigarette.

"Bet you sleep the whole night long," he said absentmindedly, thinking that he should have gone home earlier when there was a car. And now he had to walk.

"I'd like to all right!" Matvei retorted in a meaningful tone after a moment of silence. "I'd sleep all right but they don't let me . . ."

"Why? Are they stealing?" Zhukov asked ironically.

"Stealing pooh!" Matvei laughed and all of a sudden walked along more relaxed. He sort of settled down with a backward tilt like a person who had long been confined and had come out at last into open space. He didn't look at Zhukov at all, but kept peering to the sides into the twilit fields.

"Steal, they don't, fellow, but they come..."

"Girls, you mean?" Zhukov asked and laughed, remembering Lyubka and that he would see her tonight.

"Those same ones..." Matvei said indistinctly.

"That's an old man for you! Stretching it out!" Zhukov spat. "Well who?"

"The kabiasy, that's who," Matvei spoke out mysteriously and looked aslant for the first time at Zhukov.

"Well I must say you've got something there," said Zhukov jokingly. "Tell your old woman about that. And what are the kabiasy?"

"That kind," Matvei answered gloomily. "You get caught by them, and you'll find out for yourself."

"Devils are they?" Zhukov asked, making a serious face. Matvei again peered at him.

"That kind," he blurted out vaguely. "Black ones. The ones with green..."

He pulled out of his pockets two copper cartridges and blew the makhorka dust from his pocket off them.

"Look there," he said, pointing to the paper wadding in the cartridges.

Zhukov looked and saw crosses scratched on the wadding with pencil.

"Charmed!" Matvei said with satisfaction, hiding the cartridges. "I know how to deal with them!"

"They bother you?" Zhukov asked jokingly, but, catching himself again, made a serious face to show that he believed.

"Not too badly," Matvei answered seriously. "They don't

come near my blind. Instead . . . they come out of the dark
one after another and gather under the apple trees. They
make noise, they're so little and they stand in a row." Matvei
dropped his eyes to the road and moved his hand in front of
himself. "They stand there and play songs."

"Songs?" Zhukov couldn't control himself and burst out
laughing. "My! Just like in our club—amateur night! What
kind of songs?"

"Different ones . . . Sometimes awfully sad. And then
sometimes they say: 'Matvei, Matvei! Come here! Come
here!' "

"And you?"

"And I give it to them good: oh you!—with such mother
oaths . . . Beat it!"

Matvei smiled affectionately.

"And then they begin to come toward my blind and I
load up with a charmed cartridge and how I let them have
it—bang!"

"Do you hit them?"

"Hit them!" Matvei spoke out contemptuously. "Do you
think you can kill an evil spirit? I just chase them away a bit
till morning, till the first cock crows."

"Well!" said Zhukov after a little silence and sighed. "It's
bad, bad!"

"Whom?" asked Matvei.

"Things are bad with my atheistic propaganda, that's
what!" said Zhukov and knitted his brows, looking at Matvei. "So maybe you're telling this nonsense in the village and
scaring the girls?" he asked severely, remembering all of a
sudden that he was the manager of the club. "*Kabiasy!*
You're a *kabias* yourself."

"Whom?" Matvei asked again and his face suddenly became malicious and impressive. "And you're going to walk
past the forest?"

"So what? I'll walk past!"

"You're going to walk past, so watch out: lucky if you get
home."

Matvei turned away without saying anything and without even saying goodbye and went quickly across the field to the orchard which was dark in the distance. Even his figure seemed embittered.

Left alone on the road Zhukov lit a cigarette and looked about. The twilight shadows were advancing. The sky in the west grew pale. The collective farm behind was no longer visible. There were only some dark roofs among the aspens and a windmill generator.

A birch forest was on the left. It went in steps to the horizon. It was as if someone had blindly drawn strokes from top to bottom on a dark background with a white pencil. First sparsely, further on more thickly, and in the murk the horizon drew a timid light stripe crosswise.

On the left could be seen a lake lying as if it had been welded there, standing motionless on a level with its banks, the only shining thing in all the dark. On the shore of the lake burned a bonfire and smoke wafted from it to the road. Dew was already falling and the smoke was wet.

And on the right in the twilight, meadows and cuts, between the dark capes of the forest, from hillock to hillock marched latticed electric power towers. They were like a file of enormous silent beings thrown to us from other worlds and walking soundlessly with raised arms to the west in the direction of the flaring green star, their homeland.

Zhukov again looked about, still hoping that perhaps a car might come along. Then he strode down the road. He walked on and looked all the time at the bonfire and the lake. There was no one near the fire. There was not even anyone visible on the lake and the lonely fire, seemingly lit for no one and for no reason, produced a strange impression.

Zhukov went along at first uncertainly, smoking, looking back, waiting for a car or a fellow traveler afoot. But there was no one visible either before or behind as far as the horizon itself, and Zhukov finally decided and began walking along at a real pace.

He had gone four kilometers when it became completely

dark. Only the road was light, crossed in places by mist. The night was warm. Only when Zhukov moved into the mist patches did he feel a chill. But then he came back out into the warm air and these changes from cold to warm air were pleasant.

"Our people are superstitious!" thought Zhukov. He walked sticking his hands in his pickets, moving his brows and remembering the face of Matvei, how it had become malicious and contemptuous right away when he had laughed at him. "Yes," he thought, "I must, must step up atheistic propaganda. Superstition must be uprooted." And he wanted even more to talk with someone about things cultural, things intellectual.

Then he began to think that it was time for him to move to the city, to enroll in some educational institution for study. And right then he began to imagine how he was directing a chorus, not in a collective farm club where there weren't even curtains, where young people smoked in the hall and laughed across the room at each other, but in Moscow and that his chorus had a hundred persons in it—an academic capella.

As always he felt from such thoughts a glad liveliness and paid no attention to things around him, didn't look at the stars nor at the road, walked along unevenly, compressing and releasing his fists, moving his brows. He began to sing and laugh aloud, not fearing that anyone would see him. He was even glad he was walking alone without companions. It was then that he approached an empty barn near the road and sat down on a beam to rest and smoke.

Once this had been a separate farm, but soon after the establishment of the collective farm the farmhouse had been torn down and only the barn remained. It was open and empty. In it, evidently, there wasn't even a door. It was all dark and askew, and in its innards, deep inside it, there was especially deep darkness.

Zhukov sat there, placing his elbows on his high raised

knees, his face to the road, his back to the barn, and smoked. Gradually, he cooled off and thought no more about the conservatory but about Lyubka when he felt he was being looked at from behind.

He understood suddenly that he was sitting alone in the darkness, among empty fields, among mysterious dark spots that could be bushes and could be something other than bushes.

He remembered Matvei, his cruel-prophetic face at the end and the empty, mute lake with the bonfire lit for an unknown reason.

Holding his breath he slowly turned and looked at the barn. Its roof hung in the air and the stars were visible in the gap. But as he was looking, it settled on its frame and behind the barn something ran with audible footfall into the field uttering a suppressed monotonous cry: "Oh! Oh! Oh!"—ever more distant and more quietly. Zhukov's hair stood on end and he jumped out onto the road.

"Well!" he thought awestricken. "I'm a goner!" And he struck off down the road. The air whistled in his ears and in the bushes on both sides of the road something moved, sniffed, breathed on his back with a chill. "I should cross myself!" thought Zhukov, feeling how something was trying to grab him from behind. "Oh Lord God, I am in your hands..." And having crossed himself he stopped, already unable to run away farther. And he turned around.

But there was no one on the road nor in the field, and the barn was no longer to be seen. Zhukov wiped himself off with his sleeve without dropping his eyes from the road and said hoarsely, "Ha!" and shuddered, having frightened himself. Then he coughed, listened, and again said, with an effort, so his voice did not tremble:

"Ho! Ho! Ei!"

Having caught his breath Zhukov hurriedly walked along, remembering with feverish loneliness how far he still had to go, what black night lay all about, and that the forest about which Matvei had so mysteriously hinted still lay ahead.

The road dropped down to a stream and Zhukov as if in his sleep jumped in enormous leaps across the bridge over the black water and the willow thickets. From beneath the bridge there was a croak, but Zhukov couldn't even decide whether there had really been a sound or whether it just seemed to him as if there had been one. "Well, wait, I'll catch up with you," Zhukov thought with fear of Matvei, while ascending the slope on which, as he knew, the woods began.

The forest commenced with dewiness and damp. Something powerful breathed from its depths, bringing out into the warm field air the odor of rot, mushrooms, water and pines. On the right in the forest hung thick murk. On the left the field was more visible. Up above the stars shone down. The later it got the thicker they were strewn. The heaven, even though it was black, possessed a weak smoky light, and the trees stood out on its background with firm silhouettes.

From the forest murk from some branch or other an owl leaped. With a weak rustle it flew and perched on a branch ahead. Zhukov heard it, but he couldn't see it no matter how hard he tried. He saw only how, crossing off the stars, the branch on which it perched rocked.

Coming up to it Zhukov scared it off again, and it began to fly about in circles, over part of the field and immediately returning into the forest darkness. And now Zhukov saw it. On the horizon, beyond the fields, there still glimmered a remnant of the sunset, even not a remnant but simply a lighter sky, more immaterial there, and the owl, flying past, flashed there each time, a soundless, dark spot.

Looking askance at the owl Zhukov stumbled on a root and cursed it in his mind. He didn't dare to look directly into the forest or behind. And when, nevertheless, he looked ahead on the road a chill ran up and down his spine: up

ahead and a little to the left, from the woods across the road
there were standing waiting for him the *kabiasy*. They were
little, just as Matvei had said. One of them snickered just at
that moment and another groaned dolefully with the same
sound he had heard just before behind the barn: "Oh-
oh... Oh-oh..." And a third cried in the voice of a quail:
"Come here! Come here!"

Zhukov clenched his teeth and grew numb. He couldn't
even cross himself. His hands wouldn't rise.

"Ahhhhhh!" he hollered through the whole forest, and
all of a sudden he saw that they were little fir trees. Trembling like a hunting dog on a point, he took first one step
toward them, then another... Behind the firs something
rustled and started rolling with a worried cry into the field.

"A bird!" Zhukov guessed with gladness, resuming his
breathing and moving his shoulders beneath his wet shirt.
Speedily passing the little fir trees he pulled out a cigarette
and started to get out his matches, but realized immediately
that if he lit it he would be visible throughout the forest. He
didn't know who would see him and he was afraid to think,
but he knew that they would.

Zhukov sat down, looked around on all sides, pulled his
jacket over his head and thus under his jacket lit up. "I'll go
through the fields!" he decided. He could not any longer go
through the forest, on the road. And in the fields, though it
was awful, it wasn't that bad.

He roared past the nut trees beginning on the edge of the
forest and emerged into the open and walked parallel to the
forest, bypassing at a distance everything on his path which
was dark, incessantly looking to the right. The owl kept on
flying, rustling, and squeaking everywhere, and somewhere
in the very depth of the forest, among the ravines could be
heard something which wasn't quite a cry nor a groan and
which lingered long in the air, rolling like an echo through
the edge of the woods.

But there the forest ended and again the dusty light road

writhed like a snake. Zhukov came out on it and squealing with fright, without looking behind, ran at a full trot, pressing his elbows to his sides like a long-distance runner. He ran and the air screamed in his ears and the forest fell further and further behind till it became a barely noticeable dark ribbon. Zhukov had already decided there was nothing to look at and had begun to rejoice. He had begun, in rhythm with his running pace, to sing something to himself which was monotonous and unnaturally merry: "Tee-ta-ta! Tee-ta-ta!" when suddenly he again pulled back sharply and his eyes grew wide.

What he saw this time was neither tree, nor bird, such as he had already grown used to seeing, but something alive which was moving toward him across his path on a field boundary. It was neither like a man, a cow, nor a horse and had an indefinite look to it. Zhukov already clearly heard the crunching of the tall weeds on the boundary line, a soft hopping, a weak knocking.

"Who is it?" roared a resounding voice.

Zhukov didn't make a sound.

"Are you someone I know? Or not?" the voice asked from the road. Zhukov by now understood that he was being called, that a human being was approaching him, pushing a bicycle, but as before he couldn't answer. He could only breathe.

"Zhukov?" the person guessed without conviction, coming right up to him and staring at him. "That's funny. Why are you so quiet? And I thought who could it be? Do you have matches? Give me a light!"

And now Zhukov recognized Popov from the local Youth Communist League executive committee. Zhukov's hands trembled so that the matches rattled in the box when he gave them to Popov.

"Where are you coming from?" Popov asked him, after getting a light. "I, you see, lost my way. I was going to your place and missed my turn because I was thinking about some-

thing else. I finally came out over in Gorki, and then came
from that road over here along the boundary... What's
wrong with you?"

"Wait a minute..." Zhukov said hoarsely, feeling weakness and dizziness. "Wait just a minute..."

He stood there smiling guiltily and couldn't manage to
get control over his weakness. He was sweating profusely and
breathing hurriedly. There was a smell of dusty, strong roadside weeds in the air.

"Are you ill?" Popov asked with fright.

Zhukov silently nodded.

"Well, in that case sit down!" Popov said with determi-
nation and pushed up the bicycle. "Get on to the handle-
bars. Well!"

Popov pushed the bicycle in uneven pushes and jumped
into its seat, moving strongly from side to side. He blew away
the locks of hair which fell into his eyes and rolled off to
Dubki. Zhukov sat on the bar. He was uncomfortable and
ashamed. He felt how heavy the bicycle was moving along
on the dust. Popov was breathing heatedly on his back and
knocking against him with his knees.

Almost the whole way both were silent. Finally the lights
of the collective farm came into view and Zhukov stirred.

"Stop..." he said.

"Sit there, just sit there!" Popov answered breathlessly.
"It's only a little further. We'll get to the clinic..."

"No, put on the brakes..." said Zhukov wrinkling his
brows, and stretching out his foot, caught hold of the ground.

Popov braked with relief. They jumped from the bicycle
and stood for a while silently without knowing what to talk
about. Next to them was a stable. The horses heard the
people and grew impatient, tramping with their hooves on
the planking. There was a strong and pleasant odor of manure and tar from the stable.

"Give me the matches," Popov said again.

He lit up and wiped the sweat from his face lengthily and

with satisfaction. Then he unbuttoned the collar of his shirt entirely.

"Well how do you feel? Are you better?" he asked hopefully.

"Now it's nothing," Zhukov said hurriedly. "I drank some *kvas*. Probably that was it . . ."

They walked slowly down the street, listening to the quieting sounds of the big village.

"How are things in the club?" Popov asked.

"So, so . . . You know yourself. It's harvest time and people are busy," Zhukov answered absent-mindedly and all of a sudden remembered:

"Have you ever heard the word *kabiasy?*"

"What, what? *Kabiasy?*" Popov thought. "No, I've never heard it. And why do you need to know? For a play?"

"Just something that popped into my mind," Zhukov said evasively.

They came up beside the club and shook hands.

"Take the matches," said Zhukov. "I have some at home."

"Good!" Popov took the matches. "And you drink some milk—it helps a troubled stomach."

He got on his bicycle and rode off to the house of the farm chairman, and Zhukov went along the dark corridors and unlocked the door to his room. After drinking cold tea he smoked, listened to the radio in the darkness, opened the window, and lay down.

He had almost gone to sleep when everything in him turned upside down and, as if from above, from a hill, he saw the nighttime fields, the empty lake, the dark rows of power towers with raised arms, the lonely bonfire, and heard the life which filled these enormous spaces in the deaf night hours.

He began to relive over again his whole journey, all the way, but this time with happiness, with a warm feeling for the night, for the stars, for the smells, for the rustlings and cries of the birds.

He wanted again to talk with someone about cultural things, high things—about eternity, for example. He thought about Lyubka and jumped up from his cot and pattered bare-foot across the room. He pulled on his clothes and went out.

Seventh House

R. K. NARAYAN

R. K. Narayan was born in Madras, South India, in
1907 and although a frequent visitor to the United
States still lives in India. He is best known for his
novels of "Malgudi," an imaginary Indian district;
these include *The Vendor of Sweets, The Man-
Eater of Malgudi, The Guide, Swami and Friends,
The English Teacher,* and *Waiting for the Mahatma.*
In 1966 he received the Padna Bhushan award, India's highest literary honor. "Seventh House" is
taken from his 1970 collection of short stories entitled *A Horse and Two Goats.*

KRISHNA RAN HIS FINGER over the block of ice in order to
wipe away the layer of sawdust, chiselled off a piece, crushed
it, and filled the rubber ice bag. This activity in the shaded
corner of the back verandah gave him an excuse to get away
from the sickroom, but he could not dawdle over it, for he
had to keep the icecap on his wife's brow continuously,
according to the doctor's command. In that battle between
ice and mercury column, it was ice that lost its iciness while
the mercury column held its ground at a hundred and three
degrees Fahrenheit. The doctor had looked triumphant on
the day he diagnosed the illness as typhoid, and announced
with glee, "We now know what stick to employ for beating
it; they call it Chloromycetin. Don't you worry any more."

He was a good doctor but given to lugubrious humour and monologuing.

The Chloromycetin pills were given to the patient as directed, and at the doctor's next visit Krishna waited for him to pause for breath and then cut in with "The fever has not gone down," holding up the temperature chart.

The doctor threw a brief, detached look at the sheet and continued, "The municipality served me a notice to put a slab over the storm drain at my gate, but my lawyer said—"

"Last night she refused food," Krishna said.

"Good for the country, with its food shortage. Do you know what the fat grain merchant in the market did? When he came to show me his throat, he asked if I was an M.D.! I don't know where he learned about M.D.s."

"She was restless and tugged at her bedclothes," Krishna said, lowering his voice as he noticed his wife open her eyes.

The doctor touched her pulse with the tip of his finger and said breezily, "Perhaps she wants a different-coloured sheet, and why not?"

"I have read somewhere the tugging of bedclothes is a bad sign."

"Oh, you and your reading!"

The patient moved her lips. Krishna bent close to her, and straightened himself to explain, "She is asking when you will let her get up."

The doctor said, "In time for the Olympics..." and laughed at his own joke. "I'd love to be off for the Olympics myself."

Krishna said, "The temperature was a hundred and three at one a.m...."

"Didn't you keep the ice going?"

"Till my fingers were numb."

"We will treat you for cramps by and by, but first let us see the lady of the house back in the kitchen."

So Krishna found, after all, a point of agreement with the

doctor. He wanted his wife back in the kitchen very badly. He miscooked the rice in a different way each day, and swallowed it with buttermilk at mealtimes and ran back to his wife's bedside.

The servant maid came in the afternoon to tidy up the patient and the bed, and relieved Krishna for almost an hour, which he spent in watching the street from the doorway: a cyclist passing, schoolchildren running home, crows perching in a row on the opposite roof, a street hawker crying his wares—anything seemed interesting enough to take his mind off the fever.

Another week passed. Sitting there beside her bed, holding the ice bag in position, he brooded over his married life from its beginning.

When he was studying at Albert Mission he used to see a great deal of her; they cut their classes, sat on the river's edge, discussed earnestly their present and future, and finally decided to marry. The parents on both sides felt that here was an instance of the evils of modern education: young people would not wait for their elders to arrange their marriage but settled things for themselves, aping Western manners and cinema stories. Except for the lack of propriety, in all other respects the proposal should have proved acceptable; financial background of the families, the caste and group requirements, age, and everything else were correct. The elders relented eventually, and on a fine day the horoscopes of the boy and girl were exchanged and found not suited to each other. The boy's horoscope indicated Mars in the Seventh House, which spelled disaster for his bride. The girl's father refused to consider the proposal further. The boy's parents were outraged at the attitude of the bride's party—a bride's father was a seeker and the bridegroom's the giver, and how dare they be finicky? "Our son will get a bride a hundred times superior to this girl. After all, what has she to commend her? All college girls make themselves up to look pretty, but that is not everything." The young couple felt and looked miserable, which induced the parents to re-open negotiations. A wise man suggested that, if other things were all right, they could ask for a sign and go ahead. The parties agreed to a flower test. On an auspicious day they assembled in the temple. The wick lamp in the inner sanctum threw a soft illumination around. The priest lit a piece of camphor and circled it in front of the image in the sanctum. Both sets of parents and their supporters, standing respectfully in the pillared hall, watched the image and prayed for guidance. The priest beckoned to a boy of four who was with another group of worshippers. When he hesitated, the priest dangled a piece of coconut. The child approached the threshold of the sanctum greedily. The priest picked off a red and a white flower from the garland on the image, placed them on a tray, and told the boy to choose one.

"Why?" asked the boy, uneasy at being watched by so many people. If the red flower was chosen, it would indicate God's approval. The little boy accepted the piece of coconut and tried to escape, but the priest held him by the shoulder and commanded, "Take a flower!" at which the child burst into tears and wailed for his mother. The adults despaired. The crying of the child at this point was inauspicious; there should have been laughter and the red flower. The priest said, "No need to wait for any other sign. The child has shown us the way," and they all dispersed silently.

Despite the astrologers, Krishna married the girl, and Mars in the Seventh House was, eventually, forgotten.

The patient seemed to be asleep. Krishna tiptoed out of the room and told the servant maid waiting in the verandah, "I have to go out and buy medicines. Give her orange juice at six, and look after her until I return." He stepped out of his house, feeling like a released prisoner. He walked along, enjoying the crowd and bustle of Market Road until the thought of his wife's fever came back to his mind. He desperately needed someone who could tell him the unvarnished truth about his wife's condition. The doctor touched upon all subjects except that. When Chloromycetin failed to bring down the fever, he said cheerfully, "It only shows that it is not typhoid but something else. We will do other tests to-morrow." And that morning, before leaving: "Why don't you pray, instead of all this cross-examination of me?"

"What sort of prayer?" Krishna had asked naïvely.

"Well, you may say, 'O God, if You *are* there, save me if You can!'" the doctor replied, and guffawed loudly at his own joke. The doctor's humour was most trying.

Krishna realized that the doctor might sooner or later arrive at the correct diagnosis, but would it be within the patient's lifetime? He was appalled at the prospect of be-reavement; his heart pounded wildly at the dreadful thought. Mars, having lain dormant, was astir now. Mars and an unidentified microbe had combined forces. The microbe was the doctor's business, however confused he might look. But the investigation of Mars was not.

Krishna hired a bicycle from a shop and pedalled off in the direction of the coconut grove where the old astrologer lived who had cast the horoscopes. He found the old man sitting in the hall, placidly watching a pack of children climb over walls, windows, furniture, and rice bags stacked in a corner and creating enough din to drown all conversation. He unrolled a mat for Krishna to sit on, and shouted over the noise of the children, "I told you at the start itself how it was going to turn out, but you people would not listen to my words. Yes, Mars has begun to exercise his most malignant aspect now. Under the circumstances, survival of the person concerned is doubtful." Krishna groaned. The children in a body had turned their attention to Krishna's bicycle, and were ringing the bell and feverishly attempting to push the machine off its stand. Nothing seemed to matter now. For a man about to lose his wife, the loss of a cycle taken on hire should not matter. Let children demolish all the bicycles in the town and Krishna would not care. Everything could be replaced except a human life.

"What shall I *do?*" he asked, picturing his wife in her bed asleep and never waking. He clung to this old man desperately, for he felt, in his fevered state of mind, that the astrologer could intercede with, influence, or even apologize on his behalf to, a planet in the high heavens. He remembered the reddish Mars he used to be shown in the sky when he was a Boy Scout—reddish on account of malignity erupting like lava from its bosom. "What would you advise me to do? Please help me?" The old man looked over the rim of his spectacles at Krishna menacingly. His eyes were also red. Everything is red, reflected Krishna. He partakes of the tint of Mars. I don't know whether this man is my friend or foe. My doctor also has red eyes. So has the maid servant.... Red everywhere.

Krishna said, "I know that the ruling god in Mars is benign. I wish I knew how to propitiate him and gain his compassion."

The old man said, "Wait." He stood before a cupboard, took out a stack of palm-leaf strips with verses etched on them, four lines to a leaf. "This is one of the four originals of the *Brihad-Jataka,* from which the whole science of astrology is derived. This is what has given me my living; when I speak, I speak with the authority of this leaf." The old man held the palm leaf to the light at the doorway and read out a Sanskrit aphorism: "'There can be no such thing as evading fate, but you can insulate yourself to some extent from its rigours.'" Then he added, "Listen to this: 'Where Angaraka is malevolent, appease him with the following prayer . . . and accompany it with the gift of rice and gram and a piece of red silk. Pour the oblation of pure butter into a fire raised with sandal sticks, for four days continuously, and feed four Brahmins.'... Can you do it?"

Krishna was panic-stricken. How could he organize all this elaborate ritual (which was going to cost a great deal)

when every moment and every rupee counted? Who would
nurse his wife in his absence? Who would cook the ritual
feast for the Brahmins? He simply would not be able to
manage it unless his wife helped him. He laughed at the
irony of it, and the astrologer said, "Why do you laugh at
these things? You think you are completely modern?"
Krishna apologized for his laugh and explained his helpless state. The old man shut the manuscript indignantly,
wrapped it in its cover, and put it away, muttering, "These
simple steps you can't take to achieve a profound result. Go,
go. . . . I can be of no use to you."
Krishna hesitated, took two rupees from his purse, and
held them out to the old man, who waved the money away.
"Let your wife get well first. Then give me the fee. Not
now." And as Krishna turned to go: "The trouble is, your
love is killing your wife. If you were an indifferent husband,
she could survive. The malignity of Mars might make her
suffer now and then, mentally more than physically, but
would not kill her. I have seen horoscopes that were the
exact replica of yours and the wife lived to a ripe age. You
know why? The husband was disloyal or cruel, and that in
some way neutralized the rigour of the planet in the Seventh
House. I see your wife's time is getting to be really bad.
Before anything happens, save her. If you can bring yourself
to be unfaithful to her, try that. Every man with a concubine
has a wife who lives long. . . ."
A strange philosophy, but it sounded feasible.

Krishna was ignorant of the technique of infidelity, and
wished he had the slickness of his old friend Ramu, who in
their younger days used to brag of his sexual exploits. It
would be impossible to seek Ramu's guidance now, although
he lived close by; he had become a senior government officer
and a man of family and might not care to lend himself to
reminiscences of this kind.
Krishna looked for a pimp representing the prostitutes in

Golden Street and could not spot one, although the market gate was reputed to be swarming with them.

He glanced at his watch. Six o'clock. Mars would have to be appeased before midnight. Somehow his mind fixed the line at midnight. He turned homeward, leaned his bicycle on the lamppost, and ran up the steps of his house. At the sight of him the servant maid prepared to leave, but he begged her to stay on. Then he peeped into the sickroom, saw that his wife was asleep, and addressed her mentally, "You are going to get better soon. But it will cost something. Doesn't matter. Anything to save your life."

He washed hurriedly and put on a nylon shirt, a lace-edged dhoti, and a silk upper cloth; lightly applied some talcum and a strange perfume he had discovered in his wife's cupboard. He was ready for the evening. He had fifty rupees in his purse, and that should be adequate for the wildest evening one could want. For a moment, as he paused to take a final look at himself in the mirror, he was seized with an immense vision of passion and seduction.

He returned the hired cycle to the shop and at seven was walking up Golden Street. In his imagination he had expected glittering females to beckon him from their balconies. The old houses had pyols, pillars, and railings, and were painted in garish colours, as the houses of prostitutes were reputed to be in former times, but the signboards on the houses indicated that the occupants were lawyers, tradesmen, and teachers. The only relic of the old days was a little shop in an obscure corner that sold perfumes in coloured bottles and strings of jasmine flowers and roses.

Krishna passed up and down the street, staring hard at a few women here and there, but they were probably ordinary, indifferent housewives. No one returned his stare. No one seemed to notice his silk upper cloth and lace dhoti. He paused to consider whether he could rush into a house, seize someone, perform the necessary act, shed his fify rupees, and rush out. Perhaps he might get beaten in the process. How on earth was one to find out which woman, among all those he had noticed on the terraces and verandahs of the houses, would respond to his appeal?

After walking up and down for two hours he realized that the thing was impossible. He signed for the freedom between the sexes he read about in the European countries, where you had only to look about and announce your intentions and you could get enough women to confound the most malignant planet in the universe.

He suddenly remembered that the temple dancer lived somewhere here. He knew a lot of stories about Rangi of the temple, who danced before the god's image during the day and took lovers at night. He stopped for a banana and a fruit drink at a shop and asked the little boy serving him, "Which is the house of the temple dancer Rangi?" The boy was too small to understand the purport of his inquiry and merely replied, "I don't know." Krishna felt abashed and left.

Under a street lamp stood a jutka, the horse idly swishing its tail and the old driver waiting for a fare. Krishna asked, "Are you free?"

The driver sprang to attention. "Where do you wish to be taken, sir?"

Krishna said timidly, "I wonder if you know where the temple dancer Rangi lives?"

"Why do you want her?" the driver asked, looking him up and down.

Krishna mumbled some reply about his wanting to see her dance. "At this hour!" the driver exclaimed. "With so much silk and so much perfume on! Don't try to deceive me. When you come out of her house, she will have stripped you of all the silk and perfume. But tell me, first, why only Rangi? There are others, both experts and beginners. I will drive you wherever you like. I have carried hundreds like you on such an errand. But shouldn't I first take you to a milk shop where they will give you hot milk with crushed almond to give you stamina? Just as a routine, my boy. . . . I will take you wherever you want to go. Not my business anyway. Someone has given you more money than you need? Or is your wife pregnant and away at her mother's house? I have seen all the tricks that husbands play on their wives. I know the world, my master. Now get in. What difference does it make what you will look like when you come out of there? I will take you wherever you like."

Krishna obediently got into the carriage, filling its interior with perfume and the rustle of his silken robes. Then he said, "All right. Take me home."

He gave his address so mournfully that the jutka driver, urging his horse, said, "Don't be depressed, my young master. You are not missing anything. Someday you will think of this old fellow again."

"I have my reasons," Krishna began, gloomily.

The horse driver said, "I have heard it all before. Don't tell me." And he began a homily on conjugal life.

Krishna gave up all attempts to explain and leaned back, resigning himself to his fate.

II
THE MORAL LAW:
FREEDOM OR BONDAGE?

The Woman and the Mighty Bird

A. C. JORDAN

A. C. Jordan was born in the village of Mboko-thwana, South Africa, in 1906, to the Nobadula family of the Zengele clan; he died in 1968 in Madison, Wisconsin, where he was serving as Professor of African Languages and Literature at the University of Wisconsin. When he received a Carnegie Fellowship and an invitation to lecture at UCLA, the South African government refused to grant him a passport, so that after 1961 he was in effect exiled from his native land. Much of his creative and imaginative writing—novels and poetry—is in Xhosa, his mother tongue; most of his historical essays, criticism, and more didactic folk tales are in English. "The Woman and the Mighty Bird" is taken from his 1973 volume of translated and retold *Tales from Southern Africa.*

I⊤ CAME ABOUT, according to some tale, that there was a beautiful young woman who lived with her husband close to a very big forest where all the women used to gather firewood. In the depths of the forest there were very tall trees that cast fearful shadows all around. The depths were greatly feared by the whole community, and though no one ever gave the reason why, the women were constantly warned by the men never to go anywhere near the tall trees.

It so happened at one time that there was a long spell of cold, and the women had to go more frequently into the forest, bringing home much bigger bundles of firewood on their heads. Moons rolled by, and the cold spell did not pass. Wood became scarcer and scarcer, and the women took longer and longer to gather, and the bundles they brought home became smaller each day. What was to be done? The women were to be seen standing in small groups in the forest, talking in low tones and pointing towards the depths. The beautiful young woman never voiced her own opinion in these talks but always stood close and listened with interest while the older women talked at length and reminded every woman that none of them was ever to venture into the depths.

One day, when the women had scattered in all directions, each one picking up a twig here and a twig there in order to make up her bundle, the young woman stole quietly away and, holding her skirt daintily just above her knees, she tiptoed towards the depths. She went on and on, crossing streams and streamlets, until she came to the grove of tall trees that hid the sun, making day look like night. She paused and looked around, her heart beating wild.

Then suddenly, deep in the dark shadows of the great trees she saw two lights, as big as a man's head. Looking more closely, she saw a big red beak, a big long neck as big and long as the trunk of a big tall man. It was a giant bird on whose red throat was fold upon fold of flesh that hung loosely like the dewlap of a giant bull. The woman was seized with terror and would have turned and fled, but she found herself unable to move from where she was. Then, his eyes fixed on hers, the giant bird beckoned her with his wing. It was then that she noticed that the tips of the wings were white and the rest of the body black. She hesitated. He beckoned again, his red eyes still fixed on hers. She let down her skirt and walked slowly towards him.

He was sitting on a huge bundle of firewood, like a hen

sitting on its brood, and all around him were bundles and bundles of firewood of all sizes, ready to pick up and carry away on one's head. As she drew nearer and nearer, the bird puffed himself until he was many times his former size, and his eyes and beak and throat became a deeper and deeper red. The woman came to a stop in front of him.

"Be not afraid," he said in a deep voice. "Come closer!"

The woman came closer.

"You are the woman whose homestead is at the edge of this forest?"

"Yes."

"You are married to the Ndelas?"

"Yes."

"What have you come here for?"

"I—I'm looking for firewood."

"Is there no more where you usually gather?"

"There are only small twigs left, and they are so scarce that it takes a whole day to make up just a small bundle. It tires one."

"I understand. Where are the other women now?"

"They are scattered all over the usual area, picking up those small twigs."

"Do they know that you're here?"

"No. I—I stole away."

"Weren't all the women told never to come near this place?"

"Yes, we have been told many times never to come here. But as for me, I get tired of walking over that same place every day, picking up thin little twigs that do not make a good fire. And—it's so cold. So I came."

"You speak well! Now, if I give you a bundle of wood to carry home, do you promise never to tell anybody?"

"I promise."

"You will not tell the other women?"

"I promise."

"Your husband?"

"I'll never tell him."

Thereupon the giant bird puffed himself to a huge size, rolled his deep-red eyes and boomed:

Ungaz' utsho kwabakwa Ndela	You're never to say to those of Ndela
U'b' ukhe wayibon' intak' enk-ulu	That you've ever seen the mighty bird
Eqeba-liqeba lubilo-bilo!	Of manifold windpipe and manifold dewlap.

In reply, the woman sang sweetly but sadly:

Soze nditsho kwa bakwa Ndela	I'll never say to those of Ndela
Ukuba ndikhe ndayibona intak' enkulu	That I've ever seen the mighty bird
Eqeba-liqeba lubilo-bilo.	Of manifold windpipe and manifold dewlap.

The bird puffed himself to a yet greater size and boomed again:

"You're never to say to those of Ndela" etc.

The woman sang again:

"I'll never say to those of Ndela" etc.

The bird puffed himself still greater and more fearful, his rolling eyes and beak and throat a deeper red than ever, and he boomed a third time:

"You're never to say to those of Ndela" etc.

The woman sang a third time:

"I'll never say to those of Ndela" etc.

"Very well!" said the bird. "Pick up any bundle you like and carry it home. Remember! You are not tell your husband."

The woman picked up a bundle of firewood, put it on her head and went home, taking a round-about way in order not to be seen by the other women.

Her husband was surprised to see her come home so early and with such a big bundle of good firewood.

"How does it happen that you come home so early, and with such a big bundle on your head?" he asked.

"I—I've been very lucky," she replied. "I found plenty of wood in a place that the other women don't know about."

"Where's this place?" asked the husband sharply.

"In the forest."

"I know *that*. But whereabouts?"

"Somewhere—not very far from the place where we usually gather wood."

"Where are the other women now?"

"They're still gathering twigs in the usual place."

The husband said no more, but he followed the woman with his eyes as she moved about the home preparing the evening meal.

When the time came to go to the forest again, the young woman joined the other women of the community, and as soon as they had scattered, she stole away and made for the depths. She found the bird sitting on the pile of wood as if he had never moved. He beckoned her, and she came up to him. As soon as she was close enough, he puffed himself and boomed:

Ungabo'b' utshilo kwabakwa Ndela	Woe to you if you've said to those of Ndela
U'b' ukhe wayibon' intak' enkulu	That you've ever seen the mighty bird
Eqeba-liqeba lubilo-bilo!	Of manifold windpipe and manifold dewlap.

In reply, the woman sang sweetly and more brightly than before:

Mn' anditshongo kwa bakwa Ndela	I did not say to those of Ndela
Ukuba ndikhe ndayibona intak' enkulu	That I ever saw the mighty bird
Eqeba-liqeba lubilo-bilo.	Of manifold windpipe and manifold dewlap.

The bird puffed himself greater and boomed louder:

"Woe to you if you have said to those of Ndela" etc.

The woman sang sweetly and assuringly in reply:

"I did not say to those of Ndela" etc.

The bird puffed himself and boomed yet louder and more menacingly:

"Woe to you if you have said to those of Ndela" etc.

The woman sang sweetly and more reassuringly:

"I did not say to those of Ndela" etc.

Then the bird deflated and calmed himself and told her to pick up a bundle of wood and go. She cast her eye over the bundles, taking her own time, and then picked up a much larger one than before. As she turned to go, the bird again gave the warning: "Remember! You are not to tell your husband!"

When she reached home, her husband was more startled than surprised because she had returned much earlier and her bundle was noticeably bigger. Again he asked her, and again she gave the same explanation as before. He said no more, but looked more troubled than ever.

When the pile of wood was almost finished, the woman went to the forest again, and again she stole away as soon as she knew that the other women were far enough. This time she went close up to the bird without waiting to be asked, and when the bird boomed three times, "Woe to you..." each time more menacingly than before, she sang sweetly in reply, "I did not say...," each time more brightly and reassuringly than before. Then she picked up the best bundle next to the one on which the bird was brooding, and turned to go.

"Remember! You are not to tell your husband!"

On reaching home, she threw down the bundle on the usual spot and was just turning to go to the cooking hut, when her husband appeared at the door of the Great Hut and beckoned her. She walked up to him, noting that he was agitated, but not letting him see that she had noted this.

He stood aside to let her go in, and as soon as she had entered, he grabbed a pile of spears with his left hand and one glittering long-bladed one with his right, turned and faced her.

"Woman!" he said. "Twice you have told me lies. This time you're going to tell me the truth or I'm going to stab you to death. Where do you *alone* get this wood?"

And he raised his long-bladed spear threateningly.

"But what are you asking me, my husband? I told you before that I found—"

"You told me, but you told me a lie. I want the truth!"

He stepped towards her, his long-bladed spear held high in his right hand. The woman tried to run this way and that along the wall, but he caught up with her, pressed her to the wall with the blades of the spears in his left hand, and then lowered the spear in the right hand and held it close to her heart.

"Will you tell the truth or shall I kill you? Where did you get this wood?"

"Wait! Don't kill me! O, don't kill me! I'll tell the truth!"

"Speak!"

"I got it from the depths."

"From the depths!! Who gave it to you?"

"O! Mhm! O!"

"Speak!"

"It was given to me by—by—by—the mighty bird."

No sooner had she uttered these words than the great trees moved from the depths of the forest, surrounded the entire homestead and cast their dark shadows over it. The great bird emerged from the shadows and made straight for the Great Hut. His eyes and beak and throat were a terrifyingly deep red, and as he approached, he grew bigger and bigger until, by the time he reached the doorway, he was

many sizes bigger than the hut itself. The man was so terrified that his spears dropped from his hands, and he fell
senseless near the hearth. The woman crouched at the far
end of the hut, clutching her chest with her right hand and
shielding her face with her left, as if she was being blinded by
the light of the big red eyes that glared at her from the
doorway.

The great bird thundered:

Woe to you if you have said to those of Ndela
That you ever saw the mighty bird
Of manifold windpipe and manifold dewlap.

The woman sang weakly, a little out of tune:

I did not say to those of Ndela
That I ever saw the mighty bird
Of manifold windpipe and manifold dewlap.

The great bird interrupted her, thundering more fiercely:

Woe to you if you have said to those of Ndela
That you ever saw the mighty bird
Of manifold windpipe and manifold dewlap.

The woman sang more weakly, much more out of tune:

I did not say to those of Ndela
That I ever saw the mighty bird
Of—

The great bird interrupted her, thundering most fiercely:

Woe to you if you have said to those of Ndela
That you ever saw the mighty bird
Of manifold windpipe and manifold dewlap.

The woman sang very weakly, completely out of tune:

I did not say to those of Ndela
That I ever saw—

Like lightning the great bird stretched out his long red
neck right over the prostrate man, opened his great red

mouth very wide and—gulp!—he swallowed the woman alive. Then turning sharply about, he vanished in the grove, and the great trees and their shadows receded to the depths of the forest.

Every Leave That Falls

PETER DEVRIES

Born in Chicago in 1910 and for a time an editor of *Poetry*, **Peter DeVries** later became a staff member of *The New Yorker* and a resident of Connecticut. He is best known as the author of witty, sardonic novels about contemporary American life, including *Tunnel of Love* (1954), *Comfort Me with Apples* (1956), *Mackerel Plaza* (1958), *The Tents of Wickedness* (1959), *Through the Fields of Clover* (1961), *The Blood of the Lamb* (1962), *Let Me Count the Ways* (1965), and more recently *Mrs. Wallop, Into Your Tent I'll Creep, The Glory of the Hummingbird,* and *I Hear American Swinging.* "Every Leave That Falls" was first published in *The New Yorker* and is taken from DeVries's 1972 collection of humorous short pieces, *Without a Stitch in Time.*

THE OTHER NIGHT, leaving a party with a man who was in rather poor condition, I offered to see him home in a cab. It seemed like a simple enough thing to do, but what with all the cajolery, stumbling and scolding it took, and the indistinguishable replies he made to questions about where he lived and how to get there, it was a good hour before I finally delivered him to the doorman of his apartment house. I turned back into the street murmuring "Never again," and the vow struck a familiar chord. I had made the same resolution following an incident with a drunk almost fifteen years ago—an experience that should have taught me more of a lesson than, apparently, it did.

On Saturdays in the fall of 1938, I ran a taffy-apple route between Chicago and Geneva, Illinois, supplying storekeepers in a score or so of the interlying suburbs, and on two of the other days of the week serviced fifty candy-vending machines in the same general region. It was a line of work I had gone into during the depression and, finding it profitable, had continued with afterward, in order to have time for other, less remunerative projects. I had an old Chevrolet that was adequate for carrying the candy but not the taffy apples, since the apples were packed in bulky cartons and I couldn't cram in enough of them to satisfy the demand. My father helped me out, finally, by letting me use his Packard on Saturdays. I could get a third again as many apples into it, because, in addition to being larger than the Chevrolet, it was one of the models from which you could remove the whole rear seat, leaving the space between the back of the front seat and the door of the luggage compartment empty, thus converting the sedan into a kind of small truck. The only stipulation my father made was that I have the Packard home before the stroke of midnight each Saturday, since he had strong religious scruples against the commercial use of the car on Sunday.

I was making my way home one chilly Saturday night around ten o'clock when, at a turn in the road near Wheaton, my headlights picked out a dim shape in the roadside grass. I stopped, got out, and found a small man in a blue serge suit lying on his side, unconscious. Damned hit-and-run drivers! I thought indignantly, heaving him by the armpits to a sitting position. I began to worry him backward through the gravel toward my car, and he emitted a small moan. "There, there," I said. "Easy does it." He was beginning to come to, and with some help from him I finally got him into the car, propped him up on the front seat beside me, and took a closer look at him.

There was an ominous flexibility about his limbs, and I began exploring him gingerly for breaks when my hand encountered a large, round lump the shape and size of a bottle on one flank. Next an odor, imperceptible in the open air, reached my nostrils, and I began revising my inferences. Still, there was a cut over one eye, so I couldn't be sure that he hadn't really been struck by a car. Certainly something had to be done for him—or, anyhow, with him—and I looked around for a place from which to phone. There was a filling station about a hundred feet back, on the other side of the road, and I made for it, trotting carefully since my pockets were sagging with silver from the day's business.

The filling station's sole attendant was a heavy-set man of about forty, who stood with his hands in his coverall pockets, looking out of the window and inhaling from a panatela that he kept in his mouth. He clipped his sentences rather as if they were cigars, dropping the first word of every one.

"Seems to be the trouble?" he asked, not taking his eyes from the window.

"I found a man lying beside the road," I said breathlessly.

"Happened to him?"

"Well, I don't know," I said. "He seems to have been drinking, but I think he was hit by a car."

"Far from the road is he?"

"I didn't leave him lying there," I replied. "I've got him in my car."

The man turned deliberately, taking the cigar out of his mouth, and his sentences became complete. "You should never go to work and move an accident victim," he said. "Say there are broken bones. People have died of being moved by amateurs. Don't ever, ever do that again."

"Well..." I said, looking at the floor.

He regarded me a moment in silence, to let his words sink in. "Remember that," he said. Then he put the cigar back in his mouth. "Expect you better phone the Wheaton police," he said, nodding toward a phone booth.

I phoned them, and they told me to sit tight, they'd be right over. As I hung up and left the booth, I had a sudden notion that they mightn't be right over at all, and, glancing at an old overstuffed settee against one wall, I said to the attendant, "Look, it happens I'm in quite a hurry to get to the city. Could I leave him here?"

He took the cigar out of his mouth and turned to me slowly. "What, move him again?" he said. He put the cigar back, and I dropped the subject and stepped briskly toward the door. "Sake," he muttered, looking out the window. I buttoned my topcoat and opened the door. I hesitated a moment with my hand on the knob.

"I'm right over there," I said, pointing. "Will you tell the cops when they come?"

"K."

When I got back to the car, the drunk was sitting up inspecting the backs of his hands. "It must be late," he said. "I'm dirty."

I climbed in beside him and pulled the door shut.

"What happened?" I asked.

"Somebody must of hauled me in here," he said, looking around the interior. "This is nice."

I took out a clean handkerchief and began dabbing the cut over his eye, which had begun to trickle again. "No, I mean did somebody hit you?" I asked.

He reflected a moment. "You damn right," he said vengefully, speaking in thick, flannelly tones. "And I'd like to get my hands on the son of a bitch."

"So would I," I said. "There, now. Easy."

He settled himself back, evidently reassured. "I'll get him tomorrow. Yellow bastard! No. Monday."

Having brushed away some of the dirt around his cut, which seemed to be about the extent of his injuries, I made a bandage of my handkerchief, tying it around his head and knotting it firmly behind. "Say, you're all right," he said, looking at me gratefully with what focus he could command. "By God, they don't come any better." He became progressively more sentimental, finally reaching out a hand and starting to pat my face. "Cut it out," I said, drawing back.

We sat there, waiting. Suddenly, something I knew I had heard but hadn't perceived came fully into my consciousness. I looked at him out of the corner of my eye. "Who will you get Monday?" I asked.

"McCaffrey."

I rolled my window down and looked at the cars coming along the road, watching for the police. "That the guy who hit you?"

"Yeah," he said. "I'll get him at work. If he shows up."

From some mumblings that followed, I was able to piece together the events of the evening. He and McCaffrey, both of whom worked at a nearby factory, had drawn their pay and set out to hang one on at a tavern down the road, visible from the car as a streak of indecipherable neon. They had got into an argument, and McCaffrey had taken a poke at him and run—or, anyhow, had gone off and left him.

The drunk stirred, after a silence, and pulled the bottle out of his pocket. It was a half pint of Old Oscar Pepper. "Open this," he said, handing it to me. I did and had a drink. Then he took the bottle, slid his palm across the mouth of it, and drank, letting the whiskey gurgle through the neck. "Ah!" he said gratefully, smacking his lips. He passed the bottle back to me, and since it had begun to turn cold, I was far from averse to another. We emptied the half pint, and then he tried to throw it out the window, but the window was closed, and the bottle slammed against the glass and clattered to the floor. "Whoops!" he said equably. "Missed it."

"Hey, watch it!" I said, fumbling for the bottle, which I finally retrieved and threw across the road from my window. I glanced at the clock on the dashboard. Ten-twenty-five. I tapped my fingers on the steering wheel and kept watching for the squad car. The next thing I knew, the drunk was at the glove compartment, fumbling around inside it and spilling my taffy-apple records. I yanked his hands out, stuffed the records back in, and slammed the door. "Now, cut it out!" I said. "Or get the hell out of here!"

He turned toward me with a start. He shifted in his seat and regarded me for several seconds, narrowly but with a reflective air. "You've changed," he said.

The cops didn't come and they didn't come. When the drunk settled, mumbling, into the corner and showed signs of passing out again, I glanced at him and then, speculatively, at the ditch, and the thought of putting him back where I'd found him crossed my mind. I recalled a couple I knew who had tried to return an adopted baby after living with it for several months.

I didn't put the drunk out, however, and presently he began brushing dirt and wisps of grass and foliage from his clothes. "Every leave that falls shows a Supreme Being," he said, picking a leaf from his sleeve and holding it up contemplatively by the stem. "You," he said, and when I didn't respond, he pulled my sleeve. "You."

"I know," I said irritably, watching down the road.

He signed, and looked around. "Let's go somewhere else. This is no good."

I peeled the cellophane from a fresh pack of cigarettes. "We're waiting for someone," I said.

"Who?"

I wadded up the cellophane and dropped it out the window. "You'll see," I said.

I had no more than lit my cigarette when the cops arrived, scrunching to a stop behind us. I got out quickly. There were two of them—a tall, rangy, dark one, and a short, roundish towhead with horn-rimmed glasses. Apparently they were both new and were bent on going into the situation with a maximum of conscientious thoroughness.

"Now, where was he when you seen him?" the short one began, after looking briefly in at the drunk, who was muttering about seasonal cycles and design in nature. I pointed out the spot.

Meanwhile, the other cop had poked his head into the rear of the car. "What happened to your back seat?" he called. I explained, and they exchanged skeptical frowns. Openly leery of the idea that anybody would be peddling taffy apples in a Packard, they questioned me further, and I wondered whether they were thinking of the same thing I was—a recent story in the papers about a gangster who had thrown the back seat of his car into the path of a pursuing motorcycle cop, overturning him and nearly doing him in. The fistfuls of money in my pocket, which I offered in evidence, seemed only to make them more suspicious. "Let's see your driver's license," the short one said.

"Sure!" I said. I reached confidently toward the glove compartment, but my movement died in mid-air. "It's in my other car," I said.

The short one nodded sardonically and continued, "Well, then, how about the title to this automobile?"

"That I've got," I said, searching briefly in the disheveled interior of the glove compartment and producing my father's state registration. As they examined it the thought crossed my mind that perhaps, after all, I was lucky to be without my driver's license, since my father's first name wasn't the same as mine. The short cop was studying me through his thick-rimmed glasses.

"How long have you been in this line of work?" he asked. "Taffy apples."

"Seven years," I said. "Now, why don't you take this man and let me go?"

They said that if the drunk was really injured, I'd be detained for questioning in any case, and that therefore I might as well take it easy. So I told them the drunk hadn't been struck by a car at all, that he was just drunk, and they asked me sharply why I was changing the story I'd given over the phone. At that point, the drunk started muttering about what a bastard I'd turned out to be. The cops circled suspiciously around to the front of the car, where they began to examine my fenders and bumper closely, looking, as I gathered from their murmured exchanges, for bloodstains. They came back.

"Did you hit this man?" the tall one asked me abruptly.

I turned and gave the drunk a look. "Not yet," I said.

"Oh, a wise guy," the cop said.

"Now, look," I said, "I want to get the hell out of here and home. I've got to be home by twelve o'clock."

"What for?" the tall one asked.

I threw my cigarette into the ditch. "For religious reasons."

"Let's smell your breath," he said. But what he meant was that he had smelled it already, and presently we were all on our way to the station.

The tall cop drove the police car, taking the drunk with him, and the short one drove mine, ordering me into the back, where, of course, I sat on the floor. "We have to be strict with traffic violations," he called. "We're making a drive on altogether too many accidents." I squatted in the cavernous rear, preparing my defense—not so much for the police as for my father. The cops, since they were certain to phone my home to check on the car ownership, were likely to corroborate my story of the delay, but not in a way that would be found palatable at the other end: driving while under the influence of liquor, suspicion of running down a pedestrian, and operating a vehicle without a license were sure to be mentioned.

Even so, I decided to tell the truth about the car owner-

PETER DEVRIES

ship. This involved still *another* shift in my story, but it was
with at least a show of open-mindedness that, when we
reached the station, the desk sergeant put a call through to
my father.

"Do you own a Packard?" the sergeant asked. "Do you
have a son driving it around here with taffy apples?" He got
what seemed to be a satisfactory answer. "Well, we're having
a little trouble with him here," he said, and reeled off the
charges I had anticipated. A crackling response, audible all
over the room, came through the earpiece.

"Damn it, you're getting him all upset," I said. "Let me
talk to him." He handed the receiver and I explained the
complications, as much in my favor as I could, and then
hung up and turned back to the cops. They fined me fifteen
dollars for operating a motor vehicle without a license and
let me go.

I sped toward the city in a driving sleet, perfecting my
rejoinders: all the biblical quotations I could think of that
embodied a flexible view of the Sabbath. I got the car into
the garage at twenty minutes to one, and found my father
sitting in the kitchen waiting for me when I stepped into the
house.

"It's Sunday," he said, glancing at the clock.

"'What man shall there be among you that shall have
one sheep, and if it fall into the pit on the Sabbath day, will
he not lay hold on it and lift it out?'" I began, wasting no
time. "'How much is a man better than a sheep?'"

"'Abstain not only from evil, but from the appearance of
evil,'" he replied, scrutinizing me.

"'The Sabbath was made for man, and not man for the
Sabbath,'" I said.

"'Wine is a mocker, strong drink is raging,'" said my
father, still examining me narrowly.

I thought for a while. "'Drink no longer water, but use a
little wine for thy stomach's sake and thine often infir-
mities,'" I said at last. "It was cold out there. That's what

you get for trying to play Good Samaritan. I only had a *slokje*," I added, using the Dutch word, which I thought would be less jarring to my father than "snifter."

"I hope you've learned your lesson," my father said.

"I certainly have," I said. And I had. The very next Saturday, a woman flagged me and pointed at a flat tire with which she was stalled beside the road, and I shot past her without a second thought.

The Pastor

SLAWOMIR MROZEK

Slawomir Mrozek, born in Borzecin, Poland in
1930, is one of the best known of the generation
of Polish satirists that emerged after the political
"thaw" of 1956. An absurdist playwright (*The
Policeman, Tango*) as well as a story writer, Mrozek
uses ridicule, fantasy, and a Kafkaesque parable
form to attack bureaucratic and institutional hypocrisy and stupidity. "The Pastor" was a part of
Mrozek's collection *Slón* (1957), which was translated into English as *The Elephant* in 1962 by Kon-
rad Syrop.

PASTOR PETERS WAS A YOUNG MAN. He wore rimless glasses;
his soft, thinning hair was parted on the left.

Until he became a missionary, he had never left San
Francisco. His father had also been a pastor and, at the same
time, acted as the legal adviser to his religious body. Peters
senior used to deliver his sermons to a congregation of
white-collar workers, looked after the legal department and
had some shipping shares. Then he died just as his son was
leaving the missionary college.

The superiors, who had decided to send young Peters
away, had acted wisely. His average intelligence would not
allow him to occupy a leading position in the Church, but it
was sufficient for giving religious instruction to coloured
children. They sent him to Tokyo.

He spent his journey in prayer and contemplation of his

mission. His father had brought him up on strict lines and the number of prayers Peters knew was great.

In Tokyo he was told by his superiors: "You've been assigned a hard task but one that's particularly dear to Our Lord. You'll go to Hiroshima."

He remembered the name from the enormous newspaper headlines he had seen when he was sixteen years old.

When he reached Hiroshima young Pastor Peters felt sad. The city was quite unlike San Francisco.

The mission house stood among a cluster of small dwellings by the motorway.

He devoted a great deal of time and effort to the preparation of his first sermon. Though he understood nothing, Peters was unable to deliver a sermon without a thesis. For the purpose of his first public appearance in Hiroshima he formulated a double thesis: the defence of the faithful from the sins threatening them in their misery, and the parallel argument about their misery, which resulted from the war, being a punishment for their sins. As the most suitable text he chose Matthew, chapter 24.

The faithful, who numbered a few score, were recruited from the neighbourhood of the mission. The services took place once a week in the chapel, the congregation attending only for the sermon. They sat silently on their benches, and when the preacher finished they went into the courtyard where they were given some meat soup. Then they disappeared until the following Sunday.

It must be said that young Pastor Peters was nervous as he went up to the pulpit. However the familiar words of chapter 24 brought back his self-confidence. Raising his voice he read:

". . . See ye not all these things? Verily I say unto you, there shall not be left here one stone upon another, that shall not be thrown down."

He looked at the congregation. They were sitting grey and shrivelled.

". . . And ye shall hear of wars and rumours of wars; see

that ye be not troubled: for all these things must come to pass, but the end is not yet.

"For nation shall rise against nation, and kingdom against kingdom: and there shall be famines, and pestilences, and earthquakes, in divers places.

"All these are the beginning of sorrows.

"Then shall they deliver you up to be afflicted, and shall kill you...."

He raised his head because he could hear footsteps. A blind girl was feeling her way to the door. He was surprised and indignant but his eyes returned to the Book on the pulpit.

"... Let him which is on the housetop not come down to take any thing out of his house:

"Neither let him which is in the field return back to take his clothes...."

Others started to follow in the wake of the blind girl; they were going out into the street. In an orderly fashion they were filing out, those nearer to the door waiting till the aisle was clear, then turning and making intently for the exit. Young Pastor Peters watched them from the pulpit, his mouth wide open. But not in vain had prayer always preceded his meals for so many years; now it seemed to him that the only force which could arrest this exodus from the chapel was the Word, the Word printed in black on the pages of the Book that was lying open before him.

"... And woe unto them that are with child, and to them that give suck in those days!

"But pray ye that your flight be not in the winter, neither on the sabbath day:

"For then shall be great tribulation, such as was not since the beginning of the world to this time, no, nor ever shall be.

"And except those days should be shortened, there should no flesh be saved...."

He raised his head again and looked round with the eyes

of a child whose parents, in spite of their solemn promise, refuse to take him to the cinema. The chapel was empty. Only one man remained, kneeling in front of the altar. He was an old man, his head bent down to the floor. The empty chapel shook slightly as lorries passed by and from the court-yard there came the aroma of meat soup.

He read the last quotation.

"But he that shall endure unto the end, the same shall be saved."

He closed his Bible and turned to his last listener.

The old man was swaying as if he were about to fall, but somehow regained his balance just in time. He was asleep. The war had damaged his hearing. He was deaf.

Gorilla, My Love

TONI CADE BAMBARA

Toni Cade Bambara, who makes her home in Atlanta, Georgia, is the author of the short story collections *Gorilla, My Love* (1972) and *The Seabirds
Are Still Alive* (1977). She is also the editor of *The
Black Woman* (1970) and of *Tales and Stories for
Black Folks* (1971). She is currently at work on film
scripts and film productions and on a novel about
the twenty-first century. Ms. Bambara has studied
pantomime with Etienne Decroux and has studied
film at the Studio Museum of Harlem. She holds
degrees in theater and literature.

THAT WAS THE YEAR Hunca Bubba changed his name. Not
a change up, a change back, since Jefferson Winston Vale
was the name in the first place. Which was news to me cause
he'd been my Hunca Bubba my whole lifetime, since I
couldn't manage Uncle to save my life. So far as I was concerned it was a change completely to somethin soundin very
geographical weatherlike to me, like somethin you'd find in a
almanac. Or somethin you'd run across when you sittin in
the navigator seat with a wet thumb on the map crinkly in
your lap, watchin the roads and signs so when Granddaddy
Vale say "Which way, Scout," you got sense enough to say
take the next exit or take a left or whatever it is. Not that
Scout's my name. Just the name Granddaddy call whoever
sittin in the navigator seat. Which is usually me cause I don't

feature sittin in the back with the pecans. Now, you figure
pecans all right to be sittin with. If you think so, that's your
business. But they dusty sometime and make you cough. And
they got a way of slidin around and dippin down sudden, like
maybe a rat in the buckets. So if you scary like me, you sleep
with the lights on and blame it on Baby Jason and, so as not
to waste good electric, you study the maps. And that's how
come I'm in the navigator seat most times and get to be
called Scout.

So Hunca Bubba in the back with the pecans and Baby
Jason, and he in love. And we got to hear all this stuff about
this woman he in love with and all. Which really ain't
enough to keep the mind alive, though Baby Jason got no
better sense than to give his undivided attention and keep
grabbin at the photograph which is just a picture of some
skinny woman in a countrified dress with her hand shot up
to her face like she shame fore cameras. But there's a movie
house in the background which I ax about. Cause I am a
movie freak from way back, even though it do get me in
trouble sometime.

Like when me and Big Brood and Baby Jason was on our
own last Easter and couldn't go to the Dorset cause we'd seen
all the Three Stooges they was. And the RKO Hamilton was
closed readying up for the Easter Pageant that night. And
the West End, the Regun and the Sunset was too far, less we
had grownups with us which we didn't. So we walk up
Amsterdam Avenue to the Washington and *Gorilla, My
Love* playin, they say, which suit me just fine, though the
"my love" part kinda drag Big Brood some. As for Baby
Jason, shoot, like Granddaddy say, he'd follow me into the
fiery furnace if I say come on. So we go in and get three bags
of Havmore potato chips which not only are the best potato
chips but the best bags for blowin up and bustin real loud so
the matron come trottin down the aisle with her chunky self,
flashin that flashlight dead in your eye so you can give her
some lip, and if she answer back and you already finish seein

the show anyway, why then you just turn the place out. Which I love to do, no lie. With Baby Jason kickin at the seat in front, egging me on, and Big Brood mumblin bout what fiercesome things we goin do. Which means me. Like when the big boys come up on us talkin bout Lemme a nickel. It's me that hide the money. Or when the bad boys in the park take Big Brood's Spaudeen way from him. It's me that jump on they back and fight awhile. And it's me that turns out the show if the matron get too salty.

So the movie come on and right away it's this churchy music and clearly not about no gorilla. Bout Jesus. And I am ready to kill, not cause I got anything gainst Jesus. Just that when you fixed to watch a gorilla picture you don't wanna get messed around with Sunday School stuff. So I am mad. Besides, we see this raggedy old brown film *King of Kings* every year and enough's enough. Grownups figure they can treat you just anyhow. Which burns me up. There I am, my feet up and my Havmore potato chips really salty and crispy and two jawbreakers in my lap and the money safe in my shoe from the big boys, and here comes this Jesus stuff. So we all go wild. Yellin, booin, stompin and carryin on. Really to wake the man in the booth up there who musta went to sleep and put on the wrong reels. But no, cause he holler down to shut up and then he turn the sound up so we really gotta holler like crazy to even hear ourselves good. And the matron ropes off the children section and flashes her light all over the place and we yell some more and some kids slip under the rope and run up and down the aisle just to show it take more than some dusty ole velvet rope to tie us down. And I'm flingin the kid in front of me's popcorn. And Baby Jason kickin seats. And it's really somethin. Then here come the big and bad matron, the one they let out in case of emergency. And she totin that flashlight like she gonna use it on somebody. This here the colored matron Brandy and her friends call Thunderbuns. She do not play. She do not smile. So we shut up and watch the simple ass picture.

Which is not so simple as it is stupid. Cause I realize that
just about anybody in my family is better than this god they
always talkin about. My daddy wouldn't stand for nobody
treatin any of us that way. My mama specially. And I can
just see it now, Big Brood up there on the cross talkin bout
Forgive them Daddy cause they don't know what they doin.
And my Mama say Get on down from there you big fool,
whatcha think this is, playtime? And my Daddy yellin to
Granddaddy to get him a ladder cause Big Brood actin the
fool, his mother side of the family showin up. And my mama
and her sister Daisy jumpin on them Romans beatin them
with they pocketbooks. And Hunca Bubba tellin them folks
on they knees they better get out the way and go get some
help or they goin to get trampled on. And Granddaddy Vale
sayin Leave the boy alone, if that's what he wants to do with
his life we ain't got nothin to say about it. Then Aunt Daisy
givin him a taste of that pocketbook, fussin bout what a
damn fool old man Granddaddy is. Then everybody jumpin
in his chest like the time Uncle Clayton went in the army
and come back with only one leg and Granddaddy say somethin stupid about that's life. And by this time Big Brood off
the cross and in the park playin handball or skully or somethin. And the family in the kitchen throwin dishes at each
other, screamin bout if you hadn't done this I wouldn't had
to do that. And me in the parlor trying to do my arithmetic
yellin Shut it off.

Which is what I was yellin all by myself which make me a
sittin target for Thunderbuns. But when I yell We want our
money back, that gets everybody in chorus. And the movie
windin up with this heavenly cloud music and the smart-ass
up there in his hole in the wall turns up the sound again to
drown us out. Then there comes Bugs Bunny which we already seen so we know we been had. No gorilla my nuthin.
And Big Brood say Awwww sheeet, we goin to see the manager and get our money back. And I know from this we
business. So I brush the potato chips out of my hair which is

where Baby Jason like to put em, and I march myself up the aisle to deal with the manager who is a crook in the first place for lyin out there sayin *Gorilla, My Love* playin. And I never did like the man cause he oily and pasty at the same time like the bad guy in the serial, the one that got a hideout behind a push-button bookcase and play "Moonlight Sonata" with gloves on. I knock on the door and I am furious. And I am alone, too. Cause Big Brood suddenly got to go so bad even though my mama told us bout goin in them nasty bathrooms. And I hear him sigh like he disgusted when he get to the door and see only a little kid there. And now I'm really furious cause I get so tired grownups messin over kids just cause they little and can't take em to court. What is it, he say to me like I lost my mittens or wet on myself or am somebody's retarded child. When in reality I am the smartest kid P.S. 186 ever had in its whole lifetime and you can ax anybody. Even them teachers that don't like me cause I won't sing them Southern songs or back off when they tell me my questions are out of order. And cause my Mama come up there in a minute when them teachers start playin the dozens behind colored folks. She stalk in with her hat pulled down bad and that Persian lamb coat draped back over one hip on account of she got her fist planted there so she can talk that talk which gets us all hypnotized, and teacher be comin undone cause she know this could be her job and her behind cause Mama got pull with the Board and bad by her own self anyhow.

So I kick the door open wider and just walk right by him and sit down and tell the man about himself and that I want my money back and that goes for Baby Jason and Big Brood too. And he still trying to shuffle me out the door even though I'm sittin which shows him for the fool he is. Just like them teachers do fore they realize Mama like a stone on that spot and ain't backin up. So he ain't gettin up off the money. So I was forced to leave, takin the matches from under his ashtray, and set a fire under the candy stand, which closed the raggedy ole Washington down for a week. My Daddy had the suspect it was me cause Big Brood got a big mouth. But I explained right quick what the whole thing was about and I figured it was even-steven. Cause if you say Gorilla, My Love, you suppose to mean it. Just like when you say you goin to give me a party on my birthday, you gotta mean it. And if you say me and Baby Jason can go South pecan haulin with Granddaddy Vale, you better not be comin up with no stuff about the weather look uncertain or did you mop the bathroom or any other trickified business. I mean even gangsters in the movies say My word is my bond. So don't nobody get away with nothin far as I'm concerned. So Daddy put his belt back on. Cause that's the way I was raised. Like my Mama say in one of them situations when I won't back down, Okay Badbird, you right. Your point is well-taken. Not that Badbird my name, just what she say when she tired arguin and know I'm right. And Aunt Jo, who is the hardest head in the family and worse even than Aunt Daisy, she say, You absolutely right Miss Muffin, which also ain't my real name but the name she gave me one time when I got some medicine shot in my behind and wouldn't get up off her pillows for nothin. And even Granddaddy Vale—who got no memory to speak of, so sometime you can just plain lie to him, if you want to be like that—he say, Well if that's what I said, then that's it. But this name business was different they said. It wasn't like Hunca Bubba had gone back on his word or anything. Just that he was thinkin bout gettin married and was usin his real name now. Which ain't the way I saw it at all.

So there I am in the navigator seat. And I turn to him and just plain ole ax him. I mean I come right on out with it. No sense goin all around that barn the old folks talk about. And like my mama say, Hazel—which is my real name and what she remembers to call me when she bein serious—when you got somethin on your mind, speak up and let the chips fall where they may. And if anybody don't like it, tell em to come see your mama. And Daddy look up from the paper and say, You hear your mama good, Hazel. And tell em to come see me first. Like that. That's how I was raised.

So I turn clear round in the navigator seat and say, "Look here, Hunca Bubba or Jefferson Windsong Vale or whatever your name is, you gonna marry this girl?"

"Sure am," he say, all grins.

And I say, "Member that time you was baby-sittin me when we lived at four-o-nine and there was this big snow and Mama and Daddy got held up in the country so you had to stay for two days?"

And he say, "Sure do."

"Well. You remember how you told me I was the cutest thing that ever walked the earth?"

"Oh, you were real cute when you were little," he say, which is suppose to be funny. I am not laughin.

"Well. You remember what you said?"

And Granddaddy Vale squintin over the wheel and axin Which way, Scout. But Scout is busy and don't care if we all get lost for days.

"Watcha mean, Peaches?"

"My name is Hazel. And what I mean is you said you were going to marry *me* when I grew up. You were going to wait. That's what I mean, my dear Uncle Jefferson." And he don't say nuthin. Just look at me real strange like he never saw me before in life. Like he lost in some weird town in the middle of night and lookin for directions and there's no one to ask. Like it was me that messed up the maps and turned the road posts round. "Well, you said it, didn't you?" And Baby Jason lookin back and forth like we playin ping-pong. Only I ain't playin. I'm hurtin and I can hear that I am screamin. And Granddaddy Vale mumblin how we never gonna get to where we goin if I don't turn around and take my navigator job serious.

"Well, for cryin out loud, Hazel, you just a little girl. And I was just teasin."

" 'And I was just teasin,' " I say back just how he said it so he can hear what a terrible thing it is. Then I don't say nuthin. And he don't say nuthin. And Baby Jason don't say nuthin nohow. Then Granddaddy Vale speak up. "Look here, Jefferson Winston Vale." And Hunca Bubba say, "That's right. That was somebody else. I'm a new somebody."

"You a lyin dawg," I say, when I meant to say treacherous dog, but just couldn't get hold of the word. It slipped away from me. And I'm crying and crumplin down in the seat and just don't care. And Granddaddy say to hush and steps on the gas. And I'm losin my bearins and don't even know where to look on the map cause I can't see for cryin. And Baby Jason cryin too. Cause he is my blood brother and understands that we must stick together or be forever lost, what with grownups playin change-up and turnin you round every which way so bad. And don't even say they sorry.

The Face of Evil

FRANK O'CONNOR

Frank O'Connor is the pen name of Michael O'Donovan, who was born in Cork in 1903, educated by the Christian Brothers in Ireland, and immigrated to New York in the early fifties. Along with his short stories, which have been published in collections such as *Domestic Relations* (1957), O'Connor has written an autobiography (*An Only Child*, 1961) and criticism. "The Face of Evil" is typical of his writing in its Irish locale and its treatment of the problems of modern Irish life. It was first published in *The New Yorker* in 1954, and is reprinted here from *More Stories from Frank O'Connor.*

I COULD NEVER UNDERSTAND all the old talk about how hard it is to be a saint. I was a saint for quite a bit of my life and I never saw anything hard in it. And when I stopped being a saint, it wasn't because the life was too hard.

I fancy it is the sissies who make it seem like that. We had quite a few of them in our school, fellows whose mothers intended them to be saints and who hadn't the nerve to be anything else. I never enjoyed the society of chaps who wouldn't commit sin for the same reason that they wouldn't dirty their new suits. That was never what sanctity meant to me, and I doubt if it is what it means to other saints. The companions I enjoyed were the tough gang down the road, and I liked going down of an evening and talking with them under the gas lamp about football matches and school, even if they did sometimes say things I wouldn't say myself. I was never one for criticizing; I had enough to do criticizing myself, and I knew they were decent chaps and didn't really mean much harm by the things they said about girls.

No, for me the main attraction of being a saint was the way it always gave you something to do. You could never say you felt time hanging on your hands. It was like having a room of your own to keep tidy; you'd scour it and put everything neatly back in its place, and within an hour or two it was beginning to look as untidy as ever. It was a full-time job that began when you woke and stopped only when you fell asleep.

I would wake in the morning, for instance, and think how nice it was to lie in bed and congratulate myself on not having to get up for another half hour. That was enough. Instantly a sort of alarm-clock would go off in my mind; the mere thought that I could enjoy half an hour's comfort would make me aware of an alternative, and I'd begin an argument with myself. I had a voice in me that was almost the voice of a stranger, the way it nagged and jeered. Sometimes I could almost visualize it, and then it took on the appearance of a fat and sneering teacher I had some years before at school—a man I really hated. I hated that voice. It always began in the same way, smooth and calm and dangerous. I could see the teacher rubbing his fat hands and smirking.

"Don't get alarmed, boy. You're in no hurry. You have another half hour."

"I know well I have another half hour," I would reply, trying to keep my temper. "What harm am I doing? I'm only imagining I'm down in a submarine. Is there anything wrong in that?"

"Oho, not the least in the world. I'd say there's been a heavy frost. Just the sort of morning when there's ice in the bucket."

"And what has that to do with it?"

"Nothing, I tell you. Of course, for people like you it's

easy enough in the summer months, but the least touch of
frost in the air soon makes you feel different. I wouldn't worry trying to keep it up. You haven't the stuff for this sort of
life at all."

And gradually my own voice grew weaker as that of my
tormentor grew stronger, till all at once I would strip the
clothes from off myself and lie in my nightshirt, shivering
and muttering: "So I haven't the stuff in me, haven't I?"
Then I would go downstairs before my parents were awake,
strip, and wash in the bucket, ice or no ice, and when
Mother came down she would cry in alarm: "Child of grace,
what has you up at this hour? Sure, 'tis only half past seven."
She almost took it as a reproach to herself, poor woman, and
I couldn't tell her the reason, and even if I could have done
so, I wouldn't. It was a thing you couldn't talk about to
anybody.

Then I went to Mass and enjoyed again the mystery of
the streets and lanes in the early morning; the frost which
made your feet clatter off the walls at either side of you like
falling masonry, and the different look that everything wore,
as though, like yourself, it was all cold and scrubbed and
new. In the winter the lights would still be burning red in the
little whitewashed cottages, and in summer their walls were
ablaze with sunshine so that their interiors were dimmed to
shadows. Then there were the different people, all of whom
recognized one another, like Mrs. MacEntee, who used to be
a stewardess on the boats, and Macken, the tall postman;
people who seemed ordinary enough when you met them
during the day but carried something of their mystery with
them at Mass, as though they, too, were reborn.

I can't pretend I was ever very good at school, but even
there it was a help. I might not be clever, but I had always a
secret reserve of strength to call on in the fact that I had
what I wanted, and that besides it I wanted nothing. People
frequently gave me things, like fountain pens or pencil-
sharpeners, and I would suddenly find myself becoming at-

tached to them and immediately know I must give them away, and then feel the richer for it. Even without throwing my weight around, I could help and protect kids younger than myself and yet not become involved in their quarrels. Not to become involved, to remain detached—that was the great thing; to care for things and for people, yet not to care for them so much that your happiness became dependent on them.

It was like no other hobby, because you never really got the better of yourself, and all at once you would suddenly find yourself reverting to childish attitudes; flaring up in a wax with some fellow, or sulking when Mother asked you to go for a message, and then it all came back; the nagging of the infernal alarm-clock, which grew louder with every moment until it incarnated as a smooth, fat, jeering face.

"Now, that's the first time you've behaved sensibly for months, boy. That was the right way to behave to your mother."

"Well, it *was* the right way. Why can't she let me alone once in a while? I only want to read. I suppose I'm entitled to a bit of peace some time?"

"Ah, of course you are, my dear fellow. Isn't that what I'm saying? Go on with your book! Imagine you're a cowboy, riding to the rescue of a beautiful girl in a cabin in the woods, and let that silly woman go for the messages herself. She probably hasn't long to live anyway, and when she dies you'll be able to do all the weeping you like."

And suddenly tears of exasperation would come to my eyes and I'd heave the story-book to the other side of the room and shout back at the voice that gave me no rest: "Cripes, I might as well be dead and buried. I have no blooming life." After that I would apologize to Mother (who, poor woman, was more embarrassed than anything else and assured me that it was all her fault), go on the message, and write another tick in my notebook against the heading of "Bad Temper" so as to be able to confess it to Father O'Regan when I went to Confession on Saturday. Not that he was ever severe with me, no matter what I did; he thought I was the last word in holiness, and was always asking me to pray for some special intention of his own. And though I was depressed, I never lost interest, for no matter what I did, I could scarcely ever reduce the total of times I had to tick off that item in my notebook.

Oh, I don't pretend it was any joke, but it did give me the feeling that my life had some meaning; that inside me I had a real source of strength; that there was nothing I could not do without and yet remain sweet, self-sufficient, and content. Sometimes, too, there was the feeling of something more than mere content, as though my body were transparent, like a window, and light shone through it as well as on it, onto the road, the houses, and the playing children, as though it were I who was shining on them, and tears of happiness would come into my eyes, and I hurled myself among the playing children just to forget it.

But, as I say, I had no inclination to mix with other kids who might be saints as well. The fellow who really fascinated me was a policeman's son named Dalton, who was easily the most vicious kid in the locality. The Daltons lived on the terrace above ours. Mrs. Dalton was dead; there was a younger brother called Stevie who was next door to an imbecile, and there was something about that kid's cheerful grin that was even more frightening than the malice on Charlie's broad face. Their father was a tall melancholy man with a big black moustache, and the nearest thing imaginable to one of the Keystone cops. Everyone was sorry for his loss in his wife, but you knew that if it hadn't been that, it would have been something else—maybe the fact that he hadn't lost her. Charlie was only an additional grief. He was always getting into trouble, stealing and running away from home; and only his father's being a policeman prevented his being sent to an industrial school. One of my most vivid recollections is that of Charlie's education. I'd hear a shriek, and there would be

Mr. Dalton dragging Charlie along the pavement to school and, whenever the names his son called him grew a little more obscene than usual, pausing to give Charlie a good going-over with the belt which he carried loose in his hand. It is an exceptional father who can do this without getting some pleasure out of it, but Mr. Dalton looked as though even it were an additional burden. Charlie's screams could always fetch me out.

"What is it?" Mother would cry after me.

"Ah, nothing. Only Charlie Dalton again."

"Come in! Come in!"

"I won't be seen."

"Come in, I say. 'Tis never right."

And even when Charlie uttered the most atrocious indecencies, she only joined her hands as if in prayer and muttered "The poor child! The poor unfortunate child!" I never could understand the way she felt about Charlie. He wouldn't have been Charlie if it hadn't been for the leatherings and the threats of the industrial school.

Looking back on it, the funniest thing is that I seemed to be the only fellow on the road he didn't hate. They were all terrified of him, and some of the kids would go a mile to avoid him. He was completely unclassed: being a policeman's son, he should have been way up the social scale, but he hated the respectable kids worse than the others. When we stood under the gas lamp at night and saw him coming up the road, everybody fell silent. He looked suspiciously at the group, ready to spring at anyone's throat if he saw the shadow of offence; ready even when there wasn't a shadow. He fought like an animal, by instinct, without judgment, and without ever reckoning the odds, and he was terribly strong. He wasn't clever; several of the older chaps could beat him to a frazzle when it was merely a question of boxing or wrestling, but it never was that with Dalton. He was out for blood and usually got it. Yet he was never that way with me. We weren't friends. All that ever happened when we passed each other was that I smiled at him and got a cold, cagey nod in return. Sometimes we stopped and exchanged a few words, but it was an ordeal because we never had anything to say to each other.

It was like the signalling of ships, or, more accurately, the courtesies of great powers. I tried, like Mother, to be sorry for him in having no proper home, and getting all those leatherings, but the feeling that came uppermost in me was never pity but respect—respect for a fellow who had done all the things I would never do: stolen money, stolen bicycles, run away from home, slept with tramps and criminals in barns and doss-houses, and ridden without a ticket on trains and on buses. It filled my imagination. I have a vivid recollection of one summer morning when I was going up the hill to Mass. Just as I reached the top and saw the low, sandstone church perched high up ahead of me, he poked his bare head round the corner of a lane to see who was coming. It startled me. He was standing with his back to the gable of a house; his face was dirty and strained; it was broad and lined, and the eyes were very small, furtive and flickering, and sometimes a sort of spasm would come over them and they flickered madly for half a minute on end.

"Hullo, Charlie," I said. "Where were you?"

"Out," he replied shortly.

"All night?" I asked in astonishment.

"Yeh," he replied with a nod.

"What are you doing now?"

He gave a short, bitter laugh.

"Waiting till my old bastard of a father goes out to work and I can go home."

His eyes flickered again, and self-consciously he drew his hand across them as though pretending they were tired.

"I'll be late for Mass," I said uneasily. "So long."

"So long."

That was all, but all the time at Mass, among the flowers and the candles, watching the beautiful, sad old face of Mrs.

MacEntee and the plump, smooth, handsome face of Macken, the postman, I was haunted by the image of that other face, wild and furtive and dirty, peering round a corner like an animal looking from its burrow. When I came out, the morning was brilliant over the valley below me; the air was punctuated with bugle calls from the cliff where the barrack stood, and Charlie Dalton was gone. No, it wasn't pity I felt for him. It wasn't even respect. It was almost like envy.

Then, one Saturday evening, an incident occurred which changed my attitude to him; indeed, changed my attitude to myself, though it wasn't until long after that I realized it. I was on my way to Confession, preparatory to Communion next morning. I always went to Confession at the parish church in town where Father O'Regan was. As I passed the tramway terminus at the Cross, I saw Charlie sitting on the low wall above the Protestant church, furtively smoking the butt-end of a cigarette which somebody had dropped, getting on the tram. Another tram arrived as I reached the Cross, and a number of people alighted and went off in different directions. I crossed the road to Charlie and he gave me his most distant nod.

"Hullo."

"Hullo, Cha. Waiting for somebody?"

"No. Where are you off to?"

"Confession."

"Huh." He inhaled the cigarette butt deeply and then tossed it over his shoulder into the sunken road beneath without looking where it alighted. "You go a lot."

"Every week," I said modestly.

"Jesus!" he said with a short laugh. "I wasn't there for twelve months."

I shrugged my shoulders. As I say, I never went in much for criticizing others, and anyway Charlie wouldn't have been Charlie if he had gone to Confession every week.

"Why do you go so often?" he asked challengingly.

"Oh, I don't know," I said doubtfully. "I suppose it keeps you out of harm's way."

"But you don't do any harm," he growled, just as though he were defending me against someone who had been attacking me.

"Ah, we all do harm."

"But, Jesus Christ, you don't do anything," he said almost angrily, and his eyes flickered again in that curious nervous spasm, and almost as if they put him into a rage, he drove his knuckles into them.

"We all do things," I said. "Different things."

"Well, what do you do?"

"I lose my temper a lot," I admitted.

"Jesus!" he said again, and rolled his eyes.

"It's a sin just the same," I said obstinately.

"A sin? Losing your temper? Jesus, I want to kill people. I want to kill my bloody old father, for one. I will too, one of those days. Take a knife to him."

"I know, I know," I said, at a loss to explain what I meant. "But that's just the same thing as me."

I wished to God I could talk better. It wasn't any missionary zeal. I was excited because for the first time I knew that Charlie felt about me exactly as I felt about him, with a sort of envy, and I wanted to explain to him that he didn't have to envy me, and that he could be as much a saint as I was just as I could be as much a sinner as he was. I wanted to explain that it wasn't a matter of tuppence ha'penny worth of sanctity as opposed to tuppence worth that made the difference, that it wasn't what you did but what you lost by doing it that mattered. The whole Cross had become a place of mystery—the grey light, drained of warmth; the trees hanging over the old crumbling walls; the tram, shaking like a boat when someone mounted it. It was the way I sometimes felt afterwards with a girl, as though everything about you melted and fused and became one with a central mystery.

"But when what you do isn't any harm?" he repeated angrily with that flickering of the eyes I had almost come to dread.

"Look, Cha," I said, "you can't say a thing isn't any harm. Everything is harm. It might be losing my temper with me and murder with you, like you say, but it would only come to the same thing. If I show you something, will you promise not to tell?"

"Why would I tell?"

"But promise."

"Oh, all right."

Then I took out my little notebook and showed it to him. It was extraordinary, and I knew it was extraordinary. I found myself, sitting on that wall, showing a notebook I wouldn't have shown to anyone else in the world to Charlie Dalton, a fellow any kid on the road would go a long way to avoid, and yet I had the feeling that he would understand it as no one else would do. My whole life was there, under different headings—Disobedience, Bad Temper, Bad Thoughts, Selfishness, and Laziness—and he looked through it quietly, studying the ticks I had placed against each count.

"You see," I said, "you talk about your father, but look at all the things I do against my mother. I know she's a good mother, but if she's sick or if she can't walk fast when I'm in town with her, I get mad just as you do. It doesn't matter what sort of mother or father you have. It's what you do to yourself when you do things like that."

"What do you do to yourself?" he asked quietly.

"It's hard to explain. It's only a sort of peace you have inside yourself. And you can't be just good, no matter how hard you try. You can only do your best, and if you do your best you feel peaceful inside. It's like when I miss Mass of a morning. Things mightn't be any harder on me that day than any other day, but I'm not as well able to stand up to them. It makes things a bit different for the rest of the day. You don't mind it so much if you get a hammering. You know there's something else in the world besides the hammering."

I knew it was a feeble description of what morning Mass really meant to me, the feeling of strangeness which lasted throughout the whole day and reduced reality to its real proportions, but it was the best I could do. I hated leaving him.

"I'll be late for Confession," I said regretfully, getting off the wall.

"I'll go down a bit of the way with you," he said, giving a last glance at my notebook and handing it back to me. I knew he was being tempted to come to Confession along with me, but my pleasure had nothing to do with that. As I say, I never had any missionary zeal. It was the pleasure of understanding rather than that of conversion.

He came down the steps to the church with me and we went in together.

"I'll wait here for you," he whispered, and sat in one of the back pews.

It was dark there; there were just a couple of small, unshaded lights in the aisles above the confessionals. There was a crowd of old women outside Father O'Regan's box, so I knew I had a long time to wait. Old women never got done with their confessions. For the first time I felt it long, but when my turn came it was all over in a couple of minutes: the usual "Bless you, my child. Say a prayer for me, won't you?" When I came out, I saw Charlie Dalton sitting among the old women outside the confessional, waiting to go in. He looked very awkward and angry, his legs wide and his hands hanging between them. I felt very happy about it in a quiet way, and when I said my penance I said a special prayer for him.

It struck me that he was a long time inside, and I began to grow worried. Then he came out, and I saw by his face that it was no good. It was the expression of someone who is saying to himself with a sort of evil triumph: "There, I told you what it was like."

"It's all right," he whispered, giving his belt a hitch. "You go home."

"I'll wait for you," I said.

"I'll be a good while."

I knew then Father O'Regan had given him a heavy penance, and my heart sank.

And it was only long afterwards that it occurred to me that I might have taken one of the major decisions of my life without being aware of it. I sat at the back of the church in the dusk and waited for him. He was kneeling up in front, before the altar, and I knew it was no good. At first I was too stunned to feel. All I knew was that my happiness had all gone. I admired Father O'Regan; I knew that Charlie must have done things that I couldn't even imagine—terrible things—but the resentment grew in me. What right had Father O'Regan or anyone to treat him like that? Because he was down, people couldn't help wanting to crush him further. For the first time in my life I knew real temptation. I wanted to go with Charlie and share his fate. For the first time I realized that the life before me would have complexities of emotion which I couldn't even imagine.

The following week he ran away from home again, took a bicycle, broke into a shop to steal cigarettes, and, after being arrested seventy-five miles from Cork in a little village on the coast, was sent to an industrial school.

A Temple of the Holy Ghost
FLANNERY O'CONNOR

Mary Flannery O'Connor was born in 1925 in Savannah, Georgia. During her short life (she died of lupus in 1964) she won two *Kenyon Review* fellowships in fiction, a grant from the National Institute of Arts and Letters, and three O. Henry first prizes. For *The Complete Short Stories* she was awarded, posthumously, the 1972 National Book Award in fiction. In addition to the stories collected in that volume, she published two short novels, *Wise Blood* (1952) and *The Violent Bear It Away* (1960), and a collection of essays, *Mystery and Manners* (1961). "A Temple of the Holy Ghost" appeared originally in *Harper's Bazaar* (May 1954) and in the 1955 collection *A Good Man Is Hard to Find*.

ALL WEEKEND THE TWO GIRLS were calling each other Temple One and Temple Two, shaking with laughter and getting so red and hot that they were positively ugly, particularly Joanne who had spots on her face anyway. They came in the brown convent uniforms they had to wear at Mount St. Scholastica but as soon as they opened their suitcases, they took off the uniforms and put on red skirts and loud blouses. They put on lipstick and their Sunday shoes and walked around in the high heels all over the house, always passing the long mirror in the hall slowly to get a look at their legs. None of their ways was lost on the child. If only one of them had come, that one would have played with her, but since there were two of them, she was out of it and watched them suspiciously from a distance.

They were fourteen—two years older than she was—but neither of them was bright, which was why they had been sent to the convent. If they had gone to a regular school, they wouldn't have done anything but think about boys; at the convent the sisters, her mother said, would keep a grip on their necks. The child decided, after observing them for a few hours, that they were practically morons and she was glad to think that they were only second cousins and she couldn't have inherited any of their stupidity. Susan called herself Su-zan. She was very skinny but she had a pretty pointed face and red hair. Joanne had yellow hair that was naturally curly but she talked through her nose and when she laughed, she turned purple in patches. Neither one of them could say an intelligent thing and all their sentences began, "You know this boy I know well one time he. . ."

They were to stay all weekend and her mother said she didn't see how she would entertain them since she didn't know any boys their age. At this, the child, struck suddenly with genius, shouted, "There's Cheat! Get Cheat to come! Ask Miss Kirby to get Cheat to come show them around!" and she nearly choked on the food she had in her mouth. She doubled over laughing and hit the table with her fist and looked at the two bewildered girls while water started in her eyes and rolled down her fat cheeks and the braces she had in her mouth glared like tin. She had never thought of anything so funny before.

Her mother laughed in a guarded way and Miss Kirby blushed and carried her fork delicately to her mouth with one pea on it. She was a long-faced blonde schoolteacher who boarded with them and Mr. Cheatam was her admirer, a rich old farmer who arrived every Saturday afternoon in a fifteen-year-old baby-blue Pontiac powdered with red clay dust and black inside with Negroes that he charged ten cents apiece to bring into town on Saturday afternoons. After he dumped them he came to see Miss Kirby, always bringing a little gift—a bag of boiled peanuts or a watermelon or a stalk of sugar cane and once a wholesale box of Baby Ruth candy bars. He was bald-headed except for a little fringe of rust-colored hair and his face was nearly the same color as the unpaved roads and washed like them with ruts and gulleys. He wore a pale green shirt with a thin black stripe in it and blue galluses and his trousers cut across a protruding stomach that he pressed tenderly from time to time with his big flat thumb. All his teeth were backed with gold and he would roll his eyes at Miss Kirby in an impish way and say, "Haw haw," sitting in their porch swing with his legs spread apart and his hightopped shoes pointing in opposite directions on the floor.

"I don't think Cheat is going to be in town this weekend," Miss Kirby said, not in the least understanding that this was a joke, and the child was convulsed afresh, threw herself backward in her chair, fell out of it, rolled on the floor and lay there heaving. Her mother told her if she didn't stop this foolishness she would have to leave the table.

Yesterday her mother had arranged with Alonzo Myers to drive them the forty-five miles to Mayville, where the convent was, to get the girls for the weekend and Sunday afternoon he was hired to drive them back again. He was an eighteen-year-old boy who weighed two hundred and fifty pounds and worked for the taxi company and he was all you could get to drive you anywhere. He smoked or rather chewed a short black cigar and he had a round sweaty chest that showed through the yellow nylon shirt he wore. When he drove all the windows of the car had to be open.

"Well there's Alonzo!" the child roared from the floor. "Get Alonzo to show em around! Get Alonzo!"

The two girls, who had seen Alonzo, began to scream their indignation.

Her mother thought this was funny too but she said, "That'll be about enough out of you," and changed the subject. She asked them why they called each other Temple One and Temple Two and this sent them off into gales of giggles. Finally they managed to explain. Sister Perpetua, the oldest nun at the Sisters of Mercy in Mayville, had given them a lecture on what to do if a young man should—they put their heads in their laps—on what to do if—they finally managed to shout it out—if he should "behave in an ungentlemanly manner with them in the back of an automobile." Sister Perpetua said they were to say, "Stop sir! I am a Temple of the Holy Ghost!" and that would put an end to it. The child sat up off the floor with a blank face. She didn't see anything so funny in this. What was really funny was the idea of Mr. Cheatam or Alonzo Myers beauing them around. That killed her.

Her mother didn't laugh at what they had said. "I think you girls are pretty silly," she said. "After all, that's what you are—Temples of the Holy Ghost."

The two of them looked up at her, politely concealing their giggles, but with astonished faces as if they were beginning to realize that she was made of the same stuff as Sister Perpetua.

Miss Kirby preserved her set expression and the child thought, it's all over her head anyhow. I am a Temple of the Holy Ghost, she said to herself, and was pleased with the phrase. It made her feel as if somebody had given her a present.

After dinner, her mother collapsed on the bed and said, "Those girls are going to drive me crazy if I don't get some entertainment for them. They're awful."

"I bet I know who you could get," the child started.

"Now listen. I don't want to hear any more about Mr. Cheatam," her mother said. "You embarrass Miss Kirby. He's her only friend. Oh my Lord," and she sat up and looked mournfully out the window, "that poor soul is so lonesome she'll even ride in that car that smells like the last circle in hell."

And she's a Temple of the Holy Ghost too, the child reflected. "I wasn't thinking of him," she said. "I was thinking of those two Wilkinses, Wendell and Cory, that visit old lady Buchell out on her farm. They're her grandsons. They work for her."

"Now that's an idea," her mother murmured and gave her an appreciative look. But then she slumped again. "They're only farm boys. These girls would turn up their noses at them."

"Huh," the child said. "They wear pants. They're sixteen and they got a car. Somebody said they were both going to be Church of God preachers because you don't have to know nothing to be one."

"They would be perfectly safe with those boys all right," her mother said and in a minute she got up and called their grandmother on the telephone and after she had talked to the old woman a half an hour, it was arranged that Wendell and Cory would come to supper and afterwards take the girls to the fair.

Susan and Joanne were so pleased that they washed their hair and rolled it up on aluminum curlers. Hah, thought the child, sitting cross-legged on the bed to watch them undo the curlers, wait'll you get a load of Wendell and Cory! "You'll like these boys," she said. "Wendell is six feet tall ands got red hair. Cory is six feet six inches talls got black hair and wears a sport jacket and they gottem this car with a squirrel tail on the front."

"How does a child like you know so much about these men?" Susan asked and pushed her face up close to the mirror to watch the pupils in her eyes dilate.

The child lay back on the bed and began to count the narrow boards in the ceiling until she lost her place. I know them all right, she said to someone. We fought in the world war together. They were under me and I saved them five times from Japanese suicide divers and Wendell said I am going to marry that kid and the other said oh no you ain't I am and I said neither one of you is because I will court marshall you all before you can bat an eye. "I've seen them around is all," she said.

When they came the girls stared at them a second and then began to giggle and talk to each other about the convent. They sat in the swing together and Wendell and Cory sat on the banisters together. They sat like monkeys, their knees on a level with their shoulders and their arms hanging down between. They were short thin boys with red faces and high cheekbones and pale seed-like eyes. They had brought a harmonica and a guitar. One of them began to blow softly on the mouth organ, watching the girls over it, and the other started strumming the guitar and then began to sing, not watching them but keeping his head tilted upward as if he were only interested in hearing himself. He was singing a hillbilly song that sounded half like a love song and half like a hymn.

The child was standing on a barrel pushed into some bushes at the side of the house, her face on a level with the porch floor. The sun was going down and the sky was turning a bruised violet color that seemed to be connected with the sweet mournful sound of the music. Wendell began to smile as he sang and to look at the girls. He looked at Susan with a dog-like loving look and sang,

> "I've found a friend in Jesus,
> He's everything to me,
> He's the lily of the valley,
> He's the One who's set me free!"

Then he turned the same look on Joanne and sang,

> "A wall of fire about me,
> I've nothing now to fear,
> He's the lily of the valley,
> And I'll always have Him near!"

The girls looked at each other and held their lips stiff so as not to giggle but Susan let out one anyway and clapped her hand on her mouth. The singer frowned and for a few seconds only strummed the guitar. Then he began "The Old Rugged Cross" and they listened politely but when he had finished they said, "Let us sing one!" and before he could start another, they began to sing with their convent-trained voices,

"Tantum ergo Sacramentum
Veneremur Cernui:
Et antiquum documentum
Novo cedat ritui:"

The child watched the boys' solemn faces turn with perplexed frowning stares at each other as if they were uncertain whether they were being made fun of.

"Praestet fides supplementum
Sensuum defectui.
Genitori, Genitoque
Laus et jubilatio
Salus, honor, virtus quoque..."

The boys' faces were dark red in the gray-purple light. They looked fierce and startled.

"Sit et benedictio;
Procedenti ab utroque
Compar sit laudatio.
Amen."

The girls dragged out the Amen and then there was a silence.

"That must be Jew singing," Wendell said and began to tune the guitar.

The girls giggled idiotically but the child stamped her foot on the barrel. "You big dumb ox!" she shouted. "You big dumb Church of God ox!" she roared and fell off the barrel and scrambled up and shot around the corner of the house as they jumped from the banister to see who was shouting.

Her mother had arranged for them to have supper in the back yard and she had a table laid out there under some Japanese lanterns that she pulled out for garden parties. "I ain't eating with them," the child said and snatched her plate off the table and carried it to the kitchen and sat down with the thin blue-gummed cook and ate her supper.

"Howcome you be so ugly sometime?" the cook asked.

"Those stupid idiots," the child said.

The lanterns gilded the leaves of the trees orange on the level where they hung and above them was black-green and below them were different dim muted colors that made the girls sitting at the table look prettier than they were. From time to time, the child turned her head and glared out the kitchen window at the scene below.

"God could strike you deaf dumb and blind," the cook said, "and then you wouldn't be as smart as you is."

"I would still be smarter than some," the child said.

After supper they left for the fair. She wanted to go to the fair but not with them so even if they had asked her she wouldn't have gone. She went upstairs and paced the long bedroom with her hands locked together behind her back and her head thrust forward and an expression, fierce and dreamy both, on her face. She didn't turn on the electric light but let the darkness collect and make the room smaller and more private. At regular intervals a light crossed the open window and threw shadows on the wall. She stopped and stood looking out over the dark slopes, past where the pond glinted silver, past the wall of woods to the speckled sky where a long finger of light was revolving up and around and away, searching the air as if it were hunting for the lost sun. It was the beacon light from the fair.

She could hear the distant sound of the calliope and she saw in her head all the tents raised up in a kind of gold sawdust light and the diamond ring of the ferris wheel going around and around up in the air and down again and the screeking merry-go-round going around and around on the ground. A fair lasted five or six days and there was a special afternoon for school children and a special night for niggers. She had gone last year on the afternoon for school children and had seen the monkeys and the fat man and had ridden on the ferris wheel. Certain tents were closed then because they contained things that would be known only to grown people but she had looked with interest at the advertising on the closed tents, at the faded-looking pictures on the canvas of people in tights, with stiff stretched composed faces like the faces of the martyrs waiting to have their tongues cut out by the Roman soldier. She had imagined that what was inside these tents concerned medicine and she had made up her mind to be a doctor when she grew up.

She had since changed and decided to be an engineer but as she looked out the window and followed the revolving searchlight as it widened and shortened and wheeled in its arc, she felt that she would have to be much more than just a doctor or an engineer. She would have to be a saint because that was the occupation that included everything you could know; and yet she knew she would never be a saint. She did not steal or murder but she was a born liar and slothful and she sassed her mother and was deliberately ugly to almost everybody. She was eaten up also with the sin of Pride, the worst one. She made fun of the Baptist preacher who came to the school at commencement to give the devotional. She would pull down her mouth and hold her forehead as if she were in agony and groan, "Fawther, we thank Thee," exactly the way he did and she had been told many times not to do it. She could never be a saint, but she thought she could be a martyr if they killed her quick.

She could stand to be shot but not to be burned in oil. She didn't know if she could stand to be torn to pieces by lions or not. She began to prepare her martyrdom, seeing herself in a pair of tights in a great arena, lit by the early Christians hanging in cages of fire, making a gold dusty light that fell on her and the lions. The first lion charged forward and fell at her feet, converted. A whole series of lions did the same. The lions liked her so much she even slept with them and finally the Romans were obliged to burn her but to their astonishment she would not burn down and finding she was so hard to kill, they finally cut off her head very quickly with a sword and she went immediately to heaven. She rehearsed this several times, returning each time at the entrance of Paradise to the lions.

Finally she got up from the window and got ready for bed and got in without saying her prayers. There were two heavy double beds in the room. The girls were occupying the other one and she tried to think of something cold and clammy that she could hide in their bed but her thought was fruitless. She didn't have anything she could think of, like a chicken carcass or a piece of beef liver. The sound of the calliope coming through the window kept her awake and she remembered that she hadn't said her prayers and got up and knelt down and began them. She took a running start and went through to the other side of the Apostles' Creed and then hung by her chin on the side of the bed, empty-minded. Her prayers, when she remembered to say them, were usually perfunctory but sometimes when she had done something wrong or heard music or lost something, or sometimes for no reason at all, she would be moved to fervor and would think of Christ on the long journey to Calvary, crushed three times on the rough cross. Her mind would stay on this a while and then get empty and when something roused her, she would find that she was thinking of a different thing entirely, of some dog or some girl or something she was going to do some day. Tonight, remembering Wendell and Cory, she was filled with thanksgiving and almost weeping with delight, she said, "Lord, Lord, thank You that I'm not in the Church of God, thank You Lord, thank You!" and got back in bed and kept repeating it until she went to sleep.

The girls came in at a quarter to twelve and waked her up with their giggling. They turned on the small blue-shaded lamp to see to get undressed by and their skinny shadows climbed up the wall and broke and continued moving about softly on the ceiling. The child sat up to hear what all they had seen at the fair. Susan had a plastic pistol full of cheap candy and Joanne a pasteboard cat with red polka dots on it. "Did you see the monkeys dance?" the child asked. "Did you see that fat man and those midgets?"

"All kinds of freaks," Joanne said. And then she said to Susan, "I enjoyed it all but the you-know-what," and her face assumed a peculiar expression as if she had bit into something that she didn't know if she liked or not.

The other stood still and shook her head once and nodded slightly at the child. "Little pitchers," she said in a low voice but the child heard it and her heart began to beat very fast.

She got out of her bed and climbed onto the footboard of theirs. They turned off the light and got in but she didn't move. She sat there, looking hard at them until their faces were well defined in the dark. "I'm not as old as you all," she said, "but I'm about a million times smarter."

"There are some things," Susan said, "that a child of your age doesn't know," and they both began to giggle.

"Go back to your own bed," Joanne said.

The child didn't move. "One time," she said, her voice hollow-sounding in the dark, "I saw this rabbit have rabbits."

There was a silence. Then Susan said, "How?" in an indifferent tone and she knew that she had them. She said she wouldn't tell until they told about the you-know-what. Actually she had never seen a rabbit have rabbits but she forgot this as they began to tell what they had seen in the tent.

It had been a freak with a particular name but they couldn't remember the name. The tent where it was had been divided into two parts by a black curtain, one side for men and one for women. The freak went from one side to the other, talking first to the men and then to the women, but everyone could hear. The stage ran all the way across the front. The girls heard the freak say to the men, "I'm going to show you this and if you laugh, God may strike you the same way." The freak had a country voice, slow and nasal and neither high nor low, just flat. "God made me thisaway and if you laugh He may strike you the same way. This is the way He wanted me to be and I ain't disputing His way. I'm showing you because I got to make the best of it. I expect you to act like ladies and gentlemen. I never done it to myself nor had a thing to do with it but I'm making the best of it. I don't dispute hit." Then there was a long silence on the other side of the tent and finally the freak left the men and came over onto the women's side and said the same thing.

The child felt every muscle strained as if she were hearing the answer to a riddle that was more puzzling than the riddle itself. "You mean it had two heads?" she said.

"No," Susan said, "it was a man and woman both. It pulled up its dress and showed us. It had on a blue dress."

The child wanted to ask how it could be a man and woman both without two heads but she did not. She wanted to get back into her own bed and think it out and she began to climb down off the footboard.

"What about the rabbit?" Joanne asked.

The child stopped and only her face appeared over the footboard, abstracted, absent. "It spit them out of its mouth," she said, "six of them."

She lay in bed trying to picture the tent with the freak walking from side to side but she was too sleepy to figure it out. She was better able to see the faces of the country people watching, the men more solemn than they were in church, and the women stern and polite, with painted-looking eyes, standing as if they were waiting for the first note of the piano to begin the hymn. She could hear the freak saying, "God made me thisaway and I don't dispute hit," and the people saying, "Amen. Amen."

"God done this to me and I praise Him."

"Amen. Amen."

"He could strike you thisaway."

"Amen. Amen."

"But he has not."

"Amen."

"Raise yourself up. A temple of the Holy Ghost. You! You are God's temple, don't you know? Don't you know? God's Spirit has a dwelling in you, don't you know?"

"Amen. Amen."

"If anybody desecrates the temple of God, God will bring him to ruin and if you laugh, He may strike you thisaway. A temple of God is a holy thing. Amen. Amen."

"I am a temple of the Holy Ghost."

"Amen."

The people began to slap their hands without making a loud noise and with a regular beat between the Amens, more and more softly, as if they knew there was a child near, half asleep.

The next afternoon the girls put on their brown convent uniforms again and the child and her mother took them back to Mount St. Scholastica. "Oh glory, oh Pete!" they said. "Back to the salt mines." Alonzo Myers drove them and the child sat in front with him and her mother sat in back between the two girls, telling them such things as how pleased she was to have had them and how they must come back again and then about the good times she and their mothers had had when they were girls at the convent. The child didn't listen to any of this twaddle but kept as close to the locked door as she could get and held her head out the window. They had thought Alonzo would smell better on Sunday but he did not. With her hair blowing over her face she could look directly into the ivory sun which was framed in the middle of the blue afternoon but when she pulled it away from her eyes she had to squint.

Mount St. Scholastica was a red brick house set back in a garden in the center of town. There was a filling station on one side of it and a firehouse on the other. It had a high black grillework fence around it and narrow bricked walks between old trees and japonica bushes that were heavy with blooms. A big moon-faced nun came bustling to the door to let them in and embraced her mother and would have done the same to her but that she stuck out her hand and preserved a frigid frown, looking just past the sister's shoes at the wainscoting. They had a tendency to kiss even homely children, but the nun shook her hand vigorously and even cracked her knuckles a little and said they must come to the chapel, that benediction was just beginning. You put your foot in their door and they got you praying, the child thought as they hurried down the polished corridor.

You'd think she had to catch a train, she continued in the same ugly vein as they entered the chapel where the sisters were kneeling on one side and the girls, all in brown uniforms, on the other. The chapel smelled of incense. It was light green and gold, a series of springing arches that ended with the one over the altar where the priest was kneeling in front of the monstrance, bowed low. A small boy in a surplice was standing behind him, swinging the censer. The child knelt down between her mother and the nun and they were well into the "*Tantum Ergo*" before her ugly thoughts stopped and she began to realize that she was in the presence of God. Hep me not to be so mean, she began mechanically. Hep me not to give her so much sass. Hep me not to talk like I do. Her mind began to get quiet and then empty but when the priest raised the monstrance with the Host shining ivory-colored in the center of it, she was thinking of the tent at the fair that had the freak in it. The freak was saying, "I don't dispute hit. This is the way He wanted me to be."

As they were leaving the convent door, the big nun swooped down on her mischievously and nearly smothered her in the black habit, mashing the side of her face into the crucifix hitched onto her belt and then holding her off and looking at her with little periwinkle eyes.

On the way home she and her mother sat in the back and Alonzo drove by himself in the front. The child observed three folds of fat in the back of his neck and noted that his ears were pointed almost like a pig's. Her mother, making conversation, asked him if he had gone to the fair.

"Gone," he said, "and never missed a thing and it was good I gone when I did because they ain't going to have it next week like they said they was."

"Why?" asked her mother.

"They shut it on down," he said. "Some of the preachers from town gone out and inspected it and got the police to shut it on down."

Her mother let the conversation drop and the child's round face was lost in thought. She turned it toward the window and looked out over a stretch of pasture land that rose and fell with a gathering greenness until it touched the dark woods. The sun was a huge red ball like an elevated Host drenched in blood and when it sank out of sight, it left a line in the sky like a red clay road hanging over the trees.

III
REVELATION:
NATURAL OR
SUPERNATURAL?

A Young Man, Gleaming, White

JOÃO GUIMARÃES ROSA

João Guimarães Rosa was born in Cordisburgo, Minas Gerais, Brazil, in 1908, and died in Rio de Janeiro in 1967. He served as a country doctor, as a military physician, taking part in the civil war of 1932, and, after 1934, as a Brazilian diplomat. Shortly before his death he became a member of the Brazilian Academy of Letters. His published work includes *Sagarana* (1946), *Corpo de Baile* (1956), and *Primeiras Estorias* (1962), a book of short stories translated from Portuguese by Barbara Shelby in 1968 as *The Third Bank of the River and Other Stories*. "A Young Man, Gleaming, White" is taken from that collection.

ON THE NIGHT of November 11, 1872, in the district of Sêrro Frio in Minas Gerais, there occurred eerie phenomena which were referred to in contemporary newspapers and registered in the astronomical tables. According to these accounts, a glowing missile hurtled out of space, accompanied by booming blasts. The earth rocked in a quake that shook the mountain heights, made rubble of houses, and caused the valleys to tremble. Countless people were killed. The torrential rainstorm that followed caused greater floods than any ever seen before; the water in the streams and rivers rose sixty feet above its normal level. After this cataclysm the

125

features of the country for leagues around were entirely
changed; all that was left were the wrecks of hills, caves
newly blasted open, creeks shifted from their courses, forests
uprooted, new mountains and cliffs upthrust, farms swallowed up without a trace—strewn rocks covering what had
been fields. Even some distance away from the monstrous
happenings, many men and animals perished by being buried
alive or drowned. Others wandered at random, going wherever it pleased God to send them, in their confusion at no
longer finding the old roads they knew.

A week later, on the day of St. Felix the Confessor, one
of these poor fugitives, who had doubtless been driven from
his home by hunger or shock, appeared in the courtyard of
Hilário Cordeiro's Casco Ranch. Suddenly he was there, a
youth with the appearance of a gentleman but in a pitiable
state. Without even rags to cover his nakedness, he had
wrapped himself in a thick cloth like a horse blanket, which
he had found God knows where. Bashfully, he showed himself there in the early morning light and then disappeared
behind the fence of the cow pasture. He was of an amazing
whiteness, not at all sickly or wan, but of a fine paleness,
semi-gilded with light, which caused him to gleam as if he
had a source of brightness inside his body. He seemed to be a
foreigner of some kind never met with before in those parts,
almost as if he constituted a new race all by himself. They
talk about him to this day, though with a good deal of confusion and uncertainty because it was so long ago. The story is
told by the children and gradnchildren of men who were
adolescents, or perhaps even children, when they were fortunate enough to know him.

Because Hilário Cordeiro, a good, God-fearing man, was
generous to the poor, more especially in those first days after
the catastrophe in which his own relatives had died or suffered total ruin, he unhesitatingly offered the youth hospital-
ity and thoughtfully provided him with clothing and food.
The stranger was in dire need of such help, for, as a result of

the extraordinary misfortunes and terrors that he had suffered, he had completely lost his memory and even his use
of speech. In his condition perhaps the future was indistinguishable from the past: since he had lost all sense of time
and could understand nothing, he answered neither yea nor
nay. His was a truly pitiful state. He seemed not even to try
to understand gestures, or at any rate often interpreted them
to mean the opposite of what was intended. Since he was
bound to have a given name already, he could not just be
given some made-up one; but no one had any idea what his
Christian name was any more than the surname he must
have inherited from his unknown progenitors. He seemed to
be the Son of No Man.

For days after his arrival the neighbors came to inspect
him. Stupid they certainly did not find him, but he was
subject to a kind of dreamy disinvolvement, tinged by sadness. They were surprised, though, at how unobtrusively
observant he could be—noting every little characteristic of
people and of things. This odd combination of careful
scrutiny and misinterpretation only began to be understood
later on. Nevertheless, they all liked him. And the person
who was perhaps most attached to him was the Negro José
Kakende, who was a bit odd himself. This former slave of a
halfwitted musician had been touched in the head ever since
a shock he had suffered during the calamities in the county,
so that he began to wander from place to place, shouting
warnings to the people and crying out wild lunatic tales
about a portentous apparition that he swore he had seen on
the banks of the Rio do Peixe just before the cataclysm. Only
one person had a grudge against the youth from the beginning, and that was a certain Duarte Dias, the father of a
beautiful girl named Viviana. He swore the youth was a
rascal, a secret criminal, who, in better times, would have
been banished to Africa or put in irons and thrown into the
king's dungeon. But because he was known to be a hot-
tempered, overbearing man, and malignant and unjust be-

sides, with a heart of pure adamant, nobody paid much attention to him.

One particular day they took the youth to mass, and though he gave no sign of being a believer or an unbeliever, he did nothing untoward. He listened to the singing and the choral music, seriously and with considerable feeling. He was not sad exactly, but it seemed as if he felt a greater nostalgia than other people, a deeper yearning. Perhaps because he understood nothing of the service, his feeling was refined into a purer ecstasy—the heart of a dog who hears his master. His smile, which was more a matter of the lips than of the eyes and which was never broad enough to reveal his teeth, sometimes lingered on his face for long periods, as if he were thinking of some other place, some other time. After mass, when Father Bayão gave a kindly talk to the youth, he prefaced it by unexpectedly making the sign of the cross over him but found that the young man was not made at all uneasy by the holy gesture. It seemed to the priest that he floated a little above the earth, held there by some inner buoyancy denied to the earthbound. "Compared to him, all of us ordinary mortals have hard expressions, an ugly look of habitual weariness." These lines were written by the priest in a letter which he signed and sealed as a witness of the coming of the exquisitely strange wanderer and sent to Canon Lessa Cadaval of the Mariana See. In this letter he also mentioned the Negro José Kakende, who had approached him on the same occasion with loud and extravagant accounts of the vision he had had at the riverside: ". . . the dragging wind and majesty of the cloud full of splendor, and in it, swirled round by fire, a dark-yellow moving object, a flying vehicle, flat, with rounded edges, and surmounted by a glass bell of a bluish color. When it landed, there descended from it archangels, amidst wheels, flaring flames, and the pealing of trumpets." Along with the excited José Kakende came Hilário Cordeiro to take the youth home with him again, as tenderly as if he were his real father.

At the door of the church was a blind beggar, Nicolau. When the youth caught sight of him he gazed at him deeply and with his whole attention (they say his eyes were the color of a rose!) and then he walked straight up to the beggar and hastily handed him a bit of something out of his pocket. No Christian soul could see that blind man, sweating in the sun, without noting the irony of his having to bear the heat of that burning orb and at the same time be denied the ability to rejoice in the beauty of the sun or the moon. The blind man fingered the gift in his hand and then, instead of wondering what outlandish manner of money it could be and then realizing it was no money at all, brought it up to his mouth at once, only to have the child who was his guide warn him that it was not something to eat but only a seed from some kind of tree pod. The blind man angrily put the seed away and only planted it months later, long after the events soon to be related had already taken place. From the seed sprouted a rare and unexpected bluish flower, several contraposed flowers in one, all commingled impossibly in lovely confusion. The tints were of a kind not seen in our times; no two people could even agree on precisely what the colors were. But soon it wilted and withered away, producing no seeds nor shoots; even the insects had not had the time to learn to seek it out.

Just after the scene with the blind man, though, Duarte Dias appeared in the churchyard with some of his friends and servants, ready to make trouble and astonishing everyone by demanding that the youth go with him, on the grounds that because of the whiteness of his skin and his aristocratic ways, he must be one of the Resendes, Duarte Dias's rich relatives who had been lost in the earthquake; and that therefore, unless some definite news was received that the youth was no Resende, it was his responsibility to hold him in his custody. This proposal was promptly contested by Hilário Cordeiro, and the argument might easily have become a real altercation because of Dias's loud insistence, if he had not finally given in to the persuasion of Quincas Mendanha, a political notable from the capital, who was also purveyor for the Brotherhood.

Soon it became clear that Hilário Cordeiro was righter than he knew when he protected the youth so zealously. He began to be lucky in everything: all in his household were healthy and lived in harmony, and his business prospered. It was not that the youth gave him much overt help; he could hardly have been expected to do rough farm labor with his dainty, uncallused hands, as white and smooth as a courtier's. In fact, he spent most of his time dreamily wandering about here and there at will, exercising an airy freedom and a taste for solitude. People said he must be under some magic spell. Magic and delicate hands to the contrary notwithstanding, the youth did take an extremely important part in everything to do with the machinery and the tools used on the place. He was extraordinarily good at mechanics, inventing and repairing in the cleverest, most careful way. At those times he was wide-awake enough. He was also an astronomer, but one with the odd habit of continually watching the sky by day as well as by night. Another amusement of his was to light fires, and everyone noticed how eagerly he took part in lighting the traditional bonfires on St. John's Eve.

It was on that very St. John's Eve that the incident with the girl Viviana occurred, a story which has never been told accurately before. What happened was that when the youth, accompanied by the Negro José Kakende, came up and saw that the girl, though so pretty, was not amusing herself like the others, he went up close to her and gently, but startlingly, laid the palm of his hand delicately on her breast. And since Viviana was the loveliest of all the girls, the wonder was that the beauty of his deed in no way altered his vague melancholy. But her father, Duarte Dias, who had been watching, bawled out, over and over: "They've got to be married! Now they have to get married!" He declared that since the stranger, who was unmarried, had shamed his daughter, he would have to take her to wife, willy-nilly. Though the young man listened pleasantly to all this and made no objection, Duarte Dias never stopped bellowing until Father Bayão and some of the older men remonstrated with him for his nonsensical anger. Young Viviana soothed him, too, by her radiant smiles; from the moment of the youth's touch there was awakened in her an unending joy, a pure gift which she enjoyed for the rest of her life. Incomprehensibly, Duarte Dias later added to the general amazement, as we shall see.

He came to Casco Ranch on August 5, the day of the mass of Our Lady of the Snows and Eve of the Transfiguration, and asked to speak to Hilário Cordeiro. The youth was present, too, so otherworldly and graceful that he made one think of moonlight. And Duarte Dias begged them to let him take the young man home with him, not out of ambition or because he wanted to pretend to a rank he didn't have, nor out of any petty self-interest, but because he really wanted and needed to have with him one for whom his contrition and remorse had led him to conceive the strongest esteem and affection. He was so moved that he could scarcely speak, and copious tears flowed from his eyes. Those who heard him could not understand such a change in a man who had never been able to express any emotion at all except in some violent, impetuous way. However, the youth, bright as the eye of the sun, simply took him by the hand and, accompanied by the Negro José Kakende, led him off through the fields to a place on Duarte's land where there was an abandoned brick kiln. There he made signs for the men to dig, and they found a diamond deposit—or maybe a big pot of gold, as another story has it. Naturally, Duarte Dias thought he would become a very rich man after this, and he changed from that day on into a good, upright man, so his awestruck contemporaries claimed.

But on the Venerable St. Bridget's Day something more

was heard of the imperturbable youth. It was said that the
night before he had made one of his customary disappear-
ances, but this time by way of the sky, at a time of dry
thunder. All José Kakende would say was that he had secretly helped light nine bonfires in a pattern. Aside from
that, he only repeated his old wild descriptions of a cloud,
flames, noises, round things, wheels, a contraption of some
sort, and archangels. With the first sunlight, the youth had
gone off on wings.

Each one, in his own way, mourned his life long
whenever he thought of the youth. They doubted the air
they breathed, the mountains, the very solidity of the
earth—but remembered him. Duarte Dias actually died of
sorrow, though his daughter, the maiden Viviana, never lost
her joy. José Kakende had long talks with the blind man.
Hilário Cordeiro, like many others, said he felt he was half in
his grave whenever he thought of the youth. His gleam remained when he was gone. That's all there is to tell.

One Day After Saturday

GABRIEL GARCÍA MÁRQUEZ

Although **Gabriel García Márquez** was born in Colombia (1928) and studied at the University of Bogata, he has spent most of his life in Mexico and Europe, and lives at present with his family in Barcelona. His highly acclaimed novel *One Hundred Years of Solitude* has gained him many American readers. Similarly, his short story collections translated into English, such as *No One Writes to the Colonel* and *Leaf Storm,* have displayed to readers in this country an acute vision of history and the past and a sense of fantasy that characterize his art. "One Day After Saturday," from the collection *Los funerales de la mamá grande* (1962; included in the American edition of *No One Writes to the Colonel*), was translated into English by J. S. Bernstein.

THE TROUBLE BEGAN IN JULY, when Rebecca, an embittered widow who lived in an immense house with two galleries and nine bedrooms, discovered that the screens were torn as if they had been stoned from the street. She made the first discovery in her bedroom and thought that she must speak to Argenida, her servant and confidante since her husband died. Later, moving things around (for a long time Rebecca had done nothing but move things around), she noticed that not only the screens in her bedroom but those in all the rest of the house were torn, too. The widow had an academic sense of authority, inherited perhaps from her paternal great-grandfather, a creole who in the War of Independence had fought on the side of the Royalists and later made an arduous journey to Spain with the sole purpose of visiting the palace which Charles III built in San Ildefonso. So that when she discovered the state of the other screens, she thought no more about speaking to Argenida about it but, rather, put on her straw hat with the tiny velvet flowers and went to the town hall to make a report about the attack. But when she got there, she saw that the Mayor himself, shirtless, hairy, and with a solidity which seemed bestial to her, was busy repairing the town hall screens, torn like her own.

Rebecca burst into the dirty and cluttered office, and the first thing she saw was a pile of dead birds on the desk. But she was disconcerted, in part by the heat and in part by the indignation which the destruction of her screens had produced in her, so that she did not have time to shudder at the unheard-of spectacle of the dead birds on the desk. Nor was she scandalized by the evidence of authority degraded, at the top of a stairway, repairing the metal threads of the window with a roll of screening and a screwdriver. She was not thinking now of any other dignity than her own, mocked by her own screens, and her absorption prevented her even from connecting the windows of her house with those of the town hall. She planted herself with discreet solemnity two steps inside the door and, leaning on the long ornate handle of her parasol, said:

"I have to register a complaint."

From the top of the stairway, the Mayor turned his head, flushed from the heat. He showed no emotion before the gratuitous presence of the widow in his office. With gloomy nonchalance he continued untacking the ruined screen, and asked from up above:

"What is the trouble?"

"The boys from the neighborhood broke my screens."

The Mayor took another look at her. He examined her carefully, from the elegant little velvet flowers to her shoes the color of old silver, and it was as if he were seeing her for the first time in his life. He descended with great economy of movement, without taking his eyes off her, and when he reached the bottom, he rested one hand on his belt, motioned with the screwdriver toward the desk, and said:

"It's not the boys, Señora. It's the birds."

And it was then that she connected the dead birds on the desk with the man at the top of the stairs, and with the broken screens of her bedrooms. She shuddered, imagining all the bedrooms in her house full of dead birds.

"The birds!" she exclaimed.

"The birds," the Mayor concurred. "It's strange you haven't noticed, since we've had this problem with the birds breaking windows and dying inside the houses for three days."

When she left the town hall, Rebecca felt ashamed. And a little resentful of Argenida, who dragged all the town gossip into her house and who nevertheless had not spoken to her about the birds. She opened her parasol, dazzled by the brightness of an impending August, and while she walked along the stifling and deserted street she had the impression that the bedrooms of all the houses were giving off a strong and penetrating stench of dead birds.

This was at the end of July, and never in the history of the town had it been so hot. But the inhabitants, alarmed by the death of the birds, did not notice that. Even though the strange phenomenon had not seriously affected the town's activities, the majority were held in suspense by it at the beginning of August. A majority among whom was not numbered His Reverence, Anthony Isabel of the Holy Sacrament of the Altar Castañeda y Montero, the bland parish priest who, at the age of ninety-four, assured people that he had seen the devil on three occasions, and that nevertheless he had only seen two dead birds, without attributing the least importance to them. He found the first one in the sacristy, one Tuesday after Mass, and thought it had been dragged in there by some neighborhood cat. He found the other one on Wednesday, in the veranda of the parish house, and he pushed it with the point of his boot into the street, thinking, Cats shouldn't exist.

But on Friday, when he arrived at the railroad station, he found a third dead bird on the bench he chose to sit down on. It was like a lightning stroke inside him when he grabbed the body by its little legs; he raised it to eye level, turned it over, examined it, and thought astonishedly, Gracious, this is the third one I've found this week.

From that moment on he began to notice what was happening in the town, but in a very inexact way, for Father Anthony Isabel, in part because of his age and in part also because he swore he had seen the devil on three occasions (something which seemed to the town just a bit out of place), was considered by his parishioners as a good man, peaceful and obliging, but with his head habitually in the clouds. He noticed that something was happening with the birds, but even then he didn't believe that it was so important as to deserve a sermon. He was the first one who experienced the smell. He smelled it Friday night, when he woke up alarmed, his light slumber interrupted by a nauseating stench, but he didn't know whether to attribute it to a nightmare or to a new and original trick of the devil's to disturb his sleep. He sniffed all around him, and turned over in bed, thinking that that experience would serve him for a sermon. It could be, he thought, a dramatic sermon on the ability of Satan to infiltrate the human heart through any of the five senses.

When he strolled around the porch the next day before Mass, he heard someone speak for the first time about the dead birds. He was thinking about the sermon, Satan, and the sins which can be committed through the olfactory sense when he heard someone say that the bad nocturnal odor was due to the birds collected during the week; and in his head a confused hodgepodge of evangelical cautions, evil odors, and dead birds took shape. So that on Sunday he had to improvise a long paragraph on Charity which he himself did not understand very well, and he forgot forever about the relations between the devil and the five senses.

Nevertheless, in some very distant spot in his thinking, those experiences must have remained lurking. That always happened to him, not only in the seminary, more than seventy years before, but in a very particular way after he passed ninety. At the seminary, one very bright afternoon when there was a heavy downpour with no thunder, he was reading a selection from Sophocles in the original. When the rain was over, he looked through the window at the tired field, the newly washed afternoon, and forgot entirely about Greek theater and the classics, which he did not distinguish but, rather, called in a general way, "the little ancients of old." One rainless afternoon, perhaps thirty or forty years later, he was crossing the cobblestone plaza of a town which he was visiting and, without intending to, recited the stanza from Sophocles which he had been reading in the seminary. That same week, he had a long conversation about "the little ancients of old" with the apostolic deputy, a talkative and impressionable old man, who was fond of certain complicated puzzles which he claimed to have invented and which became popular years later under the name of crosswords.

That interview permitted him to recover at one stroke all his old heartfelt love for the Greek classics. At Christmas of that year he received a letter. And if it were not for the fact that by that time he had acquired the solid prestige of being exaggeratedly imaginative, daring in his interpretations, and a little foolish in his sermons, on that occasion they would have made him a bishop.

But he had buried himself in the town long before the War of 1885, and at the time when the birds began dying in the bedrooms it had been a long while since they had asked for him to be replaced by a younger priest, especially when he claimed to have seen the devil. From that time on they began not paying attention to him, something which he didn't notice in a very clear way in spite of still being able to decipher the tiny characters of his breviary without glasses. He had always been a man of regular habits. Small, insignificant, with pronounced and solid bones and calm gestures, and a soothing voice for conversation but too soothing for the pulpit. He used to stay in his bedroom until lunchtime day-dreaming, carelessly stretched out in a canvas chair and wearing nothing but his long twill trousers with the bottoms tied at the ankles.

He didn't do anything except say Mass. Twice a week he sat in the confessional, but for many years no one confessed. He simply thought that his parishioners were losing the faith because of modern customs, and that's why he would have thought it a very opportune occurrence to have seen the devil on three occasions, although he knew that people gave very little credence to his words and although he was aware that he was not very convincing when he spoke about those experiences. For himself it would have been a surprise to discover that he was dead, not only during the last five years but also in those extraordinary moments when he found the first two birds. When he found the third, however, he came back to life a little, so that in the last few days he was thinking with appreciable frequency about the dead bird on the station bench.

He lived ten steps from the church in a small house without screens, with a veranda toward the street and two rooms which served as office and bedroom. He considered, perhaps in his moments of less lucidity, that it is possible to achieve happiness on earth when it is not very hot, and this idea made him a little confused. He liked to wander through metaphysical obstacle courses. That was what he was doing when he used to sit in the bedroom every morning, with the door ajar, his eyes closed and his muscles tensed. However, he himself did not realize that he had become so subtle in his thinking that for at least three years in his meditative moments he was no longer thinking about anything.

At twelve o'clock sharp a boy crossed the corridor with a sectioned tray which contained the same things every day: bone broth with a piece of yucca, white rice, meat prepared without onion, fried banana or a corn muffin, and a few lentils which Father Anthony Isabel of the Holy Sacrament of the Altar had never tasted.

The boy put the tray next to the chair where the priest sat, but the priest didn't open his eyes until he no longer heard steps in the corridor. Therefore, in town they thought that the Father took his siesta before lunch (a thing which seemed exceedingly nonsensical) when the truth was that he didn't even sleep normally at night.

Around that time his habits had become less complicated, almost primitive. He lunched without moving from his canvas chair, without taking the food from the tray, without using the dishes or the fork or the knife, but only the same spoon with which he drank his soup. Later he would get up, throw a little water on his head, put on his white soutane dotted with great square patches, and go to the railroad station precisely at the hour when the rest of the town was lying down for its siesta. He had been covering this route for several months, murmuring the prayer which he himself had made up the last time the devil had appeared to him.

One Saturday—nine days after the dead birds began to fall—Father Anthony Isabel of the Holy Sacrament of the Altar was going to the station when a dying bird fell at his feet, directly in front of Rebecca's house. A flash of intuition exploded in his head, and he realized that this bird, contrary to the others, might be saved. He took it in his hands and knocked at Rebecca's door at the moment when she was unhooking her bodice to take her siesta.

In her bedroom, the widow heard the knocking and in-

stinctively turned her glance toward the screens. No bird had
got into that bedroom for two days. But the screen was still
torn. She had thought it a useless expense to have it repaired
as long as the invasion of birds, which kept her nerves on
edge, continued. Above the hum of the electric fan, she
heard the knocking at the door and remembered with impatience that Argenida was taking a siesta in the bedroom at
the end of the corridor. It didn't even occur to her to wonder
who might be imposing on her at that hour. She hooked up
her bodice again, pushed open the screen door, and walked
the length of the corridor, stiff and straight, then crossed the
living room crowded with furniture and decorative objects
and, before opening the door, saw through the metal screen
that there stood taciturn Father Anthony Isabel, with his
eyes closed and a bird in his hands. Before she opened the
door, he said, "If we give him a little water and then put him
under a dish, I'm sure he'll get well." And when she opened
the door, Rebecca thought she'd collapse from fear.

He didn't stay there for more than five minutes. Rebecca
thought that it was she who had cut short the meeting. But
in reality it had been the priest. If the widow had thought
about it at that moment, she would have realized that the
priest, in the thirty years he had been living in the town, had
never stayed more than five minutes in her house. It seemed
to him that amid the profusion of decorations in the living
room the concupiscent spirit of the mistress of the house
showed itself clearly, in spite of her being related, however
distantly, but as everyone was aware, to the Bishop. Furthermore, there had been a legend (or a story) about Rebecca's family which surely, the Father thought, had not
reached the episcopal palace, in spite of the fact that Colonel Aureliano Buendía, a cousin of the widow's whom she
considered lacking in family affection, had once sworn that
the Bishop had not come to the town in this century in order
to avoid visiting his relation. In any case, be it history or
legend, the truth was that Father Anthony Isabel of the Holy

Sacrament of the Altar did not feel at ease in this house, whose only inhabitant had never shown any signs of piety and who confessed only once a year but always replied with evasive answers when he tried to pin her down about the puzzling death of her husband. If he was there now, waiting for her to bring him a glass of water to bathe a dying bird, it was the result of a chance occurrence which he was not responsible for.

While he waited for the widow to return, the priest, seated on a luxurious carved wooden rocker, felt the strange humidity of that house which had not become peaceful since the time when a pistol shot rang out, more than twenty years before, and José Arcadio Buendía, cousin of the colonel and of his own wife, fell face down amidst the clatter of buckles and spurs on the still-warm leggings which he had just taken off.

When Rebecca burst into the living room again, she saw Father Anthony Isabel seated in the rocker with an air of vagueness which terrified her.

"The life of an animal," said the Father, "is as dear to Our Lord as that of a man."

As he said it, he did not remember José Arcadio Buendía. Nor did the widow recall him. But she was used to not giving any credence to the Father's words ever since he had spoken from the pulpit about the three times the devil had appeared to him. Without paying attention to him she took the bird in her hands, dipped him in the glass of water, and shook him afterward. The Father observed that there was impiety and carelessness in her way of acting, an absolute lack of consideration for the animal's life.

"You don't like birds," he said softly but affirmatively.

The widow raised her eyelids in a gesture of impatience and hostility. "Although I liked them once," she said, "I detest them now that they've taken to dying inside of our houses."

"Many have died," he said implacably. One might have

thought that there was a great deal of cleverness in the even tone of his voice.

"All of them," said the widow. And she added, as she squeezed the animal with repugnance and placed him under the dish, "And even that wouldn't bother me if they hadn't torn my screens."

And it seemed to him that he had never known such hardness of heart. A moment later, holding the tiny and defenseless body in his own hand, the priest realized that it had ceased breathing. Then he forgot everything—the humidity of the house, the concupiscence, the unbearable smell of gunpowder on José Arcadio Buendía's body—and he realized the prodigious truth which had surrounded him since the beginning of the week. Right there, while the widow watched him leave the house with a menacing gesture and the dead bird in his hands, he witnessed the marvelous revelation that a rain of dead birds was falling over the town, and that he, the minister of God, the chosen one, who had known happiness when it had not been hot, had forgotten entirely about the Apocalypse.

That day he went to the station, as always, but he was not fully aware of his actions. He knew vaguely that something was happening in the world, but he felt muddled, dumb, unequal to the moment. Seated on the bench in the station, he tried to remember if there was a rain of dead birds in the Apocalypse, but he had forgotten it entirely. Suddenly he thought that his delay at Rebecca's house had made him miss the train, and he stretched his head up over the dusty and broken glass and saw on the clock in the ticket office that it was still twelve minutes to one. When he returned to the bench, he felt as if he were suffocating. At that moment he remembered it was Saturday. He moved his woven palm fan for a while, lost in his dark interior fog. Then he fretted over the buttons on his soutane and the buttons on his boots and over his long, snug, clerical trousers, and he noticed with alarm that he had never in his life been so hot.

Without moving from the bench he unbuttoned the collar of his soutane, took his handkerchief out of his sleeve, and wiped his flushed face, thinking, in a moment of illuminated pathos, that perhaps he was witnessing the unfolding of an earthquake. He had read that somewhere. Nevertheless the sky was clear: a transparent blue sky from which all the birds had mysteriously disappeared. He noticed the color and the transparency, but for a moment forgot about the dead birds. Now he was thinking about something else, about the possibility that a storm would break. Nevertheless the sky was diaphanous and tranquil, as if it were the sky over some other town, distant and different, where he had never felt the heat, and as if they were other eyes, not his own, which were looking at it. Then he looked toward the north, above the roofs of palms and rusted zinc, and saw the slow, silent, rhythmic blot of the buzzards over the dump.

For some mysterious reason, he relived at that moment the emotions he felt one Sunday in the seminary, shortly before taking his minor orders. The rector had given him permission to make use of his private library and he often stayed for hours and hours (especially on Sundays) absorbed in the reading of some yellowed books smelling of old wood, with annotations in Latin in the tiny, angular scrawl of the rector. One Sunday, after he had been reading for the whole day, the rector entered the room and rushed, shocked, to pick up a card which evidently had fallen from the pages of the book he was reading. He observed his superior's confusion with discreet indifference, but he managed to read the card. There was only one sentence, written in purple ink in a clean, straightforward hand: "*Madame Ivette est morte cette nuit.*" More than half a century later, seeing a blot of buzzards over a forgotten town, he remembered the somber expression of the rector seated in front of him, purple against the dusk, his breathing imperceptibly quickened.

Shaken by that association, he did not then feel the heat, but rather exactly the reverse, the sting of ice in his groin and in the soles of his feet. He was terrified without knowing what the precise cause of that terror was, tangled in a net of confused ideas, among which it was impossible to distinguish a nauseating sensation, from Satan's hoof stuck in the mud, from a flock of dead birds falling on the world, while he, Anthony Isabel of the Holy Sacrament of the Altar, remained indifferent to that event. Then he straightened up, raised an awed hand, as if to begin a greeting which was lost in the void, and cried out in horror, "The Wandering Jew!"

At that moment the train whistled. For the first time in many years he did not hear it. He saw it pull into the station, surrounded by a dense cloud of smoke, and heard the rain of cinders against the sheets of rusted zinc. But that was like a distant and undecipherable dream from which he did not awaken completely until that afternoon, a little after four, when he put the finishing touches on the imposing sermon he would deliver on Sunday. Eight hours later, he was called to administer extreme unction to a woman.

With the result that the Father did not find out who arrived that afternoon on the train. For a long time he had watched the four cars go by, ramshackle and colorless, and he could not recall anyone's getting off to stay, at least in recent years. Before it was different, when he could spend a whole afternoon watching a train loaded with bananas go by; a hundred and forty cars loaded with fruit, passing endlessly until, well on toward nightfall, the last car passed with a man dangling a green lantern. Then he saw the town on the other side of the track—the lights were on now—and it seemed to him that, by merely watching the train pass, it had taken him to another town. Perhaps from that came his habit of being present at the station every day, even after they shot the workers to death and the banana plantations were finished, and with them the hundred-and-forty-car trains, and there was left only that yellow, dusty train which neither brought anyone nor took anyone away.

But that Saturday someone did come. When Father Anthony Isabel of the Holy Sacrament of the Altar left the
station, a quiet boy with nothing particular about him except
his hunger saw the priest from the window of the last car at
the precise moment that he remembered he had not eaten
since the previous day. He thought, If there's a priest, there
must be a hotel. And he got off the train and crossed the
street, which was blistered by the metallic August sun, and
entered the cool shade of a house located opposite the station whence issued the sound of a worn gramophone record.
His sense of smell, sharpened by his two-day-old hunger, told
him that was the hotel. And he went in without seeing the
sign "HOTEL MACONDO," a sign which he was never to
read in his life.

The proprietress was more than five months pregnant.
She was the color of mustard, and looked exactly as her
mother had when her mother was pregnant with her. He
ordered, "Lunch, as quick as you can," and she, not trying to
hurry, served him a bowl of soup with a bare bone and some
chopped green banana in it. At that moment the train whistled. Absorbed in the warm and healthful vapor of the soup,
he calculated the distance which lay between him and the
station, and immediately felt himself invaded by that confused sensation of panic which missing a train produces.

He tried to run. He reached the door, anguished, but he
hadn't even taken one step across the threshold when he
realized that he didn't have time to make the train. When he
returned to the table, he had forgotten his hunger; he saw a
girl next to the gramophone who looked at him pitifully,
with the horrible expression of a dog wagging his tail. Then,
for the first time that whole day, he took off his hat, which
his mother had given him two months before, and lodged it
between his knees while he finished eating. When he got up
from the table, he didn't seem bothered by missing the train,
or by the prospect of spending a weekend in a town whose
name he would not take the trouble to find out. He sat down

in a corner of the room, the bones of his back supported by a hard, straight chair, and stayed there for a long time, not listening to the records until the girl who was picking them out said:

"It's cooler on the veranda."

He felt ill. It took an effort to start conversation with strangers. He was afraid to look people in the face, and when he had no recourse but to speak, the words came out different from the way he thought them. "Yes," he replied. And he felt a slight shiver. He tried to rock, forgetting that he was not in a rocker.

"The people who come here pull a chair to the veranda since it's cooler," the girl said. And, listening to her, he realized how anxiously she wanted to talk. He risked a look at her just as she was winding up the gramophone. She seemed to have been sitting there for months, years perhaps, and she showed not the slightest interest in moving from that spot. She was winding up the gramophone but her life was concentrated on him. She was smiling.

"Thank you," he said, trying to get up, to put some ease and spontaneity into his movements. The girl didn't stop looking at him. She said, "They also leave their hats on the hook."

This time he felt a burning in his ears. He shivered, thinking about her way of suggesting things. He felt uncomfortably shut in, and again felt his panic over the missed train. But at that moment the proprietress entered the room.

"What are you doing?" she asked.

"He's pulling a chair onto the veranda, as they all do," the girl said.

He thought he perceived a mocking tone in her words.

"Don't bother," said the proprietress. "I'll bring you a stool."

The girl laughed and he left disconcerted. It was hot. An unbroken, dry heat, and he was sweating. The proprietress dragged a wooden stool with a leather seat to the veranda. He was about to follow her when the girl spoke again.

"The bad part about it is that the birds will frighten him," she said.

He managed to see the harsh look when the proprietress turned her eyes on the girl. It was a swift but intense look. "What you should do is be quiet," she said, and turned smiling to him. Then he felt less alone and had the urge to speak.

"What was that she said?" he asked.

"That at this hour of the day dead birds fall onto the veranda," the girl said.

"Those are just some notions of hers," said the proprietress. She bent over to straighten a bouquet of artificial flowers on the little table in the middle of the room. There was a nervous twitch in her fingers.

"Notions of mine, no," the girl said. "You yourself swept two of them up the day before yesterday."

The proprietress looked exasperatedly at her. The girl had a pitiful expression, and an obvious desire to explain everything until not the slightest trace of doubt remained.

"What is happening, sir, is that the day before yesterday some boys left two dead birds in the hall to annoy her, and then they told her that dead birds were falling from the sky. She swallows everything people tell her."

He smiled. The explanation seemed very funny to him; he rubbed his hands and turned to look at the girl, who was observing him in anguish. The gramophone had stopped playing. The proprietress withdrew to the other room, and when he went toward the hall the girl insisted in a low voice:

"I saw them fall. Believe me. Everyone has seen them."

And he thought he understood then her attachment to the gramophone, and the proprietress's exasperation. "Yes," he said sympathetically. And then, moving toward the hall: "I've seen them, too."

It was less hot outside, in the shade of the almond trees. He leaned the stool against the doorframe, threw his head back, and thought of his mother: his mother, exhausted, in her rocker, shooing the chickens with a long broomstick, while she realized for the first time that he was not in the house.

The week before, he could have thought that his life was a smooth straight string, stretching from the rainy dawn during the last civil war when he came into the world between the four mud-and-rush walls of a rural schoolhouse to that June morning on his twenty-second birthday when his mother approached his hammock and gave him a hat with a card: "To my dear son, on his day." At times he shook off the rustiness of his inactivity and felt nostalgic for school, for the blackboard and the map of a country overpopulated by the excrement of the flies, and for the long line of cups hanging on the wall under the names of the children. It wasn't hot there. It was a green, tranquil town, where chickens with ashen long legs entered the schoolroom in order to lay their eggs under the washstand. His mother then was a sad and uncommunicative woman. She would sit at dusk to take the air which had just filtered through the coffee plantations, and say, "Manaure is the most beautiful town in the world." And then, turning toward him, seeing him grow up silently in the hammock: "When you are grown up you'll understand." But he didn't understand anything. He didn't understand at fifteen, already too tall for his age and bursting with that insolent and reckless health which idleness brings. Until his twentieth birthday his life was not essentially different from a few changes of position in his hammock. But around that time his mother, obliged by her rheumatism, left the school she had served for eighteen years, with the result that they went to live in a two-room house with a huge patio, where they raised chickens with ashen legs like those which used to cross the schoolroom.

Caring for the chickens was his first contact with reality.

And it had been the only one until the month of July, when his mother thought about her retirement and deemed her son wise enough to undertake to petition for it. He collaborated in an effective way in the preparation of the documents, and even had the necessary tact to convince the parish priest to change his mother's baptismal certificate by six months, since she still wasn't old enough to retire. On Thursday he received the final instructions, scrupulously detailing his mother's teaching experience, and he began the trip to the city with twelve pesos, a change of clothing, the file of documents, and an entirely rudimentary idea of the word "retirement," which he interpreted crudely as a certain sum of money which the government ought to give him so he could set himself up in pig breeding.

Dozing on the hotel veranda, dulled by the sweltering heat, he had not stopped to think about the gravity of his situation. He supposed that the mishap would be resolved the following day, when the train returned, so that now his only worry was to wait until Sunday to resume his trip and forget forever about this town where it was unbearably hot. A little before four, he fell into an uncomfortable and sluggish sleep, thinking while he slept that it was a shame not to have brought his hammock. Then it was that he realized everything, that he had forgotten his bundle of clothes and the documents for the retirement on the train. He woke up with a start, terrified, thinking of his mother, and hemmed in again by panic.

When he dragged his seat back to the dining room, the lights of the town had been lit. He had never seen electric lights, so he was very impressed when he saw the poor spotted bulbs of the hotel. Then he remembered that his mother had spoken to him about them, and he continued dragging the seat toward the dining room, trying to dodge the horseflies which were bumping against the mirrors like bullets. He ate without appetite, confused by the clear evidence of his situation, by the intense heat, by the bitterness of that loneliness which he was suffering for the first time in his life. After nine o'clock he was led to the back of the house to a wooden room papered with newspapers and magazines. At midnight he had sunk into a miasmic and feverish sleep while, five blocks away, Father Anthony Isabel of the Holy Sacrament of the Altar, lying face down on his cot, was thinking that the evening's experiences reinforced the sermon which he had prepared for seven in the morning. A little before twelve he had crossed the town to administer extreme unction to a woman, and he felt excited and nervous, with the result that he put the sacramental objects next to his cot and lay down to go over his sermon. He stayed that way for several hours, lying face down on the cot until he heard the distant call of a plover at dawn. Then he tried to get up, sat up painfully, stepped on the little bell, and fell headlong on the cold, hard floor of his room.

He had hardly regained consciousness when he felt the trembling sensation which rose up his side. At that instant he was aware of his entire weight: the weight of his body, his sins, and his age all together. He felt against his cheek the solidity of the stone floor which so often when he was preparing his sermons had helped him form a precise idea of the road which leads to Hell. "Lord," he murmured, afraid; and he thought, I shall certainly never be able to get up again.

He did not know how long he lay prostrate on the floor, not thinking about anything, without even remembering to pray for a good death. It was as if, in reality, he had been dead for a minute. But when he regained consciousness, he no longer felt pain or fear. He saw the bright ray beneath the door; he heard, far off and sad, the raucous noise of the roosters, and he realized that he was alive and that he remembered the words of his sermon perfectly.

When he drew back the bar of the door, dawn was breaking. He had ceased feeling pain, and it even seemed that the blow had unburdened him of his old age. All the goodness, the misconduct, and the sufferings of the town penetrated his heart when he swallowed the first mouthful of that air which was a blue dampness full of roosters. Then he looked around himself, as if to reconcile himself to the solitude, and saw, in the peaceful shade of the dawn, one, two, three dead birds on the veranda.

For nine minutes he contemplated the three bodies, thinking, in accord with his prepared sermon, that the birds' collective death needed some expiation. Then he walked to the other end of the corridor, picked up the three dead birds and returned to the pitcher, and one after the other threw the birds into the green, still water without knowing exactly the purpose of that action. Three and three are half a dozen, in one week, he thought, and a miraculous flash of lucidity told him that he had begun to experience the greatest day of his life.

At seven the heat began. In the hotel, the only guest was waiting for his breakfast. The gramophone girl had not yet got up. The proprietress approached, and at that moment it seemed as if the seven strokes of the clock's bell were sounding inside her swollen belly.

"So you missed the train," she said in a tone of belated commiseration. And then she brought the breakfast: coffee with milk, a fried egg, and slices of green banana.

He tried to eat, but he wasn't hungry. He was alarmed that the heat had come on. He was sweating buckets. He was suffocating. He had slept poorly, with his clothes on, and now he had a little fever. He felt the panic again, and remembered his mother just as the proprietress came to the table to pick up the dishes, radiant in her new dress with the large green flowers. The proprietress's dress reminded him that it was Sunday.

"Is there a Mass?" he asked.

"Yes, there is," the woman said. "But it's just as if there weren't, because almost nobody goes. The fact is they haven't wanted to send us a new priest."

"And what's wrong with this one?"

"He's about a hundred years old, and he's half crazy," the woman said; she stood motionless, pensive, with all the dishes in one hand. Then she said, "The other day, he swore from the pulpit that he had seen the devil, and since then no one goes to Mass."

So he went to the church, in part because of his desperation and in part out of curiosity to meet a person a hundred years old. He noticed that it was a dead town, with interminable, dusty streets and dark wooden houses with zinc roofs, which seemed uninhabited. That was the town on Sunday: streets without grass, houses with screens, and a deep, marvelous sky over a stifling heat. He thought that there was no sign there which would permit one to distinguish Sunday from any other day, and while he walked along the deserted street he remembered his mother: "All the streets in every town lead inevitably to the church or the cemetery." At that moment he came out into a small cobblestoned plaza with a whitewashed building that had a tower and a wooden weathercock on the top, and a clock which had stopped at ten after four.

Without hurrying he crossed the plaza, climbed the three steps of the atrium, and immediately smelled the odor of aged human sweat mixed with the odor of incense, and he went into the warm shade of the almost empty church.

Father Anthony Isabel of the Holy Sacrament of the Altar had just risen to the pulpit. He was about to begin the sermon when he saw a boy enter with his hat on. He saw him examining the almost empty temple with his large, serene, and clear eyes. He saw him sit down in the last pew, his head to one side and his hands on his knees. He noticed that he was a stranger to the town. He had been in town for thirty years, and he could have recognized any of its inhabitants just by his smell. Therefore, he knew that the boy who had just arrived was a stranger. In one intense, brief look, he observed that he was a quiet soul, and a little sad, and that his clothes were dirty and wrinkled. It's as if he had spent a long time sleeping in them, he thought with a feeling that was a combination of repugnance and pity. But then, seeing him in the pew, he felt his heart overflowing with gratitude, and he got ready to deliver what was for him the greatest sermon of his life. Lord, he thought in the meantime, please let him remember his hat so I don't have to throw him out of the temple. And he began his sermon.

At the beginning he spoke without realizing what he was saying. He wasn't even listening to himself. He hardly heard the clear and fluent melody which flowed from a spring dormant in his soul ever since the beginning of the world. He had the confused certainty that his words were flowing forth precisely, opportunely, exactly, in the expected order and place. He felt a warm vapor pressing his innards. But he also knew that his spirit was free of vanity, and that the feeling of pleasure which paralyzed his senses was not pride or defiance or vanity but, rather, the pure rejoicing of his spirit in Our Lord.

In her bedroom, Rebecca felt faint, knowing that within a few moments the heat would become impossible. If she had not felt rooted to the town by a dark fear of novelty, she would have put her odds and ends in a trunk with mothballs and would have gone off into the world, as her great-grandfather did, so she had been told. But she knew inside that she was destined to die in the town, amid those endless corridors and the nine bedrooms, whose screens she thought she would have replaced by translucent glass when the heat stopped. So she would stay there, she decided (and that was a decision she always took when she arranged her clothes in the closet), and she also decided to write "My Eminent Cousin" to send them a young priest, so she could attend church again with her hat with the tiny velvet flowers, and hear a coherent Mass and sensible and edifying sermons again. Tomorrow is Monday, she thought, beginning to

think once and for all about the salutation of the letter to the
Bishop (a salutation which Colonel Buendía had called
frivolous and disrespectful), when Argenida suddenly opened
the screened door and shouted:

"Señora, people are saying that the Father has gone crazy
in the pulpit!"

The widow turned a not characteristically withered and
bitter face toward the door. "He's been crazy for at least five
years," she said. And she kept on arranging her clothing,
saying:

"He must have seen the devil again."

"It's not the devil this time," said Argenida.

"Then who?" Rebecca asked, prim and indifferent.

"Now he says that he saw the Wandering Jew."

The widow felt her skin crawl. A multitude of confused
ideas, among which she could not distinguish her torn
screens, the heat, the dead birds, and the plague, passed
through her head as she heard those words which she hadn't
remembered since the afternoons of her distant girlhood:
"The Wandering Jew." And then she began to move, en-
raged, icily, toward where Argenida was watching her with
her mouth open.

"It's true," Rebecca said in a voice which rose from the
depths of her being. "Now I understand why the birds are
dying off."

Impelled by terror, she covered herself with a black em-
broidered shawl and, in a flash, crossed the long corridor and
the living room stuffed with decorative objects, and the
street door, and the two blocks to the church, where Father
Anthony Isabel of the Holy Sacrament of the Altar, transfigured, was saying, "I swear to you that I saw him. I swear to
you that he crossed my path this morning when I was coming
back from administering the holy unction to the wife of
Jonas the carpenter. I swear to you that his face was blackened with the malediction of the Lord, and that he left a
track of burning embers in his wake."

His sermon broke off, floating in the air. He realized that he couldn't restrain the trembling of his hands, that his whole body was shaking, and that a thread of icy sweat was slowly descending his spinal column. He felt ill, feeling the trembling, and the thirst, and a violent wrenching in his gut, and a noise which resounded like the bass note of an organ in his belly. Then he realized the truth.

He saw that there were people in the church, and that Rebecca, pathetic, showy, her arms open, and her bitter, cold face turned toward the heavens, was advancing up the central nave. Confusedly he understood what was happening, and he even had enough lucidity to understand that it would have been vanity to believe that he was witnessing a miracle. Humbly he rested his trembling hands on the wooden edge of the pulpit and resumed his speech.

"Then he walked toward me," he said. And this time he heard his own voice, convincing, impassioned. "He walked toward me and he had emerald eyes, and shaggy hair, and the smell of a billy goat. And I raised my hand to reproach him in the name of Our Lord, and I said to him: 'Halt, Sunday has never been a good day for sacrificing a lamb.'"

When he finished, the heat had set in. That intense, solid, burning heat of that unforgettable August. But Father Anthony Isabel was no longer aware of the heat. He knew that there, at his back, the town was again humbled, speechless with his sermon, but he wasn't even pleased by that. He wasn't even pleased with the immediate prospect that the wine would relieve his ravaged throat. He felt uncomfortable and out of place. He felt distracted and he could not concentrate on the supreme moment of the sacrifice. The same thing had been happening to him for some time, but now it was a different uneasiness. Then, for the first time in his life, he knew pride. And just as he had imagined and defined it in his sermons, he felt that pride was an urge the same as thirst. He closed the tabernacle energetically and said:

"Pythagoras."

The acolyte, a child with a shaven and shiny head, god-son of Father Anthony Isabel, who had named him, approached the altar.

"Take up the offering," said the priest.

The child blinked, turned completely around, and then said in an almost inaudible voice, "I don't know where the plate is."

It was true. It had been months since an offering had been collected.

"Then go find a big bag in the sacristy and collect as much as you can," said the Father.

"And what shall I say?" said the boy.

The Father thoughtfully contemplated his shaven blue skull, with its prominent sutures. Now it was he who blinked:

"Say that it is to expel the Wandering Jew," he said, and he felt as he said it that he was supporting a great weight in his heart. For a moment he heard nothing but the guttering of the candles in the silent temple and his own excited and labored breathing. Then, putting his hand on the acolyte's shoulder, while the acolyte looked at him with his round eyes aghast, he said:

"Then take the money and give it to the boy who was alone at the beginning, and you tell him that it's from the priest, and that he should buy a new hat."

In the Blue Country

RALPH BLUM

Ralph Blum, who lives on a small farm in Connecticut, is the author of such novels as *The Simultaneous Man* (1970) and *Old Glory and the Real Time Freaks* (1972). He is co-author, with Judy Blum, of *Beyond Earth: Man's Contact with UFOs* (1976) and is currently, with his wife, writing an anthropological fiction book.

OUR WIVES STILL GRUMBLE about our annual fishing trip. But women, I have observed, tend to suspect on principle the rituals of their men. Or else to look down on them. "Then what do you do?" asks my wife. "When you're *not* fishing?" Drink, tell stories, smoke. What men always do in the woods.

Early in April the three of us went again to the Karelian Peninsula to fish. We took the same boat we had last year. The owner, an old Finn with a screwy eye, told us that almost nobody was in the woods. He charged less for his boat, saying that soon he would use it for firewood.

A soft wind was blowing as we stowed our gear. Columns of cloud dragged across a sky as gray as a prison mattress. The Finnish sky is an empty bloodless affair at this time of year. The landscape is boring, with not a duck flying, and big pines reduced to furry matchsticks stuck onto the horizon. Who cares how vacant everything is? I am weary of the hammerlock winter has on Leningrad. I am sick of slogging over icy pavements and fighting for a place on trams whose drivers chop off the line of people waiting to board like excess sausage. I am fed up with government offices, *papkas* stuffed with lab reports, steam heat. I hate my own scarf more each time I wind it around my neck. I long for that "spirit of spring and of decay" the poet Blok described; for the day when that army of stout women in cloth boots will come to work without their padded *vatniki* and, exchanging their shovels for brooms, begin brushing down the sidewalks with metronome arms. My teeth ache for spring. So I cherish the few days Volodya, Bob, and I spend in Karelia, out here where nobody fusses at nature.

The others feel the same way. Take Fedin, my colleague at the Institute. Alexandr Alexandrovich, whom everybody calls "Bob," is a tough guy of the old school. And solid Russian despite that nickname—there are spaces in his passport that attest. We have even that in common. Together we passed our ten-year course, defended Leningrad together, and then, still together, sat our years in the eastern camps. As Bob says, "The years use men like candles."

Vladimir Romanovich is our Institute carpenter. He is a master fisherman. We are all on "thee" terms, all friends. I often give him clothes and books for his boy. I think he realizes my nose is not stuck in the air. That counts, after all, between friends. Volodya, too, is familiar with life in the eastern oblasts.

More than two hundred and fifty islands are strewn among these lakes, whose Finnish name is Vuoksi, which means "a stream." Actually, Vuoksi is a collection of little lakes with flowing water between. Bass and trout aplenty. And because of the falls and rapids and the strong currents, salmon make their way from lake to lake.

In late March, the smaller lakes still wear a skin of ice. Volodya crouched in the bow and, with an extra oar, cracked open a path for our boat. Bob and I did the rowing. After a time, Volodya growled, "Eh! Look there!"

Over my shoulder I saw another boat. It was coming from the south: two men pulling hard in our direction, as though eager to greet us. "Never mind," I said. "They're leaving."

"Row," said Volodya, and began whacking the ice.

Bob and I laid hard on the oars. We managed to escape an encounter by a good sixty meters. Still, I could see the buck teeth of one fellow, and the turned-up nose of the blond girl who sat in the stern. She was smoking a *papirós*: I even saw how she had crimped the long filter-end twice, at right angles, the way men do. The men shouted, but the wind took charge of their shouts. And as our boats drew apart, we had only to wave. Then they were gone, back down our channel. And the lake with its islands lay undisturbed ahead of us.

"Just the same"—Volodya sprayed us both with water—"what do they want, bringing a girl here at this time of year?"

It was near dusk when we chose our island. We came ashore and picked out a mossy spot in a stand of tall pines as our campsite. While Bob and I lugged up the tent and provisions, Volodya stood scanning the water, as if to reassure himself that the other boat really had gone for good. Then he came slowly after us, boots squelching: a short man with a fighter's face and black hair that the wind combed as he walked.

Both Bob and I had on heavy sweaters and wind-cheaters over. Volodya wore his leather jacket unbuttoned, his throat bare to the chilling tail of winter. As I unbuckled the rucksacks, he yanked the ax from where Bob had imbedded it in a fallen log, and stood muttering to himself as he ran his thumb along the blade.

"What are you fussing at?" Bob was fashioning stones into a hearth. He said, "Their holiday is over."

Volodya said, "It displeases me when women smoke."

Bob said, "Nowadays all women smoke."

I said, "My wife smokes. Even the girls she teaches at the Filfak smoke."

"That one in the boat," Bob said, "perhaps she has a rough time at home. A bitch for a mother-in-law. So, when she goes camping—" He shrugged.

Volodya seemed to have discovered a nick in the ax blade. He held it close to his eye. He is a man for whom surfaces count. Bob gave me a look and continued wedging the stones.

"That is the way with the *meshchanstvo*," Volodya said and wandered off to collect logs.

Sometimes Volodya sounds like an old Bolshevik. He has no tenderness for the *meshchanstvo*, "the vulgar bunch," as he likes to call people of whom he disapproves. The term, which was popular with poets of our Revolution, has lost its exclusive aroma of class accusation. Nowadays, anyone can belong: Lieutenant-Colonels, factory directors, even members of the Central Committee, if you like. What qualifies a man for inclusion in the *meshchanstvo?* What he values, I suppose. What he lives for. Still, as I see it, Volodya is entitled to hold his stiff opinions. I don't think he minded so much the girl's smoking; it was just that she and her two friends had been here before us.

I went and put a bottle of vodka in the lake. During the war, I commanded a big gun whose recoil mechanism was cushioned by a supply of high-grade alcohol. You fire, then, thanks to that alcoholic bed, the gun settles back with a whooosh! My crew taught me how to siphon off some of that "private stock." Not so much that the gun shook itself to death; but enough to make its action like that of a tram coming to an emergency stop. Enough to keep us from freezing more than once. Later, in the camps, I learned from a man like Volodya about *politura*, furniture polish, a well-established joiner's drink. But not even the two-hundred-proof stuff readily available at our Institute can match the taste of a bottle of "Stolichnaya" purchased from Eliseef's Gastronom on our own Nevsky Prospekt, and iced in Vuoksi waters.

I had the ground sheets laid and was ready to set up the tent, when Volodya dumped a great log onto the ground and hefted the ax. "What men do—" he swung; the ax flashed through the twilight, struck and caught—"and what is seemly in women—that's two different stories." White lips smiled from the pine log. Volodya swung the ax again, widening the smile. He said, "There is the matter of dignity."

After that, Volodya worked in ferocious silence. The way he raged through log after log, it was as though one of their ends had served that girl to strike her match.

The light was failing. The afternoons are short in March. Soon the wood was stacked. Volodya helped me mount the tent and fix the pegs. I considered fishing but decided to wait for morning. In times such as these, it seems best not to leap into pleasure.

Bob had the fire going, and soon I could hear water bubbling in the pot. He took a bag of *pelmeni* from his rucksack. Kneeling on the ground, he began to separate the tiny frozen parcels of meat and dough.

"I met an Italian once, a physicist," Bob said, "who called *pelmeni* 'Siberian ravioli.' How about that? Do you remember how we made them up? Hundreds of *pelmeni*, soon as winter started?"

"All winter long," I told Volodya, "we kept a barrel full of frozen *pelmeni* outside the door. That was a good winter. Just step out and reach in, and you had dinner."

"Before I caught Natasha," Bob said wistfully, "I kept a pot at my window, hanging in a mesh sack."

Bob was married only four months back. Until then, he always lived alone in a communal apartment on Mokhovaya Street. In the evenings, when I visited him, I sometimes found him in the kitchen making soup, tending his pot while old Moldavian ladies with faces like sunburned sailors squabbled as they cut up fat meat pies. Hurrying home to my own dinner, it used to depress me like hell to think of him. We work all day developing plastics for Russia. Then Bob would have to wait in line to get a kilo of soup meat. A week before his wedding, I found him in his room, legs apart, stripped to the waist, leaning over a big tin tub. He was so concentrated on rubbing and squeezing his underwear that he did not even hear my knock. It is a good thing that Bob finally married, and got a woman who does what a woman should. Oh, not just to relieve him of feminine chores. But because men like us have spent too long on our own, chained to our basic needs. Some of Russia's finest scholars and artists and scientists could double as laundrymen and cooks.

It was dark when Bob called us to eat. Stars were out, and the throat of the vodka bottle had a necklace of frost. The wind blew in from Finland's gulf, scissoring a skein of black water back and forth across the ice. The passage we had cut was almost sealed again.

Steam from the *pelmeni* mounted with swirling wood-smoke, and the wind fed above us in the trees. Out on the lake I saw—thought I saw—the white wing of a gull. In the woods, an owl screeched. We drank the vodka from special plastic cups Bob made for us in the lab. We drank to the fish we would take in the morning. We toasted dead friends and loved ones. Each time, we poured a few drops onto the hard ground, and Bob said, "May the earth lie lightly over them."

The wind fell and the trees became still. By the time we had drunk our tea, and Volodya got out his pipe, the peace of the Blue Country had settled over us.

"Who smokes a pipe in Russia today?" Volodya settled his back against a tree. "Writers smoke, and sailors. A few old Jews like Efim Abramovich. He showed me once," Volodya added, puffing between phrases, "a fine old pipe carved from cherry wood. His own work—what loving care! And

polished by the years . . . but I can count on my fingers the
youngsters I've seen . . . pulling at a pipe."

"New times, new habits," said Bob.

I could smell Volodya's *makhorka,* a homegrown shag his
wife detests. Somehow, all we could talk about was cigarettes
and pipes, tobacco and smoking. I got it started again, without even thinking, when I said to tease Volodya, "I promised
your wife I'd buy you a packet of something good like Golden
Fleece."

"I release you from your promise," said Volodya, and we
all laughed, and Volodya sat puffing contentedly and gazing
up at the skies.

Every time I have visited Volodya's home, his wife,
Tamara Alexeievna, seizes the opportunity to whine about
the stink. She has a point: *makhorka* gets into the draperies,
and hers are already a frightening mustard-colored velvet.
Yes, Tamara Alexeievna, the joiner's wife, is of the
meshchanstvo. You have only to examine the sentimental
pictures on her walls, the Meissen shepherdesses that simper
behind the locked doors of the china cabinet. But if Volodya
realizes the truth, he does not complain. Loyalty comes in
more cuts and qualities than tobacco.

Almost as if he had been tuned in to my thoughts, Volodya said, "A man grows accustomed."

"Accustomed?" said Bob.

"Forming habits takes a while, and at first things bite
into the heart. Only before you realize, you have become
affectionate toward your own ways. But the wife can't
fathom that. 'Here, Vladimir Roman'ich,' she'll tell me,
'take these few kopecks extra, buy Golden Fleece and give
me a rest from that filthy stuff.'" Then Volodya looked at me
and Bob, grinning as he said, "For Tamara Alexeievna, life's
good things are always separated from what is miserable by
the distance of a few kopecks."

"She may well be right, you know," said Bob.

"Tell me, what makes them give such fancy names to their tobacco?" Volodya frowned. "Now, if she only would plead with me to buy Kapitansky, I just might. But they put me off with their Golden Fleece."

Bob said, "Ah, but just listen to the sound of those round words. Summon up the picture of fine yellow strands of tobacco—"

Already, after that one simple meal, I felt we had been in Vuoksi a week. The magic of the Finnish night, the invading airs from across the frontier, our wandering minds—that is my joy in these lakes.

"The King of Colchis had set a dragon to guard it . . ." In lyrics to go with the night, Bob told about the *Argo*, her crew, and Jason, the captain; he showed us that white-sailed ship, never out of sight of islands; he dotted the seascape with porpoises and strange African birds; and finally, the place in Asia Minor, the sacred grove, that miracle of a fleece hanging in a tree. "And when the sun set," Bob added, "the fleece kept its golden glow. Like the Admiralty Spire, and those giant gilt pretzels that still hung outside the bakers' shops when I was a kid."

Volodya mused, "But all that, it must have happened long ago. In the time of the first Tsars."

"Long before that," sighed Bob.

"How long?"

"Before Russia and before Rus. Before Rurik came from Sweden and taught the tribes of our forebears better manners."

"History, poetry," Volodya said, shaking his head.

"Wooagh! I just remembered!" Bob was up, rifling through his rucksack. He turned then and, in a startling movement, his hand shot out and sent something—a silvery tube—sailing in my direction. I caught it and saw the imprimatur: *Romeo y Julieta*. Bob said, "I was given a box of them today."

Bob already had another of the elegant milled canisters

in his hand. He waved it like a magic wand. Me, I just held mine in my hand and consorted with mystery: the cigar inside, guaranteed to have come all the way from Havana; the promise of rich aromas and a blue-gray vine of smoke soon to hang on the cold peninsular air. Not an experience to rush.

I unscrewed the cap and removed the cigar in its shroud of paper-thin sandalwood. The moon strolled between the pine branches. The wind came up and gently displaced the boughs; even the moon was curious. As I freed the cigar, the night seemed to hover on the frozen shell of spring.

"Beautifully made, aren't they? Look how the outer leaf is tight, snug," said Bob.

The cigars were brown as the faces of those Moldavian *babas* I have seen hovering over pies in Bob's kitchen. I watched how, with savage precision, he bit off the end of the cigar and spat it into the fire. Then, dainty as a girl selecting a bonbon from a crystal dish, he lifted a glowing coal and set it on a rock. Kneeling and leaning forward so that his hair fell over his eyes, Bob bowed the cigar to the coal.

Stroked by the breeze, the coal glimmered and paled. I lit my cigar, then we sat back, smoking and talking about the place where such tobacco is grown, the soil of Cuba. "One small region only," Bob told us, "has perfect conditions. They call it the *Revuelto Bajo* . . ." He told us about *fincas* and cane fields crackling in the sun, and about the Hispanic *ganaderías* where bulls like locomotives made the earth shake. What a pleasure there is in a word such as *ganadería*.

"D'you inhale?" Volodya was refilling his pipe.

"You can. But the smoke is strong," said Bob.

"Cubans must have great lungs," said Volodya.

"Have you never heard Fidel make a speech?"

The first time I saw Fidel, I remember, was in a photograph in *Izvestia*. There was Fidel, his fierce beard and raised fist, giving testimony at a mass rally. The picture was hazy and mulled by inadequate printing. Still, he looked almost courtly in his jungle garb—like an Apostle snatched from a dark time. And around him, his lieutenants: babies with scrawny beards and dark glasses. "The Children's Revolution"—that's what Bob once called Cuba. Yet we have seen identical dark glasses masking the eyes of soldiers holding automatic pistols in the streets of Guatemala and men releasing dogs from leashes in the cities of Mississippi. Was the common denominator nothing more, really, than the glaring sun?

The night birds began to talk in the woods. Of Fidel, Bob said, "He may not make it. But he is serious."

I said, "Do you suppose Fidel sometimes smokes a *Romeo y Julieta?* People must offer him cigars all the time. Just because they like him."

Volodya said, "My wife says the Cubans are a very religious people. I suppose she is right?"

"A lot of Cubans are believers," Bob said. "In Fidel's country, it is not a question of closing the churches."

"And are there still many Cuban popes?"

"Many. Like taxi drivers and bartenders, they are called *gusános,* which means 'worms.' But Fidel allows them to go on about their business—so long as they do not talk against the Revolution."

I got up, stretched, and went inside the tent. I unlaced my boots and took them off. As I climbed into my sleeping bag, I thought of Tamara Alexeievna's ikon: a slug of shrapnel lopped off St. George's left leg during the Blockade. She goes to church Christmas and Easter. She is friendly with the *prosvírka*—an old woman who stands in church selling communion bread—and with the pope himself. Volodya rarely speaks about his wife's religiosity, but I know it annoys him.

"And are they rich?" Volodya's voice drifted through the tentflap.

"No, they are like the people. They live like the people, but being popes, they do not believe in the Revolution."

"And Fidel—does he believe in God?"

Bob did not answer immediately. I could see him across the fire: elbows resting on his knees, chin against his knuckles—the way he used to sit before an exam and behind the gun mount, awaiting orders from Divcom—a huddled Rodin, a Thinker from the Petrograd Side. Lying snug in my warm cave, I thought I knew what he would answer Volodya. But he is a strange man, our Bob; one who loves to observe the growth of crystals, a live-and-let-live believer with a powerful punch. Bob surprised me.

"Believe? He just might, you know. I sometimes think that if God is anything, he is the lot. The works. Not just everywhere, but everything. The stuff from which is made our toenails and blue eyes. And our belief." Bob took a stick and gave the fire a prod. Then, in the tone he so often uses to end an argument, he said, "Well, if God is God, he's the DNA molecule, too."

"The popes are no revolutionaries," Volodya said with angry certainty. "You know their idea of God's command? To keep their own lives running smooth as a lathe."

I think Volodya meant to say God's commandment. He is not schooled except in adzing and beveling. I lay back, one arm behind my head, thinking how blue the smoke from my *Romeo y Julieta* looked; the way the islands and woods and water of Vuoksi would look at first light. It is because of that early morning haze that we call this the Blue Country. And I thought how much I love this country of mine. Oh, not great Mother Russia. Not all of her. But certainly this bit: the island; the fish dozing under the water; Volodya's habit of sitting for hours with his big boots crossed near the fire; and the way Bob can still surprise me after thirty years.

"Did I ever tell you," Volodya was saying, "about the time I sold lottery tickets to a pope?"

Bob chuckled. "How many did he buy? One?"

"That was many years back, when I was a *Fininspektor* in the Internal Revenue System." Volodya always starts a story at the beginning. "In those times, people like dentists still

did private work. I had to help that sort to assess their in-
come, so they would pay the proper tax. Anyway, on my
lists, I had the popes of several village churches."
  Bob asked, "Did popes earn enough to be taxed?"
  "Sssss! Did they!"
  "As much as dentists?"
  "Listen, a pope once paid me sixty-five thousand rubles
in one year. If that was the *tax,* imagine how much he put
away in his mattress. Oh, I tell you, brothers, they live a
glorious life, some of those country popes!"
  "Was that the pope who bought the tickets?"
  "No, another."
  "And was the lottery ticket pope rich?"
  "So everyone said. Well, I had lottery tickets to sell. It
was part of my job just then. So I asked myself: Why not sell
that pope a hatful? In those days, I had a motorcycle. It was
twenty-five kilometers to that village, over winter roads. But
never mind that. Only when I arrived, no pope . . ." Volodya told his story like a man showing you points on a road
map: here is the house of the *prosvírka,* who told him the
pope was not in church, and when he asked which was the
pope's house, she pointed across the snow-covered square, at
a blue-walled cottage: there were other wooden houses, the
barns, the bakery; the *prosvírka* had a brown shawl over her
shoulders and steam for breath. "She let me get halfway there
before shouting that only the *popadyá* was there . . ." The
pope's wife was very ill, dying, so everyone said; no cause to
trouble her. "And then I got mad," Volodya said. "I shouted
at her to stop playing the fool and tell me where her damned
pope was. She stopped being snotty fast enough, I can tell you.
  "Where was he then?"
  "Another twelve kilometers on down the road. At a
place with six houses, not even a village. He'd be with his
mistress, Agrippa Innokentievna. Thinking about the tickets, I told myself, might as well add the extra kilometers. So
I set off over what was hardly worth the name 'road' . . ."

I pictured that nameless village: the *popadyá* alone in a dark room; the callousness of the pope, twelve kilometers away, rolling on top of the stove with the Agrippa Innokentievna—likely the daughter of a pope herself with a name like that—while his wife lay dying. A scene you would expect to find in the Anti-Religion Museum.

But Volodya told just the facts; they were natural enough, human enough; and the only thing that made him mad was the arrogance of that *prosvírka*. And I could see her, skirts hitched, scurrying through the snow to answer the questions of her neighbors even before Volodya had roared his motorcycle off into the forest.

Somewhere an owl got to hooting. I heard the cry of a wolf, and I imagined him, snout lifted, teeth whitened by moonlight, saliva on the short fur around his mouth, howling.

"The girl was well made. She was outside, beating a carpet. The old pope was there too, standing in the door, touching his beard and watching her body swing with each stroke. That old man, well, he greeted me kindly, so I said, Batiushka, I have tickets to sell you, for the lottery. They will give marvelous prizes, I told him. You are old now, I said politely, and the distance you walk between your village and here is far for one of your years. So why not try to win first prize, an automobile?"

"And if he had won? Who was to drive him?"

"We did not get onto that. The pope, he wiped his eyes with his sleeve and took a good squint at the wad of tickets I held out. His mistress, she came over and stood shyly at the bottom of the steps, watching us but not saying nothing. How much, the pope wanted to know, would your tickets be? I told him, three rubles each, and he said he would have six. But he looked worried and wanted to know: could he be certain of winning the automobile with half a dozen tickets—"

Volodya knocked the ashes from his pipe by tapping it

against a log. Then he shook his head. "Not a chance, I told him respectfully. Well, both of us stood there, looking sad. And the pope, he was watching the girl's face, dreaming of the pleasure she would take in that automobile. I gave it a moment before pointing out that if he took say, well, two hundred tickets—it would be like a guarantee from the Ministry. Hell, then the wintry light crackled in his eyes. Go in, add wood to the stove, he told the girl; prepare tea. And soon, smoke clean as Manila hemp was climbing straight up to heaven. That pope stood down from the porch, watching it like it was Jacob's ladder. Says he, 'Expensivish...' But already he was a man trying to chip away the price on a piece of goods. Like he'd read that ladder of smoke for a sign..."

Smoking first; then tobacco itself: myths of strange places like Havana and Colchis appeared smoky through the distance; *makhorka* smoke and the smoke of brown Cuban leaf, smoke blue as the Vuoksi mists. And now it was God, another kind of smoke.

"That was when I really started to work on him," Volodya said, "telling him what it cost to produce an automobile—just take the tires, the leather for seats, gears and cam shafts and such... Well, you know, didn't he buy two hundred and fifty tickets... him at least eighty, and the girl maybe twenty-seven... And still, that pope came those twelve kilometers to her on foot."

"And did he win an automobile?"

"He did not win a mouse."

Both of them laughed and then fell silent. All at once, I felt drowsy and drugged. I gave my cigar a toss toward the fire. Then I lay back and listened to the flames snapping around a new log. The wind came up again; not strong; just enough to tighten the tent ropes. It was a funny story for bedtime: the tale of the pope, the *prosvírka*, and Agrippa Innokentievna.

"Did you ever see that pope again?" Bob asked.

"No, but the next time I passed through that village, there was the coffin! The pope had it leaning against the wall of his house."

"Then it was true, about the *popadyá* dying."

"True. Only she did not die right away as everyone had expected. She lived on through the year, and until the winter came back. And all that time there stood the coffin. Nearby was a great hill of snow. The village kids got hold of the coffin and used it for a sled . . . Well, it wasn't until the following spring—this time of year—that the *popadyá* died. The old pope took her coffin back from those kids, cracked it open, and buried the *popadyá*—all scarred the coffin was, but freeze and thaw would have done as much in the ground . . ."

I never heard the end. Or maybe that was the end. I was asleep when the two of them came into the tent. Once I awoke and heard them whispering. But the subject had gone from smoke and God to the camps where we had been prisoners. ". . . I have built an entire house with my hands: a plane, a saw, but no nails. Imagine . . ." The air was spicy with night breezes. The wind hung around, strumming the tent ropes, and I dreamed about that owl, milky wings spread, circling through the night above our tent.

In the early light, I was the first to awake. Quietly, I got out of the tent—I wanted a moment or two alone.

All the ice was gone from the lake. The water was black, and the sky was just collecting lilac in the east. But the air was the way Vuoksi air should be: blue and smoky; as though the wind, which had swept the water clear of ice, had granted a dispensation to our blue Havana smoke to stay and multiply, until it looked like Nature herself had been puffing at *Romeo y Julietas* through the night.

In the trees, black grouse were talking. I went to the shore and got down on my knees. I splashed water on my face. Still kneeling, I shouted to the others. They came slowly, rubbing their eyes, bootless like me.

The black grouse never stopped their talk. The wind blew up salty off the Finnish Gulf. Oh, how we fished! And talked! And every night, after the meal, Bob and me, we filled the air of Vuoksi with our Havana smoke. Volodya stuck by his pipe and told us stories a man would have to travel some distance to even hear equaled, especially in times like these.

The Kool-Aid Wino

RICHARD BRAUTIGAN

Richard Brautigan was born in the Pacific Northwest in 1935 and now lives in San Francisco. His published work includes poetry (*The Pill Versus the Springhill Mine Disaster*, 1960), stories (*Revenge of the Lawn*, 1971), and several works of long fiction, including *The Abortion, A Confederate General from Big Sur, In Watermelon Sugar,* and *Trout Fishing in America* (1967), from which "The Kool-Aid Wino" is taken.

WHEN I WAS A CHILD I had a friend who became a Kool-Aid wino as the result of a rupture. He was a member of a very large and poor German family. All the older children in the family had to work in the fields during the summer, picking beans for two-and-one-half cents a pound to keep the family going. Everyone worked except my friend, who couldn't because he was ruptured. There was no money for an operation. There wasn't even money to buy him a truss. So he stayed home and became a Kool-Aid wino.

One morning in August I went over to his house. He was still in bed. He looked up at me from underneath a tattered revolution of old blankets. He had never slept under a sheet in his life.

"Did you bring the nickel you promised?" he asked.

"Yeah," I said. "It's here in my pocket."

"Good."

He hopped out of bed and he was already dressed. He had told me once that he never took off his clothes when he went to bed.

"Why bother?" he had said. "You're only going to get up, anyway. Be prepared for it. You're not fooling anyone by taking your clothes off when you go to bed."

He went into the kitchen, stepping around the littlest children, whose wet diapers were in various stages of anarchy. He made his breakfast: a slice of homemade bread covered with Karo syrup and peanut butter.

"Let's go," he said.

We left the house with him still eating the sandwich. The store was three blocks away, on the other side of a field covered with heavy yellow grass. There were many pheasants in the field. Fat with summer they barely flew away when we came up to them.

"Hello," said the grocer. He was bald with a red birthmark on his head. The birthmark looked just like an old car parked on his head. He automatically reached for a package of grape Kool-Aid and put it on the counter.

"Five cents."

"He's got," my friend said.

I reached into my pocket and gave the nickel to the grocer. He nodded and the old red car wobbled back and forth on the road as if the driver were having an epileptic seizure.

We left.

My friend led the way across the field. One of the pheasants didn't even bother to fly. He ran across the field in front of us like a feathered pig.

When we got back to my friend's house the ceremony began. To him the making of Kool-Aid was a romance and a ceremony. It had to be performed in an exact manner and with dignity.

First he got a gallon jar and we went around to the side of the house where the water spigot thrust itself out of the ground like the finger of a saint, surrounded by a mud puddle.

He opened the Kool-Aid and dumped it into the jar. Putting the jar under the spigot, he turned the water on. The water spit, splashed and guzzled out of the spigot.

He was careful to see that the jar did not overflow and the precious Kool-Aid spill out onto the ground. When the jar was full he turned the water off with a sudden but delicate motion like a famous brain surgeon removing a disordered portion of the imagination. Then he screwed the lid tightly onto the top of the jar and gave it a good shake.

The first part of the ceremony was over.

Like the inspired priest of an exotic cult, he had performed the first part of the ceremony well.

His mother came around the side of the house and said in a voice filled with sand and string, "When are you going to do the dishes? . . . Huh?"

"Soon," he said.

"Well, you better," she said.

When she left, it was as if she had never been there at all. The second part of the ceremony began with him carrying the jar very carefully to an abandoned chicken house in the back. "The dishes can wait," he said to me. Bertrand Russell could not have stated it better.

He opened the chicken house door and we went in. The place was littered with half-rotten comic books. They were like fruit under a tree. In the corner was an old mattress and beside the mattress were four quart jars. He took the gallon jar over to them, and filled them carefully not spilling a drop. He screwed their caps on tightly and was now ready for a day's drinking.

You're supposed to make only two quarts of Kool-Aid from a package, but he always made a gallon, so his Kool-Aid was a mere shadow of its desired potency. And you're supposed to add a cup of sugar to every package of Kool-Aid, but he never put any sugar in his Kool-Aid because there wasn't any sugar to put in it.

He created his own Kool-Aid reality and was able to illuminate himself by it.

Don't You Remember Me?

GLENN MEETER

Glenn Meeter was born in Hammond, Indiana, in 1934 and has taught writing and literature at the University of Southern California and Northern Illinois University. His short stories have been published in *The Atlantic, Redbook, Epoch, The Chicago Review, The Ohio Review,* and other magazines, and in various anthologies, including *Innovative Fiction* (1972) and *Redbook's Famous Fiction* (1977). "Don't You Remember Me?" originally appeared in the Spring 1968 issue of the *South Dakota Review.*

HE COULDN'T REMEMBER HER. That was the problem. An important problem, considering he was going to marry her in two weeks. Sometimes at night in a rush of longing he hugged his pillow and called her name, and his imagination would bring him a single, isolated feature that flickered into consciousness and faded: an eyebrow, a wisp of her hair. Brown hair, plain brown like a table top, though he knew her hair was not just brown; it had *highlights,* he had told her so many times. But that was the best he could do. Brown. Beyond that, nothing. The freckles hidden under her skin, the tiny freckles he had traced with his fingers and his lips: gone, nowhere, only the words left. "Hidden freckles": he could invent it by putting two abstractions together, just as he could invent mountain of gold, purple cow, brass

monkey. Or eternal love. He could invent it, but he could
no longer remember it.

A common complaint of separated lovers—loss of memory. He supposed there were psychological explanations. But
it would be a complaint also of those who loved no longer.
Why should it happen now, with two weeks to go, when he
most needed to know that he loved her?

How light had flashed from her limbs! Once, reading
Herrick's couplet about his mistress Julia's legge, that was "as
white and hairless as an egge," he had written a couplet of
his own. Something about Marian's silken or golden thigh,
the apple of his eye. Corny, but accurate; now he could not
have said whether egg or silk or canvas were the more appropriate image; he couldn't remember. She used to complain
that he had no eye for style, he never noticed a new dress;
now as he searched for her image the most vivid thing in his
head was, perversely, the clothing she had worn. He could
have drawn as well as a designer her flared skirts, her plaid
pleats, her puffed sleeves, cuffed sleeves, scoop necks, square
necks, stripes, prints, spikes, flats, the red belt with golden-
arrow buckle, the golden chain with simulated lock and key,
the belt made of corks, the brooch with the blue-eyed deer
and the lotus ivory ear-rings. His imagination could have
filled her closet, as if for six months she had been no more
to him than a department-store dummy. As for Marian herself—if she had been lost or kidnapped he could have told
the police only that she was of, well, average height, average
weight, give or take a little, had whitish skin, pinkish lips,
and the usual number of teeth. And that he used to think her
smile, when he saw it every day, was very nice.

Their courtship had been too compressed, only the last
half of their senior year, back at school in Michigan. Now
that he was home in Wisconsin, and she in Dakota, waiting
for the summer to end, they referred to their past geograph-
ically. "Back East," she would write, "when you bought the
ring," or, "when I had to have a lot of winter clothes, back

East. . . ." She might have said the Far East. His photographs of that time began with one of Marian in the Homecoming hierarchy. It was at Homecoming that he first noticed her. She was standing on a lower level from the Queen, and wearing a gown of a different color, for she was only part of the Court. She was the Queen to him, he told her. Now the picture gave him no memory. She had never worn that gown again, and inside the frame on his bureau she looked like the others: darkish hair, brownish eyes, average height. The snapshots were like that also. Bob and Marian alighting from a bus in winter; Bob carrying Marian over a spring puddle; Bob and Marian engaged (his joy mixed with relief at being accepted by a medical school); Bob and Marian at track meets, band concerts, beaches, picnics—all in two dimensions, mostly black and white, and, worst of all, all representing a kind of unreality, a lost world of white pillars, ivy, pink blossoms, philosophy, and love. Even the best photographs made him wonder whether he had loved Marian —Marian herself—or only that romantic haze with which in retrospect he saw that he had invested everything "back East."

And now this summer of separation. In May it had seemed a sensible thing to do; they had jobs and could earn a little money; they could say good-bye, for two and a half months, to the families they would not see again for a long time, and never again when they were single. Perhaps they had thought a little separation would do them good. What was ten weeks, after all, in the history of their love? It was seventy days, one three-hundred-sixtieth of a man's life, a moment's loneliness before an eternity together—a test of their seriousness and faith. So they had kissed each other good-bye until the wedding, and separated.

Meanwhile he had his work; he was a leader of children's games on a city playground. He bandaged cut knees and bathed swollen temples, practicing those virtues of firmness, patience, and compassion which he told himself he would need in his life hereafter. And he had friends. They gave him a party, a stag party at which he drank the required amount and sat through a dirty movie which someone apparently thought would make him happy before his marriage. The truth was that the party was for themselves. His former friends had gone to different colleges from his, or had gone to school from work; none of them knew Marian; his future was in the South, far away, and they were writing his friendship off.

"Not Texas," he would say to someone busy planning his own future. "Nashville."

"Nashville? Well, look, let's keep in touch, and if you and, ah, Marilyn are ever in Texas..."

He felt as alone at the party as he did on the Fourth of July, when he walked at night past the bushes quivering with birds, and the golf course where nightcrawlers twined on the greens, and the steamed windshields of parked couples—all by himself, his eye fixed on the future, while the rest of the city celebrated with rockets and noise. Living this way on faith and hope, he saw that if he didn't love Marian, he was left with nothing at all.

He needed her letters. It was a thirst; his throat tightened as he opened the envelopes. They came at the rate of one a day, none on Sunday but two on Monday. When he came home from work his mother said immediately, "It's on the desk"; he would do nothing until he had read the letter. He read each one several times over. He tried to read them in private; if he read them in the living room his teenaged brother and sister would tease him.

"Look, Bob's on it again."

"Should we confiscate his letter? For his own good?"

"He'd scream and kick. He'd go into delirium. He'd see snakes."

"Why don't we intercept his mail? Put him on cold turkey?"

"It wouldn't do any good. He's got a case of letters

stashed away somewhere. I've seen him take a nip or two
before he goes to bed."

It was true; he read them at night in his room. But
secretly the letters disappointed him. No matter how warmly
she spoke of their love, or how moved he was by her picture
of their linked futures, the disappointment lingered. For one
thing, he had liked what he thought was her streak of
whimsy and irony; but the letters seemed completely serious.
Then there was her penmanship—round and perfect, like a
first-grade teacher's. She was in fact a first-grade teacher,
and intended to put him through school by teaching—but
somehow he had never thought of her in just that way before. And the exclamations, her frequent underlining, her
use of "cuz" for "Because"—these, he supposed, were characteristic of college girls. But Marian wasn't a college girl, she
was a graduate, she was Marian, she was going to be his wife!

He spent hours at the desk every evening, working on his
replies.

"Look," his brother and sister would say, "Bob's at his
devotions again."

"Shall we get him a kneeling bench?"

"Look, he's got his eyes closed! He's looking at the ceiling! He's communing with her!"

"No, he's trying to spell. You want a dictionary, Bob? Or
a hair shirt?"

"Bob, have you ever tried fasting?"

Yesterday (he would write) *the paper said it was a hundred
degrees in Nashville. Well, today I got a heavy-duty radiator
which I think I can install myself. That's not so easy to find for a
'48 Chevy but I finally found one. I think I'll put in brand-new
hoses. I'm trying to get new tires but fifteen-inch tires are getting
hard to find too* . . . His feelings had to be compacted into the
signature: *All my love, Robert.* Once he tried to express something deeper. He wrote that her letters sounded different
from the way he remembered her. He asked whether she
thought they had changed. Oh Bob, she wrote back, I wish

you hadn't written that! I love you, I really do. I'm the *same!* I won't ever change, I promise! Maybe it's only your conception of me that's changing? I hope not, I love you as madly as ever. No, you don't sound stuffy in your letters. I love them, every word. Of course it's not really *you!* But I can wait. If I don't joke any more maybe it's cuz everything is so *close* now. Do you have any ideas about the music? I don't want Mendelssohn, but I want something that sounds joyful. . . .

On the night of the Fourth he called her up. Just to hear her voice. The line was busy for a long time, and then: the party does not answer. Of course not; she was out with her parents, visiting relatives; she wrote about it in her next letter. But something in him made it into a test; next time he would let her call him. So he waited, she didn't call, and he didn't hear her voice.

But sometimes the joy they had had came flooding back—as when he passed somebody's lawn-sprinkler and smelled the wet grass and remembered a spring day when they had walked on the yellow hills and smelled the sun burning off the dew. Or when he planned their trip, checking and rechecking his maps—in a strange way the maps gave him a more pure and unmixed pleasure than Marian's letters. The journey was west, first of all, in the direction of explorers, and also, paradoxically, a journey toward the past, toward a rural land where, as it happened, his mother had been born. And then south, in that strange double life so difficult to imagine, south to live on a different parallel of the globe, among a people with a different way of life. Wisconsin travellers went east or west, sometimes to California or Florida, but no one went just south: that was uniquely his, his and Marian's. It was a real pleasure to work on his car, to get his last hometown haircut, to purchase the wedding ring, to buy a summer suit, for the South, and summer shoes with mesh tops. It was a pleasure to remind Miss Nikkerson, down at the city Recreation office, that he was leaving, and to hear her sourly wish him every joy. Miss Nikkerson, his boss for the summer, was tough, ugly, old, cranky, born to die single; though he couldn't remember Marian he sometimes reconstructed her from the fact that Miss Nikkerson was in every way her opposite. It was a pleasure to get his teeth fixed, and to get himself licensed and checked by the lugubrious old family doctor, who told him, after testing for hernia, that he had nothing to be afraid of.

His mother laughed. "Remember Edna's wedding, last summer? The poor groom, he looked like an absolute corpse! And she didn't look much better. Of course they were trying to do too much, everything between semesters, they were both taking exams and then they must have been on tranquilizers or something for four straight days. Do you believe that, Robert? Tranquilizers?"

"Maybe after I've been to medical school," he said, "I'll be able to form an opinion."

"But talk about your deathly pallor! It was comical! Now when you were born, Robert"—she apparently felt no need for transition between topics of death, marriage, and birth—"when you were born I thought I was going to die."

"She did it natural childbirth," his father said. "Without anesthetic."

"I know," Robert said.

"Now they call it natural childbirth. When I did it it was just without anesthetic. I wanted to do it the way my mother did. I'm from South Dakota too, you know."

"I know."

"But that part was wonderful, it didn't bother me. It was the heat that got me down. You talk about heat! I don't know what the temperature was but it must have set a record. I just hope it's cooler for your wedding. Wisconsin is nothing compared to Dakota. South Dakota in August is no place for a wedding, believe me."

"Bob's depending on air-conditioning," his brother said. "Right, Bob?"

"But when they held you up, Robert"—his mother was

knitting, and she pointed at him with the knitting needle—when they held you up, and I could see you, kicking and crying—"

"He looked like a frog," his father said. "All mouth, no chin at all."

"—and all these other women were lying around, drugged, you know, like absolute corpses—you talk about your deathly pallor, believe me, they had it—but I was radiant—"

"That's the truth," his father said. "She never looked better in her life."

"—and all these other babies were being carted off to their glass cases, while the poor mothers were lying there just as stiff as logs, with their mouths open, just so much senseless lumber, with their babies torn away, and I could *see you*, Robert—"

She was laughing and crying together; his father, for comic relief, said, "Screaming. A screaming, wet, red, naked frog."

"—then I felt like I could never die. I was wild with happiness. I felt like I would never die. Robert, I want you to promise me"—she threw down her knitting and looked at him with her face blotched strangely red beneath the eyes— "I want you to promise me, if you ever go into obstetrics— now let me finish!—I want you to promise me you will remember that these are not your babies. They don't belong to the doctor. Or the nurse, or the hospital. And it's not your birth, either. Do you understand? You're just supposed to be an agent. A *tool*. Will you remember that?"

"I'll remember," he said.

"Just let the poor women get some satisfaction out of bearing them," she said, "before they have to lose them," and, to his dismay, a week before he was to leave for his wedding, she began to weep steadily, and had to leave the room for Kleenex.

Two days later he went to see his pastor. He had tended

to ignore this man since his catechism days, but the pastor had married hundreds of couples. To him Robert confessed that he sometimes didn't feel ready for marriage; he didn't feel old enough. He wondered whether many bridegrooms felt this way.

"Sometimes they do," the pastor said. "Sometimes when they aren't sure they love the girl."

He was white-haired and shrewd; Robert used to feel that he could look into a person's soul. He answered immediately.

"I do love her. I know it. But sometimes—I can't remember her."

The minister laughed. It'll come back to you. Maybe a letter, maybe a picture, maybe a dream. Suddenly you'll remember. Why don't you call her up?"

He wanted to. He wanted one last evidence that it was all for the best. And then, on his last night home, as he was about to call her, she called him. He could hardly believe it; he wondered if something had gone wrong. When at last the operators cleared away he could hear Marian's voice.

Hi?

Hi, he said. Marian?

Yes. Bob?

Yes. Hi!

Hi! I can hardly hear you! You sound so far away!

You sound pretty far away yourself.

Oh Bob, I can hardly wait! Just one more day!

The voice was Marian's—though not, somehow, the voice he remembered. A gigantic storm seemed to shake the wire from end to end, causing it to whisper hollowly.

Just one more day, he said. It's been a long summer.

Do you have any more ideas about music?

Just something stately, he said. You know. But joyful.

Something what?

Stately. Stately, but—

I can hardly hear you. We must have a bad connection.

Stately. You know, dignified.

Oh, stately. I thought you said shapely!

He knew that she spoke not for his ears alone but for all those others that listened in on a party line in the great, friendly West. As for him, now that they were almost one flesh, he was conscious of how much it was going to cost; he asked her to call the operator and make a note.

I will, she said. Did you get my map?

I got it. It came yesterday.

You won't forget to stop for the gown?

I won't.

And don't look at it!

I won't look, he said.

Shortly afterward they hung up. It was not a private or satisfactory call, but the fact that she had done this, had responded in this way to his need, gave a lift to his soul. That night he had a dream in which Marian was vividly real. He was swimming in a stream, and on the shore Marian sat in profile: he saw the exact, remembered curve of the small of her back, and of that soft length, under the skirt, from hip to knee; and she smiled at him with the sun full on her face bringing out the brown flecks in her cheek and the red-gold highlights in her hair. He swam to her eagerly, though the current swung against him. As he reached the bank she turned to him with joy and he saw that it was—clearly a mistake—Miss Nikkerson from the city Recreation office. Miss Nikkerson, with her shark's mouth, her tough bony calves fringed with hair, her veiny arms, was grasping at him and saying, Love is not love which alters when it alteration finds, or bends with the remover to remove, oh no! it is an ever fixed mark, that looks on tempests and is never shaken, and she was shaking, shaking, shaking him by the shoulders.

He woke suddenly in the dark. His mother, yawning, was telling him she had packed a lunch for him and would see him in a few days at the wedding. Downstairs his father was kicking the tires and wishing him luck and Godspeed. He shook his father's hand and kissed his mother good-bye. The sun would soon be up; ready or not, it was time to go.

The trip would take him seven hundred miles west, and, less perceptibly, seven hundred feet up, from an elevation of 680 on the green, right-hand edge of the map, to one of 1450 on the left, where green turned brown on the way to the mountains. It would be a long day's drive.

Morning slipped by easily. Whitewashed trees with red reflectors fastened to them rushed at him from the dark; then black and white cows swam by, grazing in mist, walking in grass gray as the sea; then on a long hill west of Whitewater the dawn blinked red in his mirror; and then past Fort Atkinson the full sun hammered gold the dry streets of little towns familiar since boyhood. Signs pointed toward Beaver Dam, where the basketball team was so poor that he, on the second string, always got to play. He crossed route 51, the romantic highway he never crossed without longing to go straight north beyond Wasau, Tomahawk, and Minoqua to where the Indians still fished the wild lakes for rice. He passed Devil's Lake, where he had gone rowing with a girl named Schmidt, Cheryl or Sheila or Sharon, and had kissed her, closing his eyes prematurely and locating her mouth, finally, by the smell of the spearmint she chewed. Ah, good-bye to the ferns, rocks, and birches of Wisconsin! Near Sparta he had a flat, and changed tires gladly in the windy, blue-gold morning. It was not until he sat in a country restaurant, waiting for the Shell station to finish his work, while a bare-armed Swedish girl gave him coffee, that he remembered he had thought of the wedding hardly at all. He was enjoying the trip itself, as if it had no destination.

After that it was work. Crossing the Mississippi, a milestone disappointingly small, he chose route 16 instead of 14. How his freedom had shrunk, it seemed, since his birth twenty-two years before, a male child of infinite possibility! All the earth had offered brides, self-contained Asiatics,

each joint subtly crafted, faces smooth with repose, dark
Africans rich in grace and music, all Europe from blonde
sunbathing north to the lustrous-eyed Mediterranean where
skins were white as milk—and from this wealth he had chosen two for consideration, one from New Jersey who couldn't
pronounce things right ("Do you live on a form?" she asked,
the first time they met), and the other Marian, whom he had
loved. Now his alternatives were 14 or 16, and he had chosen: more pigs, fewer cows; Herefords, not Holsteins; more
pork less butter, more corn less rye, more SuperValu and less
Red Owl, Grainbelt instead of Rainier, more Champlin and
less Co-op, more Methodist less Lutheran, elm instead of
pine—a narrow strip of life. Yet it was his and he loved it.
Oh Marian I love you, he sang, I'm always dreaming of you.
But down by the cool though shrunken Root River, through
Hokah, Houston, and Rushford, he bent his thoughts forward and west—not to the wedding but to the wedding
gown, for which he would have to reach Sioux Falls by five
o'clock, or the stores would be closed. The overtaking sun
heated his roof and left elbow; a wind came against him,
slowing the Chevy but helping to cool it. He could do sixty-
five without overheating. He knew his car, knew it in every
vibrating bone and in his blinking eyes; on a glaring curve he
stopped to put black tape on his dashboard chrome. He
played games; the trick now was to stay awake. There was
the mystic's game, where you made every experience your
own: speeding between Austin and Albert Lea he could sing
without regard for whatever reality inspired the town's
names,

> Albert Lea and Austin, rough and hearty,
> Invite you to their Austin-Lea party.

There was the scientist's game in which you surrendered to
the objectivity of experience (though keeping an eye at the
same time on your own road racing ahead to a five o'clock
deadline): three Clabber Girl, four Harold's Club, five Wall

Drug, one very old Plough Boy, and, at intervals of twenty-five miles, the flying wooden goose of Kozy Kampground, counted down finally west of Blue Earth, where tents were being pitched for the night although he, with miles and miles to go, couldn't stop. As a budding medical man he could play a third game, combine mystic and scientist, inner and outer, and so he colored life as it came to him through the nose: skunk (dark), hayfield (dry and winy), horse manure (rich and wet), cow manure (dry and clean), sheep manure (harsh), fresh paint (sharp), Hormel plant (musty), diesel fumes (heavy), carbon monoxide (light, sick), gasoline (penetrating), a state park (mud and dead fish, simple decay).

> The Bride
> Can't Wait
> To See
> His Face
> But First
> He'll Have
> To Clear
> A Space.
> *Burma Shave*

It did not amaze him that inner and outer worlds corresponded; he believed that they should. He rubbed his twelve-hour beard. Marian would forgive him, she knew he couldn't stop.

> Lover,
> Wait
> 'Til You
> Get Home.
> Careless
> Drivers
> Love
> Alone.

Now it took distraction to keep him travelling awake. If it were not for a pack of cigarettes, stops for rest in dirty rest rooms, the St. Louis Cardinals, and the ups and downs of hog prices, he would have pulled off to the side of the road, cut his engine, and sunk gratefully to sleep. He put Minnesota finally behind him and crossed the Sioux River. His tongue was as hot as his tires, his eyes were red, and his nerves jumped with nicotine, Frankie Yankovic's polkas, and the rushing of a seventy-mile-an-hour wind. But he entered Sioux Falls in triumph, like a great man, a success: it was twenty minutes before five. He had finished the course. He was on time. He had arrived.

He stood in front of Fantle's Department Store on the warm sidewalk, his back aching, and looked through the glass doors, darkly, at a scene of perpetual winter. Frozen mannequins, cut off at the legs, wore corduroy, wool, and fur. The lights were out, the store was empty, the glass doors locked tight. Where had he gone wrong? *During the month of August,* he read, *the management of Fantle's will close one hour earlier.* Between his waking and arrival, someone had changed the rules.

But all the world, he knew, loves a lover. The force of his love made the black man emptying trash in the alley give him the manager's phone number; it made the manager, who arrived smelling of beer and sausage, jangling his keys, call a clerk; it inspired the clerk to direct the manager, by phone, in the folding of the gown, so that the bridegroom could observe custom and remain ignorant until the last second of the shape his prize would take.

"So I've got this separate floating panel in my left—okay, then the bodice, that's the top, right? Okay, so I've got this bodice in my right hand . . ."

Now he could rest. With the gown in its box in its plastic bag in his trunk, safe, he ate chicken and blueberry pie in Sioux Falls, watching slow folks move on brick streets and tennis players, in the watery green park, play their spotless game. There was no pressure, now, to hurry on; there was reason to rest. Yet fits of longing broke across his body like a chill, in the hot restaurant, and it seemed intolerable that the sun, arcing once and looking back, should sink and see him still alone. He had wandered among Fantle's plastic and cardboard females like Solomon neglecting his riches; these love-shadows made him ache for Marian, her incomplete memory more substantial than their presence. Outside, on twenty-two heavy tires, a silver truck-and-trailer rumbled by, loaded with freight, its running lights, turned on against the evening, starring its outline under a crest of smoke. It wore the many-colored tags of a dozen states, and the slogan it carried—the bravely ridiculous syllable *PIE*—was an abbreviation of everything swift and high and far: Pacific Intermountain Express. Its driver flung a hand against the sun. It shuddered at a stop sign, sighing like a wanderer who should never stop, and in the silence it left behind it Marian's last sentence echoed: *one more night and you'll be in my arms.* He paid his bill with a lover's, not a husband's tip, and went for his bug-stained car.

She was more present to him now than she had been since the day he kissed her good-bye. This was her state, her wide free sky and quiet pasture: in the shadows of trees he saw her standing, dressed in white, waiting with cool brown arms. With the wind gone in the gathering dark he pushed the Chevy to seventy, seventy-five, singing to keep awake.

> Work and pray!
> Live on hay!
> You'll get PIE in the sky by and by!

He closed his windows and imagined Marian's warmth. Then, at the last of dusk, bending northwest toward Mitchell, with a shiver he slowed for an accident. A train coming out of the north was stopped across the highway. The Pacific Intermountain Express was twisted into it, jammed, as if someone with great strength had tried forcibly to attach one to the other. From the west, where the body would be, a red light throbbed, glaring with the dying sun from the freight-train's wheels. Crates of eggs, smeared with gasoline, dripped a hundred feet into pasture, where sheep, never frightened long by any angel, already grazed. He backed up to detour on dirt roads; there was nothing else to do.

Now the fragility of life kept him rigid in his seat. On high-crowned gravel he hit the brakes to spare a jack-rabbit. He searched every headlight for messages of his mortality. Oh Marian, Marian! The thought of his journey's end existed now merely as a negative, an alternative to being rubbed senseless into the pavement. Darkness at last fell complete. West of Mitchell, towns became insignificant and ceased. Fences, telephone wires, fell back into the dark. The white centerline disappeared. The radio brought only noise. Rushing through alien, dry-weather grass, humiliated by a sea of unreachable brittle points of light, he was alone with two human things, the green glow of his dash and, once, the flicker of a sign that told him what he already knew, this was pheasant country. What if he had turned wrong, south or north, by mistake? His tires hummed three syllables, *forever, forever*. His backbone was a worn rope, each vertebra a center of fatigue. Headlights appeared at last, hurting his eyes, though they guided him safely off 16 onto a road he thought he had missed. Feeling more like a mole than a bridegroom, he slipped south along the hills east of the Missouri, a river he would not cross, though it loomed dark on his map, until after his marriage.

The last twenty miles were the hardest. Near Henley, long since darkened in sleep, he found the turnoff marked on Marian's map, a dark dirty road down which he sneezed violently. He had entered her county and found that he was allergic to it; at last he drove with his face masked, like a bandit's or surgeon's, in a handkerchief. It was stubbornness more than love which held his foot on the accelerator and made him keep breathing. Almost there, he skidded on a turn, and on the last dusty mile his heart flapped with fear. A boulder, then the shadow of a windmill on the stars, then a mailbox with her father's name fading on it (dust caught and covered him as he stopped to look), and then he was in her yard. He had no sense of direction. It was all he could do, as a dog barked and a light went on far away and someone, Marian, came toward him whiter than darkness, to avoid hitting anything, then stop the car, kill his engine and lights, and wait. She opened the door and he fell into her arms.

"Marian! Marian!"

"Get down, Pal!" she said. "Down! Can't you see? It's Robert!"

They held each other. It made no difference, there in the glittering dark with rays of yellow light falling thinly from the kitchen, that she was almost a stranger: he stood up to hold her better, kissing first her forehead by mistake, then her eyes and chin; the smoothness of her skin, the smell of her hair, the strength of her waist as her body moved against his and soothed it, all was new and yet familiar. Surrounded as they were by dust, her touch settled every nerve, her fingers swept weariness away. He kissed her lips. His blood rose astonishingly, red and eager in his eyelids as if he would never be tired again.

They held each other for a long time, until the dust settled around them and the dog, Pal, stopped sniffing and went away. "Don't you remember me?" she said at last, and he remembered her wide, bright smile. She moved as if to take him to the house, where they could see each other's faces.

"Wait," he said.

He held her to his chest and laughed aloud at a simple forgotten glory: beyond the curve of hip and thigh, in the dust on which they stood, the grace of her feet in sandals.

"I never forgot you," he said. "Not for a single minute."

Oh Happy Eyes

INGEBORG BACHMANN

Born in Klagenfurt, Austria, in 1926, **Ingeborg Bachmann** gained recognition in the fifties for her existential lyric poetry influenced by Heidegger and Wittgenstein, the subjects of her doctoral dissertation at the University of Vienna. She also wrote highly praised radio plays, essays, and short stories (including *The Thirtieth Year* collection, 1961), taught for a time at the University of Frankfurt, and spent the latter years of her life in Rome, where she died in 1973. "Oh Happy Eyes" was published in German ("Ihr glücklichen Augen") in her collection *Simultan* in 1972. The translation below is by Robert Detweiler and Nancy Dingus.

It HAD BEGUN WITH two and a half in the right and three and a half in the left, Miranda recalls, but now she has, harmoniously, seven and a half diopters in each eye. Thus she has become abnormally nearsighted, and her long-range vision has also decreased. At one time she wanted to memorize the prescription for her glasses so that she could have new ones made immediately in case of an accident, for instance, on a trip. She let it go because she has astigmatism as well, which complicates the details, and the second deformity frightens her, because she can't altogether understand why her meridians are unequally curved and never show equal

194

refractions. The terms astigmatism and distorted vision also sound ominous to her and she says to Josef in a self-important voice, astigmatism, you know, is worse than being blind.

But there are occasions when Miranda feels that her diseased optical systems are "a gift of heaven." She is quick to hand with such expressions, those dedicated to heaven, God, and the saints—yes, they are a gift, if only, perhaps, an inherited one. For it astonishes her how other people endure what they see and have to witness daily. Or don't the others suffer as much from it because they have no other means of viewing the world? It's possible that normal sight, including normal astigmatism, dulls people's senses totally, and Miranda shouldn't reproach herself anymore for her privileged existence, her mark of distinction.

Miranda would certainly not love Josef any the less if she had to see his yellow-stained teeth every time he laughed. She knows, from close up, what these teeth are like but thinks uncomfortably about the possibility of having them "constantly in view." It probably wouldn't bother her either to be startled by the map of wrinkles around his eyes on those days when he is fatigued. But she would still rather be spared such acute vision, so that her sensibilities won't be affected and weakened. She notices immediately in any case—because she receives messages on other wave lengths—whether Josef is tired, why he is tired, whether his laughter is carefree or forced. She doesn't need to face him as sharply focussed as others, she scrutinizes no one, doesn't catch people with a candid glance through her glasses but rather paints them in a style of her own, influenced by other impressions, and Josef, finally, really worked for her from the start. For her it was love at first sight, although every oculist would shake his head over it, because Miranda's "first sight" could produce catastrophic errors. But she insists on her first sight, and of all men Josef is the one her early sketches of whom, and later more detailed studies—those in the light, in darkness and in all conceivable situations—totally satisfy Miranda.

With the aid of a tiny correction done via a concave lens—with a gold spectacle frame stuck on her nose—Miranda can see through to hell. This inferno has never lost its terror for her. Therefore, always on guard, she glances carefully around her before she puts on her glasses in a restaurant to read the menu, on the street when she wants to call a taxi, because if she's not careful something will cross her field of vision that she'll never be able to forget: she'll see a crippled child or a dwarf, or a woman with an amputated arm, yet these figures are really only the most garish, the most obvious amidst a debris of unfortunate, malicious, doomed faces—faces marked by humiliations or crimes unimaginable visages. And their vapors, those global emanations of ugliness, force tears to her eyes, cause the ground beneath her feet to vanish, and to prevent that she reads the menu quickly and tries in a flash to tell a taxi from a private car, and then puts her glasses away—she needs only minimal information. She wishes to know nothing more. (Once, to punish herself, she walked for a whole day throughout Vienna wearing glasses, through several districts, and she does not consider it appropriate to repeat this course. It exceeded her capabilities, and she needs all her strength to cope with the world she is familiar with.)

Miranda's excuses for not acknowledging people or returning a greeting are not taken seriously by some, are labelled by others as silly subterfuges or viewed as a special brand of arrogance. Stasi says, almost spitefully,

So put on your glasses!

No, never, never, Miranda responds. I can't bring myself to do that. Would you wear them?

Stasi retorts: I? Why should I? I can see properly.

Properly, Miranda thinks, why properly? And, a bit dejected, she probes further: but you'd grant that a person might not out of vanity?

Stasi gives Miranda no reply, and that means: it's not just this fantastic self-delusion; she's also vain, and this fantastic luck, on top of it, that she always has with men, assuming it's true, but it was impossible to fathom this cautious Josef.

To Josef Miranda says:

Stasi is more relaxed these days, she used not to be so nice; I think she's in love; at any rate, it must be something good for her. What does he actually want from her now, the divorce and the child? I don't understand the whole business.

Josef is distracted, as if he didn't quite know what was being discussed. Yes, he agrees, Stasi has become more pleasant, almost tolerable; it might be the result of Berti's medical finesse or on account of Miranda and all of them, because Stasi had been simply worn down, had already turned quite despicable from all that misfortune, but now the custody of the child is going to be awarded to her. Miranda hears that for the first time, and she hears it from Josef. She'd like to ring up Stasi and announce her happiness, but then she feels a chill for a second, she checks if the window is open, but it's closed. Josef turns back to the newspaper, Miranda to the roof opposite. How gloomy it is in this narrow lane, too expensive and too gloomy in all these houses on the place of execution from the good old days.

Miranda has waited in the Arabia-Espresso Cafe, now it's time, she pays, leaves, bangs her head against the glass door of the cafe, rubs her forehead, that will leave a bump where the old one has barely healed, she should have a piece of ice at once, but where would she get ice now? Glass doors are more impossible than people, for Miranda never ceases to hope that people will look out for her the way Josef does, and she is already smiling again, trustfully, on the pavement. She could be wrong, however, because Josef either wanted to go first to the bank and then to the bookstore, or the other way round, and thus she stands on the Graben and tries to locate him among all those traversing the Graben, and then positions herself on the Wollzeile, eyes swimming and wide-open. She looks alternately in the direction of the Rotenturmstrasse and in the direction of Parkring, she thinks she sees him approaching, then in the distance—ah, there he's coming from the Rotenturmstrasse after all, and she rejoices over a total stranger who is then dismissed abruptly from her favor when he emerges as Not-Josef. Then the anticipation starts again, gets ever livelier, and there is at last, in her foggy world, belatedly, a kind of sunrise after all, the curtain of misty tears parts, for Josef is there, she takes his arm and goes off happily.

The veiled world in which Miranda wants something specific, namely Josef, is the only one, in spite of everything, where she feels at ease. The more precise one, by the grace of the Viennese Optical Studio and of their foreign rivals Söhnges and Götte, whether out of lead-glass, lightweight glass or plastic, or viewed through the ultra-modern contact lenses—Miranda will never accept it. She makes the effort, she tries, refuses abruptly, gets headaches, her eyes water, she has to lie in a darkened room, and once, before the opera ball, truly only to surprise Josef, she had sent for these expensive German contact lenses from Munich and read the advertisement on the bill: Always keep your eye on the good. Bent over a black cloth she tried to insert the tiny things, memorizing the directions, blind from the benumbing eye-drops, and then one of the lenses did get lost, never to be recovered in the bathroom, hopped into the shower drain or shattered on the tiles, and the other one slipped under Miranda's eyelid, way up on the eyeball. Nothing worked in spite of the flood of tears until Berti arrived, and then still nothing for another hour in spite of Berti's expert hands. Miranda doesn't like to recall how and when Berti found the lens and got rid of it, and still declares now and again, well, I did do my best. Josef also forgets sometimes, when he converses with her, that he isn't exactly involved with a blind person but with someone on the borderline and that familiar things aren't quite familiar to Miranda, yet that her insecurity is productive. Although she appears timid, she is not weak but independent, precisely because she knows full well what is brewing in the jungle she inhabits and because she is prepared for anything. Because Miranda can't be corrected, reality has to ensure her temporary alterations. She enlarges, minimizes, she directs tree shadows, clouds, and admires two moss green clumps because she knows it must be St. Charles Church, and in the Vienna Woods she doesn't see the trees but the forest, breathes deeply, tries to orient herself.

Look there, Mount Bisam.

It's only Mount Leopold, but it doesn't matter. Josef is patient. What did you do with your glasses again? Aha, forgotten in the car. And why shouldn't it be Mount Bisam for a change, Miranda asks herself and pleads with Mount Leopold to do her a favor someday and be the right mountain.

Tender and blindly trusting and always half-nestled against Josef's lean frame she takes the next root hurdle in her path. "Tender" means not merely that she feels that way at the moment but that everything about Miranda is tender, from her voice to her groping feet, including her overall function in the world, which could be simply tenderness.

When Miranda boards a Viennese tram and sways between people in an AK or BK coach without noticing that pure hate reigns between the conductor and the old woman with the wrong ticket, that the shovers have been infected with rabies, and those who haven't yet exited have murderous gleams in their eyes, and when Miranda reaches the exit with many "excuse me's," glad to have discovered the Schottenring in time, and finds her way down the two steps unassisted, then she thinks that people are really all "terribly nice," and these other people in the AK coach who are disappearing, heading toward the university, don't know why the mood is better, the air breathable again; only the conductor notices that someone didn't take his change, probably the woman who got off at the Stock Exchange or at the Schottenring. A smart-looking woman. Nice legs. He gathers up the money.

Miranda loses many things, while others have them stolen, and she'll walk by a person untouched instead of colliding with him. Or she will run into him, but then it was a mistake, purely an accident, her fault. She could have masses read for all the drivers who didn't run over her, could light candles at St. Florian's shrine for each day on which her apartment did not burn from the lighted cigarettes that she puts down, hunts and then, thank God, finds even if a hole is already burned in the table.

Sad too, really, a little sad, how many spots, scorch marks, overheated stove burners, ruined casseroles, can be found in Miranda's flat. Yet it always turns out all right, and when Miranda opens the door, because someone rang, and a stranger is standing there unexpectedly, she has her usual good luck. It will be her Uncle Hubert, her old friend Robert, and she'll throw her arms around Uncle Hubert and Robert or whoever. True, it could have been a salesman, or thief, or Killer Novak, or the rape-murderer who is still terrorizing the first district; but only the best of friends visit Miranda in the Blutgasse. The others, whom Miranda doesn't recognize anyhow, at larger gatherings, at parties, at the theatre, and in concert halls, surround a not unsociable Miranda with their sparkling presence or suspicious absence. She just can't tell whether Dr. Bucher acknowledged her from over there or maybe didn't acknowledge her after all, and it is also possible that it was, judging from the size and girth, Mr. Langbein. She reaches no conclusions. In a world of alibis and proscriptions Miranda puzzles over—certainly not global problems but over nothing important. Only: does the hazy outline intend to be Mr. Langbein or does it not? It remains a secret. Everyone strives toward clarity, but Miranda withdraws. No: she has no such ambitions, and where others smell secrets, behind the back and behind everything and everyone, there is for Miranda just one secret in the direction she's facing. Two meters distance suffice, and the world is already impenetrable, people impenetrable.

Her face is the most relaxed one at the music society, an oasis of peace in a hall where she is seen by a good twenty gesturing persons and herself sees no one. She has learned to forego nervousness in rooms where people observe, assess, write up, ignore, ogle each other. She doesn't dream, she simply relaxes. For what to others is rest for the soul is for Miranda rest for the eyes. Her gloves slip off quietly and fall under the seat. Miranda feels something on her leg, she's afraid she's accidentally brushed her neighbor's leg and murmurs, "Excuse me." A chair leg has fallen in love with Miranda. Josef picks up the program. Miranda smiles uncertainly and tries to hold her legs stern and straight. Dr. Bucher, who is not Mr. Langbein but Mr. Kopetzky, sits three rows behind her, feeling insulted and groping for the reasons for this woman's fickleness, for whom he would have, at one time, done almost anything, really anything—

Josef inquires.

Have you got your glasses?

Of course, says Miranda, and digs in her handbag. She seems also to have had gloves with her, but she'd better not tell that to Josef, no, her glasses, it's curious, she must have... in the bathroom, or right beside the front door, or in her other coat or, Miranda doesn't comprehend it, but she says quickly:

No, listen, I don't have them. But I don't need to see at a concert.

Josef is silent, guided by his leitmotif regarding Miranda: My guileless angel.

Other women have no defects in Miranda's view, they are beings who have hair neither on their upper lips nor legs, who are always well-coiffed, who have no pores or roughnesses, no pimples or nicotine-stained fingers—no, she struggles alone against her imperfections in front of the shaving mirror that once belonged to Josef and in which she sees what she hopes Josef might mercifuly overlook. After that, after Miranda has practiced self-criticism, she poses in front of the gentle Biedermeier mirror in the bedroom and judges herself to be "passable," "all right," it's not really that bad, and she deludes herself in that too, but Miranda exists among a dozen possibilities for deluding herself, and she balances between the most favorable and the most unfavorable every day of her life.

Miranda owns, in good times, three pairs of glasses: a pair of prescription sunglasses with a gold, black-inlaid frame, then a light, transparent, cheap pair for around the house, and a reserve pair in which one glass is loose and which allegedly doesn't become her. Besides, she could fall back on an old prescription, because Miranda sees everything askew through this reserve pair.

There are times when all three pairs have been simultaneously mislaid, have vanished, are missing, and then Miranda is at a loss. Josef arrives before 8 a.m. from Prinz-Eugen-Strasse and searches through the whole flat, he scolds Miranda, he suspects the maid and the workmen, but Miranda knows that no one steals, that it is simply all her fault. Because Miranda can't stand reality yet can't function without a few points of reference, reality undertakes, from time to time, little campaigns of vengeance against her. Miranda grasps this, she nods complicitly to the objects, the stage scenery around her, and the funny wrinkle she has, where she should not yet have any, from the strain of opening and closing her eyes, grows deeper on such days. Josef promises to go immediately to the optician, because Miranda can't exist without glasses, and she thanks him, suddenly embraces him full of fear and wants to say something, not just because he has come and helped her but because he helps her to see and to cope. Miranda doesn't know what's the matter with her, and she wants to say, just help me please! And she thinks, inconsequently, she's simply more attractive than I am.

During the week in which Miranda has to wait and can't go out and loses her perspective, Josef has to go out to eat twice with Anastasia, in order to advise her on the divorce. Stasi phones after the first time, not after the second time. Yes, we were at the Römischer Kaiser restaurant. Awful. It was bad, the food, and she was cold. And Miranda cannot reply, for to her the Römischer Kaiser is the loveliest and best place in Vienna, because Josef took her out to eat there the first time, and now all at once it's supposed to be the worst—Miranda, are you listening? Well, as I was saying. Afterwards, in the Eden Bar. Horrible. What a clientele!

There must certainly be something to Stasi's concept of a clientele, but what could it be ? Miranda breathes easier again. She has never been to the Eden Bar with Josef, that's a tiny comfort. Does she just act that way or is she like that?

Stasi assures her after another half hour of details. In any case, you didn't miss anything.

Miranda wouldn't put it like that, "didn't miss anything," because she's afraid to miss everything these days. The week won't end, and each day has an evening on which Josef is tied up. Then the glasses are ready. He brings them from the optician a few hours later, but it happens again immediately. Miranda is upset, she has to lie down, wait and figure out when Josef has arrived at his Prinz-Eugen-Strasse flat. She finally gets hold of him, she doesn't know how to start, how to tell him that her glasses fell in the sink.

Yes, you know, in the washbasin. I feel like an invalid, I can't go out, I can't see anyone. You know what I mean.

Josef says, speaking from in the fourth district:

A lovely mess. But you've often gone out without your glasses.

Yes but. Miranda can't think of anything convincing to offer. Yes, but now it's different; I usually have them in my purse, at least.

No you don't. I beg to differ.

But we don't want to . . . because of that, Miranda whispers. Why do you sound like that?

How should I sound?

Different. Just different.

And when no reply comes she says quickly:

Listen, my love, I'll come along, I just feel so insecure, yesterday I almost fainted, well nearly; not altogether, really, it's hideous; I've already tried the reserve pair. Everything looks wrong, blurred. You understand what I mean.

When Josef remains silent like that, then he has not understood.

I'm very sorry to say that I don't follow that logic, Josef says, sounding different, and hangs up.

Miranda sits guiltily in front of the telephone. Now she's given him another reason, but for what? Why do her glasses fall into the sink, why is Josef and why is the world, oh God, it can't be true. Is there no other restaurant in Vienna? Does Josef have to take her to the Römischer Kaiser? Does Miranda have to cry, must she live in a gloomy cave, walk along the book shelves, press her face close to the book spines and then find a book, De l'Amour? After she has read the first twenty pages, laboriously, she feels dizzy, she sinks deeper into the easy chair, the book covering her face, and topples with the chair to the floor. The world has turned black.

Because she knows that her glasses did not fall into the sink by accident, because she has to lose Josef and would rather lose him voluntarily, she goes into action. She takes the first steps toward a finality that she will one day, blind with fright, recognize. That she is permitting Josef and Anastasia to drift toward each other they dare not know, least of all Stasi, and thus she has to invent a story for all of them that is more tolerable and attractive than the real one: she will have never much cared for Josef, this above all; she starts to learn this role. Josef is a dear good old friend, nothing more, and she will be happy for them, she'll also have guessed it all along. She simply doesn't guess what the two are actually doing and planning, how far they have already gone, and what sort of resolution they have in store for her. Miranda phones

Ernst, and after a few days he calls back, encouraged. She makes some obtuse comments to Stasi, then half-confessions: Ernst and I, one can't look at it that way, who says such a thing? No, it was never quite over, that is really . . . to you I can . . . yes, true, always been more than one of those affairs that one just has, you know—

And she murmurs something else, as if she had already said too much. Anastasia, confused, learns that Miranda still has not got free of Ernie and no one, as usual, had an inkling of that in this city where everyone is supposed to know everything about everyone.

Miranda manages a rendezvous with Stasi, timed so that she'll be seen with Ernst at the front door where she proceeds to kiss the indecisive and embarrassed Ernst and, laughing vivaciously, asks if he still remembers how to unlock her front door.

Stasi discusses the front door scene with Josef in detail. She saw everything clearly. Josef doesn't say much about it, he doesn't feel like reflecting, with Anastasia, on a Miranda in Ernie's arms at her front door. Josef is convinced that he is the only one for Miranda, but the next morning, after he has made breakfast for Anastasia, he becomes jovial. He discovers that this isn't so bad, also a relief, and Anastasia is after all very clever and discerning. He'll get used to the idea that Miranda needs other men, that Ernst also suits her better, ultimately, because of common interests, and he can even imagine her with Berti or with Fritz, who talks about her so abominably only because he never got anywhere with her and who would still come running if she wanted him. Miranda has a new attractiveness for Josef that he hadn't recognized in her, and because Anastasia starts in on it once again, he believes, almost with pride, that Miranda would know how to cause real devastation.

Fritz, the poor fellow, he's been drinking ever since.

Josef is not as sure about that as Anastasia, for Fritz also drank before. At one point he defends Miranda feebly. Stasi dissects Miranda's character and claims above all that she has none, that she changes constantly. Sometimes one will see her elegant, at the theatre, then at other times she is unkempt, her skirt hangs awry, or she hasn't been to a hairdresser for weeks. Josef says:

But you don't understand. It depends on whether or not she just found her glasses, and then it depends on whether or not she puts them on.

Stupid goose, Stasi thinks, he is still stuck on her; no, I'm the stupid goose, because I've got my hopes set on Josef, and now he doesn't know what he wants, what does he want anyhow? Yet that's really crystal clear, this foxy, sloppy, dumb, this—Stasi is at a loss for words—she has him in complete control through her helplessness that Josef wants to protect, and who'll protect me?

And she weeps two tears into her orange juice out of her lovely, properly functioning blue eyes and swears to herself that she will never again cry in her whole life, at any rate not this year anymore and not because of Josef.

Josef's holy Miranda, intercessor for all borderline cases, is roasted, dismembered, skewered and burned by Stasi, and Miranda feels it on her body although she'll never hear a single word about it. She no longer dares to leave the house, sits there with the second new pair of glasses—she doesn't want to go out into the street. Ernst comes to tea, and they make plans for the Salzkammergut, and Berti comes by once to check, he thinks she has a vitamin deficiency. Miranda regards him trustingly, she also believes this, and she suggests to Berti on her own initiative that she might eat a lot of raw carrots. Berti says, filling out a long prescription form:

Besides, they're good for your eyes.

Miranda says gratefully:

Of course, you know, my eyes are most important of all to me.

Only she can barely look at Josef anymore. She always looks to the right or left or past him somewhere, so that her glance meets the void. She'd like most of all to hold her hand in front of her eyes, because the biggest temptation for her is still to watch him fervently. The act he's putting on for her benefit simply hurts her eyes—not, as with others, her heart, or stomach or head, and her eyes must endure the whole pain, because seeing Josef was for her the most important thing in the world. And it now happens daily: seeing Josef less. Seeing less of Josef.

Miranda puts ice cubes in Josef's glass and Josef lounges around as casually as ever, only he talks about Stasi as if they had always talked about her. Sometimes he says formally: Anastasia. Miranda, for whom Josef keeps getting in the way, looks at her manicured fingernails. Porcelain, that was the polish that accompanied the Josef era, but now that Josef gives her hand only a cursory kiss when he arrives and leaves and no longer admires and studies the porcelain, she can perhaps give up the polish. Miranda jumps up, closes the window. She is over-sensitive to noise. Lately this city consists only of noise: radios, television sets, barking puppies, and these little delivery trucks, well, Miranda is offended by them but she can't wish, in addition, poor hearing on herself! And even then she'd still hear the sounds loudly, but no longer, with any clarity, the voice she wants most to hear.

Miranda says pensively:

I absorb everything through the ear, I have to like a person's voice, otherwise it won't lead to anything.

But doesn't she claim to like only handsome people? No one knows more beautiful people than Miranda; she attracts them, for she prefers beauty above all other qualities. If she is abandoned, and Josef is in the process of abandoning her, then simply because Anastasia is prettier or especially lovely. It is the explanation for all alterations in Miranda's life.

(Do you understand, Berti? She was simply prettier than I.)

But what was Josef talking about the whole time, of course about her once again, if she's not mistaken.

It's a very, very rare thing, Josef says.

Oh? Do you think so? — Miranda still does not com-prehend what he said. She listens to him less and less.

Yes, he says, but with you it's possible.

So that's where he's heading, and now Miranda looks at him for the first time in weeks. Oh yes, she'll transform this terrible pious lie into the truth. Doesn't he catch on? A friendship—Josef, she, and a friendship?

Well, Miranda says, it's not all that seldom, a friendship. And another Miranda, turned inward and less sublime, can't believe it: my God, is this man retarded, he's too utterly stupid, doesn't he notice anything and will it be like this through all eternity, and why must the only man who ap-peals to me be like this!

Naturally they'd go together to the Sunday concert, Josef explains offhandedly. Miranda no longer considers it to be natural. But since Stasi has to go to her husband on Sundays in order to "have it out" with him once again over the child, a Sunday is left over for her.

What, Mahler's Fourth again, so soon? she says.

No, it's the Sixth, I said. Do you still remember London? Yes, Miranda says, her confidence has returned, she'll listen to Mahler one more time with Josef, and Stasi couldn't de-stroy a note of it for her and also couldn't compete with her for Josef on the staircase of the music society, as long as she had to be gone on Sundays to "have it out."

Josef does come along to Miranda's after the concert, as if it were not the final time. He can't tell her, in a couple of weeks she'll have caught on, she seems so sensible. He puts his shoes on slowly, then looks for his tie, which he ties with an absent-minded expression and jerks straight without look-ing at Miranda a single time. He pours himself a Slirowitz, stands at the window and looks down at the street sign, I. Blutgasse. My guileless angel. He takes Miranda in his arms for a moment, he brushes her hair with his mouth and is unable to see or feel anything other than the word "Blut-

gasse," "Blood Lane." Who does all this to us? What do
we do to each other? Why must I do it? And he'd like to
kiss Miranda but he can't, and then he thinks only that
executions are still carried out, it's an execution, because
everything that I do is a monstrosity, the deeds are the mon-
strosities. And his angel looks at him with wide eyes, keeps
her eyes open questioningly, as if there were still something ultimate to be recognized about Josef, but finally gives
him an expression that annihilates him still further because
it releases and pardons him. Because Josef knows that no one
will look at him like that again, not even Anastasia, he
closes his eyes.

Miranda has not noticed the door falling shut, she only
hears a garage door slamming below, a bawling from a distant
tavern, drunks on the street, the musical cue to a radio
program, and Miranda does not wish to live any longer in
this prison of noise, this prison of light and darkness; she has
only one entry left to the world, through a pounding
headache that presses shut her eyes held open too long.
Whatever was it that she saw last? She saw Josef.

In Salzburg, in the Bazaar Cafe, they meet again. Anastasia and Josef enter as a couple, and Miranda trembles only
because Stasi looks so angry or unhappy, my, what's the
matter with her, how should I—and Miranda, who has always flown to Josef, hears him say something mocking,
funny, upon which Stasi heads gloomily in her direction.
While Josef taking flight (certainly not away from her?) has
to acknowledge old Councilor Perschy and then the Alten-
wyls and the whole clique, Miranda stands up in her sandals
with a jerk, and flies clumsily to a pale Stasi and murmurs,
with a red sheen on her face, after she's kissed Stasi on the
cheek, blushing with hypocrisy and an exertion of will:

I'm so happy for you and Josef, naturally, yes, the card,
yes, thanks, I got it.

She shakes hands with Josef briefly, laughing, hello, and
Stasi says generously, come on, Josef, give Miranda a kiss.

Miranda acts as if she didn't even hear it, she takes a step backward, draws Anastasia along with her, murmurs and whispers, increasingly red in the face, listen, this is quite some mix-up here in Salzburg, no, no, nothing bad, but I have to... afterwards right away... with Ernst, he's unexpectedly... you know how it is. Break it to Josef somehow, you'll manage it all right.

Miranda is in a hurry, she still sees that Anastasia nods comprehendingly and all at once looks lovable, but suddenly also has this redness in her face. Yet it could also be that only she is so feverish and that her sense of a sullied world has got the upper hand. But she'll make it back to the hotel with this scarlet fever, this hot shame all over her face and on her body, and she still sees the swinging door but doesn't see that the panels don't want to swing with her; instead a panel of the door swings against her and she thinks at the last, as it flings her down under a hail of broken glass, and as she gets still warmer from the blow and from the blood that spurts out of her mouth and nose: always keep your eye on the good.

IV
COMMUNITY: COVENANT OR CONVERSION?

Shōjū

NOBUO KOJIMA

Nobuo Kojima was born in 1915 in Gifu on Honshu. He studied English literature at Tokyo University, spent the Second World War as a soldier and intelligence officer in China, and after the war began a career as teacher and creative writer in Japan. Much of his fiction, such as his 1965 novel *Hōyō Kazoku* (for which he received the Tanizaki Prize), consists of self conscious and ironic explorations of ordinary persons trying to survive the fragmentation of postwar life. "Shōjū," Kojima's first published story, appeared in 1952 and again in Kojima's 1967 collection *American School*. The translation below is by Elizabeth Baldwin.

I RELISHED MY GUN-GRIPPNG SHADOW. Marching into the sun, I would suddenly find myself searching for my own gun in the forest of rifle shadows appearing in the dust clouds kicked up by army boots. Frequent explosions accompanied that moving forest. Locating my rifle's shadow creeping along the ground, I pined for the similar earth of my homeland.

In early spring dirt spouts leaped into the sky in the Mōkyō area. When caught nearby, we cocooned ourselves in blankets, but saw nevertheless a fine film of sand cover our guns. My fingers sliding along the dome-like breechblock cover left a clear trail. The much thicker layers accumulating inside turned cleaning into an arduous task.

Peering from behind the muzzle, I yearned through the glittering spiraled barrel for a point in the bright sky and began to feel faint. Opening my hidden ammunition case I polished the interior as though it were a woman's secret place. Grasping the grip firmly I cleaned dirt out of the slit in the fish-eye—my name for the screw holding the butt plate— removed the oil, and breathed again as I wiped the barrel. I can't describe how this wiping operation warmed me. One by one I counted and filed in my mind the worn blemishes, each with its own history. For example, my right hand could feel a blunt, round flaw on the belly and a little above, a barren one, constricted as though by surgical treatment. Near the left-handed grip was a wound like a slashed Buddha's eye. Some-how in the grip's center was a raised area dotted with mole-like specks, pimples in shadow, as if during some military operation a substance like apricot candy had attached itself and been forever bonded by a sweaty and feverish clutch, like bark on a tree. Many times a day I touched this spot, that one. Each time I would remember a woman; I touched it to remember.

When I was twenty-one and about to leave my own country, I wanted all I could get from a twenty-six year old married woman carrying the child of her husband who was at the front. I joined her on her way to her parents' home; we fell in together at an old lodging house where we chanced to stop over in a cold way-station town. After seven months of stroking her white, swollen abdomen and choking my sobs in the hollows of the ups and downs of her skin we parted. When I pleaded, "Let me touch you; we'll both be gone soon," she would instead, her eyes closed, cautiously grasp my hand and, with force meant to atone, refuse to let go. The ambivalence of her touch, her smell, her moles, all held me.

Seizing the grip, I certified the reality of my existence; I saw my life flowing towards me. It felt like the waist of a pre-pregnant woman. I shut my pain into the slender hips of my thirty-eight caliber rifle. It hurts, it hurts! Shin Chan, stop! It's no good. I could almost hear that voice. The strength of what I desired and could not get entered my elbow and turned towards my gun. Having a fair amount of elbow strength, I would raise the rifle by the grip directly to a perpendicular position and maintain it with ease for some time.

The rifle became my woman—an older woman, even. The locked-in wounds, the full underside, an actual older woman. Pawed by an unknown man, my gleaming gun.

They indulged my unwillingness ever to exchange my E62377 for another rifle. No one with the same length of service surpassed me in marksmanship. Born into the house of a cabinet maker, I acquired while playing an accurate eye. Aiming at a target, I saw a woman's lips begin to speak.

Shin Chan, you'll surely be loved. You're a person who will be loved. That's a great relief. It's not just me. That's a great relief. I feel better about him too. This is a secret, but it feels like this child isn't his. I'd like to think that. If it's a boy he'll take your name. To tell the truth I was scared. But now I'm nearly unable to feel our age difference. If that happens it's the end. If you start to love me. Understand, okay? But I'll always be by your side, as your pistol.

I discharged my heart into the barrage towards the target. Five times bullets piled onto each other in one tiny mark.

* * *

As the training period of the new recruits ended, the regular soldiers returned in a bloodthirsty state from their efforts to subjugate the area. The day after their arrival we followed our regular training regimen, which began with a trot toward a ruined castle courtyard that was our practice ground. White poppies of the kind used for opium bloomed around the crumbled walls, piled up like so much rapeseed.

The gun forest passed a roadside stand in which dust hovered over a bubbling kettle of pig feet and hooves. As in countless earlier runs, I was consumed by my private pleasure. On my shoulder my rifle shouted with joy.

Dig a hole! About this wide, two meters deep. Finish in two hours!

Turning, Squad Leader Oya described a circle with a stick of wood as he gave this order.

(This is how I'll do it. Wait a second and it'll be done. I'm faster than the others.)

Speaking to my rifle, I lifted my shovel. Hard labor—any kind of pure hard labor was gratifying to me.

As we were finishing an odd-looking group appeared. Wearing Chinese clothing and shoes, the men in bound leggings, they included one woman. Their hands were tied behind their backs, and two were shouldering a pole between them. Chinese soldiers, soldiers like us. Feeling a sudden sense of familiarity welling up, I had to stifle the urge to call out a greeting. And more compelling still, the woman—how I wanted a woman. I wanted her for my own. My hands stilled the shovel, and my eyes pored over her as if to taste her. Suddenly stunned, I swallowed my voice. And I had thought they had been brought here for forced labor!

After the group came to a stop, no one moved again.

"Tie them up!"

I looked up in a frenzy of anxiety at the squad leader's smile. I was familiar enough with that smile.

"Hey, you're really good, you know that? I'd say that rifle of yours has some kind of devilish power. Let me see that thing a second. Say, it's like a living thing." Saying that, he would turn it over, hit it on its white fish-belly and stand it on its end, all with a smirk that managed to be tender.

None of the seven prisoners made a move towards the edge of the hole. Like willful children they doggedly resisted the order until rifle bayonets pushed them. The bayonet's jab did not kill, but moving to the hole was the last step before death. Some screamed and others bent like bows in response to the jab and the unwillingness of their feet. I must have been the only one staring at the woman. She turned to me the color of unabashed pleading. Unprepared for that, I instinctively nodded, for having once made contact, I now could not avert my eyes. She never wavered her gaze from its direct line to me.

Her hair fell over her grimy forehead with the evenness of a bamboo shade. For whose sake had it been so neatly cut and arranged? That face—yes, it was my woman from home. Lengthen the jaw a little bit and there she stood, not just the face either. That woman was pregnant. How many painful miles had they been prodding her along without a bite to eat? A woman walking all this distance at military speed in her lightly soiled pants stretched over a slight abdominal swelling. Come to think of it, she was probably no soldier but a worker in a factory under military contract.

"Sir!" That had come from me. Whatever strength I had left was instantly transformed into a rage of shock. The squad leader turned, picked up a rock, took aim at me, and hurled it. Then he laughed.

"You! Get out of the hole. You're all alone in there. Maybe we should bury you." Only at those words did I realize where I still stood.

The squad leader probably knew what I wanted to say and that there was no possible response to it. He was fond of me but wanted to kill the milksop in me.

"Well, what is it? What is it? Tell us! Get over here and say it in front of everyone. Now what is it? Everyone listen! Just what do you want to say?"

I loved Squad Leader Oya. The complete soldier, there was nothing he couldn't do. The second degree black belt I got in kendo during business school didn't come close to the martial skill he had picked up in the army. He even surpassed my mastery of the abacus. "Can't tell us, can you? So it's a matter you'd rather keep quiet about. All right then, you kill that woman!"

Mindlessly I turned and looked at her.

"Shoot her at one hundred meters. Then fasten your bayonet and drive towards her. At fifty meters you begin your charge and stab her. Double quick! Move!"

I turned about-face and began running. Sand hot enough to grill an imprint crumbled beneath my boots. Under me was a ruined field of watermelon fruit that would never ripen. Smashing them as I trampled through, I wanted the one hundred meters never to end.

"Stop!"

The voice rode to me on a sweltering wind. I did another about-face.

"Take position! Rifle!"

Instinctively I stilled my breath and took the stance. That my object this time was not a target but a female figure tied to a stake I realized at that moment. Tensed muscles performed the actions impelled by the orders. I hurried to line my target properly in my sights. When the muzzle and rear sights squared with each other, I saw the woman's framed fluttering lips whispering.

I'd be glad if this were your child. But just one thing I want clear, I'm sure I'll start to want you to love me. If that happens it's the end. The end as far as I'm concerned. Do you understand?

I felt giddy. As my eyes started to swim, it suddenly struck me that my way to her was the path of the bullet. That straight line was my transport to the depths of her chest, of her heart, to the center of her stomach.

"Fire!"

My E62377 leaped on my shoulder. I attached the bayonet and began running. I saw her hanging head and red-stained chest as I ran. Gradually human forms grew larger. As I ran I became a tool, a mere rifle with weight,

strength, and direction. The distance covered, my arm shot
out by itself, spontaneously, exactly as I had learned. My
duty was over, the exercise completed.

"Great!"

"Impressive. One shot."

The squad leader pounded my shoulder triumphantly.
"You can call yourself a man now."

Breathlessly receiving that adulation was the rifle. In my
hand the E62377, bathing in spattered blood, was being
flattered by its master. Anger began to surge in me.

Not Squad Leader Oya, but my own instrument had
blinded me to the fact that this time our shooting game held
at stake a human life. Wrath backed up the blood in my
vessels and I fainted.

*   *   *

Every day I ate on the run—practicing kendo, marching.
Always when evening came my remaining strength dissolved
into fear of an old desire newly attached to the face of a
Chinese woman whose name I didn't know. I had become in
fact half a man. However I tried to stir up my fervor towards
my rifle, the bubbling passion had turned tepid. When I was
alone, I poked the cleaning rod in the snout—pulling, jabbing, scraping the interior. I watched the butt plate rust and
left the rear sight permanently detached. The wooden part I
had loved so much I now trampled under foot with the mixed
force of hatred and yearning for my distant woman. In the
end I threw the rifle on top of the straw mat. A whore who
sucks a man's blood, I said—I, who still had never known a
woman. Lying there on its side. That I should look at! How
do I like that! Pouncing, I was shaking it when my shouts
diffused into a quiet chuckle that seemed to exhale through
my pores. Well, if that's the case, I thought to myself, and
began spreading on grease until it lay deep inside its oily
makeup.

In the course of daily living, the woman from home died

in my mind and I ceased to suffer from dreams of a woman in Chinese clothes. However, I became weak. Probably it was a twenty-one year old's caprice that led me to spend my vacations learning how to play with women. As a result of an all-consuming effort to bring pleasure to Korean women, my bodily strength was exhausted. I picked up a dishonorable disease and, like many new recruits, was laid up in a hospital in downtown Daido—I don't know how many miles away. My E62377 taken away, I was issued instead a rude, fairly new yet inferior rifle. Holding its seven and a half pounds in my hands, I saw at a glance that the center of gravity was way off. Resting a familiar part on my palm, I could tell that its lopsidedness was obvious. So recently made, the mouth should have been spherical; but peering into the barrel, I saw that light and shadow were not spaced evenly through the coils of the cylinder. I would not waste my disgust and self-reproach on such a rifle.

* * *

With my warped rifle, heart and body, I returned to the home regiment. One day leaving the mess line, I was asked to carry the squad leader's meal to him. Previously I had eagerly volunteered for this kind of thing. As a twenty-one year old I enjoyed being favored for my quickness to respond, to swing into movement. At around this time, the squad leader, as was the custom, in a loud voice read a letter from a woman addressed to me and said: "When I'm back home collecting the new recruits I'll pay her a little visit in your stead. How about doing me the favor of finding me a good one too? I'll bet she has a younger sister, doesn't she?"

He carried on at my expense in that vein. Of course I was no longer receiving letters from that woman. I figured he was just trying to get to me, but I could arouse no hatred towards him.

When he heard my "I've brought your meal, Sir!" he shut the door in my face. Fearing my voice hadn't carried the proper military ring, I repeated my message numberless times in a booming manly voice. When the door suddenly opened I stared at his expressionless face as he lifted up the tray to dash it against the stone flooring in the courtyard. Bewildered, I clambered around gathering the fragments until a blow from a soldier who charged out from the office of domestic affairs sent me flying. As earnest and sober as I had been previously, I still wouldn't have stood for that kind of thing because I had confidence in my arm. Now I stood vacantly where he had left me.

Because the squad leader failed to get his supper, we were all denied ours; immersed in hostile stares from the others, I walked through the mess area to return the can that the meal had been in. I figured out later the source of the whole scene. I had been walking around with no breechblock on my gun. Someone must have taken it because I couldn't find it anywhere. I had no memory of it of any kind; for all I knew it could have been missing a long time. When I had the E62377 I had only to touch the bolt or latch to feel the difference between someone else's and mine. I had no grounds for defense. Squad Leader Oya, who could have stood up for me, seemed determined to take the lead in chastising me. I was put into the guardhouse. When my offense was announced to the assembled troops, a red cloth was hung onto the end of my incomplete rifle and I was made to present arms. My steps in this procedure had always been so flawless that I was considered a model. My one gesture of rebellion at this time was to execute the movements with flair and refinement appropriate to a soldier of high standing.

The meaning of the red cloth was "This man wears a woman's colors," but to my bitter eyes it signified a woman's blood.

Everything became distant from me. My weapons, my clothing, the other soldiers, even my homeland. Merely for my one failing the others began pushing me around in all situations. If a mere needle were missing or a lice outbreak

occurred, suspicion settled on me. The group that had de-
lighted in my marksmanship now enjoyed my deficiency.
The test for officer candidacy had been given long ago, but
even if it were to be offered now I would not have been
allowed to take it. I was not perturbed. Left behind as the
others passed on, I became a second-rate soldier.

At that time, because of my reputation as a marksman I
was chosen to represent our company in the national target
contest. It was probably my squad leader's last hope for me. I
asked to borrow my old E62377, which was consigned to a
sergeant-major with seniority. Having managed to get it for
me, my squad leader tossed it lightheartedly into my arms.

"This time you're going to work for those points and win
that match. Remember our training period? No one could
touch you then. I got special permission from the com-
mander so you could enter. Don't let me down."

With unashamed emotion he cried bitterly. My back
turned to him, I examined the rifle. It had changed in its
journey from one man's hands to another's. Holding it to my
chest, I saw that the grainy moles I had been fond of remembering had been cleanly stripped off. Entrusted to the care of
all the soldiers to whom it had been assigned, the rifle revealed filth as if from inside the ear, scum from the gums,
dirt visible in hair in bright sunlight.

Shutting out my squad leader's passionate words, I
laughed shortly and tossed aside the rifle. That was a habit I
had recently acquired.

"You've lost your bearings now, huh? Clever or not."
With that he struck me on the face with my military boots
for my slighting of the emperor in that way.

I burst out. "This breechblock, Sir, is the one that was
lost from that other rifle. It is not the one belonging to
E62377."

"What are you talking about, man?"

"Nothing at all. I beg your forgiveness. However, I am

unable to represent our company in this match."

"Unable to represent? Unable to represent, huh? It's not up to you; it's been decided. And you claim you won't enter."

"I'll enter, I'll enter."

"You sure will. Look at the star on your shoulder. If you don't, I'll commit suicide, I swear I will. Someone does here every year, you know."

I participated in the shooting match. My score was the worst—near zero. Without aiming I was merely firing in the general direction of the target.

*   *   *

When that year was deep into autumn we were sent out in groups to subdue the surrounding area, hiking and carrying pistols. If anyone had been asked about his goals in the venture, he would have replied "eating and resting." If you happened to bump into one of your comrades, the excursion turned into a fight. Such was the nature of the conquering force. Oblivious to this meanness, the gun forest wound around serpentine river beds. The Kadagawa was a clear river that started in the distant Gori mountains and flowed whitely beneath us towards Tenshin. Plodding along in the silent forest, I found myself wanting to scream. A ghostly aura drifted from the seven and a half pound piece of baggage in my arm. "In a lonely place like this, without a rifle there's nothing to rely on. This thing is a protecting deity," Oya's unexpected voice came from somewhere in the forest. The gun was, to the contrary, the cause of my unbearable pain.

Catching my reflection in the river I started. I saw not myself but a pale woman, tied to a stake, entreating me.

At that moment my body was violated with fever and my feet became entangled. I found myself lying face down in the river inhaling water, and lifted my eyes up to mountains of rock looming like those painted by the Nanga school. I lost all hope. Beside me rifles with brass muzzle-caps marched single file further and further up the mountain. Wearing socks on their feet, dolled up in bandages and coverings, all were decked out as if for a parade. I'll light a fire and burn them up. Standing at the foot of the mountain, I screamed in my heart. I dragged my feet until I was at the tail of the line. *Yoischo, Yoischo*—from the belly of the mountain their baiting voices flourished in the air.

I heard in them the devilish power of the rifle coming to torture me. Instantly furious, I tried to curse to stifle the sound, but my voice was still.

Suddenly I saw I was being shoved upwards by someone. Whirling around I almost fainted. Jabbing me in the tail was the butt of my old rifle, in turn being pushed by Oya. My own rifle, forcing me into forward leaps. I felt a morbid fear and the intended humiliation together.

"Squad Leader, Sir, please kill me."

His face was an expressionless sea with no island to grab hold of.

"There have been some who did the job themselves," he intoned.

After that I was forced to continue on a mule. Only by the animal's grunting did I remain aware that my head was higher than the others and that my feet were not doing the walking. I had a sense of inevitability about the rifle bound onto my back and digging into my flesh.

As evening bore down, twilight on the treeless mountains gave off a sinister glow. A ruined village came into sight as in a dream. Anti-Japanese slogans painted boldly on rows of houses greeted our conquering army. Suddenly gunshots rained down from the mountain tops and reverberated in the valley.

Immediately the gun forest toppled; the mountain swallowed the bullets as we twisted up its slopes. The festival has started; I think I'll blow on my flute. Good, here's a mask. Hey, dance, let's dance. Going on in this vein, I was abruptly jerked to the ground, and realized that I had still been atop the mule.

*   *   *

After that my memory ceases for awhile. The end of the war found me in a military prison with seventeen years left to serve.

That night, they tell me, I laid my rifle on some straw and set it on fire. My squad leader, who had been keeping an eye on my condition, came at me with a knife, but I warded off the blow with the rifle. The safety was off and my finger accidentally caught in the trigger sent a bullet into his stomach. I was wounded in the shoulder.

The year after the war ended, I awaited the day I could cross the water on a Tenshin freighter. I was boxed into a tiny cell, and my knees came to find sitting preferable to standing. Attached to a sergeant-major in charge of judicial affairs, I was sent to the war criminals reception accommodation in Nankin. Immediately upon arriving with the warden's personal effects in a rucksack, I began forced labor for the Chinese. The newly claimed thirty-eight caliber rifles arrived stacked in trucks every day. Just as they were, they were now to be handed over to their new masters. Like a machine I began my daily job of catching them as they were hurled down.

"Hoi, hoi." Performing the hurried motions in lifeless rhythm I suddenly felt in the palm of my grasping hand a rush of blood. Looking down, I saw my hands had recognized my old E62377 when my eyes had not.

Our long journeys had brought us to this chance meeting.

Upon examination, I saw that all the metal from the butt to the breechblock was rusted out, the grip was dried and cracked. The screw on the butt plate creaked loosely. I wondered what had happened to that woman. Was she embracing her just-returned husband or fading towards death like this rifle? What had happened to her? I whistled as I caught one weapon after another.

Shin Chan, I don't want to be loved. What I want is to give love. So please understand.

The Chinese soldier gave me a look of pure hate and raised his whip.

The Deacon

JOHN UPDIKE

John Updike was born in Shillington, Pennsylvania, in 1932. In addition to books of poetry (including *Telephone Poles and Other Poems*, 1963) and light essays (for example, *Assorted Prose*, 1965), he has written many novels and books of short stories. Notable among them are the novels *Rabbit, Run* (1960), *The Centaur* (National Book Award winner in 1964), *Of the Farm* (1965), *Couples* (1968), *Rabbit Redux* (1971), and *A Month of Sundays* (1977). His short story collections include *The Same Door* (1959), *Pigeon Feathers* (1962), *The Music School* (1966), *Bech: A Book* (1970), and *Museums and Women and Other Stories* (1972). "The Deacon" is taken from *Museums and Women* and originally appeared in *The New Yorker*.

HE PASSES THE PLATE, and counts the money afterward—a large dogged-looking man, wearing metal-framed glasses that seem tight across his face and that bite into the flesh around his eyes. He wears for Sunday morning a clean white shirt, but a glance downward, as you lay on your thin envelope and pass the golden plate back to him, discovers fallen socks and scuffed shoes. And as he with his fellow-deacons strides forward toward the altar, his suit is revealed as the pants of one suit (gray) and the coat of another (brown). He is too much at home here. During the sermon, he stares toward a corner of the nave ceiling, which needs repair, and slowly, reverently, yet unmistakably chews gum. He lingers in the vestibule, with his barking, possessive laugh, when the rest of the congregation has passed into the sunshine and the dry-mouthed minister is fidgeting to be out of his cassock and home to lunch. The deacon's car, a dusty Dodge, is parked outside the parish hall most evenings. He himself wonders why he is there so often, how he slipped into this ceaseless round of men's suppers, of Christian Education Committee meetings, choir rehearsals, emergency sessions of the Board of Finance where hours churn by in irrelevant argument and prayerful silences that produce nothing. "Nothing," he says to his wife on returning, waking her. "The old fool refuses to amortize the debt." He means the treasurer. "His Eminence tells us foreign missions can't be applied to the oil bill even if we make it up in the summer at five per cent interest." He means the minister. "It was on the tip of my tongue to ask whence he derives all his business expertise."

"Why don't you resign?" she asks. "Let the young people get involved before they drop away."

"One more peace-in-Vietnam sermon, they'll drop away anyway." He falls heavily into bed, smelling of chewing gum. As with men who spend nights away from home drinking in bars, he feels guilty, but the motion, the brightness and excitement of the place where he has been continues in him: the varnished old tables, the yellowing Sunday-school charts, the folding chairs and pocked linoleum, the cork bulletin board, the giggles of the children's choir leaving, the strange constant sense of dark sacred space surrounding their lit meeting room like the void upholding a bright planet. "One more blessing on the damn Vietcong," he mumbles, and the young minister's face, white and worriedly sucking a pipestem, skids like a vision of the Devil across his plagued mind. He has a headache. The sides of his nose, the tops of his cheeks, the space above his ears—wherever the frames of his glasses dig—dully hurt. His wife snores, neglected. In less than seven hours, the alarm clock will ring. This must stop. He must turn over a new leaf.

His name is Miles. He is over fifty, an electrical engineer. Every seven years or so, he changes employers and locations. He has been a member of the board of deacons of a prosperous Methodist church in Iowa, a complex of dashing blond brick-and-glass buildings set in acres of parking lot carved from a cornfield; then of a Presbyterian church in San Francisco, gold-rush Gothic clinging to the back of Nob Hill, attended on Sundays by a handful of Chinese businessmen and prostitutes in sunglasses and whiskery, dazed drop-out youths looking for a warm place in which to wind up their Saturday-night trips; then of another Presbyterian church in New York State, a dour granite chapel in a suburb of Schenectady; and most recently, in southeastern Pennsylvania, of a cryptlike Reformed church sunk among clouds of foliage so dense that the lights are kept burning in midday and the cobwebbed balconies swarm all summer with wasps. Though Miles has travelled far, he has never broken out of the loose net of Calvinist denominations that places almost every American within sight of a spire. He wonders why. He was raised in Ohio, in a village that had lost the tang of the frontier but kept its bleak narrowness, and was confirmed in the same colorless, bean-eating creed that millions in his generation have dismissed forever. He was not, as he understood the term, religious. Ceremony bored him. Closing his eyes to pray made him dizzy. He distinctly heard in the devotional service the overamplified tone of voice that in business matters would signal either ignorance or dishonesty. His profession prepared him to believe that our minds, with their crackle of self-importance, are merely collections of electrical circuits. He saw nothing about his body worth resurrecting. God, concretely considered, had a way of merging with that corner of the church ceiling that showed signs of water leakage. That men should be good, he did not doubt, or that social order demands personal sacrifice; but the Heavenly hypothesis, as it had fallen upon his ears these forty years of Sundays, crushes us all to the same level of unworthiness, and redeems us all indiscriminately, elevating especially, these days, the irresponsible—the unemployable, the riotous, the outrageous, the one in one hundred that strays. Neither God nor His ministers displayed love for deacons—indeed, Pharisees were the first objects of their wrath. Why persist, then, in work so thoroughly thankless, begging for pledges, pinching and scraping to save degenerate old buildings, facing rings of Sunday-school faces baked to adamant cynicism by hours of television-watching, attending fruitless meetings where the senile and the frustrated dominate, arguing, yawning, missing sleep, the company of his wife, the small, certain joys of home. Why? He had wanted to offer his children the Christian option, to begin them as citizens as he had begun; but all have left home now, are in college or married, and, as far as he can tactfully gather, are unchurched. So be it. He has done his part.

A new job offer arrives, irresistible, inviting him to New England. In Pennsylvania the Fellowship Society gives him a farewell dinner; his squad of Sunday-school teachers presents him with a pen set; he hands in his laborious financial records, his neat minutes of vague proceedings. He bows his head for the last time in that dark sanctuary smelling of moldering plaster and buzzing with captive wasps. He is free. Their new house is smaller, their new town is white. He does not join a church; he stays home reading the Sunday paper. Wincing, he flicks past religious news. He drives his wife north to admire the turning foliage. His evenings are immense. He reads through Winston Churchill's history of the Second World War; he installs elaborate electrical gadgets around the house, which now and then give his wife a shock. They go to drive-in movies, and sit islanded in a sea of fornication. They go bowling and square dancing, and feel ridiculous, too ponderous and slow. His wife, these years of evenings alone, has developed a time-passing pattern—

television shows spaced with spells of sewing and dozing—
into which he fits awkwardly. She listens to him grunt and
sigh and grope for words. But Sunday mornings are the
worst—blighted times haunted by the giddy swish and roar of
churchward traffic on the road outside. He stands by the
window; the sight of three little girls, in white beribboned
hats, bluebird coats, and dresses of starched organdie, scam-
pering home from Sunday school gives him a pang unholy in
its keenness.

Behind him his wife says, "Why don't you go to church?"

"No, I think I'll wash the Dodge."

"You washed it last Sunday."

"Maybe I should take up golf."

"You want to go to church. Go. It's no sin."

"Not the Methodists. Those bastards in Iowa nearly
worked me to death."

"What's the pretty white one in the middle of town?
Congregational. We've never been Congregationalists;
they'd let you alone."

"Are you sure you wouldn't like to take a drive?"

"I get carsick with all that starting and stopping. To tell
the truth, it would be a relief to have you out of the house."

Already he is pulling off his sweater, to make way for a
clean shirt. He puts on a coat that doesn't match his pants.
"I'll go," he says, "but I'll be damned if I'll join."

He arrives late, and sits staring at the ceiling. It is a
wooden church, and the beams and ceiling boards in drying
out have pulled apart. Above every clear-glass window he
sees the dried-apple-colored stains of leakage. At the door,
the minister, a very young pale man with a round moon face
and a know-it-all pucker to his lips, clasps Miles' hand as if
never to let it go. "We've been looking for you, Miles. We
received a splendid letter about you from your Reformed pastor in Pennsylvania. As you know, since the U.C.C. merger
you don't even need to be reconfirmed. There's a men's supper this Thursday. We'll hope to see you there." Some min-

isters' hands, Miles has noticed, grow fatty under the pressure of being so often shaken, and others dwindle to the bones; this one's, for all his fat face, is mostly bones.

The church as a whole is threadbare and scrawny; it makes no resistance to his helpless infiltration of the Men's Club, the Board of Finance, the Debt Liquidation and Building Maintenance Committee. He and a few shaggy Pilgrim Youth paint the Sunday-school chairs Chinese red. He and one grimy codger and three bottles of beer clean the furnace room of forgotten furniture and pageant props, of warped hymnals and unused programs still tied in the printer's bundles, of the gilded remnants of a dozen abandoned projects. Once he attends a committee meeting to which no one else comes. It is a gusty winter night, a night of cold rain from the sea, freezing on the roads. The minister has been up all night with the family of a suicide and cannot himself attend; he has dropped off the church keys with Miles.

The front door key, no bigger than a car key, seems magically small for so large a building. Is it the only one? Miles makes a mental note: have duplicates made. He turns on a light and waits for the other committee members—a retired banker and two maiden ladies. The furnace is running gamely, but with an audible limp in its stride. It is a coal burner converted to oil twenty years ago. The old cast-iron clinker grates are still heaped in a corner, too heavy to throw out. Should be sold for scrap. Every penny counts. Pinching and scraping. Miles thinks, as upon a mystery, upon the prodigality of heating a huge vacant barn like this with such an inefficient burner. Hot air rises direct from the basement to the ceiling, drying and spreading the wood. Fuel needle half gummed up. Waste. Nothing but waste, salvage and waste. And weariness.

Miles removes his glasses and rubs the chafed spots at the bridge of his nose. He replaces them to look at his watch. His watch has stopped, its small face wet from the storm like an

excited child's. The electric clock in the minister's study has
been unplugged. Bogus thrift. There are books: concor-
dances, daily helps, through the year verse by verse, great
sermons, best sermons, sermon hints, all second-hand, no,
third-hand, worse, hundredth-hand, thousandth-hand, a
coin rubbed blank. The books are leaning on their sides and
half the shelves are empty. Empty. The desk is clean. No
business conducted on it. He tests the minister's fountain
pen and it is dry. Dry as an old snakeskin, dry as a locust husk
that still clings to a tree.

In search of the time, Miles goes into the sanctuary. The
1880 pendulum clock on the choir balustrade still ticks. He
can hear it in the dark, overhead. He switches on the nave
lights. A moment passes before they come on. Some shaky
connection in the toggle, the wiring doubtless rotten
throughout the walls, a wonder it hasn't burnt down. Miles
has never belonged to a wooden church before. Around and
above him, like a stiff white forest, the hewn frame creaks
and groans in conversation with the wind. The high black
windows, lashed as if by handfuls of sand, seem to flinch, yet
do not break, and Miles feels the timbers of this ark, with its
ballast of tattered pews, give and sway with the fierce
weather, yet hold; and this is why he has come, to share the
pride of this ancient thing that will not quite die, to have it
all to himself. Warm air from a grilled duct breathes on his
ankles. Miles can see upward past the clock and the organ to
the corner of the unused gallery where souvenirs of the
church's past—Puritan pew doors, tin footwarmers, velvet
collection bags, Victorian commemorative albums, cracking
portraits of wigged pastors, oval photographs of deceased
deacons, and inexplicable unlabelled ferrotypes of chubby
cross children and picnics past—repose in dusty glass cases
that are in themselves antiques. All this anonymous treasure
Miles possesses by being here, like a Pharaoh hidden with his
life's rich furniture, while the rain like a robber rattles to get
in.

Yes, the deacon sees, it is indeed a preparation for death—an emptiness where many others have been, which is what death will be. It is good to be at home here. Nothing now exists but himself, this shell, and the storm. The windows clatter; the sand has turned to gravel, the rain has turned to sleet. The storm seizes the church by its steeple and shakes, but the walls were built with love, and withstand. The others are very late, they will not be coming; Miles is not displeased, he is serene. He turns out the lights. He locks the door.

A City of Churches

DONALD BARTHELME

Donald Barthelme was born in Philadelphia in 1931, grew up in Houston, and now lives in New York. Many of his numerous short stories first appeared in *The New Yorker* and in such periodicals as *New American Review*, *Paris Review*, *Contact*, and *New World Writing*. Collections of his stories include *Come Back, Dr. Caligari* (1964), *City Life* (1970), and *Sadness* (1972), from which "A City of Churches" is taken. He has also written a short novel, *Snow White* (1967), and a book for children, *The Slightly Irregular Fire Engine* (1971), which won the 1972 National Book Award.

"Yes," MR. PHILLIPS SAID, "ours is a city of churches all right."

Cecelia nodded, following his pointing hand. Both sides of the street were solidly lined with churches, standing shoulder to shoulder in a variety of architectural styles. The Bethel Baptist stood next to the Holy Messiah Free Baptist, St. Paul's Episcopal next to Grace Evangelical Covenant. Then came the First Christian Science, the Church of God, All Souls, Our Lady of Victory, the Society of Friends, the Assembly of God, and the Church of the Holy Apostles. The spires and steeples of the traditional buildings were jammed in next to the broad imaginative flights of the "contemporary" designs.

"Everyone here takes a great interest in church matters,"
Mr. Phillips said.

Will I fit in? Cecelia wondered. She had come to Prester
to open a branch office of a car-rental concern.

"I'm not especially religious," she said to Mr. Phillips,
who was in the real-estate business.

"Not *now,*" he answered. "Not *yet.* But we have many
fine young people here. You'll get integrated into the community soon enough. The immediate problem is, where are
you to live? Most people," he said, "live in the church of
their choice. All of our churches have many extra rooms. I
have a few belfry apartments that I can show you. What
price range were you thinking of?"

They turned a corner and were confronted with more
churches. They passed St. Luke's, the Church of the
Epiphany, All Saints Ukrainian Orthodox, St. Clement's,
Fountain Baptist, Union Congregational, St. Anargyri's,
Temple Emanuel, the First Church of Christ Reformed. The
mouths of all the churches were gaping open. Inside, lights
could be seen dimly.

"I can go up to a hundred and ten," Cecelia said. "Do
you have any buildings here that are *not* churches?"

"None," said Mr. Phillips. "Of course many of our fine
church structures also do double duty as something else." He
indicated a handsome Georgian façade. "That one," he said,
"houses the United Methodist and the Board of Education.
The one next to it, which is Antioch Pentecostal, has the
barbershop."

It was true. A red-and-white striped barber pole was attached inconspicuously to the front of the Antioch Pentecostal.

"Do many people rent cars here?" Cecelia asked. "Or
would they, if there was a handy place to rent them?"

"Oh, I don't know," said Mr. Phillips. "Renting a car
implies that you want to go somewhere. Most people are
pretty content right here. We have a lot of activities. I don't

think I'd pick the car-rental business if I was just starting out in Prester. But you'll do fine." He showed her a small, extremely modern building with a severe brick, steel, and glass front. "That's St. Barnabas. Nice bunch of people over there. Wonderful spaghetti suppers."

Cecelia could see a number of heads looking out of the windows. But when they saw that she was staring at them, the heads disappeared.

"Do you think it's healthy for so many churches to be gathered together in one place?" she asked her guide. "It doesn't seem . . . *balanced,* if you know what I mean."

"We are famous for our churches," Mr. Philllips replied. "They are harmless. Here we are now."

He opened a door and they began climbing many flights of dusty stairs. At the end of the climb they entered a good-sized room, square, with windows on all four sides. There was a bed, a table, and two chairs, lamps, a rug. Four very large bronze bells hung in the exact center of the room.

"What a view!" Mr. Phillips exclaimed. "Come here and look."

"Do they actually ring these bells?" Cecelia asked.

"Three times a day," Mr. Phillips said, smiling. "Morning, noon, and night. Of course when they're rung you have to be pretty quick at getting out of the way. You get hit in the head by one of these babies and that's all she wrote."

"God Almighty," said Cecelia involuntarily. Then she said, "Nobody lives in the belfry apartments. That's why they're empty."

"You think so?" Mr. Phillips said.

"You can only rent them to new people in town," she said accusingly.

"I wouldn't do that," Mr. Phillips said. "It would go against the spirit of Christian fellowship."

"This town is a little creepy, you know that?"

"That may be, but it's not for you to say, is it? I mean,

you're new here. You should walk cautiously, for a while. If you don't want an upper apartment I have a basement over at Central Presbyterian. You'd have to share it. There are two women in there now."

"I don't want to share," Cecelia said. "I want a place of my own."

"Why?" the real-estate man asked curiously. "For what purpose?"

"Purpose?" asked Cecelia. "There is no particular purpose. I just want—"

"That's not usual here. Most people live with other people. Husbands and wives. Sons with their mothers. People have roommates. That's the usual pattern."

"Still, I prefer a place of my own."

"It's very unusual."

"Do you have any such places? Besides bell towers, I mean?"

"I guess there are a few," Mr. Phillips said, with clear reluctance. "I can show you one or two, I suppose."

He paused for a moment.

"It's just that we have different values, maybe, from some of the surrounding communities," he explained. "We've been written up a lot. We had four minutes on the C.B.S. Evening News one time. Three or four years ago. 'A City of Churches,' it was called."

"Yes, a place of my own is essential," Cecelia said, "if I am to survive here."

"That's kind of a funny attitude to take," Mr. Phillips said. "What denomination are you?"

Cecelia was silent. The truth was, she wasn't anything.

"I said, what denomination are you?" Mr. Phillips repeated.

"I can will my dreams," Cecelia said. "I can dream whatever I want. If I want to dream that I'm having a good time, in Paris or some other city, all I have to do is go to sleep and I will dream that dream. I can dream whatever I want."

"What do you dream, then, mostly?" Mr. Phillips said, looking at her closely.

"Mostly sexual things," she said. She was not afraid of him.

"Prester is not that kind of a town," Mr. Phillips said, looking away.

They went back down the stairs.

The doors of the churches were opening, on both sides of the street. Small groups of people came out and stood there, in front of the churches, gazing at Cecelia and Mr. Phillips.

A young man stepped forward and shouted, *"Everyone in this town already has a car! There is no one in this town who doesn't have a car!"*

"Is that true?" Cecelia asked Mr. Phillips.

"Yes," he said. "It's true. No one would rent a car here. Not in a hundred years."

"Then I won't stay," she said. "I'll go somewhere else."

"You must stay," he said. "There is already a car-rental office for you. In Mount Moriah Baptist, on the lobby floor. There is a counter and a telephone and a rack of car keys. And a calendar."

"I won't stay," she said. "Not if there's not any sound business reason for staying."

"We want you," said Mr. Phillips. "We want you standing behind the counter of the car-rental agency, during regular business hours. It will make the town complete."

"I won't," she said. "Not me."

"You must. It's essential."

"I'll dream," she said. "Things you won't like."

"We are discontented," said Mr. Phillips. "Terribly, terribly discontented. Something is wrong."

"I'll dream the Secret," she said. "You'll be sorry."

"We are like other towns, except that we are perfect," he

said. "Our discontent can only be held in check by perfection. We need a car-rental girl. Someone must stand behind the counter."

"I'll dream the life you are most afraid of," Cecelia threatened.

"You are ours," he said, grippng her arm. "Our car-rental girl. Be nice. There is nothing you can do."

"Wait and see," Cecelia said.

Conversation with My Child on the Nazis' Deeds in the Jungle

URS WIDMER

Urs Widmer was born in 1938 in Basel, Switzerland. Although he remains a Swiss citizen, he now lives in Frankfurt am Main in the Federal Republic of Germany. He has published stories, plays, essays, and two novels: *Die Forschungsreise* (1974) and *Die gelben Männer* (1976). "Conversation with My Child on the Nazis' Deeds in the Jungle" is taken from his 1977 collection *Vom Fenster meines Hauses aus* and is translated here by Robert Detweiler.

TODAY WE ARRIVED IN THE JUNGLE. I stand beneath the overhanging roof of our grass hut and look out across our clearing. The sun sets slowly behind ancient trees— mammoth trees, palms, vines. Monkeys scream. Our dog, a white poodle, scampers through the tomato plants that grow in our clearing. I slice a melon and gesture with my juice-smeared hand to my child who comes trotting through the tall grass. The child is wearing a T-shirt emblazoned with "University of Alabama" and has a cap pistol in his hand.

Yellow sulfurous air lay over the city we came from. In

the office building across from our living quarters men paced back and forth with dictaphones in their hands; their hands trembled, they telephoned, and at night they rushed to the air conditioning unit and pressed their mouths against the stream of air until they thought, now we look refreshed and won't be fired.

I used to watch old movies now and then. I stared with moist eyes at the young women who acted in them. They were blond, pale, and incredibly passionate. Today, I imagine, they live in one-room apartments in Los Angeles and have a dog to whom they say, when they let him out on the terrace, "we love each other, don't we, Sam?"

I think that here in the jungle I will grow tomatoes, distill schnapps, build a chimney, construct a xylophone, analyze mushrooms, cook ratatouille, explore the woods, dig a well, set out lime twigs, make love to my wife. The child stands in front of me and watches me. He puts the cap pistol in the holster on his belt and stretches out his hand. I give him a slice of melon. "In Florida," I tell him, "Negroes ride high waves foaming with black spray. The whites sold them their surfboards and now ski in the Himalayas, seven thousand meters up in virgin snow."

"I know," I say, "what death smells like. I shudder when his odor reaches my nose. My grandfather sat down in the bathtub and slit his wrists. He had cancer, and the plague ravages India, where millions are starving." The child watches me. He puts out his hand, and I give him another slice of melon. He bites into it. Juice runs down his chin and onto the T-shirt. I notice that his cap pistol is set on single-shot.

"In San Francisco," I tell him, "a man jumped from a large suspension bridge. The reporters asked him, well, how was death? I was never happier than during the few seconds in the air, the man said. Now they all watch him from the corners of their eyes to see if he'll try it again, but he plants his feet on the asphalt as if he might lose all support at any moment."

"Martin Bormann, namely, stepped out of this very grass hut early one morning three months ago. Monkeys screamed. Martin Bormann sniffed. Such good air, he thought. As of now I shall get up at five o'clock, that is an order. Martin Bormann stood at attention. He paced back and forth, happy, almost young. When his men reported for morning inspection they found a completely transformed chief. He shone. He steamed. He glowed. They looked at him astonished, then at each other. They grinned. They clapped each other on the back with their prostheses. They rushed back to their huts and polished their boots, and the forest echoed with the sound of their marching. Their whips cracked as never before. Life is a hedgehog race, murmured Martin Bormann as he walked through his tomato patch with a sprinkling can and twine.*

But now, he shouted into the forest, I am standing at the end of the rows again. Whoever races there will die of a heart attack. Good times are coming, I feel it, shouted Martin Bormann, child."

"Then, about two months ago, I sailed on a ship. The waves were many meters high and icy. I stood far below deck at the bar of the economy class. I listened to the groaning of the cargo that had torn loose from its fastenings and was crashing

---

*In the Low German tale of the hedgehogs and the hare, the hedgehog challenges the hare (who constantly boasts of his speed) to a race from one end of the field to the other. The hedgehog's mate is hiding at the far end, and when the hare arrives she pops up and says, "I'm already here!" The confused hare keeps racing back and forth, trying to beat what he thinks is a single hedgehog, until he drops dead from exhaustion (translator's note).

against the ship's sides. Do you hear that? I said to my wife. She nodded. She stroked your head. We emptied our glasses. Then the ship listed suddenly. The glasses skidded across the floor. We ran gasping through the corridor to the tilting stairs. Silent people hastened hither and yon. Half-awake heads peered out of cabin doors as if from manhole covers, because of the ship's strange angle. Water foamed down the stairs, and we screamed. I let go of my wife's hand. I was swept through the corridors, and I don't know how I escaped."

"If it were my choice," I said to the child, "I wouldn't be sitting here now in this clearing among the tomatoes. I would rather walk across an endless plateau, under a hat as wide as a wagon wheel, into the setting sun. Old women or men would walk ahead of me, black shadows. Then I would sit with them in front of a hut, we would drink wine and talk sparely and quietly, and I would barely recognize their faces. We would eat together, and no one would get a choicer piece of meat. Sometimes our hands would touch."

"But it wasn't my choice, child. Nonetheless I thought again and again about my dream: that Martin Bormann stepped out of a grass hut into a clearing in the midst of the jungle, and that he looked reborn. My wife and I ran our forefingers for hours over the map of South America until we found a clearing that looked exactly like the one in my dream. We packed our knapsacks feverishly: socks, underpants, candy for you, mosquito spray, a net, a map, an Iron Cross, a photo of Martin Bormann. We went to the train station dressed in boots and spurs. It turned into a long journey, especially because of the last stage that we covered clinging to a piece of the railing. Cold and shivering we climbed up a sea wall of Santa Cruz harbor in Argentina. We sat down on a coil of rope and looked out over the ocean. A customs official approached us. He leafed through our passports and compared our real ears to those on the photos. He shifted the net back and forth in his hands uncertainly. *Porchè utilizar usted esto filho*, he said, or something like that. I wanted to tell him that I intended to capture Martin Bormann with it, but then I saw that he had discovered the Iron Cross in my knapsack. His eyes lit up. He offered me his hand and laughed. I laughed too. Then we went through the harbor installation, among rolls of cable and trucks. I studied the map. Jungle, jungle, jungle everywhere. There was the clearing. It had to be."

"You know," I said to the child, wiping the melon juice from his chin, "I would never travel alone through the jungle. I do not wish to smash any mandolins nor decorate any towels with the banners of my madness. I do not wish to annihilate the will of others with a thunderous shout. Oh," I said to the child staring at me, "I like to yell. I would like to juggle seven balls. I love the gentle sighs of women and the invited guests clapping their hands. I would like to walk a high wire sometime across Niagara Falls, child. I would look down into the teeming spray, up into the blue sky, ahead to the silent people standing on the rocky banks. I might take you along. I would spring up and down on the wire, harder and harder, my feet would get wet below and my head would disappear above in the clouds. With luck we could grasp the feet of a crane sweeping by. A light plane would also do, one with a lot of gas, so that we wouldn't have to land right away in Houston, Texas or Cleveland, Ohio. Because a two hundred pound man in uniform is waiting there. He wears a gray-blue shirt, moves slowly, and chews with a jutting jaw. Hello, he says; identification. He toys with his revolver as he reads my passport page by page. When he reaches the page with the photo he turns the passport around. He spits out the chewing gum. His lips move. I hold you in my arms, child, because you don't yet have your own passport. Your child? says the official. Yes, I say. Writer? he says. Yes, I say. That must be, the official says, a fascinating but also lonely trade, right, sir?"

"Every morning for thirty-one years Martin Bormann walked in his tomato patch, until a month ago. He stood there erect and looked over the clearing that he and his men had freed of trees. The sun burned. Martin Bormann removed his straw hat and wiped the sweat from his forehead. He looked up at the sky repeatedly, daily, until he saw a little black cloud, very high, scudding past. He had dreamed about it. He trembled. He had never been able to stand the sight of ashes. Sighing, he put his hat back on and petted his dog. Perhaps sometime later you'll look up to the sky, he said softly to him, and then you'll see two black clouds travelling from horizon to horizon, the ashes of my friend and me in our orbit."

"Day after day we fought our way through the jungle: you, my wife and I. We slashed paths through the vines with machetes, we ate mushrooms and drank coconut milk and sucked out each other's snakebite wounds. I was unshaven and stank, my wife had a red face and tangled hair, and you were full of mosquito bites. Finally we collapsed exhausted at a little pond. We've lost our way; we'll die here, I whispered; we can't go on. My wife nodded. Then we stared glassy-eyed straight ahead, hand in hand. Suddenly we jumped up as if on command. Very clearly we heard the singing of male voices, and we recognized the song. I grasped my wife by the arm. That's him, I whispered. We sneaked Indian file through the ferns on tiptoe and fingertips, so that we would leave no trail."

"In Nagasaki, namely," I say, as the child and I watch the dog chase a monkey through the tomatoes, "in Nagasaki on that day a man travelled two hundred miles north on business. He heard about it up there. His wife, his child, his father, his mother, his sister, his friends: dead. He had photos of none of them. The photos had melted. The man from Nagasaki forgot what his wife and children looked like. He could not remember their voices. He tried to for hours at a time. Only now and then, like a bolt of lightning, he heard them: clearly, close by, and vivid. That is all true."

The child looks at me. "Another slice of melon," he says, and points the cap gun at the dog standing under a palm tree and barking. "No," I say. I see how the child's face muscles start to twitch. "In Japan," I say quickly, "Japanese are already being built who no longer have their cameras swaying in front of their bellies. They have them built in. When they wink an eye a picture is snapped. Each night they pull the exposed film from their assholes and review the day."

"Or shall we hike down a long, narrow serpentine path someday, high above the settled areas—you, your mother, and I? In an earlier age, when our fathers returned from Spain, they were thrown in jail. They had lost. Up there in the mountains, we'll assume, the fascists are powerless; we can't imagine that the mountain dwellers heed their slogans. They are stubborn, but they have a good instinct for false frills. They cut off their sons' tails if they catch them with Mother in the hay, but they don't care for law and order and uniforms at all. The peasants in the highest mountain village will notice at once that in spite of our hiking shoes and violin cases we're no travelling orchestra. An old jeep will drive us down to the train station. We arrive at a meeting point not far from the place where the leader of the last regime was hanged. We don't want to hang anyone; we don't want to be hanged; we want to stay together. We'll take a picture of ourselves. We will recall the many stories of final partings. The lovers never saw each other again. We will think: someday, suddenly, they will be stories no more. We will see each other for the first time, as never before."

"But in reality, my child, we lay among the fern growth at the edge of the clearing. Flies buzzed around our heads. I parted the weeds and saw Martin Bormann's men marching away in double columns, in ragged polished boots and with wooden truncheons on their shoulders. They thrust their legs straight ahead as they went and jerked their heads around as they passed Martin Bormann. He stood on a box. Look at that man there, you yelled. I held my hand over your mouth and hissed, you'll get an electric train if you keep your mouth shut just this once. I freed my net from the knapsack. The jungle was completely still. I saw how Martin Bormann, along with a dog, went to a tomato bed. He remained standing, removed the straw hat from his head, looked up at the sky a long time, sighed and drew his hand across his forehead. The dog also looked up. I cast the net. I yanked it tight. The three of us pulled the squirming bundle toward us in the fern bushes, and then Martin Bormann lay before us, along with his dog and a few tomatoes. He groaned. Not a sound, I hissed in German, or you'll get it. Martin Bormann and his dog stared at us slack-jawed."

"We walked for hours across sun-baked plains, among cactuses and boulders under which snakes vanished. I went first, then Martin Bormann followed attached to a rope, next his dog on a leash, then my wife, then you with your cap pistol, the safety released. Cawing birds circled above us. We perspired. I fumbled the canteen loose from my belt, took a drink and gave it to Martin Bormann. He drank and stuck it in the dog's mouth. The dog drank like crazy.

'How are things in Europe now?' Martin Bormann said abruptly.

'Nothing is like it was in your day,' I said.

'Hm,' said Martin Bormann. 'Isn't there anyone who thinks the way we think?'

'By no means,' I said. 'You're the last of those.'

Martin Bormann was silent. He slowly took the canteen out of the dog's mouth. He screwed it shut and gave it to me. He looked old, sweaty, and sad.

'What will you do with me?' he said softly.

'I'm taking you to Germany,' I said.

Martin Bormann sighed. He looked up at the sky. Then he knelt and scratched his dog behind the ears.

'Didn't I tell you,' he said."

"We travelled in the hold of a ship that was carrying rum. It was pitch dark. The air was thick. So that we would have no fear of each other we held hands and sang songs, first mine and then Martin Bormann's. We drank. We embraced. Then I heard that you were no longer singing, then my wife stopped singing, and then the dog was silent. As Martin Bormann collapsed and slid out of my arms I took a last swallow and lay down on the planks of the tossing ship.

When I awoke the ship was no longer rocking, and light fell on us from an open porthole. Martin Bormann lay beside me, snoring open-mouthed. I arose. My head was throbbing. 'Get up!' I yelled. Martin Bormann sprang erect and pressed his hands against his trouser seams. My wife, you and the dog opened your eyes astonished. I looked at the lot of you: Martin Bormann had an unruly beard, a torn shirt, red eyes. My wife had lost her shoes, her hair looked like chicken wire, and her face was smeared. You were covered with rum from head to toe. The dog was black. In this condition we entered the closest police station: first me, then Martin Bormann on the end of the rope, then the dog on the leash, then my wife, and finally you with your weapon. The official on duty stared at us. 'Yes?' he said.

'I have captured Martin Bormann,' I said.

'Who?' said the official and looked back and forth between me and Martin Bormann.

'Martin Bormann,' I said.

'Bormann, Martin,' the official said and leafed in a fat book. He looked at me. 'Not here. Identification.'

I gave him my passport. He paged in it, looked at the picture, then at me. Then he paged in the book again. 'We haven't got your name either,' he said. He looked at us, at the rope between us, at the dog. He took down my personal data and threw the paper behind him on a table where an official in a green shirt sat facing the screen of a computerized tracer. The two of them exchanged glances. The the official shrugged his shoulders and returned my passport to me.

'I . . .,' I said.

'That doesn't interest us,' said the official. 'This one time I'll let it pass, young man. Just leave quietly with your friend and don't ever show your face here again.'

'But . . .,' I said.

'And I mean today,' said the official, sitting up straight. I nodded and left through the door of the police station with Martin Bormann at the end of the rope and holding the dog on the leash. I heard you emptying the magazine of your cap pistol behind us. Outside the sun shone. We stood on the sidewalk and looked at the high-rises, the cars, the pizza parlors.

'So that's how it looks nowadays,' said Martin Bormann and scratched his head.

'Yes,' I said as I loosened the rope. 'Well then. Take care.'

I beckoned to my wife and to you. We left, walking past a self-service gas station. You reloaded your cap pistol. After a time I turned around and saw Martin Bormann standing with his dog in front of the police station. He scratched his head and looked up at the sky. At last he trotted off in the opposite direction."

"When we arrived home a man was waiting at our door.

'I'm from the immigration service,' he said, and in a flash turned up his collar. 'Can I have a look at your passport?'

'Certainly,' I said. I opened the door to the house, nodded to him and followed him into the house. A thick cloud of dust hung in the hallway. I gave the official my passport.

'So you're a foreigner,' he said, and watched me.

'Yes,' I said.

'And why do you fool with the internal affairs of the Federal Republic of Germany?' he said.

'I?' I said. 'Do I do that?'

'Indeed you do,' he said, and extracted a file from his briefcase.

'I have your dossier here. You have four tickets for illegal parking. You know a teacher who belongs to the German Communist Party. Once you ate at a Portuguese restaurant. Sometimes you stay in bed until nine a.m.'

'Excuse me,' I said. 'I meant no harm.'

'All right,' he said. 'Forget it. But under these circumstances I cannot, of course, grant you an extension to stay in the country. You'll certainly understand that.'"

"As we were packing our bags at two in the morning the doorbell rang. It was Martin Bormann. He had washed and gone to a barber. He wore gray flannel pants, a white shirt, a dark-blue tie with a coat of arms, and a blue blazer. The dog was clean as a whistle—a poodle.

'Excuse me,' he said, sitting down and crossing his legs, 'for bothering you at this late hour.'

'It doesn't matter in the least,' I said and smiled.

'I've found someone to take care of me,' he said. 'I'm going to live in the Black Forest.'

'How nice,' I said.

'And now I have a favor to ask,' he said. 'Couldn't you take care of the dog? I'd like to get myself a bigger one again.'

'Well, actually,' I said, 'I'm leaving tomorrow anyhow.'
'Oh really?' said Martin Bormann. 'Don't you like it here
with us?'
  I kept silent. We looked at each other.
  'Well then,' said Martin Bormann, and got up. He
stretched out his hand. I placed mine into his, and he shook
it. Then he went out the door. I heard his heavy footsteps as
he went down the stairs. I stood there rigid; then I gave the
suitcase a kick. I went over to the dog and scratched him a
little behind the ears."

  "It wasn't especially nice there where we were living anyhow," I said then to the child as we head hand in hand to our
grass hut where my wife stands in the doorway wearing a red
apron and holding a steaming pot. "The yellow sulfur fumes
in the air. The arsenic in the drinking water. The strontium
90 in the pool where you and your playmates swam. Recently
someone forgot that an old people's home was standing in an
apricot plantation where bark beetles were to be destroyed.
The old folks, who are now all blind, watched with interest
as the airplane flew over them spraying a fine blue rain."
  The child stands still and looks at me. "You promised me
an electric train," he says. He aims his pistol at me and his
face muscles twitch.
  "I know," I say. "I can't always do what I want." The
child starts to cry. I bend down to him and caress him.
"We'll clear the jungle together," I say. "We'll distill
schnapps and build a chimney and construct a xylophone
and put on a new roof and dig a well and set out lime twigs
and make love to my wife, that is to say to your mother."
  The child looks at me with reddened eyes. He swallows,
then he murmurs, "I want to become a general, or a pastor."
  "What?" I say.
  "Then I would have a great responsibility," the child
says. "I could set off an atomic blast, or, if I were pastor, I

could pass unhindered through a hail of bullets and free the poor hostages."

I nod. "Of course you can become a general or pastor," I say. We enter the grass hut and sit down at the table on which a steaming corn mush is standing. The child lays the cap pistol beside his plate. We eat in silence, not having said grace.

The Suitor

LARRY WOIWODE

Larry Woiwode was born in Sykeston, North Dakota, in 1941. He is the author of two novels, *What I'm Going to Do, I Think* (1969) and *Beyond the Bedroom Wall* (1975), and recently a book of poems, *Even Tide*. His fiction has achieved both critical and popular success in the United States and also in Europe. Chapters of his novels, particularly of *Beyond the Bedroom Wall*, have often appeared earlier (though in substantially different form) as short stories in a number of magazines. "The Suitor" appeared first in *McCall's* (January 1970), was reprinted in *The Best American Short Stories* (1971), and served as the basis for the chapter called "New Year" in *Beyond the Bedroom Wall*.

HE DREAMED HE'D BEEN SLEEPING in the catacombs, those cold tombs he'd heard of only from nuns' lips. The shuffling of a pair of slippers traced a series of paths and passageways through his sleep, the sound of a dropped object struck deep into his dream, and somebody in the kitchen (who?) whispering to somebody else in an insistent tone, rapidly, rapidly, like rain, had washed out a great cave, the hollow where he now lay. Moving toward the border of wakefulness, he became aware of the cold, a numbness in his nose, ears, and fingertips, and then conscious that his body was constricted, encased in something unnatural. And then he remembered that he was still fully dressed.

There was a sound of coals being shaken down at a cookstove. He opened his eyes and saw a pattern of cracks, intricate as a web, in the leather back of the horsehair sofa. January 1, 1939, registered in his mind. He closed his eyes. That date could mark the beginning, not just of a new year, but of a new life. Oh, let it. He sighed and covered his head with the quilt. Until he knew Alpha was up and had come downstairs, he didn't want the Jensens to know he was awake. He'd never faced both her parents at the same time, alone, without Alpha present, and the prospect of that made him more uneasy than ever. The night before, sitting in front of the Jensens' fireplace, he had asked Alpha to be his wife. Now he lay in the front room of their house, her house, the house where she, at this moment, was deep asleep. A smile of pleasure appeared on his face.

Time and the elements themselves, as though they knew of his purpose, made the setting of the proposal a perfect one. First, the New Year. Then, the weather. When he had left home after lunch yesterday, the sky was clear, pale blue against the white line of the plain, and the air was still and brilliant, but soon small flakes started falling, a wind hit, and by the time he pulled into the Jensens' drive, a distance of just five miles, the white stuff was up to the axle hubs of his Model A.

The blizzard blew the rest of the afternoon, wrapping the house in blackness, and the windmill clattered and shrieked in the distance, because no one could go shut it off, for fear of getting lost. Kerosene lamps were lit, rags stuffed around doors, logs brought in from the back porch, along with two lumps of coal, precious coal, and blankets were hung over all the windows.

Except for telling God, in variations of His name, what He was doing to the livestock with the storm, Alpha's father maintained a strange silence. It was her mother finally spoke the holy words; when there was no letup in the storm and it became obvious that he, the suitor, would have to spend the night, her mother, who was at the cookstove making supper, sighed, shrugged her shoulders, and without turning to him, said, "The couch will be yours," and Alpha, who was behind her mother, turned and winked at him.

Then the fire. In front of it on the hooked rug, their faces fevered with its heat. Popcorn and divinity in bowls between them. Their fingertips touching. The whine of the blizzard outside and the feeling it brought—that they were privileged beings, spared and put down on an island in the sea of it. Alone. On the O of the hooked rug. An oasis. The O of love, with them in its center. Lowering their voices when her parents, with several good-nights and a great deal of commotion, went into the bedroom. A long silence as they stared at the fire, and then the question, alive in him for two years, rising of its own accord.

"If you ever asked," she whispered, "I knew it would be tonight."

"How?"

"I knew."

"I've been afraid," he said.

"I know. *I've* been afraid."

"Of what?"

"Me. You." A glance toward her parents' bedroom. "What makes a man afraid?"

"I don't know. Everything. What you?"

"I'm not, really, now that you asked."

"Then will—" It was impossible for him to repeat it. The wind rose, and the flame swayed toward the left.

"Yes," she whispered.

Or did he imagine it? At that moment, her mother, wrapped in a robe, appeared in the doorway, saying, "Alpha, it's past time you were in bed." Then, "Here"—holding out bedclothes at arm's length, so he had to rise, go to her, and since she kept a firm grip on a quilt, look level into her eyes as she said, "*This* is to keep you warm."

Alpha's footsteps retreating up the stairs while her mother ignoring his offers to help, saying, "Shoo! Shoo!" in a strange tone—was she being playful?—piled more logs on the fire and then stood with her back to the flames, facing him, her palms open at her sides to catch the heat. He couldn't see, from the couch, the expression of her face or know whether or not she had heard. "I sleep light," she said, and turned and left the room.

The floorboards groaned and creaked above him, and he tried to visualize Alpha upstairs, and when he did, so vividly, he realized it was a sin, and then tried not to. He said three Hail Marys. He said an Our Father. Out of habit, his boyhood bedtime prayers went through his head. He discovered that there were five buttons on his shirt, and pausing at each button, gripping it tight, he ran his fingers down his shirtfront—five Hail Marys—then ran them up it—a decade of the rosary—and touched his Adam's apple for an Our Father.

What did she do so long, moving around up there, before she went to bed? Then there was a sound of springs as she settled into bed, and that was worse. He lost track of the times he'd touched his Adam's apple and rolled on his side in agony and said an Act of Contrition.

Had she said yes, or was it the wind and fire? Her hand said yes, the angle of her head, bowed so that her dark hair concealed her features, showing only her high brow bronzed by fire; the fold of her legs beneath her dress, her bare feet, her tipped shoes lying beside them—all this said, *Yes, Yes,* but did she?

Yes.

Alpha Sommerfeld. Alpha and Martin Sommerfeld. The names belonged together. But if it were so, if she said yes, then it would be hard for them from this day on. The families lived on neighboring farms, but neither parents had ever

been in the others' house, and that was not common in this
part of the country, not a good sign.

His mother going to the mailbox, over three years ago, and
seeing a stranger walking down the railroad tracks and then
coming back into the house and describing him—"so little I
thought it was a kid at first, and also because he wasn't
wearing a hat, not even a cap, mind you, but his hair was
gray on the sides, all mussed up like a madman's, flying in
the wind, and his eyes were wild, and he was making a
beeline for town like there was a train behind him!"—and
wondering who it could be, a bum, or somebody she should
know about?

"O, that's Ed Jensen," his father told her. "He just
moved in at the old Hollingsworth place."

That same night, the household woke to the sound of
someone singing and shouting obscene songs, and they
looked out to see a figure weaving down the tracks in the
moonlight; Ed Jensen on his way home.

Why did his mother have to be so pious and straitlaced
and use her religion to measure everybody else? Why did she
have to be that way? They were all adults; some of the songs
were amusing. After a few weekends of the same kind of
singing, she started calling Alpha's father "the Jensen devil"
or "that insane atheist down the road," and she demanded
that the men of the house, her son or her husband, one of
them, go tell that drunk to use the roads like everybody else.
He and his father going to the tracks and intercepting the
man with the wild hair and wild blue eyes.

"I haven't got a car," Jensen said to them, "and I'll be
damned if I'll waste the wear and tear on a good team just to
go into town to get boozed, and that's where I'm bound.
These tracks are the straightest shot I know from those two
sections of quack grass back there, which some piker pawned
off on me as a farm, to the front door of the closest gin mill.
And after farming quack grass for a week straight with no

help, no sons, I don't mind saying I like a snort or two. For
the nerves. What do you folks do about quack grass? I've
never seen it grow so thick. I beat it with a hoe, I keep the
wife and daughter after it, I pull it up by hand—roots, run-
ners, and all—and I even burn the stuff. That's right, you
laugh, but I do, by Christ, I burn a hayrack of it every day,
and the next morning it's up thick as ever, choking my
wheat."

The Hollingsworth place was one of the last pieces of
land in the area to see the plow, they told him; the sod was
turned under just ten years ago, and only two or three crops
were put in before the Depression.

"So that's it. It'll take me five years, then, or more,
before all the buried stuff comes up where I can kill it.
Damn! Well, I'll just keep at it till I win. It's part of my fault
I got took on the land. I left my old place for this Hollingsworth one because of the barn. Have you ever been in
it? It's a beauty! It's built better than a brick— Well, it's the
best barn I've seen in my life, and I've always said that if a
man can't sleep in his own barn, it's not a fit place for any
kind of livestock. We make use of the poor beasts their
whole lives, we beat them—I do we make money off them,
we don't let them run wild the way they did, so the least we
can do is not lock them up inside some drafty, stinking,
dirt-floored, jerrybuilt shack that's never warm and you can't
ever keep clean, isn't it?" They nodded.

The three of them talking a long time—rather, Jensen talking while the two of them, silent by nature, listened, blinking at the outpour, until they heard from the house: "Alfred!
Martin! *Dinner!* Alfred!" Jensen saying good-bye, saying he
hoped to see them soon, shaking their hands, and then the
two of them going in to dinner, where his father said,
"There's nothing the matter with that man. I like him and
he can walk where he wants."

So his mother quoted back at his father one of his father's

favorite maxims: "You are judged not by who you are or what you are but by the company you keep," and from that time on, his father, though trying not to be unkind about it, shied away from Ed Jensen.

And Jensen sensed it from the first; nevertheless, he was always friendly to him—the neighbor boy, the suitor, "the big hulk," as Jensen called him—or was almost always friendly, anyway. Alpha's mother never was. All her mother ever said to him, it seemed, was hello and good-bye, and if he was in the same room with her, she managed to keep her back to him most of the time.

And when he finally finished college, working his way for five years, and took a job with the state, an accomplishment he thought would soften her mother, her mother instead became even more aloof and ironic. "It's the *educated* one," she would call to Alpha, and walk out of the room.

Then, learning later, from Alpha, that her mother had been brought up a Missouri Synod Lutheran and could not believe that any Catholic was worth a grain of salt. Lord in heaven, angels and saints, pray for us all.

He listened for footsteps upstairs. Nothing. Silence.

Alpha's father liked him, though, or at least seemed to. Yes, liked him. Every time the Model A came into the yard, her father rushed out, so exuberant it was like a welcoming party in one, and was garrulous and personal, calling him "Martin" and "boy," clapping him on the shoulder—ha!—and speaking to him as an equal about Roosevelt and Landon, the repeal of Prohibition, horses (Jensen's passion) as opposed to mechanized farming, and, with a sly wink, subjects that caused the college graduate to blush.

Inside the house, however, Alpha's father was often as silent as his own father, remote and morose, and responded only with a nod, or else turned away to the radio. Why? So outspoken most of the time, on any topic, around anyone, even his daughter and wife, and then this silence in the house; why? The walls around him? The furniture—none of which, massive as it was, looked capable of containing the energy of his wiry body? Why no words?

Even Alpha couldn't explain. She knew very little of her father's past life, was uncertain about his behavior and person—"I don't know if he's mean. I don't know if he's kind"—and spoke to him as though he were an enigma to respect and beware of.

Then there had been the incidents. Two summers ago, in June, driving to the Jensens' and taking Alpha to a baseball game (five to three: home team lost) and on the way home, Alpha asking him to stop the noise of the car so they could talk. Pulling off the road, close to some tall weeds, and killing the engine. "What is it, Alpha?"

She leaned her head on his chest and didn't talk. He settled in the seat and put his arm over her shoulder. It was starting to turn dark, and a dove was mourning in the distance—yes, a dove, its three notes, the first two to proclaim the two of them together, You and You, the last one stretched out and desolate it was like the plain around them, an *Oooo* that moved in a downward curve, solitary and final as a falling star. Heart, heart, does it have to end there? No. Yes. No. Holy Mary, sanctuary of—Fingertips under her chin, lifting her face close, her pupils were enlarged and her eyes dark, and then, for the first time, kissing her on the lips.

Something hit the windshield, and they jumped back. Thirty feet away, high above them on the railway embankment, stood Alpha's father. The old man let some pebbles fall out of his fingers, put his fists on his hips, and stared at them for a long time. Finally, in humor or disgust—who could know?—Jensen turned away and kept on walking down the tracks toward town.

Alpha was terrified, in tears, and she held him by the arm all the way to her place, making him promise to stop by the next day to help her explain, to protect her if need be, to stand by her no matter what happened. Going to the Jensens' the next day, pale and afraid, and seeing the look of wonder on Alpha's face; nothing had happened.

The two of them lived in fear for a long time, thinking it would come out after one of Jensen's return trips from the tavern, but it never did. Apparently, Jensen told no one, not even his wife—certainly not his wife. Nothing ever came of it.

Unless that incident explained the other. Once, when Martin came for Alpha, Jensen was talking to a neighbor, Ray Peterson, in the front room, so he waited for Alpha in the kitchen, standing in the door next to the cookstove. Alpha's mother was at the kitchen table in her familiar attitude, her back to him, wetting her fingers and paging through the new Sears, Roebuck catalogue.

Suddenly he caught a phrase of conversation from the front room—"those damn mackerel snappers"—in Peterson's voice, he thought, and he started to cough and clear his throat, to let them know he was inside the house.

Then the voice of Alpha's father was saying, "Show me a Catholic and I'll show you a hypocrite. They're the most lying, sanctimonious band of—" Were they drinking? Or drunk? He coughed and tried to make more noise, but there was a deliberate rise of volume in Jensen's voice: "They could maim or kill a man and call it okay, because they're the chosen, and there's no way around it. They know how to pray right, you see, and we don't. They use the *beads*. Then they got those little stalls where—"

Alpha's mother rose and went into the front room, to put a stop to it, he thought, but her footsteps carried through to the bedroom. "Like rabbits, the way they breed. You wonder when they got time to go to church! The daughter here is going with one, you know. Oh, he's all right by me, a fine boy, but someday if she doesn't watch it, I say"—more volume and a change in tone, as though he'd lifted his head toward the bedroom—"I say, 'Alpha! One of these days you're going to have a dozen kids running around in the same room, none of them over the age of ten, and the whole bunch swinging those beads like lassos. Whoop-ee, Ma! Whoooo-PEE!' "

On weak legs, he made it through the door, out the back porch, and into the fresh air. No doubt about it; Jensen had to be drunk. He went to the pump and wet his head and wiped his face and wrists with his handkerchief, then got into the car and waited for Alpha. When she finally came out, her face was flushed, her eyes cast down, and she was silent most of the afternoon, wadding and squeezing a kerchief in her lap, and later in the day, when he tried to bring up the subject, she said, "No. Don't. He didn't mean it. He's bitter because he has no sons."

That was more than a year ago, and neither of them had ever mentioned it since . . .

There was a sound of logs rumbling into the woodbox, and Martin rose out of the luxury of half-sleep, aware now of the morning coldness in the marrow of his bones, and a filmy sensation over his skin from sleeping in his clothes. He heard more whispering in the kitchen, a bang of the back door, and the sound of water starting to boil, the wet bottom of the kettle stuttering on the stove top. He strained to hear Alpha, but the floorboards above him were silent, the bedsprings were too. The back door opened, it closed, and footsteps started across the kitchen, cold snow screaking underneath them on the linoleum.

("Ed!") A piercing whisper.

("Yes?") *He* could whisper?

("What do you think you're *doing?*")

("Taking this in there.")

("No you're not.")

("He should be up by now.")

('I mean, not like that, not with those snowy boots.")

"Oh, that," he said coming out of the whisper. "It's clean snow. To hell with it."

The footsteps proceeded into the front room, passing so close Martin could smell the cold of outdoors on foreign clothes, and then logs tumbled onto the hearth. There was a squeak of rubber, the crack of a knee joint, and some grunts and muttered curses as the wood was put in place.

Martin waited through a long silence, expecting the fire to start, anticipating its warmth, and then sensed Jensen's eyes on him.

"Hey, boy, aren't you up yet?"

Martin uncovered his head. "Yes."

Jensen stood in front of the fireplace in a sheepskin coat and fur cap, and when he saw Martin was awake, he started stomping his felt-booted feet as though dancing and slapping together his leather mittens. It was so cold in the room Martin could see his own breath. Wasn't he going to make a fire? Couldn't they afford one in here until night? Alpha must be freezing.

"Well!" Jensen said. "I finally got that windmill shut off before it rattled its damn brains out. The wind let up at four, and I ran out then. It's a good thing you're going into business and not farming, is all I can say. Do you know what time it is? It's almost eight o'clock."

"Oh."

"You're damn tootin'! And it's twenty below out."

"Oh."

" 'Oh, oh.' Didn't you hear what I said?"

"Yes. I mean—*what's* that you said?"

"It's almost eight."

"Oh." So? He was baffled by this cheerful small talk from Jensen, here in the house, and then the old man moved closer, a scowl on his face, his black eyelashes fringed with big beads of ice that had begun to melt, his eyes questioning and fierce, and Martin, shivering at how cold it must be, was sure that something must be wrong.

"You're positive you're awake?" Jensen asked.

"Yes."

"Then you better get up and give me a hand."

"The stock?" Martin asked, and pushed off the quilt and sat.

"Stock, hell! That's done hours ago. We have to get your car out of the snow."

"Oh," Martin said. "Oh, my car." Puzzled by this, by Jensen's attitude, in a daze, Martin reached for a shoe with his curled toes, pulled it close, slipped his stockinged foot into its cold sheath, and bent to lace it. Ooooo. His bladder felt big as a pumpkin.

"Model A's!" Jensen exclaimed. "I tried cranking the son of a—"

"Ed!" From the kitchen. "Watch that tongue."

"I tried cranking it for a half-hour and couldn't even make it go poot. How do you adjust your spark?"

"A quarter down."

"No wonder!"

Then Martin felt weak and started trembling, and it wasn't from his physical condition or the cold. The Jensens were turning him out, on purpose, before he had a chance to see Alpha. He finished tying his shoes and looked up into Jensen's excited eyes, and tried to find calm and straightforward words to tell of the proposal. But had she said yes?

"Come on, come on, boy, what is it?" Jensen said, and clapped his mittens close to Martin's head. "I've never seen a man move so slow in my life!"

"I wanted—" Martin lowered his eyes.

"Are you sure you're still not asleep?"

"No."

"Then let's get going!"

Reluctant, Martin rose from the couch and followed the old man into the kitchen, where Alpha's mother was waiting. Her large gray eyes, usually as vague and glazed as those of a convalescent, were bright and understanding, Martin noticed. She gave him a brisk nod, and said, "Good morning. Sorry you can't have breakfast."

So that was it; she had heard him propose.

She took his overcoat from the shelf of the cookstove, shook it hard, and held it out for him by the shoulders. He looked at her, feeling his lips tremble, then at Jensen, a master study of impatience, then at the coat, then at her newly bright eyes. Please, God, couldn't Alpha appear now?

"Come on, come on," said Jensen, "you're acting like a sheep! Let's get a move on."

Martin turned, holding his hands out behind him, and the overcoat, its sleeves heated from the stove, slipped up his arms. He pulled it in place and buttoned it, and its warmth drew the chill from his bones. He turned to Alpha's mother. "Thank you," he murmured. "I—"

"No need for thanks." She handed him his cap. "And no time. Good-bye."

Martin tugged the cap over his ears, stalling for time, and was about to speak when the old man, muttering something, grabbed him by the elbow, opened the door, pulled him onto the porch, and kicked the kitchen door shut. The windows and door of the porch were covered with tar paper, and it was nearly dark as night inside it.

"My overshoes," Martin said.

"Right there, beside the separator. Better get them on and hurry it up."

The rubber overshoes were frozen stiff, difficult to bend, and they were icy against his ankles and shins. Oh, if he had to bend once more—His fingertip froze to a buckle. He jerked it loose, leaving a strip of skin, and felt anger and humiliation start rising in him. He took his gloves out of his pocket and drew them on while the old man clucked his tongue, and said, "What's the matter with you? You know you should have had those on first."

He finished buckling his overshoes and rose, standing tall above Jensen, and decided now was the time to speak; but the old man swung open the outside door, and it was as if two sharp objects, icicles, had been driven home above the tops of Martin's eyes, and his lids pinched shut against the brilliance of the snow. When he'd finished blinking and his vision adjusted, he saw his car standing in a drift that came up to the running board. A team of black Percherons, nodding against the traces, blowing frosty plumes from their nostrils, their broad backs steaming, was hitched up to the car's front bumper.

"I know it looks bad here," Jensen said, and took hold of his arm, leading him down the steps, dragging him through drifts, "but I've walked up to the main road, and it's already been traveled, so there won't be any trouble once we get there, or if there is, I'll pull you all the way in. Right there is the team that can do just that!" Jensen turned to him and gave a grin of pride, but it fell away, and his expression changed to consternation. "Damn it to hell," he said. "A tie. Do you need one?"

"Tie?"

Jensen stepped back a step, and his eyes narrowed, but not from snow glare. "What's the matter with you this morning, boy? Aren't you well, or didn't you sleep all last night, or what? I'm not up on all your rigamarole, but today is Sunday, for Christ's sake, *Sunday*, and I do know you've got to get to church. Now, do you need to borrow a tie or not?"

"Oh, no. No tie. I—"

"The wife, she was a regular churchgoer once, you know, so she's been on my tail for an hour to get you there. I guess she wants to keep you pure, now that you've proposed to the daughter. You don't have to look that way. It's all right. I know about it, and I'm proud to say I was the first to know. The daughter—she finally gave out, or I suppose she'd be here helping us, that's how she is—she was so excited she couldn't sleep the whole night, so she came downstairs about five, right after I got the gag on that windmill, and told me the news, and I want you to know that both of us, the wife and I both, realize you've got a fine mind and body and everything will work out for the best. But do you want to know something?"

Martin felt that if he spoke, it would come out in a howl.

"Hold on, now," Jensen said. "Keep a hold of yourself. I'll tell you. With all the churchgoing and hymning and whatnot the wife has had—this is on her—and the praying for my soul and for this and for that—with all that, guess what? She forgot it was Sunday. *I* was the one that remembered. Now, what do you think of that?"

Jensen nudged Martin, winked an ice-fringed eye, and said, "You think I might be Christian?"

Lazarus

LAWRENCE DORR

Lawrence Dorr is the pseudonym of a native Hungarian born in Budapest and now living in the United States. Following World War II, in which he served on the Eastern Front, and political exile from Hungary, the multi-lingual Dorr eventually made his way to Florida, where he lives and works as an editor and free-lance writer. Dorr has composed fiction in Hungarian, French, and German as well as in English. His collection of stories *A Slow, Soft River* was published in 1973. "Lazarus" appeared originally in *The Reformed Journal* in September 1973.

IT WAS COLD WITH THE DAMP, bone-chilling cold of Florida winter days. They never lasted longer than two or three days at a time, but on days like those the sun would be dying hidden behind a dirty white blanket. The wind was blowing, making the cedars whistle, rattling the leafless branches of trees and the remains of the corn.

The corn stood behind the house next to the vegetable garden close enough for the waterhose to reach. It was a frame house with peeling white paint, rusting tin roof, and a front porch worn grey by the sun and rain. Looking along its side from front to back, the house was the image of a Primitive Baptist Church; yet the front with its Neo-Gothic roof and Victorian stained glass was pure Church of England. Before being planted among the trees on a forty-acre farm, it had been an antique shop in town.

The house had been rented to a family of four. Some of the neighbors thought that the family had come from England, others that they came from South Carolina. But it didn't really matter since the closest neighbors lived a mile-and-a-half away and were not inclined to visit. They saw the children at the side of the road waiting for the school bus every school day and they glimpsed the wife driving to work. She was a small woman with auburn hair and a sweet face. The children must have taken after her. The husband was big. He had black hair, brown eyes, and wide cheekbones. He didn't go to work anywhere as far as anyone knew. He did a little dirt farming and bought the groceries. He had an accent, but nobody knew what kind since it wasn't Cuban.

Once when he was at the grocery store and was asked about his nationality he said: "I am an American," and scowled.

Now he was in the kitchen waiting for the water to boil so that he could make tea for his daughter Sibet, who was home with a sore throat. He shouldn't have been glad but he was. As a tiny girl she followed him around like a puppy dog and he loved her with a love that overwhelmed him since he first saw her. The nurse had brought her out from behind a glass wall and he had asked to hold her. Holding her in his arms looking at this perfection he lifted her to thank God. The nurse took her away.

The kettle began to whistle. He made tea, enjoying the steam warming his face. The only heat in the house came from the kerosene stove in the alcove populated by two dogs, between the bathroom and the children's bedroom.

"Here is your tea, Sibet," he said.

"Thank you, Daddy." She was nine years old with a lovely nose, green-grey eyes, and dark-brown hair in pigtails. The room was painted sky blue, which made it seem filled with light. One window looked out on the desolation of the vegetable garden.

"How is your throat?"

"Much better."

"Shall we talk about our donkey cart or the four ponies who will pull our little stagecoach?... Twenty-five cents a ride."

"I think Johnny should be the driver and you and I will be the bandits who hold up the stage," she said. "Of course we just pretend holding it up."

"Of course."

They talked realistically about feed prices and the likely stagecoach passengers and the names of the ponies, who were all pinto. By 11:30 the stagecoach route was extended to cover all the schools in town, and the business provided income to build a seventy-five-foot schooner, the *Flisabeth*. It was painted the same blue as the room and had red sails like the Thames coal barges. After six weeks of uneventful crossing (*no, no,* the girl said, *we saw porpoises dancing*), they glimpsed the Devon coast and were guided in by the blinking light that stood on Jubilee to direct the fishermen of Beer.

"The light is at the bottom of Jubilee next to the men's room, Daddy."

"You are right.... Should we run the boat up on the shingle?" He was surprised that he was thinking seriously about the landing. The fishermen used to nose into shore, jump out, attach the cable, get the rollers under while the winch was slowly pulling up the boat. But would that be possible with a seventy-five-foot schooner?

"I can smell it," the girl said, happily hugging her knees. So could he. The odor of drying seaweed, nets, and lobster pots; the salty wind that with the changing of direction became a fish & chips concentrate; the pine smells and the kale too that came down from the surrounding fields.

"Where we picked mushrooms," the girl said.

The fields divided by hedges were a huge eiderdown with deep green dominating the pattern. Seagulls circled the church steeple crying a harsh, heartbreaking, homesick cry to be answered by a flock of sheep grazing by Castle Rocks. Their mouths were full of dry winter grass, yet they sounded as if it were cotton wool. Above all, or perhaps around it all, was a rhythmic panting like an engine waiting at a railway station; the sea rolling the shingle.

"You left out the two little lambs, Daddy."

"To tell it, it has to be winter." He looked out of the window. The walnut was a stark, grey Vishnu against a stark, grey sky. When the wind blew hard the Spanish moss swung out almost horizontal like acrobats on a flying trapeze. "And we need snow." There was another problem. "And Johnny should be along too."

"This time he won't be with us when we meet the two little lambs because he is in school," the girl said. The man marveled how easy it was for the child to move back into the past and alter it so that the present would fit it. He saw the day too, but for him nothing had changed: snow on the ground and piled up on the hedges, Grandfather in his grey tweed shooting cape walking straight-backed, his curly white hair uncovered, followed by Freya the collie, John, Sibet and himself bringing up the rear. The gulls were swooping and diving, wisps of cloud against the church steeple. He remembered and felt the affection they had for each other and he thought that if needed he would die for them, knowing that the proof he used was absurd yet it could not be helped. And testing, testing, he again stood before the wall facing the alien soldiers and their guns letting the horror wash over him to make sure that if he must he could do it. Then without any preliminaries he was in the oddly shaped drawing room. The sun rays touching the curtains turned into pink splotches on the wall opposite. There were flowers in the marble fireplace. Grandfather sat next to them on a low chair.

"Where there is a spark of love there is a spark of spiritual life," he said. Outside the gulls were crying.

"Daddy," the girl said, "you still didn't tell it." And

because the man was lost in thought she told it herself. "Grandfather stays behind so that Freya should not scare the sheep and you and Sibet go down toward the flock of sheep and two little lambs come jumping and skipping toward the little girl. . . . Can you see it, Daddy?"

"You put your arms around them," he said, noticing that her face crumpled. "What's the matter?"

"My head hurts," she said, lying down. He brought two aspirins and a glass of water.

"This is pink children's aspirin."

The girl choked on the second aspirin but in the end got it down. "They were not cuddly, Daddy."

"Who?"

"They were not cuddly and they felt damp and oily and stuck together. The wool wasn't soft the way it looked." She began to cry.

"Why didn't you tell us if it mattered so much?"

"I didn't want Johnny to know. He was such a sweet little boy." She cried in earnest now.

"He still is, starting second grade." He touched her forehead. "You have fever and that is why you feel bad. I'll go outside with the dogs and let you sleep awhile."

As soon as the dogs heard "outside" and "dogs" their tails beat on the kerosene stove. He went to get his gun, thinking that as the world judged he was a failure because he couldn't get a paying job and work itself was not honored so that his farming counted for nothing, yet he was happy and felt whole. His wife, his children, his dogs loved him, the soil in their garden was rich and there was always enough to eat.

Of course that did not account for the sense of his own value that allowed him the joy of others' successes or to feel the pain of their tragedies. He reached the gun rack and the next instant there was an illumination. It could not be called anything else. What he saw was a box very much like the boxes he had seen in the National Gallery at Trafalgar Square, boxes fabricated by seventeenth-century Dutch artists, containing different rooms, some with their owners in them, all done in perfect scale. His own box was open at the back and he was looking toward the nave where four people were kneeling. He recognized himself, his wife and children. The dogs were there too, their ears softly relaxed, their forepaws piously crossed. Then he looked at the great light at the altar, a golden light, and his heart began to beat with the slow booming of bells just brought into motion. Instead of the chalice and the ciborium he saw the Lord standing there surrounded by this curious light that made him finally understand the word *Glory*, and he longed with an infinitely sad longing to touch His feet. He reached out feeling tears well up.

Outside it was bleak, the damp cold making him shiver. The dogs ran through the pecan grove. Gusts of wind tore at the Spanish moss; then he was through the grove and into an old field. It was there that the dogs struck, their voices high, excited, going toward the swamp, disappearing in it then coming back. He saw them coming toward him but there was no rabbit in front of them. Not far from him they stopped, sheepishly looking from him to a clump of grass. He couldn't read the dogs at all. Then he saw them too and breaking the gun open pocketed the shells. The three little rabbits kept perfectly still. Looking at them close up was an affirmation of Dürer's mastery. They were grey-brown-white in color. One had dark fur inside its ears. They looked soft.

A second later he scooped up the rabbits and put them into the front pocket of his sweatshirt, knowing that now the mother would never come back for them but not thinking of this. He thought of his daughter. The rabbits felt soft like butterflies palpitating on yellow flowers.

* * *

The man was driving back from town with the groceries and a bagful of slightly spoiled greens. The greens were for the rabbits who had survived feedings with dolls' baby bottles and the dogs' sanitary lickings and were now ready to be turned loose.

The car turned off Highway 441 onto a side road, passed a log house with a TV aerial, a quonset hut seemingly filled with baying hounds, then Sunshine Stables, and turning left by a pond covered with duckweed drove up to the house. Seeing it the dog hanging over his shoulder began to lick his face. The other one lying on the back seat sat up ready to leave the car. They were home.

Up the front steps carrying the grocery bags, across the house into the kitchen—vegetables into the icebox, staples into the larder—then he was ready with a handful of lettuce. The rabbits lived in a basket in the alcove. They were not in their basket but that was all right; jumping out of the basket was a sign of progress. He found two of them under his son's bed and put them back into the basket. Their noses wrinkled as they nibbled the lettuce.

After awhile the man stopped watching and decided to get the third rabbit, the one with the dark fur inside its ears.

By the time he searched the bathroom, feeling the cracked linoleum against his face as he peered under the tub, it ceased to be a routine getting the rabbits back into the basket. The rabbit with the black ears was definitely lost.

He went outside to get help from the dogs, but they had gone hunting on their own. Back again in the house he was assailed by nameless fears starting in his body that froze like a bird dog coming up on a covey. He knew that this was ridiculous, thinking of the real horrors catalogued and presented in neat pablum jars for five minutes of every hour in the ceaseless litany of a fallen world. He was looking only for a lost rabbit. Then he noticed the back door of the kitchen ajar and there was new hope, the back porch was screened in and its door always closed.

The floorboard creaked under his feet. He looked down. The rabbit was lying on its side stretched out, rigor mortis already set in.

"God," he said aloud. "God." The rabbit in his hands felt like a wet glove frozen dry. He thought of his children he wanted to shield but could not, remembering their faces when they were told that their only living grandfather was dead.

Tomorrow was Saturday, and the whole family would have taken the rabbits to Oleno State Park, where there was no hunting, and turned them loose. Just one more day. Seeing their joy that had never been—the rabbits disappearing in the woods, the children jumping up and down, and the two of them standing together watching all this like reading poetry together—he moaned.

He should have gone outside to get a shovel, but instead he went inside to the alcove. The two rabbits were in their basket on a table next to the kerosene stove. There was a smaller basket on the table, and he put the dead rabbit in it. With God everything is possible he thought not believing it. He stood there not feeling or thinking any more. Then he screamed. The dead rabbit had jumped at his chest. He was holding it in his hands now, away from himself feeling a revulsion he had not felt with the dead body and put the dark-eared rabbit with the others. He knelt ponderously, his body almost bent to the floorboard as if heavy weights were pushing down on his shoulders. His lips said thank you, but he was thinking that he was an ordinary man who forgave himself too much for too many things, a man who hated injustice so much that in turn he was unjust himself. He had asked not expecting an answer and he had been answered. He had seen his own Lazarus. It was unbearable.

* * *

On Saturday it was sunny and the river glinted as they walked over the suspension bridge. There were a lot of people at Oleno. Families cooking hot dogs and hamburgers, the smoke of their fires going up straight toward the sky. There were young people everywhere and even some Northern visitors braving the river. His children carried the basket on the bridge but once they were over he asked them for it. He lifted the kitchen cloth looking at the rabbits. They all seemed to have black fur inside their ears. He couldn't tell them apart.

He walked to the edge of the woods and gently dumped them out of the basket. His children were jumping up and down. He was standing beside his wife watching the rabbits disappear into the woods.

#6 (from Stories and Texts for Nothing)

SAMUEL BECKETT

Samuel Beckett, a winner of the Nobel Prize for Literature, is an enigmatic giant of twentieth-century writing. Born in Dublin in 1906 but for decades a resident of Paris, Beckett has composed drama, fiction, and critical prose in English and French. His characters are often comic and pathetic figures who engage an intractable language for the impossible task of communicating in an absurd and pointless universe, as in his famous *Waiting for Godot* (1956; original French *En attendant Godot,* 1952). Our selection, Number 6 from *Stories and Texts for Nothing* (1967; *Nouvelles et textes pour rien,* 1955), presents a typical self-absorbed linguistic probing by an immobile character in an ambiguous setting to locate his own identity and meaning.

How ARE THE INTERVALS filled between these apparitions? Do my keepers snatch a little rest and sleep before setting about me afresh, how would that be? That would be very natural, to enable them to get back their strength. Do they play cards, the odd rubber, bowls, to recruit their spirits, are they entitled to a little recreation? I would say no, if I had a say, no recreation, just a short break, with something cold, even though they should not feel inclined, in the interests of their health. They like their work, I feel it in my bones! No, I mean how filled for me, they don't come into this. Wretched acoustics this evening, the merest scraps, literally. The news, do you remember the news, the latest news, in slow letters of light, above Piccadilly Circus, in the fog? Where were you standing, in the doorway of the little tobacconist's closed for the night on the corner of Glasshouse Street was it, no, you don't remember, and for cause. Sometimes that's how it is, in a way, the eyes take over, and the silence, the sighs, like the sighs of sadness weary with crying, or old, that suddenly feels old and sighs for itself, for the happy days, the long days, when it cried it would never perish, but it's far from common, on the whole. My keepers, why keepers, I'm in no danger of stirring an inch, ah I see, it's to make me think I'm a prisoner, frantic with corporeality, rearing to get out and away. Other times it's male nurses, white from head to foot, even their shoes are white, and then it's another story, but the burden is the same. Other times it's like ghouls, naked and soft as worm, they grovel round me gloating on the corpse, but I have no more success dead than dying. Other times it's great clusters of bones, dangling and knocking with a clatter of castanets, it's clean and gay like coons, I'd join them with a will if it could be here and now, how is it nothing is ever here and now? It's varied, my life is varied, I'll never get anywhere. I know, there is no one here, neither me nor anyone else, but some things are better left unsaid, so I say nothing. Elsewhere perhaps, by all means, elsewhere, what elsewhere can there be to this infinite here? I know, if my head could think I'd find a way out, in my head, like so many others, and out of worse than this, the world would be there again, in my head, with me much as in the beginning. I would know that nothing had changed, that a little resolution is all that is needed to come and go under the changing sky, on the moving earth, as all along the long summer days too short for all the play, it was known as play, if my head could think. The air would be there again, the shadows of the sky drifting over the earth, and that ant, that ant, oh most excellent head that can't think. Leave it, leave it, nothing leads to anything, nothing of all that, my life is varied, you can't have everything, I'll never get anywhere, but when did I? When I laboured, all day long and let me add, before I forget, part of the night, when I thought that with perseverance I'd get at me in the end? Well look at me, a little dust in a little nook, stirred faintly this way and that by breath straying from the lost without. Yes, I'm here for ever, with the spinners and the dead flies, dancing to the tremor of their meshed wings, and it's well pleased I am, well pleased, that it's over and done with, the puffing and panting after me up and down their Tempe of tears. Sometimes a butterfly comes, all warm from the flowers, how weak it is, and quick dead, the wings crosswise, as when resting, in the sun, the scales grey. Blot, words can be blotted and the mad thoughts they invent, the nostalgia for that slime where the Eternal breathed and his son wrote, long after, with divine idiotic finger, at the feet of the adulteress, wipe it out, all you have to do is say you said nothing and so say nothing again. What can have become then of the tissues I was, I can see them no more, feel them no more, flaunting and fluttering all about and inside me, pah they must be still on their old prowl somewhere, passing themselves off as me. Did I ever believe in them, did I ever believe I was there, somewhere in that ragbag, that's more the line, of inquiry, perhaps I'm still there, as large as life, merely convinced I'm not. The eyes, yes, if these memories are mine, I must have believed in them an instant, believed it was me I saw there dimly in the depths of their glades. I can see me still, with those of now, sealed this long time, staring with those of then, I must have been twelve, because of the glass, a round shaving-glass, double-faced, faithful and magnifying, staring into one of the others, the true ones, true then, and seeing me there, imagining I saw me there, lurking behind the bluey veils, staring back sightlessly, at the age of twelve, because of the glass, on its pivot, because of my father, if it was my father, in the bathroom, with its view of the sea, the lightships at night, the red harbour light, if these memories concern me, at the age of twelve, or at the age of forty, for the mirror remained, my father went but the mirror remained, in which he had so greatly changed, my mother did her hair in it, with twitching hands, in another house, with no view of the sea, with a view of the mountains, if it was my mother, what a refreshing whiff of life on earth. I was, I was, they say in Purgatory, in Hell too, admirable singulars, admirable assurance. Plunged in ice up to the nostrils, the eyelids caked with frozen tears, to fight all your battles o'er again, what tranquillity, and know there are no more emotions in store, no, I can't have heard aright. How many hours to go, before the next silence, they are not hours, it will not be silence, how many hours still, before the next silence? Ah to know for sure, to know that this thing has no end, this thing, this thing, this farrago of silence and words, of silence that is not silence and barely murmured words. Or to know it's life still, a form of life, ordained to end, as others ended and will end, till life ends, in all its forms. Words, mine was never more than that, than this pell-mell babel of silence and words, my viewless form described as ended, or to come, or still in progress, depending on the words, the moments, long may it last in that singular way. Apparitions, keepers, what childishness, and ghouls, to think I said ghouls, do I as much as know what they are, of course I don't, and how the intervals are filled, as if I didn't know, as if there were two things, some other thing besides this thing, what is it, this unnamable thing that I name and name and never wear out, and I call that words. It's because I haven't hit on the right ones, the killers, haven't yet heaved them up from that heart-burning glut of words, with what words shall I name my unnamable words? And yet I have high hopes, I give you my word, high hopes, that one day I may tell a story, hear a story, yet another, with men, kinds of men as in the days when I played all regardless or nearly, worked and played. But first stop talking and get on with your weeping, with eyes wide open that the precious liquid may spill freely, without burning the lids, or the crystalline humour, I forget, whatever it is it burns. Tears, that could be the tone, if they weren't so easy, the true tone and tenor at last. Besides not a tear, not one, I'd be in greater danger of mirth, if it wasn't so easy. No, grave, I'll be grave, I'll close my ears, close my mouth and be grave. And when they open again it may be to hear a story, tell a story, in the true sense of the words, the word hear, the word tell, the word story, I have high hopes, a little story, with living creatures coming and going on a habitable earth crammed with the dead, a brief story, with night and day coming and going above, if they stretch that far, the words that remain, and I've high hopes, I give you my word.

Afterword

THE COMMENTS THAT FOLLOW should not be taken as the "correct" analysis of the stories but rather as interpretations to stimulate or enhance the reader's own responses. They suggest, further, an overall four-fold pattern to our twenty-five choices for this collection that may help the reader to organize his or her fictive world more clearly.

Our first group of stories we have gathered under the heading of *Powers Governing the World: Providence or Fate?* The six fictions raise the question of whether a benevolent God or demonic forces determine our existence—or whether it is guided and determined at all. Kaatje Hurlbut's subtle story "Eve in Darkness" achieves its complex effect through a gradual accumulation of images rather than through dramatic plot development. The images depend on a twoness that inhabits all elements of the tale, beginning with a double articulation: the teller is a mature woman recalling her impressions as a five-year-old. This dual voice, conveying innocence from the ironic perspective of experience, finds its focus in the little marble figure, appropriately ambiguous in its identity: the adult narrator, looking back, thinks that the nude "may have been Aphrodite," yet at the time, as a small child, she accepted her cousin's judgment that it is Eve, the first woman. Immediately the conflict between classical and Judeo-Christian matrices is established, and in the forcefield of this tension the controlling images are introduced and modulated. The statuette, apple, darkness, brightness, Christ child, and Molly's daughter's baby emit childish formulations of guilt, sorrow, fear, mystery, beauty, and joy. Above all, these images blend into an impression of sin, which itself never becomes a concept but remains a sensual/sensuous cipher. Without ever reaching the stage of intellectual definition, sin is transformed—made lovely by the sheer presence of form (the very sound of the word, the statue's intuited beauty)—which form is then given depth by an image of incarnation—the infant Christ who also ("with his arms flung out and his palms open") anticipates the crucifixion and as the *second* Adam (again the twoness) redeems the *first*. But one need not look so hard for such a theological key to appreciate the tale. On an easier and just as "grace-full" level, the vitality of the five-year-old's innocent imagination turns the intuited sorrowfulness of evil into celebration. The final triumphant cluster of images, that strange trinity of King David, the baby, and the statuette whirling brilliantly through the carousel of the child's mind, projects (in a fine example of Freudian condensation and displacement) the mysterious balance of *eros* and *agape* through which sin is indeed rendered beautiful.

Borges has remarked, in conversation, that "The Gospel According to Mark" is one of his own favorite stories. One reason perhaps is that it blends more adeptly than is usual even for Borges his characteristic play with tradition, his fascination with the mystery of language, and his deceptive simplicity of narration. The audacity of taking as his title the name of the oldest New Testament Gospel indicates that Borges is not inviting a search for cryptic religious symbolism: the clues are all manifest, particularly those that accrue to fashion the thirty-three-year-old Espinoza into yet another Christ avatar and the Easter setting into the scene for a new crucifixion. Rather, the game with the Judeo-Christian tradition broadens into universal mythic dimensions, and the reader becomes absorbed in tracing archetypal figures and events: the reading of the sacred book as a ritual act, the pampering and readying of the sacrificial king for his execution, the cohabitation of a virgin with a "god." But all such mythic designs are tempered by the artist's irony that corrupts, instructively, the naivete of real myth. Espinoza begins the fateful reading of the English Bible to the illiterate Gutres "as an exercise in translation" and comprehension; as it turns out, their understanding is as perfect on a pre-conscious level as it is wrong on the literal-historical. The reading of the text inspires a pre-textual, even pre-reflective reflex. An irony just as telling is that Espinoza finally condemns himself by supplying the narrative details of the Christ story and its theology that confirm the Gutres in their compulsion to execute him. This drive to reenact the crucifixion may be a surfacing of the old Calvinist instincts in the Gutres (originally Scotts Guthries), as the narrative suggests, but it is also an effort to escape what Mircea Eliade has named the "terror of history," the fearful sense of time leading to an end, to natural catastrophe and individual death. The most intense irony of all, then, is that Jesus' death as a central moment of Christianity, intended to resolve the conflict between myth and history by helping mankind to face the ultimate reality of death, is transformed here into a primitive ritual that negates its residual theological power.

But this does not mean that the story is anti-gospel. Rather, its spare, direct style and its inexorable drive toward the climax (very different from Hurlbut's tale) are reminiscent of the Marcan narrative itself. Also somewhat like the original versions of that Gospel, Borges' story does not conclude with a resurrection account but leaves the reader facing an uncompleted action. In Saint Mark's Gospel one is left with the mystery of the empty tomb, in Borges' tale with the space of time before a crucifixion. The empty space in the New Testament Gospel demands a kerygmatic fulfillment; the empty space at the end of Borges' "gospel" also asks for the imagination's filling in. Thus irony provokes new vision in the best Borgesian fashion.

If Borges' story portrays a pre-reflective reflex, John Barth's "Night-Sea Journey" employs the mythic mode to return to a literal pre-conscious setting: the narrator-hero is a sperm cell on its way to the uterus to fertilize an ovum. This elementary life form, given a consciousness by the author, is a fanciful attribution that lends the tale its creative tension. For this bizarre situation is a version of an old literary sub-genre, the mock-heroic epic. "Night-Sea Journey" exhibits many of the mock-epic traits: a diminutive scale that produces a comic effect, a grand journey involving the voyage of a mass of people (here the millions of sperm), a high-flown rhetoric, and a pervasive sense of fate. As the first of thirteen stories constituting the *Lost in the Funhouse* collection, it introduces a number of others that also evince mock-epic qualities. Further, the tales in the collection taken in sequence form a progression from the pre-conceptive moment of human life (the sperm approaching the ovum in "Night-Sea Journey") to the old marooned Greek minstrel awaiting death in "Anonymiad," the final story. The whole collection, then, constitutes a kind of antic mock-epic of human existence, and the narrative of the sperm on its precarious voyage in the first piece prefigures in miniature the combined pathos, absurdity, and hope of the human passage through time, just as the singular hero himself experiences a whole duration of existence in the few seconds of travel to the womb. Philosophizing incessantly along the way, the skeptic-sperm rehearses many of the classical and modern arguments for and against God's existence, on life's meaning, the nature of reality, chance, fate, and providence. Audaciously, Barth invents this strange setting and narrator to stage theological (not only philosophical) discourse, and yet this discourse is merely the literal level, the content of the tale. Beneath (or above) the comic, inflated rhetoric of the unlikely narrator is the drama, as in all of Barth's fiction, of the force of love versus the recognized horror of existence. "Night-Sea Journey" is a post-modern version of *Heart of Darkness*. Here the journey into the dark interior also leads to a sense of hell on earth, and the hero's plea to "terminate this aimless, brutal business" is not far from Kurtz's "Exterminate all the brutes!" in Conrad's novella. And, as in Kurtz's case, the involvement with the erotic and with death reveals how the whole self—body and spirit—and the totality of nature and the person are caught up in the quest for a meaning that is not just knowledge but also fulfillment. "Night-Sea Journey" is unique teleological fiction.

The terror of history and horror of eternal recurrence are transformed into a different kind of concern with temporality in Cynthia Ozick's "The Butterfly and the Traffic Light." This virtually plotless story offers a central impression: how the lack of an awareness of the past alters human experience. This impression is developed through the four sections of the narration. The first section, which shows traits of the informal essay rather than of the short story, expounds on how ageless and myth-laden cities like Jerusalem contrast with modern towns, especially American ones, in which a sense of the past has barely begun to be felt and in which the missing past is compensated for through an elaborate celebration of individual streets—one need only think of the scores of famous American street names, such as Fifth Avenue, State Street, Pennsylvania Avenue, Basin Street, to recognize the truth of the argument. The brief second section represents a narrowing of focus and a partial shift from essay to story format. The shallow history of the main street of an unnamed midwestern American town is recounted, an etymology that confirms the thesis of the first section. The third and fourth sections, then, constituting the story proper, concentrate on that single street, Big Road, in a 1949 setting, and in the dialogue between Fishbein and Isabel the problematic nature of one's relation to the past is dramatized. Fishbein, apparently a European Jew unwillingly transplanted to this banal middle-American context, argues with often specious logic that a monotonous sameness infects American civilization, rendering it superficial and transitory. But Isabel, Fishbein's protégé and perhaps his lover, reminds him that such obsessive homogeneity is after all the culmination of culturizing impulses with roots in Hebrew monotheism—an observation that Fishbein dislikes, although he is much attracted to the midwestern girls and their repetitious prettiness.

The traffic light and butterfly, images of technological replication and ephemeral beauty, Fishbein confronts with the caterpillar, image of "beautiful change"; yet this image seems to have no correlative in the real world, not even in a "divine city" such as Jerusalem. It is ironic that Fishbein, so arrogantly quick to detect the illusion producing disillusion in American life, won't recognize the illusion of his own vision. The past is, in any case, what one makes of it, but it should not be an objective force that determines the present.

The regulatory quality of technological life that Fishbein rails against is even more compellingly portrayed in "Kabiasy," and is embodied there in a pervasive modern myth—that of the Marxist gospel of a classless utopia. Although this piece lacks the subtlety of those previously discussed, it possesses a power drawn from the folklore that is a part of its subject matter. Even though the geographical and social setting are strange for American readers, the tale should evoke familiarity, for it is a version of the ghost story popular for generations in the English-speaking world. The account of the gullible youth who has to undertake the fearful journey through the demon-filled forest at night (Ichabod Crane, Tam O'Shanter) is practically a cliché in British and American folk literature, so that the attraction of "Kabiasy" is not in any originality of plot but in discovering how it is adapted to the socialist framework. Predictably, perhaps, instead of serving to unsettle Western empirical attitudes or religious creeds, superstition here in the Soviet context undermines a materialist rationality. The young man who considers himself beyond such foolishness is reduced to primitive terror by suggestion and environment—precisely those forces that he has been relying on to educate his compatriots toward a more enlightened world, and, not incidentally, to better his own situation. That the human psyche cannot be so easily purged of its irrational fears is the lesson of his ordeal, but whether he absorbs it remains, at the end, in question. He does, at least, exhibit some human warmth that is a healthy balance to his programmed behavior otherwise, and the concluding paragraph conveys with comic ambiguity his irresolution: wishing to discuss "high things" with someone, he gets out of bed at night to find his girlfriend, but one doubts the nocturnal visit will produce spiritual intercourse.

In contrast to the *kabiasy*, the little goblins, are the giant power towers, "like a file of enormous silent beings thrown to us from other worlds and walking soundlessly with raised arms to the west in the direction of the flaring green star, their homeland." This awesome and almost hieratic simile, providing a sense of the alien gods that rule the technological landscape, would by itself nearly justify the remainder of the story. It can also stand as a contrast to the primarily organic imagery of our final story in this first series, set in India, Soviet Russia's still mysterious neighbor to the south. "Seventh House" seems at first to take one totally out of the West ("Kabiasy" might be seen as a transition tale) and to the Orient; here one discovers the rich and bewildering plurality of things, the polytheism that Fishbein in Ozick's story praises as an anodyne to modern, spirit-deadening monotony. Yet one also learns that this very plethora produces existential chaos. Even more instructive is that Krishna, the harried husband of Narayan's tale, is one of the new, liberated generation attempting to live a life free of the vast Hindu apparatus of prescriptions and restrictions, so that here, after all, a struggle is depicted between the progressive but neurotic West and the overwhelming immutability of the East. Indeed, this clash of cultures and eras is the central drama of this poignant fiction, and one is tempted to allegorize: the perplexing sickness of the wife as the sickness of Mother India, the doctor and the astrologer as two kinds of half-concerned adjuvants, Krishna as the educated Indian considering promiscuous relationships (various native panaceas) in despair and finally giving himself over to destiny. But the story is more rewarding on a personal-artistic level, where the interplay of ironies and bitter-comic elements emerges. For example, Krishna can't prepare the elaborate ritual meal prescribed by the astrologer as part of the cure for his wife because he would need his wife to help him make it. Similarly, he is advised to betray his wife in order to save her, but he cannot negotiate the logistics of adultery and is at last lectured to by a stranger on connubial responsibility as if he were guilty of unfaithfulness *de facto* and not only in thwarted intention.

Krishna's resignation, at the end, appears as a predictable, even natural response to a society that frustrates and enervates its members as a matter of course. Indeed, the climax of this story coincides with its denouement: the decisive and most intense moment is Krishna's surrender to fate, for this act (or non-act) resolves, ambiguously, his whole dilemma; he must now hope that fate will prove to be either providential or nonexistent, and he is stretched between two extremes. If it is providential, then he is caught all the more tightly in the web of tradition. If it is nonexistent he is abruptly faced by nihilism. Even ancient India leads one round to the crisis of belief.

How might one view these six stories as an interpretative unit in terms of "powers governing the world?" We offer the following possibilities. "Eve in Darkness" suggests the cosmic drama of the Old Testament: God the creator has his creation threatened by Satan, purveyor of sin, so that providence in the fundamental sense is challenged by fate; goodness is corrupted by evil. "The Gospel According to Mark," in contrast, recalls the drama in its emergent Christian framework: something demonic attaches to the Gutres' need to execute Espinoza; unlike the conventional view of Jesus' crucifixion as a providential event through which a sinful world can be reconciled to God, Espinoza's death seems a fateful mistake, an accident brought on by superstition and natural disaster. In Barth's "Night-Sea Journey" the ever recurring miracle of conception is depicted as a massive catastrophe in miniature; millions of sperm die on their journey to the womb, and only one arrives—certainly a compelling biological image of fateful action. Do the dynamics of chance at the moment of genesis set in motion a lifetime of hazard? Ozick's tale restates the question in terms of myth and history: Can Jerusalem, the mythic city of God, be revived in the chaotic multiplicity and technological impersonality of modern urban life, or is the metropolis fated to destruction, Babel-like, through proud and selfish striving, through radically overreaching itself? Or to put it another way, can technological society, attempting to improve on divine providence by devising its own kinds of surety, create a safe and sane humanity, or must such attempts produce a bondage that is worse than the elemental danger it seeks to subdue? "Kabiasy" dramatizes the problem in simplified form. In the Soviet framework, providence is secularized and appears as the socialist master plan designed to guarantee equality and security for all; yet this grand design is unsettled—at least briefly in the mind of a minor functionary—through the demons, figures of the uncontrolled, irrational world. One could argue that the demons appear *providentially* to challenge the *fateful* drift of the socialized state toward a depressing and debilitating sameness, the *telos* of which is not utopia but a bureaucratic and paranoid stasis. Fate itself is the explicit theme of "Seventh House." It is merged with providence in ways almost impossible for the Western mind to grasp or differentiate. The gods are capricious, even malevolent, and must be humored. But they *can* be manipulated, just as they manipulate human beings, and rituals take shape that embody hope and seem to mitigate the brutality of an often marginal existence on the harsh subcontinent.

We should not forget that the concepts of providence and fate, of powers that rule the world, are active not only in the subject matter of these stories but in the psychology (perhaps we could say ontology) of their composition as well. The artist plotting his tale is a model of the providential agent, and in tracing the games he or she plays with the personae the reader glimpses the fearsome freedom of any creator who becomes, in turn, bound by his/her own creation. The mystery of Genesis is recapitulated in every good fiction.

We have organized the second set of stories under the heading of *The Moral Law: Freedom or Bondage?* These tales reveal the difficulty of forging valid codes of ethical behavior, codes that are just, viable, and inspired by a moral force worthy of obedience. A. C. Jordan's version of the Zengele folktale "The Woman and the Mighty Bird" might lead one through its seemingly naive format to regard it as an example of a simplistic morality story, a notion that would be dead wrong. Actually, the careful observance of the folktale convention and the ritual songs indicate a complex and rigid law dictating the behavior of the society in which the action takes place. It is not just that the young wife breaks a taboo by entering the forbidden forest and incurs swift punishment for her disobedience. Rather, this initial sin begins a sequence of increasingly constricting encounters that can culminate only in the woman's death. The fatal action proceeds via a number of interacting triangulations that give the tale its artistic intricacy compounding the moral convolution. The young wife, her husband, and the mighty bird (marked by three main traits—eyes, beak, and throat) constitute a triad of characters involved in a three-stage action (three meetings between the woman and the bird, three confrontations of wife and husband), within which a threefold ritual is performed and resulting in three sins committed by the woman: breaking the taboo, telling a lie, and betraying a trust. Yet none of these strikes us as particularly heinous, certainly not deserving of death, so that the key to the enormity of the woman's crime must be sought elsewhere. The strong male sexual imagery, mainly in the depiction of the phallic bird, and the male-dominated action suggest that her transgression is at base social-sexually oriented: her actions threaten a masculine code, and for this she must die—appropriately through being devoured by the monstrous supermale figure. The only freedom for the woman under the law of this men's world, secured by sacred myths of male divinity, is precarious and is achieved, if at all, through deception and seduction. Female bondage, in other words, is virtually complete. One can at least point to an irony in the modern rendering of the tale: it was certainly intended in its original folk form as part of a societal pattern of female repression, and yet Jordan's recent retelling of it gives it a place among contemporary fictions for liberation.

Peter DeVries' well-known ambivalence toward his own strict Dutch-Calvinist background determines the moral ambience of "Every Leave That Falls." DeVries has made his reputation as a satirist. Since satiric and moralistic writing have always been closely associated, one is not surprised to find the combination in this comic-bitter story. As does Jordan's adaptation of the African folktale, this narrative also displays an oppressive moral authority that controls those subject to it mainly through fear and awe. The difference is that in DeVries' story that authority is already in eclipse, failing through its own obduracy, and is being replaced, it seems, by a self-protective cynicism. Thus the freedom that emerges here from the demise of the law might not be authentic freedom but merely a reflex against a set of prohibitions.

As in most of his fiction, DeVries here too interlaces

plots of moral dilemmas with humor. Yet it is not a mitigating humor. The slightly damaged drunk, the bizarre circumstances causing the police to suspect the young protagonist, the competitive Bible-quoting toward the end are all at least mildly funny, but they do not relieve the severity of the narrator's (and DeVries') judgment. When in the final paragraph the narrator flippantly declares his "lesson"—that the legalistic morality of his father has taught him to forego acts of compassion—one is saddened rather than amused. But, of course, the lesson that the reader is to gain from this ironic exemplum is precisely that a moral code inhibiting mercy must be degenerate. It is fitting that the moral tension in the tale appears most articulately between father and son, for the son's rejection of the father's Pharisaism opens the space for a new and effective "fraternity" that is not just a negative reaction. One finds evidence at the start of the tale that the son has not, fortunately, learned his lesson: fifteen years after the incident constituting the central action, we find he is still involved in gestures of kindness, and although he vows "never again," one suspects that the laws of compassion are more binding for him than those of his father's creed.

The Polish writer Slawomir Mrozek is also known mainly as a satirist (on occasion a hazardous profession in Eastern-bloc countries), but the satiric quality of his short piece "The Pastor" is subordinated to a tone of moral condemnation. This story exists, in fact, on the periphery of what has come to be called, in recent years, holocaust literature, fiction treating mainly the great decimation of Jewry in the Second World War but sometimes addressing other catastrophes and atrocities, such as the nuclear bombing of Japanese cities. Mrozek's approach to the Hiroshima cataclysm is certainly not subtle, but it is sufficiently oblique, in artistic design, to project a substantiality quite out of proportion to the tale's brevity and transcending the propaganda of anti-war sentiment. It is sound strategy to have as the pastor of the mission congregation an American neophyte too young to have participated in the war. His innocent arrogance is, as a result, all the more outrageous, an extension of the church's unabashed trafficking in humiliation by forcing the indigent Japanese, in their own country, to listen to a foreigner's audacious exhortation before receiving their food. The plot recalls a criticism of Americans not uncommon in some otherwise sympathetic countries and having to do with the damaging effects of our "hideous vigor," as John Updike puts it in an early story. Our technological superiority has led us to assume a moral righteousness as well, sometimes even in the face of appalling evidence of American brutality and baseness, and too often the churches of America have themselves identified with this perverted sense of supremacy rather than condemning it as immoral. The fact that the only person left in the mission chapel at the end of Pastor Peters' Bible reading is an old deaf man is symbolically important, of course, but not just because of the concluding irony the situation affords. One thinks rather of a possible inversion of Jesus' words following *his* citation of scripture: "He who has ears to hear, let him hear." When religious proclamation is corrupted in the name of false morality, it is better not to have "ears to hear."

One might wish to challenge the license of an Eastern European writer to criticize American morality, but it would be hard to deny the aptness of Toni Cade Bambara's criticism of her own country, especially as it expands to embrace a broader ethical concern, in "Gorilla, My Love." We might hesitate to call the story delicate, since the earthy—and very funny—vernacular makes it actually quite robust, and yet the fragility of childish trust, which is the narrative theme, definitely generates a tone of vulnerability and hurt that is at variance with the bravado of the language, and this opposition of inner feeling and outer statement produces the tension that makes the story live. The theme of children betrayed by adults is an old one in the American literary tradition; we recall readily its treatment by, for example, Hawthorne, Twain, Sherwood Anderson, Richard Wright, and J. D. Salinger, and Bambara upholds the tradition in what is literally and figuratively a new idiom. Indeed, "Gorilla, My Love" is very reminiscent of some of Salinger's narratives with adolescent characters but without the cloying sentimentality and self-conscious cleverness of Salinger's style; the novelty of Bambara's fiction, well represented in this tale, is the elevation of sub-literate English into an efficient and fortuitous art form. Yet, paradoxically, this language of authenticity is used mainly to transmit illusions and finally to expose the duplicitous nature of much adult behavior. The illusory quality of cinema (the "dream factory") generally, the play with names, the narrator's fantasy involving her family and the crucifixion, the deception with the movie title on the marquee (a play on the romantic title "Girl of My Love"), and finally the broken trust, in the child's mind, between her and her uncle all produce an atmosphere of shifting reality and human capriciousness that can make adolescence a time of anxiety and pain. The pose of toughness that the narrator strives to maintain does not disguise her moral absolutism—typical of children—that accounts for both her toughness (her survivor mentality) and her vulnerability. The illusion of love that she has nurtured behind her precocious cynicism, and that is destroyed at the end, is just as much a betrayal by her own immaturity as by the adults in her life. Nevertheless, the juxtaposing of scenes in the story signals how love persists through banality, monstrosity (the gorilla-love theme implied in the title), barbarity and suffering (the crucifixion), and disappointment to determine at last one's mode of being—and how it persists precisely through these obstacles rather than by avoiding them. Such love is capable of creating a liberating morality.

Frank O'Connor's "The Face of Evil" seems to begin as a fairly obvious satire on the hypocrisy of sainthood but then modulates into a version of the literary "epiphany." The epiphany as James Joyce, O'Connor's famous fellow Irish countryman, initiated it in the short stories of *Dubliners* emphasizes not a dramatic revelation but rather a quiet but insistent recognition of life's stubborn patterns, and in this sense it records a maturation experience, a growing into a realization of how things inexorably are. The recognition for O'Connor's narrator, as he interprets the events of his youth that constitute the story, was the initial realization "that the life before me would have complexities of emotion which I couldn't even imagine." This awesome knowledge—awesome because it anticipates an intensity of feeling yet to be experienced—destroys the cool innocence of his narrow boyish saintliness, wrecks his little world of self-improvement exercises (fundamentally a very selfish sphere), and opens him up to forces he cannot control. If this is the point at which he abandons sainthood, it is because of his intuition (only later an articulated awareness) that saintliness, at least as he has conceived it, is too small a vocation with which to meet the power of emotionality that he has just glimpsed. Thus "the face of evil" does not merely represent the pole of a moral confrontation; instead, it refers to the moment of the loss of innocence, which is a stage of normal maturation, and "evil" is a term for the fascinating and terrifying unknown before one.

Yet O'Connor (who has had experience with the theater) speaks elsewhere of the dramatic qualities of the short story, so we should take the hint and pursue the traces of drama that persist even in the epiphanic mode. They are quite apparent in the attraction-repulsion relationship between the young narrator as practicing saint and Charlie Dalton as the epitome of juvenile corruption. What looks, then, like the stock dramatic confrontation of morality fiction—Good meets and struggles with Evil—deepens here into a more subtle and profound encounter. The characters who have understood themselves as simple representations of good and evil discover how alike—and complex—they are, so that one of them, at least, is jarred loose from his clichéd self-definition. This insight is both dramatic and epiphanic, and if it cannot halt the tragic decline of the one youth, it provides the impetus toward authentic selfhood for the other. But is the new freedom of the one bought through the continued bondage of the other?

Flannery O'Connor's "A Temple of the Holy Ghost" could be read as a counterpart to Hurlbut's "Eve in Darkness." Here too a young girl is attracted to the mystery of the forbidden, which is connected to "evil" and sexuality, and focussed on an incomprehensible figure. And like the child protagonist of Hurlbut's tale, O'Connor's heroine is further confused by other adolescent misinformation. Vital differences also exist between the stories, however. The girl (unnamed) is twelve years old, precocious, and thus much more self-conscious and reflective than the five-year-old of "Eve in Darkness." Further, O'Connor's story is more robust, in terms both of its lively characters and theme and of her vigorous artistic style. Because O'Connor's personae tend to voice strong opinions and assume unequivocal stances, because the very terrain of her Southern settings often seems to emanate a stark judgmental aura, and because her narrative idiom conveys a toughness of will, her fiction transmits an acute awareness of moral law. But moral law here translates into a moral dilemma that is also a theological embarrassment: if the human body is, in the language of Christian metaphor, "a temple of the Holy Ghost" that should not be desecrated by sinful (meaning mainly sexual) misbehavior, how can the hermaphrodite's condition—a genital aberration—be justified as an expression of the perfection of divine creation, or at least as an expression of divine will? But the thrust of the story, the purpose of its artistic design, is not to resolve that problem, which is finally a theological one. Rather, O'Connor employs the drama of the hermaphrodite's self-exposure as a key element in the girl's inchoate maturation, and the beginning of her emergence from innocence supplies in good part the structure and substance of plot and action. The child's puzzlement, which is also (purposely) never resolved, takes form in her dream, where she connects the circus freak's abnormality with her own unloveliness, and contrasts his pious submissiveness to her own "sass"; although she never seems to recognize these relationships consciously, the experience inspires both a ripening toward adulthood and her resolution to better her behavior, and in this way the complexities of moral problems provoke moral growth. Her encounter, both literally and symbolically, with the Eucharist toward the end prefigures how such—indeed all—maturation must occur: through suffering, sacrifice, and the support of one's community.

All of the stories in this section, gathered under the concept of the moral law, have something in common that we have not yet remarked on: all employ language in some unusual fashion in order to draw attention to a moral situation. "The Woman and the Mighty Bird" presents formulaic phrases (actually a song) repeatedly to stress the earnestness of moral and social transgression. "Every Leave That Falls" uses Bible-quoting in a comic way to underscore the antagonistic moral views of a father and son. Mrozek in "The Pastor" introduces Biblical passages in a church service framework ironically to show the moral immaturity of the one who reads them. In "Gorilla, My Love" an often funny colloquial language exposes the deceitfulness of words, sometimes those that adults use to dissemble with children. In "The Face of Evil" O'Connor has the religious confessional act as the language that hinders rather than aids a delinquent young Catholic in his sudden resolve to lead a moral life. Flannery O'Connor's "A Temple of the Holy Ghost" contrasts the illiterate argot of "redneck" dialect with liturgical Latin to portray the diverse forces that prompt the heroine's moral resolve. All of these tales, in other words, not only invite an interpretation of the dynamics of moral acts and situations but also point to the primary role of language in expressing and sometimes even determining such acts and situations.

Our third set of stories we have arranged under the heading of *Revelation: Natural or Supernatural?* We have placed them in a sequence that moves gradually from supernatural manifestation to a worldly expression of new insight—although other readers may disagree that divine revelation appears in any of the six tales. The Brazilian writer João Guimarães Rosa's "A Young Man, Gleaming, White" is a fine example of the Latin American literary tradition of "magical realism," a frustrating kind of narrative by North American standards, in which impossible events are depicted in an otherwise credible context, yet one fraught with mystery and enigma. The story is very evocative, but its parts do not cohere into a neat interpretive pattern. The setting suggests the apocalypse found in religious literature, the catastrophe dealt with in realistic writing, and the extraplanetary invaders from science fiction. The central character is clearly intended to recall Christ (with José Kakende as his John the Baptist), but he also could be an angel or an alien space traveller, and he fits the archetype from myth and folklore of the mysterious youth as well, the *puer aeternus,* reminiscent of, for example, Melville's *Billy Budd* and Hesse's *Demian.* That the story must depend on such multiple evocations is apparent from the absence of any rigorously structured plot. Unlike most fiction, in which the protagonist undergoes an evolution of some sort—a maturation, an education, or change of fortunes—in Rosa's tale the luminous stranger remains a completely static character. Such action as there is results from the response of the other characters to him, and it is they who change: Duarte Dias becomes an upright man, Cordiero's luck shifts for the better, and Viviana is made enduringly joyful. Ironically, then, in this story of revelation, the subject never discloses his identity, yet the other characters are revealed to themselves and each other; they do not learn whether they have experienced a divine or human visitation, but they have been touched and their lives made fuller, and in this way they have shared in transcendence, whether from another realm or from within them.

"One Day After Saturday," by the Colombian writer Gabriel García Márquez, in contrast, is an example of magical realism that is very intricately plotted to produce a concurrence of crafted and existential revelation; things are arranged and timed so that the reader's moments of recognition coincide with those of the characters in the story. As is typical of such fiction, meticulous regard is devoted to accurate historical data, but in the midst of them inexplicable things occur—here the eerie mass death of the birds—that counteract the seeming reliance on reality. The artistic revelation results from the author's strategy of bringing the central characters together in a crucial scene, constituting the climax of the tale, and suddenly transforming the drifting particles of the apparently chaotic plot into a unified instant of disclosure. The convergence of the aged priest, the old widow, and the confused young man in the church induces the reader to find the common element among them, which appears in a symbolic fourth character, the Wandering Jew, who is related to each of the trio in a different but revelatory way. To the senile priest, who sees the legendary figure, he is a confirming sign of the imminent apocalypse, for Ahasuerus (the Jew) is condemned to wander the earth until the Last Judgment as his punishment for mocking Jesus at the crucifixion. To Rebecca, the widow who has probably murdered her husband, the news of the Jew's appearance fills her with the fear inspired by her guilt and drives her into the church where she comes otherwise only for annual confession. The panicky young stranger who has missed his train is not aware of the Wandering Jew at all, but his presence in the town at this particular time causes one to connect him to that condemned figure, especially since the Wandering Jew archetype is often also related to that of the Eternal Youth, a symbol of immortality. The "existential" revelations of the story's characters, then, are rare, charged moments that pierce their defenses and generate a terrifying knowledge of human vulnerability. The reader, in turn, learns that revelation is but the culmination of unaware experiencing, a disclosure of the self to the self.

Blum's "In the Blue Country" does not, for all of its nature celebration, attempt to apotheosize the natural nor use it as a context for deific revelation. Revelation here is mundane but nonetheless of a high order, formed out of meditation and fraternity. Its craftsmanship makes the story one of the finest of our collection, without a false word or phrase, and yet it is built on a mild deception: Blum is an American; the tale is not a translation from Russian or Finnish; and its content is wholly a fiction. Yet the deception is in a way appropriate, for the story is actually *about* fictions. The three men on their yearly fishing trip partake of an elaborate ritual the center of which is narration, story-telling, and it is the act of narration as much as the content of the tales that gives importance to this sojourn in the barren border region of southeast Finland. The ritual is characteristic of male secret societies as described, for example, by Eliade: the group is select, women are unwelcome, alcohol (vodka) and tobacco are necessary elements, isolation is imperative. Above all, sacred stories are retold—except that here, among these citizens of technologized and secularized Russia, the stories are not truly sacred but are merely about "sacred" personages (clergy and charismatic figures) and events. More exactly, the good cigars that the three men in Vuoksi smoke elicit and sustain a long train of associations that focusses on religious themes, yet not in a context of belief but of trust—one that inspires anecdotal entertainment, in a relaxed atmosphere, among friends. Precisely this memory is cherished by the narrator: the beauty and the solitude of the landscape, the companionship, the luxuries of food, drink, and tobacco, and especially the fascination of casual tale-telling create a rich, fulfilling episode worth crystallizing in another story, the one that the narrator relates. In this sense the story is its own revelation: the teller wishes to convey the force of the narrative act in its ideal environment.

Brautigan's slight and eccentric "The Kool-Aid Wino," for all its whimsy, delivers an effective social and spiritual commentary not unrelated to our theme of revelation. As is usually the case with Brautigan's fiction, a playful spirit imbues a harsh reality here, a tactic evident in the title. "Wino" suggests poverty and addiction, conditions adhering to society's failures and outcasts, but a "Kool-Aid wino" has to be someone whose vice is merely an obsession, so that "wino" is a metaphoric rather than a literal label. But once the serious ramifications of addiction, and the implications of the Bowery bum, are introduced, one discovers further parallels between actual debauchery and the condition of the disadvantaged playmate from the narrator's childhood. Both the genuine wino, implied here as a figure for comparison, and the adolescent in the story cannot function in the real world, both exist in impoverished circumstances, both scrounge for money to pay for whatever they need to help them escape the real world, and both use that something systematically, even ritually, to enter a fantasy world. But beyond these aspects the parallels end and the contrasts become instructive. The boy's innocuous drink, obviously, unlike the alcoholic's has no innate power to make his environment more bearable, so what does improve his meager life must be the rituals he invents. Further, these rituals in themselves are meaningless, but the boy gives them meaning through the elegance and precision of his performance. Even the meanest of conditions, one sees, can offer the place and the ingredients for celebration, and the transforming force is the intrepid imagination. The initial comparison between the real and the Kool-Aid wino shifts to an utter opposition.

Whereas the alcoholic languishes in a subworld of gradual disintegration, the adolescent celebrant's obsession is a relatively positive one. He shapes, with the earnestness of play, his survival from the shabby elements of his surroundings. He makes his own revelation and can perhaps redeem his future.

Meeter's "Don't You Remember Me?" gives evidence that the quest and journey motifs remain strong in recent literature. Those motifs interacting with the still lively myths of the frontier and open space in the American imagination help produce a tale that has elements both of romance and irony—and together they generate revelation. The story shows romance qualities, for example, in characterization, plot, and action: the two main figures are youthful lovers, the plot offers deepened insight into the nature of their affection, and the action consists of events that bring them back together following a "test" of separation. But romance is also active on a literary-archetypal level in ways we have already suggested: Robert is a modern version of the knight errant undertaking the perilous adventure to win his lady, and with this realization irony comes into play. The knightly hero's dignified preparatory rituals before the journey are fussy and prosaic here. The elaborate ordeals of the mythic voyage are reduced in this variation to the protagonist trying to stay awake during a marathon trip by car; the acquisition of a symbolic romance object (the virginal wedding gown) takes place in a comic atmosphere rather than in one of proper reverence. Above all, the young lover's "suffering," consisting of his inability to remember his fiancée's features and of his fretful passion for her, recalls a bit of T. S. Eliot's "memory and desire" as poeticized in "The Waste Land," itself a mythicized fiction of romance and irony; the paralyzed memory and the thwarted desire of Eliot's neurotic modern mindscape are the emotional baggage of Meeter's story as well. Yet a kind of midwestern health also pervades the narrative, and herein lies the revelation. A purity of feeling, even an innocence, shines through behind and beyond the irony that might be vulnerable to the ridicule of cynics but that helps the young man rediscover the real self in the other.

What is lost, by contrast, in inauthentic love relationships, where the ego dissembles, is dramatized in Bachmann's "Oh Happy Eyes"—the title comes from the "Tower Song" in Act Five of Goethe's *Faust* II. Here, obviously, irony overwhelms romance at every turn, and the literally shattering finale is utterly apt. One is tempted to identify Miranda's misfortune with Bachmann's own—one of the most gifted German-language artists of the postwar era, she died in 1973 at the age of forty-seven. We may not legitimately make that identification, however, beyond suggesting that the author may have suffered as did her Austrian protagonist from a heightened sensitivity toward the world's harshness and from an attendant anxiety that hinders one's functioning. The story offers, at any rate, a marvelously acute character portrayal in good part from the perspective of the disintegrating heroine. Whereas in "Don't You Remember Me?" the action consists of a convergence, a coming together, here it is the opposite, a depiction of separation, of coming apart both in terms of Miranda's loss of Josef to Anastasia, her rival, and in terms of her personal dissolution. Much of this is accomplished through the central image and metaphor of poor vision, so that our theme of revelation assumes here a different physical and symbolic quality. Miranda's weakened eyesight gives her a false view of the world, but she also consciously uses her handicap to keep from experiencing sights too grim for her. She controls her "revelation," in other words, by reducing her vision, just as her poor sight corrupts her "*in*-sight." This narrowed perspective and inpaired vision she tries to turn into a way of manipulating others, especially her lover, but that strategy becomes her undoing, for Josef tires of being her constant protector and transfers his attention to the perhaps less complicated and more independent Anastasia. As the romantic triangle develops, irony takes over. By playing the helpless one Miranda (who is an ironic contrast to her ingénue namesake in Shakespeare's *The Tempest*) actually becomes that way; her deceitfulness erodes and then destroys the only more or less authentic love relationship she has been able to sustain. As Bachmann's artful narrative technique reveals, Miranda's half-blindness has its counterpart in a falsity of language and behavior that steadily reduces her to a shallow and reflexive *poseur*. Her thought after her final (and perhaps fatal) accident is a fitting and concluding pun that we have not been able to carry over into English. "Immer das Gute im Auge behalten," she thinks—the advertising slogan of a contact lens laboratory: literally, "Always keep the good in your eye," or, as we would say more idiomatically, "Always keep your eye on what's good." This Miranda cannot, in any sense, do.

Common to the six stories in this section is that they all deal with revelation in some relationship to ritual—even those that do not portray any divine disclosure. In the first two tales of this section, those by Rosa and Márquez, supernatural events—the appearance of the angelic young man and the birds falling from the sky—precipitate the practicing of religious rituals as one would expect. But the other four tales, those presenting secularized situations, also stress ritual, as if attempts were being made to induce revelation through ritual rather than using ritual to celebrate revelation. The revelations that do appear are slight, ephemeral, and (as in "Oh Happy Eyes") not always good news; their connection to ritual perhaps points to cultures deprived of a traditional transcendent experience still trying to engender moments of profound recognition that duplicate, or reoriginate, or substitute for the old sacred manifestation. However, it could just as well be that in these latter stories of "natural" revelation a sense of the sacred *within* the world is still quite strong, so that the rituals accompany and channel an abiding immanent holiness. We should not dismiss too quickly the world's hieratic force.

Our final group of stories we have arranged under the heading of *Community: Covenant or Conversion?* We have theorized that according to the "Canaan" ideal of community the individual must remain integrally a part of his or her fellowship in order to achieve or maintain wholeness, whereas according to the "Rome" ideal one must leave the community in order to discover a true self. Our stories illustrate this opposition, and various complications of it, in a particularly rich fashion perhaps because in the late twentieth century genuine community has become so rare that we are unusually alert to its configurations.

The inclusion of Kojima's "Shōjū" (which means "rifle"), the only Far Eastern tale in our collection, may perplex some readers, since its sensationalized action and overt symbolism are traits unlike those found in most modern Japanese fiction made available to a Western audience. Yet it represents another kind of respected Oriental narrative, a sort not merely exotic but also instructive in its depiction of the young World War II soldier's agonized vacillation between allegiances to groups and individuals and his fluctuating fortunes of acceptance and rejection. The Japanese capacity for intense communal fidelity is marked here; the hero's attachment to his company is so central that other, personal loyalties are made to seem like betrayals that should be excised. His tragedy is that he is doomed whichever choice he makes, or more subtly, by the conflicting dimensions of his desire, intensified by the wartime exigencies. The young man, still undergoing the pangs of maturation, longs for his homeland, for sexual fulfillment, for the woman who was his security, yet wishes also to win the respect of his squad leader and fellow recruits. The symbolism of the rifle as a phallic

weapon is too blatant to have the effect it might have had,
yet it is not without impact or skillful design. The rifle-
symbol is made to embody the whole complex of the young
man's dilemma. It is, variously, his comfort, his passion, his
talisman—both as erotic and sacred object for him—but also
becomes an image of faithlessness, brutality, and lost innocence; as all of these it is the metaphor that unifies the sweep
of time and emotion in the story, just as it is the instrument
of coincidence (perhaps too much for Western readers) that
links the scattered strands of action. Yet the gun as symbol or
literal object does nothing to solve the problem of community the soldier struggles with; it rather brings them into
clearer focus and enlarges the vision of suffering that occurs
when brotherhood fails.

   "The Deacon" reminds one of how adept Updike has
been at creating individual character studies that draw
additional power from depictions of the communal context.
Updike's protagonists are often weak people who are sympathetically yet critically portrayed, and the deacon Miles
seems at first not to fit this mold; he appears as a strong
figure, a self-reliant, resourceful, and dedicated person who
becomes a pillar of a succession of churches. One might take
him to be the model of what a deacon (*diakonos* in Greek:
"servant, minister") should be. But Updike would not, we
are sure, offer us that simple and straightforward a portrait,
and the crux of the story lies in our gradual recognition of the
main character's weakness. Miles is, we discover, an activist
with little spiritual substance, a kind of ecclesiastical trouble-
shooter who approaches problems of the church with the
same pragmatic attitudes he maintains in his electrical engineer's profession. He is practical, conscientious, cautious,
and thrifty—readily accepted virtues by religious folk—but
has no genuine sense of the sacred or numinous. One begins
to suspect him when the question insinuates itself: if he is so
ideal a deacon, why has he moved so restlessly from church
to church? The reason is nicely ironic: Miles, in the midst of

the Christian community, seems unable to practice true fellowship. His serving of the church is a kind of imperialism whereby he gains control of the congregation. When he has thus "conquered" a church it loses its attraction for him, and he is ready for a new one. Significantly, the closest he comes to an experience of the sacred is when he pauses *alone* in the New England church during the storm. This hegemonic trait, of which he is no doubt unaware, makes a travesty out of the concept of community. Miles does not find wholeness or true self either within or outside the Christian community, for he merely uses, however unwittingly, the church to sustain a tenuous and selfish life style. Nevertheless, a faintly positive note in the story is sounded toward the end when Miles, alone in the wind-lashed church, feels "the pride of this ancient thing that will not quite die." Although he probably means the literal church building, one thinks at the same time of Christendom as a whole. If men and women like the deacon Miles do not serve it well, at least they witness to its residual force that they need for their lives and that still could engender vital fellowship.

Barthelme's surreal "A City of Churches" contrives another travesty of the concept of community. Here one finds community with a vengeance. It is not a single church member but a whole religious institution that dominates, in a subtly totalitarian fashion, the individuals. In fact, true to totalitarian form, the hegemonic institution here tries to destroy individuality in the name of a supposed greater good, and in this way the church, or better said, the town of Prester as a religious entity, is presented as demonic. As is typical of Barthelme, he selects clichés and develops them into absurd situations that convey effective social criticism. Two of the clichés here are the title phrase, "A City of Churches" and "the church of their choice." "A City of Churches" has been used traditionally to describe wholesome and God-fearing American towns. But Prester is comprised only of churches, a state of affairs drastically (and comically) askew that must inevitably prove destructive. People live "in the church of their choice," a weird fulfillment of the American democratic ideal that we all attend "the church of our choice" and that is also dangerous because, as Cecelia learns, it leaves no provision for those who wish the freedom to attend no church at all. The ultimate danger of such achieved community is its bland uniformity. "They are harmless," Mr. Phillips says of the churches to Cecelia, and that is just what is wrong. The town, an image of Christianity at its worst, does nothing but try to maintain its static condition by absorbing everyone and everything into its impotent, hypocritical sphere. The community is a pseudo-community. Its members are concerned only with their security, although Mr. Phillips speaks loftily of perfection. The rebel Cecelia threatens Prester's precarious equilibrium because she insists on settling there but on her own terms; she will not join the false community. Her wholeness will derive neither from accepting nor from leaving this "community" but from the process of trying to change it.

"Conversation with My Child on the Nazis' Deeds in the Jungle," by the Swiss author Urs Widmer, is fully as surreal as "A City of Churches" but adds to the surrealism a degree of whimsy that produces a different kind of tale. Widmer's treatment of the notorious Nazi SS officer Martin Bormann in a whimsical fashion might be offensive to some readers, those who believe that subjects such as war crimes and death camps are too terrible for comic manipulation, but here the effect justifies the author's strategy. The whimsicality gradually accrues to and deepens into a black humor that helps to render this story one of the most profound in our collection. The combination of whimsy and black humor may, in fact, be the most appropriate way of dealing with the horrors of our century, for it translates the capriciousness and outrage of human behavior at its worst into emotions we can bear (who can face, without some kind of mediation, the ghastly truth of the Holocaust?) and keeps us from forgetting, or wishing to forget, what we know we are capable of. In the guise of an adventure tale narrated to a child, Widmer has his narrator trace the continuity of technologized and bureaucratized man from the era of World War II to the present. It is the same mentality that can exterminate millions from "impure" races with mechanical efficiency, or hail the nuclear bomb as a great achievement of science, or claim to forget decades later who Martin Bormann was. The image in mid-story of the Japanese cyborgs—those with the built-in cameras—is perfect for delineating this modern man estranged from himself: he needs constructed objects to sustain, or even locate, a fugitive selfhood, threatened as he is by a dehumanized environment and a recent heritage of atrocities. To counteract all of this, the fragile defenses of the family—another kind of community—are mounted. The story's final, idyllic domestic scene, although it excludes a recognition of divinity (they ear "not having said grace"), witnesses to the resources of the family as a community of care and concern where one still can work modestly toward wholeness even in a hopelessly fragmented world.

Woiwode's "The Suitor" also treats the family as community but against a background of confessional prejudice involving Roman Catholicism versus Protestantism. The plot for a while imitates a classic structure: the boy and girl in love but hindered in their romance by unreasoning relatives and by tradition. Woiwode, however, does not carry through the "star-crossed lover" action but alters it instead to fashion a surprise happy end. The resistance from the girl's parents fades, they endorse the youthful lovers' marriage plans, and the suitor—a Roman Catholic interloper—is accepted into the privileged circle of the girl's family. Since the archetypal fated-lovers situation usually results in the pair's suicide or least separation, the denouement here is an obvious departure from the traditional one and is apt for the practical, realistic spirit said to be characteristic of the American midwest, particularly in the late Depression setting (1939) in which the story takes place. The Jensens, who through the farmers' life of battling nature are used to compromising with the inevitable, accept their future son-in-law graciously—perhaps even in a spirit of ecumenism—once it is apparent that Alpha and Martin are serious in their affection, and the tension of the narrative is resolved. What seemed at the start to have tragic tendencies turns out to be comic romance. It is "comic" in the sense both of an affirmative ending and of the humorous elements. It is a romance, in spite of the realistic setting, as a love story and as a tale depending heavily on the main characters' idealized concept of love. The stylistic success of the story lies mainly in the author's ability to convey, deftly and credibly in the uninhibited 1970s, the chaste excitement of the lovers and the fragility of emergent sexuality in an earlier era still controlled by sexual taboos. Wholeness in "The Suitor" is sought through acceptance into a family-community and through the promise of deepening and widening that community in a new marriage.

Dorr's "Lazarus" could be discussed profitably under the heading of Revelation, but it is even more appropriately treated as still another tale presenting the family as a redemptive unit. A sequence of three illuminations structures this strongly autobiographical (as is much of Dorr's writing) story. The first of these occurs with the father's and daughter's joint renarrating of the family visit to Devon and consists of the recognition of the deep sacrificial love of the family members for each other. The second, more intense than the first, consists in the abrupt and unmediated revelation of "glory" that the father experiences, in which he sees his family and himself as part of a sacred tableau. The third, most forceful of all, is of course the incident with the revived rabbit, a humbling moment for the father that strikes him with the awesome omnipotence of grace. The whole narrative, in fact, bodies forth the energy of grace at play in receptive interludes yet where it still breaks in by surprise.

Grace is the unexpected gift, and here its value seems all the more exorbitant because it appears through the ordinary and mundane—a child sick in bed, a pair of dogs, a dead rabbit—and transforms these into the extraordinary, the numinous. Such evocation of grace in the everyday is effected by Dorr's highly sensuous writing that moves through the visceral to a hallowing of the body's capacity to make contact with the world. The tactile imagery, for instance, should be appreciated: the skillful mustering of literal feeling that is most apt for a tale on corporeal resurrection. Wholeness permeates the family of this story, in spite of material insecurity, because its members have learned to accept and share life's ordinary richness.

It is not inappropriate to conclude this section on community and our collection as a whole with a short story by Samuel Beckett, Number Six (otherwise untitled) from *Stories and Texts for Nothing*. Beckett's characters, often caught in situations of desperate loneliness and isolation, try to function in a world marked by both nihilism and tenacious hope, a world where individuals simultaneously reject and long for the Other. Beckett's celebrated enigmatic style, moreover, evinces many of the elements said to constitute recent experimental fiction, sometimes called "post-modern," so that our attention turned to him now, toward the end, reminds us of an influential direction of contemporary literary art that is responsive to an analysis based on religious awareness.

It is not necessary (although a fascinating challenge to literary puzzle-solvers) and probably not possible to distill a single and reliable storyline from Beckett's cryptic paragraphs. What one should attempt to understand is *how* the narrative is obscure, and that is not difficult. Beckett's narrator, for instance, offers no clear information about himself or his environs, so that one cannot situate the story with certainty in any familiar time or location. Another way of explaining the obscurity is to point out that the speaker gives us not too little but too much information and thus overloads our capacities for explanation. We find it hard to offer our version of the story because the speaker provides so many alternatives of his own at every stage of the telling. The best we can say, then, is that the narrator, in what is part interior monologue and part direct address to an unnamed "you," ponders his dilemma of isolation—in a prison, or hospital, or even as a corpse—longs for escape and normalcy, and comes to focus on the vitality of words and of storytelling as a way of enduring, perhaps overcoming, his condition. Important for our considerations is to recognize his relentless desire to connect—with his past, his deepest self, with the others— and to name "the unnameable" through a tale.

So here at the last we find another relationship between narrative and the community. It was, after all, a story, the "good news" of the gospel (gospel: from Old English *godspell,* meaning "good news") that inspired the foundation of the early Christian community, just as the retelling and celebration of the gospel story still draw the *koinonia*—the fellowship—together. The narrator's loss of words in Beckett's tale, the lapse into grim intervals of silence, occurs in a time—our age—when the gospel story *as story* is also too seldom heard, when all is analyzed but little is related in its fullness. Likewise, the religious interpretation of fiction should above all nurture the hearing and sharing of the story rather than a mere explaining of it. For through such sharing we are constrained to offer our own stories—the personal fictions that define us—and thereby shape the *ethos* and *telos* of our being. We hope that this collection helps its readers to recall and relate their individual and common stories and thus to renew the wholeness of themselves and their communities.

R. D.